BETTER ANGELS

A CONVERSION

Timothy Strongin, PhD

Better Angels

John A. Logan's Conversion

print ISBN: 978-1-66788-966-5
ebook ISBN: 978-1-66788-967-2

Printed in the United States of America

CONTENTS

ACKNOWLEDGEMENTS

To Barbara. We met when I was a teenager adrift, and you believed in me. You taught, led, encouraged and inspired me. You shared with me and patiently allowed me to explore, imagine and talk. You indulged me for over a decade as I tiptoed up to the edge of writing but always stepped back. You opened your life and heart, blessing me with fifty three years (so far) of love, adventure and growth. I am blessed beyond measure by being married to you.

Thank you, John Gluck, for pulling me out of line and teaching me to think. For teaching me the essential value of moral responsibility and commitment to both practical and transcendent purposes. Your inspiration and constant friendship, encouragement and wisdom have transformed my life. To Kevin Sheehan for taking the risk (for a steely-eyed fighter pilot) of making friends with a psychologist, then including me in the adventure. You showed me a perspective I never imagined, and I'll always treasure the memory of seeing the earth from 50,000 feet while moving at twice the speed of sound.

There are shelves of books on my walls and piles of notes from scholars who did the real work of discovering and preserving the past for people like me to explore and imagine. P. Michael Jones and the John A. Logan Museum of Murphysboro, Illinois were wonderfully generous with their time, knowledge, and encouragement. Thank you for keeping the memory of JAL so vibrant.

The *American Battlefield Trust*, not only finds and preserves the places where the war took place but provides indispensable interpretive and educational resources. Standing on the same ground as the people in the story inspired appreciation, understanding and the certainty that we share their hopes, humanity, and heartache. I am grateful to countless librarians and museum curators who allowed me to develop relationships with the people in the story.

I am deeply moved by the willingness of abolitionists, suffragists, and healers to step into the inferno of our second revolutionary war. Without their sacrifices, we would have foundered and become part of an unsalvageable Western Hemisphere.

I hope this story honors generations of enslaved Americans and their descendants. As my distant ancestors overcame centuries of enslavement, so did very recent generations of Americans. Victimized but not victims, enslaved Americans preserved faith, love, hope, resilience, creativity, wisdom and passion. I am profoundly grateful to them and to those who preserve their memories. I hope this story encourages readers to work with other willing Americans, to fulfill the promise for which countless others gave their lives.

Finally, I give this book to my children: Matthew, Kyle, Sarah, Tristan, Emily, Eric and to my grandchildren, Liam and Gabriel. You inspire me and bless me with a profound sense of gratitude for my life. I am immensely proud that each of you, in remarkably different ways, has joined the struggle to make our country and our world better. I hope to write more, but if I don't, please remember that you and your family will always be part of the story.

Finally, to all the readers. Thank you for taking time with this story. I didn't write for money, recognition or art, but with the same goal as when I took up painting: to help me see the world in a new way, to create something for the pure joy of the effort and to pass some time. I wrote to learn, and I hope to share with anyone who will take a look. If you're looking, thank you!

Tim Strongin, January 2023

FOREWARD

I can't recall how I came across a history of the 78th Ohio Veteran Volunteer Infantry Regiment. I read it and the story sat in my mind for several years. When I reread the book, I met John A. Logan and his story introduced me to the 31st Illinois Veteran Volunteer Infantry.

I don't know where I first encountered Mary Ann Bickerdyke either, but her story is profound. She met and influenced Grant, Sherman, Logan, and countless others. Mary Ann's values and actions were part of a tide that transformed Logan from a vehement racist to an outspoken advocate for civil rights.

John A. Logan and Mary Ann Bickerdyke lived at the same time and spent much of the war in the same places. Logan's 31st Illinois Volunteer Infantry and Mortimer Leggett's 78th Ohio Volunteer Infantry participated in nearly every campaign in the Western Theater of the Civil War. Bickerdyke came from Eastern Ohio where the 78th Ohio Volunteer Infantry originated and led nursing services for Grant's and then Sherman's Armies through every stage of the war.

Bickerdyke's contributions to the welfare of the soldiers earned her the nickname "Mother" and although she is little remembered today, her commitment to abolition, suffrage, temperance, women in medicine and the welfare of soldiers had profound influence on those who met her. Together, Mary Ann Bickerdyke and John A. Logan made incalculable contributions to process of reconstruction. Their war began in 1861, fighting ended in 1865 and important aspects of the struggle continue today.

A Note on Characters

Most of the people named in the book are real and their stories deserve careful attention. Mortimer Leggett, Doff Ozburn, Lewis Garrard, Miss Hartstock and dozens of others still speak for themselves each time an interested reader with a computer and a library card visits them.

This is a novel. I put words in the mouths of historical figures to guide the reader through events. I invented other characters for the same reason. There are brief notes about historical persons at the end of the book.

A Note on Language

When modern characters speak, we don't often attempt to render their accents. Instead, we respect their thoughts by communicating their ideas in contemporary language. For the same reason, I use modern American English in this story.

A Note on Black Lives

I'm unable to do justice to the generations of enslaved people, abolitionists, fugitives and free people who overcame the weight of history. Their stories would suffer if I tried to tell them. I hope the Black characters in this story stimulate the readers' interest and that they will explore and seek to understand the generations of people who, despite having their lives and futures stolen, triumphed over unspeakable abuse. They continue to bless our country with their talent, energy, and hope. Their story deserves a better telling than I can offer.

PROLOGUE

Outside Tiffin, Ohio, 1850

The house stood on a small rise amidst a rolling landscape. Oaks and maples were allowed to grow on three sides of the house, offering shade and some protection from wind. With a pitched, shingled roof and clapboard siding, the house had always been painted white with black shutters. It overlooked a bend in the river that marked one boundary of the farm. That river fed and watered the family. A path of smoothed stones led away from the covered porch to a small, orderly farmyard.

The house had been in the family for three generations. Like thousands of veterans of the Revolutionary War, the great grandfather received the land as bounty for service in the Revolution. He built the house during his first years on the land, long before Ohio became a state. In his haste to establish his claim his farm and his family, he rushed the construction: Using wood instead of stone, stone instead of bricks and mortar instead of cement.

On one end of the original house was a large fireplace, suitable for cooking. Two rooms provided a starting place for the first, growing family. Years later, when the old soldier's son took over the house, the younger man added three rooms across the back, converting the large, open fireplace into several "Rumford" fireplaces, moving the cooking fire to an outbuilding. When original builder's grandson took the house, he installed a cast iron cook stove and used the old kitchen as a smokehouse. Although the farm matured, none of its inheritors amended the foundation.

Changes to the heating and cooking places were compromises between necessity and resources. Over the years and slowly at first, the house settled; then shifted. Mortar decomposed. Gaps opened. The flue cracked. Despite knowing there were problems, the inheritors delayed necessary repairs. Discussions devolved into arguments. Lately and because they believed there was time, the grandson and his wife simply avoided conversations about repairing the foundation.

One night, the house made its claim. The structure could no longer control the fires that had once made it livable.

In those silent hours, thin wisps of smoke escaped from a gap between the plastered wall and the old chimney. The sound of raindrops spattering across shingles punctuated the sluice of water sheeting from roof. Rain was welcome after the dry autumn but the fire that crept between the wall and the rafters didn't care about rain.

The couple awoke to their own coughing, eyes burning from smoke and panic immediate. Crackling flames danced madly through the kitchen, silencing doubts and questions. Billows of hot, black smoke rolled from windows heralding a holocaust.

On his feet in an instant, the grandson had the presence of mind to wrap his wife and baby in a quilt as he turned to dash the few steps to their children's room. His wife seized the infant with both arms, head down, following her husband out of the bedroom. "The children!" she howled over the roaring flames, even as he dashed through their door.

He turned only his head, coughing and shouting back to her, "Take the baby! I'll meet you at the front!"

He said nothing more, but grabbed-up the two half-asleep children. Taking one under each arm like sacks of wet grain, he clambered through the side door only a step behind his choking wife, stumbling on the last step and catching himself as he pressed the children roughly to their mother. In the first flush of relief, they sagged. Hearing the rising bellow of the fire, dread engulfed them.

Both knew they had waited too long to repair the ancient foundation. Now it was too late. Fire claimed the house and consumed it.

Raging and mindless, it devoured everything it reached, and it reached for everything. Telling the oldest child to keep hold of the other children and to stay under the quilt, the couple ran to the hopeless errand of drawing water.

The wife worked the pump with every bit of her strength as he attacked the flames with two, pitifully half-filled buckets. Facing the wall of flames and stepping first to his right, then looking to his left, he could find no place to launch his meager assault. Finally, in rage and despair, he heaved the buckets at the middle of the monster.

Even as he ran back to the pump, he realized the home had yielded absolutely. Beams groaned and cried out in submission. The roof, and then the walls lost shape: first transformed into flames, belching great roars of thunder and cascading embers.

Only when the monster had consumed everything that might support life, and died, did the couple turn their backs, leaving the remains of the house to fall unobserved, like so many heaps of charred bone. The couple surrendered to the inevitable, accepting the solace of neighbors who took them in.

Throughout the night, and long after the family went to the safety of their neighbors' home, the gentle rain continued. As if nothing had happened. A fog-streaked dawn revealed heaps of steaming ash and charred timber. Only the smooth stone path, the small orderly farmyard and the river remained.

Later that morning, the rain ended, and couple returned silently, with their children and their friends. The family was not hopeless nor without resources, but they could only gaze at the remains of their home.

Low clouds and occasional light rain persisted for two days after the fire. Sunday morning was gray. Walking side-by-side, two eleven-year-olds followed their shortcut through an overgrown woodlot between their homes and the recently burned place.

There were strong scents of fallen leaves and wet soil. The boys didn't mind the mud accumulating on their work boots as they followed the packed-down wagon track. It was Sunday after supper, and they had a few hours to explore before sundown. They wanted to see what remained of the old house and whether they could salvage a few boards for their raft.

A low hill and the woods obscured their view of the farmstead. Breaking out of the shrubs, Mathan and his friend followed a narrow trail rising between the neighbor's cornfields. The boys exited the cornfield and confronted the sodden remains of Mathan's neighbors' farmhouse.

Except for a light breeze rustling a few leaves, it was silent as they stood at the foot of the front path. The taller boy, Peter, glanced at Mathan. The magnitude of the destruction shocked them both and temporarily sapped their enthusiasm for adventure. A cow mooed from the barn. Chickens pecked on the side of the hill. No people seemed to be about.

"They're probably with his brother's family," suggested Peter as he took a slow step forward and scanned the farmstead for its owners.

Rivulets of rainwater drew black veins down the hillside. Mathan murmured almost to himself, "Let's go see." The scent of wet, burned wood grew stronger with each step toward the heaps.

Reaching the spot where the front steps once stood, a sound froze them. It was a rustling sound, issuing from somewhere in the pile. The boys froze, looked at each other, then back at the heaps of ashes.

On the far side of the foundation, a man's head and shoulders rose slowly up from the largest part of the pile, one that wasn't completely disintegrated. The man saw the boys and froze. He looked at each boy in turn, then beyond them, scanning for the presence of others. No one moved.

They couldn't tell whether the man was Black, soot-covered or both. Emerging slowly while keeping his eyes on the boys, the slightly built man took three tentative steps backward. His clothes were tattered. He appeared to have been in the pile for some time. A partially filled, darkly smudged, cloth bag hung across his chest.

The boys sensed the gleaner's fear and uncertainty. Their eyes locked for a final moment before the young man made an abrupt turn and jogged away.

In his turning, the boys saw that he clutched forged nails in each hand, these having been carefully prized from the remains of the house. The man's silent, bare feet bore him quickly away from the two boys.

Mathan spoke first, "I wonder if he's on the run or from that black town they built past Tiffin."

"Don't know," answered Peter softly. "He sure left in a hurry."

"Wouldn't you?" asked Mathan in a low tone, not moving but surveying the scene. "He doesn't know us, and he doesn't know if we're trouble." After a pause he added, "Probably going to use those nails on his own place. Stepping toward the pile his visage brightened and he smiled up at Peter adding, "Maybe we can find some too!"

With that, the boys began to pick through the charred boards on the edges of the pile. Their hands were quickly chilled and sooty. About to give up their search, Peter came across a long piece of what may have been a shutter or door frame.

Peter was holding one end of the charred wood as Mathan picked up the other end and looked at it admiringly. It revealed six, ancient, drawn nails forged decades before from iron bars. After a minute or two of banging the board with stones, each boy had three heavy, rectangular nails. Stuffing their treasures into their pockets they hunted for another source like the one they'd uncovered. "He must have got the rest of them," suggested Peter.

"Yeah," replied Mathan softly. "I don't see any more." He stood up and looked at the remains of the Wilsons' home. Softly he said, "It's sad."

Peter looked at Mathan and nodded in agreement. With that, the boys retraced their steps to the edge of the cornfield but followed a different path leading past the river that flowed beside both the Wilsons' and Mathan's family farm. "Let's go check our raft!" suggested Mathan.

The leaden, rain-gorged River seemed to ooze slowly past its banks. The boys ducked beneath low branches and between trees that sheltered a cut in the bank. Black alders canopied their small, muddy beach and bushes added to the sense of a secret intersection of land and water. Here, the boys often waded, fished, and hunted frogs.

Peter had agreed to visit the river, but only to clean his hands and boots, trying to hide evidence of their explorations. His head was down as he focused on scrubbing soot from his palms. The risen river had enlarged and deepened their little cove. Swirling his boots in the shallow water, Mathan's attention was drawn to the small raft they'd cobbled together from salvaged planks and board ends.

Raising his boots from the water, Mathan excitedly suggested, "Let's try it! We have time!"

Peter looked up at Mathan, then turned doubtfully to the little raft. "But, we need to get home in a few minutes," he said. "Better not."

Mathan looked in the direction of their hidden path, then at the sky and concluded firmly, "We have at least an hour. I'm gonna try it."

The raft was little more than a five-by-five-foot accretion of scrap wood. In the boys' minds, it was merely a smaller, but no less worthy version of the barges and lumber rafts they'd seen on the river all their lives.

With determination, Mathan placed his boots on a small shelf of soil, turned and stepped into the chilly, ankle-deep water. Grasping a length of rope that extended from the side of the raft, Mathan stepped backward, tugging the raft after him. He was surprised and nearly lost his balance as the grassy bank yielded the little craft.

Catching himself before he fell, Mathan kneeled onto the makeshift raft. He was careful to climb as far toward the middle as he could and nearly capsized twice. He waved an arm for balance and clutched at the pole he would use for propulsion with the other.

Scooting towards the center of the raft, an inch or two at a time, Mathan soon found the balance point. After a minute of self-admiration and growing confidence, he extended the pole into the muddy bank and pushed to the center of the cove. The raft scooted forward and settled about ten feet from where Peter watched admiringly. Framed by alders and a willow, Mathan's smile infected Peter who exclaimed, "It works! It's good!"

As quickly as it had appeared, Peter's smile evaporated. He looked past Mathan's shoulder to the swollen surface of the river beyond their little cove. "Be careful, Mathan, stay closer in," said Peter, less possessed by Mathan's excitement than he had been a moment before.

Mathan rotated the raft with his pole, then scooted himself further towards the mouth of the cove with growing confidence. "This is fun! It really goes!" he said. "I'm gonna take it over by the river!"

Peter watched but amusement evaporated and envy became concern. Silently and without permission, the river drew the raft from the cove and into its current. Peter felt the cold stab of alarm.

Mathan leaned forward to clutch at the low branch of the last tree he passed; but lost both his pole and his balance. As the edge of the raft dipped, Mathan spilled onto his face. Instinctively, he scooted back to balance the raft and flattened himself across it, maintaining his place, but completely out of control. The river pulled Mathan into the fastest part of its flow.

The boys' eyes met as the distance between them grew. "Peter!" shouted Mathan, "Reach me from the bank!"

Peter leaped back into the overgrowth trying to find a place on the bank where he might catch Mathan's hand. The branches tripped him, and he slid on his knees. As he regained his feet, Peter glimpsed Mathan rotating away and down the river.

Breaking out of the dripping brush, Peter reached a path and ran fifty yards to the next clearing. He arrived breathless, only to see Mathan hopelessly far from the bank and moving out of sight.

Peter turned and ran wildly in the direction of Mathan's house, less than a quarter mile from the river. He knew only that he had to tell a grown-up. It took a couple of minutes for him to reach the house, to find and to tell Mathan's mother her son was being swept downriver.

Mathan was far from the banks, experiencing a kind of silent calmness. He could no longer locate his friend. He was unused to seeing the riverbank from this vantage point. The featureless, gray sky and the broad greenish river merged into a borderless sphere with only a dark fringe along the banks providing a faint reference.

Mathan had no sense of hearing and felt as if he were quite still with the banks sliding silently behind him. He had no fear for his life, but only that his parents would wonder where he'd gone.

Mathan sensed slow rotation of the raft. Cold water reached up, between the loose boards of the little raft, and chilled him. With the cold, fear seeped in. Swirling further from home, he didn't know how he'd get to shore, how he'd get home or what his parents would say and do when he finally returned. He hadn't yet realized he might never get home.

Several hundred yards beyond Mathan, the pastor of the town's American Methodist Episcopal church was knee-deep at the edge of the river, guiding one of many white-clad people into the river as the rest of the congregation sang.

A tall man for his time, Pastor Alexander Allen had the broad shoulders and corded muscles of someone who worked much and ate only enough. Cradling a young woman's neck and shoulders, he gently guided her entire body beneath the surface of the river, leaving her submerged for a moment. Glancing up, he saw something unfamiliar floating toward them. With a jolt of recognition, he made sense of it and raised his new (and gasping) member of the church. He blessed her and added quickly. "Go stand with our sisters."

Turning from his congregation to gaze at the approaching boy, he raised a hand. "Wait!" he said, causing the next woman to freeze in her tracks. The congregation's eyes followed Pastor Allen's upstream.

The silence gave way to murmurs, then to shouts. "There's a little boy floating there!" "Oh, Lord, help him!" and "Is he alive?" Mathan heard the voices and raised his head, looking at the worshipers. "He sees us! Jesus! Help him!"

As the cluster of freemen and fugitives crowded into the water, Pastor Allen pulled his robe and shirt over his head in a single motion. Tossing them towards the bank and taking three strides into the deepening water, he made an arching dive in the direction of the raft. He surfaced with a strong stroke, mindful not to kick too hard, knowing better than to become exhausted by excitement.

Feeling himself redirected by the current as he swam, the pastor adjusted his direction toward the boy's path, leaving room to readjust after reaching midstream. Other members of the congregation realized their pastor and the child might be swept past them before the rescues could be completed. They began to run down the banks of the river to stay ahead of the drama on the water.

Pastor Allen's younger brother, Thad, stood above the congregation on the shore and took in the scene. "Marcus!" he shouted to the man nearest him. "Get over to the wheelwright's and get his boat to bring them in!" With that, Thad followed his brother into the water, progressing with the same confidence and steady stroke.

Mathan tried to rise to his knees, but the little raft wobbled so that he dared not try again for fear of pitching off. He raised his head and called as loudly as he could, "Here! I'm here! Help me!"

Pastor Allen didn't hear Mathan over the rush of water in his ears. Familiar with swimming in rivers, he made rapid progress towards the interception. At least there was daylight. He often brought fugitives across this water in pitch darkness.

In thirty seconds, Pastor Allen reached mid-stream and looked up, readjusting his place in the flow to give him the best chance of connecting with the raft and its passenger. Using a survival stroke with his head above the surface, he noticed Thad swimming towards him, twenty yards away and stroking steadily.

In a few seconds, Thad pulled up next to his brother and assumed a similar position in the water. "Let's spread out a little," said Thad breathlessly. "Grab the raft when he comes by."

They realized that they were now in the same current as the boy and had to swim against it to close the distance. Breast-stroking steadily, the gap between the men and the boy closed. They were nearly out of the sight of the congregation on the shore.

When Mathan was still several yards upstream, Pastor Allen shouted to him, "Boy! Stay on the raft! Don't try to move! We'll get to you!" Thad was nearer the raft now and the two men reached opposite sides within a second of one another, grasping the wood and catching their breath as they smiled.

"Let's just hang on and kick it to the bank," said Thad with renewed breath. Pastor Allen nodded and moved to Thad's side. Both began a frog-like kick, slowly working the raft towards the shore. The cold water took a toll on their muscles. By now, they were nearly past the small town where they lived and ministered.

Both brothers saw the prow of the wheelwright's rowboat pulling toward them. In it, sat a very tall, broad-shouldered, white man. His shaggy blonde hair curled from beneath a battered, Mexican War forage cap. Axel Himmelstoss had huge arms and a thick German accent. He said he kept this boat for fishing but he, Pastor Allen and Thad also used it to move fugitives.

Again, the rowboat would be a life saver. Glancing over his shoulder after every third stroke, the wheelwright was quick to bring his boat aside the swimmers. Smiling, he asked, "You fellas doing OK in that water?"

Thad and Pastor Allen checked with one another then turned back to him smiling. "We're OK here. Let's get the boy into the boat with you. We'll hold onto the transom while you take us all home."

With that, the big man boated his oars and grabbed Mathan's belt. Mathan waved his arms as all four limbs left the raft simultaneously. The big man quickly and unceremoniously transferred the weight of the dripping, dangling boy from the center of the raft to the center of the rowboat. Mathan's eyes looked from Himmelstoss to the raft and to the two men in the water. The big man didn't inquire about Mathan's welfare. He just moved confidently to his seat in the bow.

By now, Pastor Allen and Thad released the little raft and hooked elbows over the transom. With his back to the prow and a broad smile on his red face, Himmelstoss set his oars, winked at his friends and began to pull for the riverbank.

The abrupt acceleration surprised Pastor Allen and his brother Thad, who slipped back into the water. "Hold tight my brothers! We'll be to the bank in a minute, and we'll dry you off and get us some beer maybe, OK!?"

Trailing behind the boat and holding on with both hands, the men glided behind until they judged their feet would reach the bottom. Rising, the brothers splashed to the bank, behind the rowboat.

A score of townspeople milled excitedly along the low riverbank, offering congratulations, and watching the boatman bring the little crew ashore. Working his way to the front of the onlookers was a newly arrived physician with hopes of a lucrative practice and a political career in this small but rapidly growing town. "Well done Mr. Himmelstoss!" shouted Dr. Heilman, stepping to the front of the crowd and extending his hand toward the oarsman, adding, "You saved the boy!"

Hopping out of the boat into shallow water. He kept his eyes on the boat and the swimmers. In a matter-of-fact tone, Himmelstoss said, "No, Doctor, I rowed, they swam. Those men saved the boy. I just gave them a tow."

Ignoring the doctor's still-outstretched hand, Himmelstoss took the painter[1] in both hands and leaned back, dragging the rowboat, containing Mathan, onto dry land. When Axel backed himself near enough to the Doctor, he looked over his shoulder and added, "Pastor Allen would have had him up here in a few minutes anyway."

Pastor Allen and Thad were still on the bank behind Himmelstoss who walked back to embrace both of them heartily.

Thad reached into the boat. With strong hands, he took Mathan under the arms, swinging him out of the boat and onto the bank. Still dripping and chilled, Mathan's eyes searched the little crowd for someone he knew well. Seeing no one, he instinctively moved a step nearer Thad and Alexander. He followed them as they carried the rowboat with Axel, back to the wheelwright's shop.

---

1 A rope at the front of the boat.

BETTER ANGELS

Murphysboro, Illinois, 1846

In 1793, John and Elizabeth Logan, brought their five-year-old son, also named John Logan, across the Atlantic to the United States, just after Kentucky had been admitted as the 15th state. The younger Logan became a physician, moved beyond Kentucky to Missouri on the Mississippi and married Mary Berthiaume in 1814. Tragically, their first two children died in infancy.

In 1824, Dr. Logan married Elizabeth Jenkins, the daughter of a prosperous, Illinois family. The doctor re-crossed the Mississippi and settled in Jackson County, in southern Illinois. Two years later, the couple welcomed their first son, the third John Logan who was called "Jack." Eventually, Elizabeth gave birth ten times and endured the deaths of six of her children.

In 1843, when Jack was a teenager, his father lost the drawing to determine which politician would give his name to the new seat of the Jackson County government. Undaunted, Dr. Logan donated 20 acres of land for the new courthouse and the surrounding town. Other landowners complained when they weren't permitted the honor of donating their land because the honor was accompanied by a dramatic increase in the value of any nearby land they chose not to donate.

In addition to increasing his wealth, Dr. Logan's political influence grew as rapidly as the population of his county and state. Between 1820 and 1840, Illinois' population grew from around 50,000 to nearly 500,000. Dr. Logan was Jackson County's doctor and its preeminent politician.

Jack was average in height, and slight of build in his youth. A vigorous, verbal, and virile teenager, he had thick, black hair, a broad forehead, and a strong, round chin. His eyes were as dark as his hair and his skin responded to the sun, giving him a complexion matching his bay horse. Alcohol didn't sharpen his wits, but it soothed his better judgment and contributed to his reputation as a boisterous companion, fearless horseman and willing pugilist.

Lazing in the afternoon sun on one of his father's pastures, young Logan watched the clouds floating past. Jack's friend, "Doff" Ozburn had grown up with him. Hard-headed and very attracted to Jack's cousin, Diza, Doff was Jack's steady companion. "Are you going to join the Regiment?" Doff asked. "They're leaving for Mexico pretty soon and I want to go."

Jack looked at him sarcastically. "Aren't you getting married next month? You want to marry Diza and enlist before you've been married a month?"

"Come on Jack, if we don't enlist now, they'll fill the Regiment and we won't be able to go!"

"Easy Doff, I can't leave this year. You know my father's in the legislature and I have to stay with the family."

Doff pulled up a clump of grass and looked at it as if there were an answer in its roots. It was difficult to tell whether Doff was in deep thought or merely distracted by the worms wriggling in the turf. "I know, I'm sorry about the little ones."

"Thanks," Jack answered with resignation. "My mother is so low. Three babies gone in a year. It's broken her heart."

"Not easy for you either, I expect."

Jack surprised Doff with the intensity of his reply, "I *am* going to Mexico and I'm going to be part of this. I'm not going to be my father's errand boy forever!" Then he added, "I've told my father I'm going, and he said he'd help me get into the next Regiment, next summer if I help out now."

"But it'll be all over by then!" bawled Doff.

"No, it won't, Doff. It'll take a year to even get an army down there! My father knows the right people and he'll take care of it," said Jack with resignation. "Now, why don't you get back to Diza? She's only fifteen and has no idea about how to run a house. Better see to her before you take off for Mexico."

Jack's words carried more than general concern for the girl. Diza had grown up in Jack's home and was more Jack's sister than his cousin. Jack was worried that his friend Doff, was too impulsive and emotional to give Diza the life she deserved. The best thing he thought he could do for her, now that her mind was made-up, was to keep Doff close and help him as best he could.

Ignoring Jack's concern for his fiancé, Doff changed the subject. "Come on, Jack. Let's get over to the courthouse. There's a trader there with a string of horses. Won't hurt to look them over, even if we can't buy one now."

Their enlistments were put off over the winter. The war continued as Jack hoped it would. During dinner one evening in the Spring of 1847, Jack decided to ask his father for support. "I'm twenty now, and I've decided I don't want to be a physician," said Jack calmly. "I need to go to Mexico," he added with resolve.

His father looked down at his plate. He'd seen this coming, and he looked up to see tears welling in his wife's eyes. She cried easily and often. The death of her children robbed her of whatever youth she had left as well as any enthusiasm for life. Jack noticed too.

Jack caught his father's eye and pressed him. "We knew there was a war coming since Texas became a republic and asked to join the country. It's been going on for nearly a year already and I need to be part of it."

Doctor Logan said, "Our first soldiers are already there, Jack. They'll need to be relieved this summer and I know you want to go with them."

Almost pleading Jack went on, "I need your help to get a place in the Regiment. I was hoping to get started soon. They're going to make Captain Newby the new commander of the Regiment."

"Are you aware you'd be going to Santa Fe and not further South?" asked his father. Without a word, Mrs. Logan left the table. The younger children, Jack, and Dr. Logan watched her go.

"There's been a revolt in Santa Fe, and they killed the governor in front of his family," said Jack, hoping the urgency of the situation would move his father to action. "We have to put down the revolt and there are sure to be more!"

Dr. Logan looked at his son with a mixture of sadness, pride and resignation. Jack was still slender and beardless, but his father knew him well enough to understand that argument would not dissuade him a second time.

"I understand," said Dr. Logan admitting defeat. Then he added, "I also think you should take Doff with you. You can look out for him and maybe Diza won't have children until he returns. She's so young." His voice trailed off.

Days later, Jack was at the second meeting of the new Regiment, to be led by the local Sheriff, John Cunningham, who had been appointed by the governor as their Captain and Company commander. Thus far, there had been no election of officers and Jack was intensely committed to becoming the Captain's First Lieutenant.

More than ten years older and a head taller than the young man standing in front of him, Captain Cunningham shook his head and explained again, "Don't be in such a hurry, young Jack. The Regiment isn't leaving for a while yet. When the time comes to choose Lieutenants, we'll vote on them. You can talk to the men, and they'll decide. Pushing me won't make any difference, son."

Jack clenched his fists but kept them at his sides, instead, raising his chin in defiance. Cunningham's indulgent smile raised Jack's ire and challenged his self-control. "You can appoint your own officers if you want!" said Jack angrily. "And quit treating me like a boy! My name is John, not Jack!" he added.

Turning in his direction Cunningham said, "Your father is Dr. John Logan, right?"

"Yes, he is." Before the Captain turned away the younger man added, "His father was named John Logan. John A. Logan is my name and that's what I want you to call me. Lieutenant John A. Logan!"

"Well Mr. Logan," drawled the Captain. "Does your father know you're taking his name back?"

Angry and stifling a self-defeating insult, the younger man glared at Cunningham and said slowly, "John A. Logan, sir. John A. Logan."

The younger man became even more irate when Cunningham said nothing, turned his back and walked away. The older man shook his head, chuckled, and said, "If you want to be John A. Logan, I suppose you can call yourself anything you want."

Fists still clenched and veins now bulging from his neck, all five and half feet and 125 pounds of John A. Logan could do nothing more than shout after Cunningham, "I'll fight you, or wrestle you … or race you for it!" shouted Jack.

The challenge didn't alter Cunningham's pace as he mounted his big, gray trotter, shook his head in resigned disbelief and cantered away.

John glared at the Cunningham's back. Ignoring the smirks of Doff and the other volunteers, he shifted his weight back onto his heels and relaxed his fists. A secret smile crossed John's face as he backed toward his bay horse. Calmly swinging himself into the saddle, John didn't look at his friends. He coaxed his saddle horse into a trot, kicked him to a gallop, jumped a split rail fence and charged across the pasture towards town.

A week later, the new Company met to elect officers. Despite his best efforts, John lost the election to be First Lieutenant. To his relief and with his Captain's support, John succeeded in being elected the "Second" Lieutenant. Doff was made First Sergeant. It was the first of a long line of elections for John and while only half the volunteers would serve in Cunningham's Company, John and Doff were among those who traveled with him along the Santa Fe Trail to New Mexico.

Very soon, John was with the newly appointed Colonel Newby's 1st Illinois Volunteers just across the river from Illinois, in St Louis. By July, the volunteers had crossed Missouri and set out on foot from Independence along the Santa Fe Trail.

The column was spaced out to reduce the burden on grass, water sources and livestock. They crossed Kansas where the landscape was at first, lush and interesting. It soon gave way to flat, treeless plains crossed by days of monotonous marching. In a hurry to reach Santa Fe, the Regiment took the southern route across arid and often dangerous Comanche

Country instead of the higher, cooler, better watered, and safer route along the Arkansas River. Captain Cunningham's Company reached the high plains of New Mexico without significant trouble, rested in the village of Las Vegas and arrived in Santa Fe by October 1847, just days after the last local men, charged with rebellion, were hung.

SANTA FE, NEW MEXICO, 1847

During the long crossing, John had become friends with Cunningham. Both were surprised at the appearance of Santa Fe. It seemed as if the town were really a broad harbor of brown dirt nestled between high mountains. The imaginary harbor looked as if it were filled with flat, brown, rectangular barges. On a hill above the town stood rows of tents behind earthen walls. John and the others soon learned that the buildings in town were nearly all made of large, sunbaked bricks called adobe. With thick walls and high windows, adobe was easy to warm in the winter and slow to overheat in the summer when high altitude caused the temperature to fall as quickly as the sun set.

At 7,000 feet, exceptionally dry air revealed a cloudless cerulean sky that stretched unbroken to every horizon. Autumn days were crisp and the air was heavily scented by pinon fires. Before they got too comfortable in Santa Fe, Cunningham and his quartermaster, Second Lieutenant Logan took five men and were sent North to resupply the garrison at Taos.

It was an arduous trip, requiring a week of rough travel through rocks, canyons and increasingly high terrain. Although the trip was uneventful and the garrison was happy to accept the supplies, Cunningham and John were relieved to be able to visit a cantina before bedding down.

Taos was home to an ancient community that more recently served traders, troops and teamsters. Captain Cunningham and John entered the cantina through a low, heavy door. The room was lit by small windows and an oil lamp over the short bar. A few of the tables were occupied by mountain men. The newcomers chose the table furthest from the front, with a clear path to the back of the building and seats allowing a clear view of the front door.

Though they had only been in New Mexico for a few days, Captain Cunningham had immediately embraced the local flavors and knew what he wanted to eat. He ordered "huevos divorciados," a plate with two eggs divided by a scoop of beans; since it was autumn, there was fresh roasted green chile from farms to the south. Chopped chile covered one egg. The second egg was smothered in a sauce made of dried red chile, onion, garlic, oregano and cilantro.

Warm tortillas reminded him of biscuits. John was slower to develop a taste for the local food, but the quartermaster Sergeant at the Taos garrison told him the cantina's cook would leaven tortillas with sourdough and serve ham and pancakes covered with a mixture of molasses and honey. Now, John was as enthusiastic about supper as the others. They were sipping coffee when a teenager and two mountain men took the next table.

John nodded at the new arrivals and all three nodded back. The oldest of them was a short, broad man with a rust-colored beard and stringy red hair flowing from beneath a brimless, coyote-skin, head cover. He stared at the two officers and said, "We're glad you're here." He didn't glance away or turn back to his colleagues when the two young officers nodded and grunted their thanks. The red-haired man just continued to stare blankly at them.

Captain Cunningham and John glanced at the other mountain man who was also looking at them. They noticed the youngest of the trio. He didn't look like at all like his companions. He couldn't have been 20 years old and dressed like an American from home.

The teenager smiled through chipped teeth and said, "We came to help our friends and stayed to see the hangings." He looked from Captain

Cunningham to John and back at the Captain. "Are you replacing some of the soldiers here?" he asked excitedly.

"We're only here for a short stay," answered the Captain, taking a bite of his tortilla and reaching for his coffee cup.

The red-haired man had not averted his eyes and asked in a louder voice, "Did you get to Santa Fe in time to see the hangings?"

Cunningham didn't answer and went back to his meal. John shook his head saying softly, "No, we arrived a few days after." He decided to prompt the mountain man. "Why were they hung?"

Hoping to be asked, the red-haired man sat back and blew out his breath. He looked at the Captain and decided to give his full attention to John who seemed to be more interested. "Surprised you don't know about all that." he said suspiciously.

"Well," said John, looking down at the other two before turning back to Red-Hair, "We've heard some, but I wouldn't mind hearing your view of it."

Cunningham glanced at John and went on with his meal. John leaned forward on his elbows and asked, "What happened?"

With that, the two mountain men looked at the younger of their company and Red-Hair said, "Ask Garrard here. He come down with us from Bent's Fort when we heard about the revolt, and he watched all the trials here in Taos and the hangings too."

John looked at Garrard, who wore the woolen shirt and trousers of a recent arrival. His face was covered with the red spots of a teenager and his sandy hair was matted over his head. "My name is Lewis Garrard and I'm here from Cincinnati to write about the trail to New Mexico and the war."

He smiled as Captain Cunningham raised his eyes but not his head to watch the young reporter. "I was at Bent's Fort when we heard about the revolt and how they murdered the men at Arroyo Hondo we came down through the pass to help fight 'em."

Red-Hair and his friend grunted and finally, began to eat their plates of stewed goat. Garrard began, "We heard they mobbed Governor Bent's house in Taos and scalped him in front of his wife and children before they killed him. And we heard they also killed his wife's brother, the judge's son, the sheriff, a lawyer and the mayor before they went after our friends and every other American they could find."

Garrard added, "That's pretty much how it started." The mountain men nodded as they continued to eat.

The revolt had been a topic of frequent conversation at the fort and Governor's Palace in Santa Fe, but John wanted to hear more. "How come they did that?" asked John innocently, Cunningham's eyes on him now.

"This wasn't their first revolt," began Garrard who went on to describe how a man named Montoya had stirred up a revolt against the Mexican authorities in Santa Fe, ten years before. "That time, Montoya turned over his friends to the governor for punishment. A condition of the 'peace' agreement, I guess."

Garrard was enthusiastic in his descriptions of the revolt and the military trials that followed. He thought there might have been some who deserved to be hanged but many who did not. "The Army rides into Santa Fe, reads a proclamation declaring that New Mexico belongs to the United States and then hangs a man for treason because he didn't agree that Mexico had lost the war! This war is still on! How can a fighter from the other side commit treason?" he asked with indignation.

Captain Cunningham looked up at the three men and asked slowly, "So, you think things here are quiet again?"

Red-Hair looked up quickly and placed his hands, palm down on the table in front of him as he leaned forward with an intense and aggressive glint. "Quiet? Yeah, it's quiet." He didn't move his hands or his eyes for the moment and he added, "For now."

Only then did he look to the second mountain man for affirmation. Receiving a nod of assent, he turned back to the Captain. "It's not over. They hate Americans. If you know the locals and do business with them, you can be alright, even friendly, but if they don't know you, they just look at you like you're there to take their women, their land and to knock down their churches. They've been on their own so long up here, they're not Mexicans, they're Norteños. They've been living with the Pueblos and fighting with the Utes, Navajo, Comanches and Apaches forever."

He leaned back and shook his head when the second, older mountain man spoke up. "There's only one thing you could do to settle them down." He waited to be sure he had both the Captain's and the Lieutenant's attention, then added "Stop the Navajo, Ute, Comanche and Apache raiders and slavers."

As the second mountain man finished speaking, a young native girl came to take their plates from the table and offer them more coffee. Red-Hair nodded at the girl. "She's Navajo. These Norteños take 'servants' from them too. Been doing it for hundreds of years up here. Ain't gonna stop unless you stop it."

The Captain and John looked at the girl with compassion as she walked to the rear of the cantina. The cantina's door creaked open and Doff said the mules were tended and the men had been fed.

Taking a deep breath and rising from the table, Captain Cunningham said, "Thank you for your views gentlemen, the Lieutenant and I have work to do. We wish you all a good evening." He nodded at Jack who left coins on the table then followed Cunningham out the door without looking back.

The mountain men turned to their plates with a shrug while Garrard watched the officers all the way across the small plaza.

As John, Doff and Captain Cunningham walked, John asked, "Did he say the Mexicans take slaves from the Indians?"

"Well, that's one way to look at it," said Cunningham, sounding annoyed. "The natives steal women and children from other tribes and the tribes steal women and children from the Mexicans. You know they'll take them from our people too, if they can." As they passed the guards at the front of the camp he concluded, "They want us to put a stop to the Indian raids, but they want to keep their 'servants,' the same thing Southerners call the people they own."

Doff said, "Indians are just wild N---ers. The Mexicans should round all of 'em up and put 'em to work," he pronounced as if no sane person could disagree. Then he added, "Or kill the ones they can't."

John Logan didn't disagree with him because to that point, he accepted the world as his people saw it: one naturally and justly controlled by white people; for the benefit of white people.

Cunningham walked into the tent he'd been sharing with the local commander, shaking his head and muttering with disgust, "Servants."

Cunningham, John, Doff and five soldiers got back to Santa Fe within a week. Colonel Newby called Cunningham and John into his office. "Colonel Price is sending half the men to El Paso. We'll stay in Santa Fe. Lieutenant Logan, I'm adding Adjutant to your duties as quartermaster. We'll stay in control of things here in Santa Fe until we get other orders." He looked up from his papers at the two young officers and asked, "Any questions?" There were none.

Standing outside the Palace a few minutes later, Jack cursed then exhaled with a groan. "Adjutant at Santa Fe," he scoffed. "The revolt ended before we got here, the fighting is all a thousand miles south of here, and I'm counting beans and blankets!"

"Have you seen what bullets can do to a man, John?" asked the Captain softly.

John didn't answer but shook his head and looked away. The older man went on. "Don't be too hasty for action John. I was a sheriff before we left Illinois. I saw more than I care to remember."

Seeing that John was unconvinced he went on, "I've seen men's faces smashed into their skulls by the butt of a musket. I've seen 'em cry while they try to push their guts back into their bellies after they're slashed, and I've seen 'em crying themselves to death while blood pools around 'em." He paused. "I'm OK with watching the town."

Looking back at John who wore a chastened face, Cunningham looked down for a moment. Without saying anything he began to walk in the direction of the hill above the Palace toward Fort Marcy.

That Fall was uneventful for Jack. Word of victories in the South reached the garrison and there was little evidence of the insurrection that shattered Northern New Mexico the winter before. Colonel Newby was busy trying to suppress the Navajo raids west of Santa Fe and the Comanche and Apache raids on the east. He was unsuccessful because the slower, heavier mounted infantry he commanded were much too slow to catch the Native warriors mounted on nimble ponies. In their place, he commissioned mountain men and Mexicans to suppress native raiders. This only intensified the conflicts and convinced the Indians that the American government differed from the Mexican one only in wealth, numbers and extremity of violence. Although Santa Fe and the surrounding towns were quiet, bitterness seethed.

Winter brought an unfamiliar coldness to the soldiers in Santa Fe. It snowed sometimes, but the sun came out quickly and melted whatever snow it touched. If the air was still and a person stood in the sun, it felt almost warm. But a puff of breeze or a cloud would bring the cold in an instant. Because of the high altitude and dry air, the nights were very cold. Tents were almost useless, stopping the wind but retaining no heat during freezing-cold nights.

"They're sick with measles," reported the camp surgeon to Captain Cunningham. "Too close together and too little air circulation in these mud houses. We're going to lose some of them."

"I've had 'em," said Cunningham to the surgeon.

John swallowed hard enough to draw the attention of everyone in the small room. He was looking at his boots.

Turning to John the surgeon asked, "You have not?"

"No. I don't think so," said the young man, looking up at the surgeon, then Cunningham. Finally, returning his gaze to his boots.

"Well, Lieutenant," said the surgeon moving to the door and looking down at the anxious young man. "You'll know soon enough." Then he said to Cunningham, "I'll keep you informed, Sir. I expect there will be more. Should quiet down when the weather improves."

The measles appeared shortly after Newby's men arrived, probably acquired from the troops already in Santa Fe.

On John's birthday, his friend, the quartermaster Sergeant, Slade, died of measles. A few days later, John was burning with his own fever. He looked to the next bed to see how Doff was doing: afraid to lose another friend even as he had lost three young siblings only two years before. John and Doff had both been sick for over a week and a few more boys died. John and Doff recovered without apparent consequences but they lost nine friends that winter.

John never felt invulnerable again, but he dealt with uncertainty by exaggerating traits he'd developed in his teens. He became more active in seeking support from his men. He worked diligently at his job. He fashioned himself a warrior and volunteered for whatever tasks would take him away from the fort and closer to action.

As quartermaster, John's close association with the merchants and farmers in Santa Fe helped him learn some Spanish. By Springtime, he could do most business by himself. On a cold evening after leaving his paperwork with the Colonel at the little, adobe Governor's "Palace" on the Plaza, and before walking back to Ft. Marcy, he and Doff decided to visit their favorite cantina on the plaza. They ordered posole and tortillas and sipped a glass of beer: a drink that had become popular since the Americans arrived. "How is your family?" Jack asked the proprietor in Spanish.

His host rested his hands on the back of a chair and smiled sadly. "That's kind of you to ask Lieutenant." He paused waiting to see whether John was truly interested or merely trying to be polite. When John held his eyes and said nothing, the owner went on, "My wife and children are well, thank you."

John recalled the Cunningham's admonition after one of John's particularly blustery outbursts, "Why do you think God gave you two ears and one mouth?" Cunningham had asked sarcastically. "Listen at least twice as much as you talk." So, Logan sat quietly and waited for more."

Doff, who spoke no Spanish, rolled his eyes at the "Mexican gibble-gabble," and concentrated on his food, eating noisily while making impatient faces and sighing audibly.

Seeing that he was welcome to tell John the rest, the owner said, "My niece and her mother were taken last week by Navajos." Tears welled in the man's eyes. "They took them from their farm near Abiquiu. They took them and their sheep and just disappeared to the West. We can't go get them back." Then he looked intensely at Jack, "Can you and your soldiers go get them? Can you bring my niece and my brother's wife back to us? And the others they've taken?"

John listened to the man's story. The older man's anguish stirred something in the younger man's heart and there began a change in John's youthful view of the troubles that plagued New Mexico. Although he could recognize the man's pain, he still couldn't acknowledge the grief and terror that accompanied it. John lacked insight into the consequences of ten generations of violence and loss.

John continued to view New Mexico as a beautiful, desolate and wild place. He saw its inhabitants as barely civilized or utterly uncivilized people. "His" Army could suppress revolts, but there weren't enough soldiers to secure the towns or control the natives. And he believed that it would be impossible to reform the society into one that was familiar, safe and American without five times as many soldiers. It would take years and John was already planning his return to Illinois in the Autumn. It wouldn't be his problem anymore.

John's eyes moved from the man telling his story to the native girls in the back of the cantina. "You are looking at our servants," said the owner with understanding. "It is not the same."

The owner shook his head while looking at the children who were working in the back. "We bring these children into our families. We take them to church where they are baptized and we find them husbands so they can be part of a Christian community. The ones in the tribes are savage. Do you know some of them torture captives for sport! It is not the same."

John liked the man and agreed with him. He genuinely wanted to ease the man's distress. "I'm very sorry, Señor," he said softly. "Colonel Newby may do something soon. I cannot say more now." He looked meaningfully into the man's eyes adding, "Preserve your hope."

After the owner excused himself to serve another customer, John explained the conversation to Doff. Unimpressed by the story, Doff replied, "Any Christian home, even if it was papist, is better than growing up with damned savages. Living in this mud-brick rookery is better than running wild on the prairies or in the mountains!"

John nodded in thoughtful agreement adding, "Well, we're talking about Indians and Mexicans. Seems to be the same problem as Black Africans."

Ozburn dropped back in his chair, rolled his eyes and groaned, "They're all brown, they're pagan. Or worse, Papist!" Chuckling at his own joke, "They're not educated. Even your father told me education was the first step toward freedom. And these people," he said sweeping his arm to include all of Santa Fe, "aren't even *capable* of being educated!"

John felt uncomfortable with Doff's comments, he couldn't bring the idea into consciousness, let alone into the conversation. He looked vaguely downward as he began, "Doff, do you remember Wilkinson?" The servant who came to Egypt[2] with my father a couple of years before I was born?"

"So?" Ozburn rolled his eyes, "Didn't your father sell him off when we were about ten?"

John sat up and raised his eyes to Doff. "You know you can't sell people in Illinois. Wilkinson was an indentured servant and father sold the contract to Wilkinson's father when Wilkinson was about 16." John paused, recalling the older boy teaching him to tend to horses, to find places the fish would bite, even on warm summer afternoons.

The scent of grilled onions, fresh tortillas, and piñon smoke brought him back to the cantina. "Well, he only made Munday Dumbaly pay half the going price for Wilkinson's contract. I missed him, but my father said Wilkinson's best chance was with his own people and Munday was Wilkinson's father."

Completely missing the point, Ozburn pounced. "You said 'sold!' there's no difference. Contract or title, sold is sold because they're not fit for life without an owner and that's a fact!"

Colonel Newby soon realized the mountain men and Mexican paramilitary groups he'd deputized to protect the population were using their authority to plunder livestock and kidnap people to be sold into slavery elsewhere. There were very few retrievals of kidnapped Mexican people, but plenty of violent reprisals against natives. The settlements outside Santa Fe remained insecure and the hatreds festered.

At the beginning of May and a few months before leaving New Mexico, Jack managed to accompany Colonel Newby and about 200 men who wound their way into the mountains southwest of Santa Fe. Newby had come to stifle Navajo raids on settlements near the Jemez Pueblo. The

2 The triangular, Southern tip of Illinois has long called itself "Egypt." The term "Little Egypt" was substituted late in the 19th century by writers who seem to have been influenced by a stage name, used much later, by several exotic dancers.

narrow valleys and high, red rock mesas around Jemez created a maze with small streams, box canyons and impassable mountains. When the soldiers arrived and saw what appeared to be Navajo horsemen in the distance, the Colonel sent a dozen of his best riders in pursuit.

It was a futile and frustrating chase. The soldiers' mounts, burdened by extra equipment, weren't up to the task of running down the natives. After hours of futile tracking and just before dark, John and the rest of the small detachment returned to camp.

Early the next morning, several leaders of the Navajos they'd been chasing approached the camp with a white flag of truce. Over the next couple of days, Colonel Newby and the native men reached an agreement. The Colonel wrote a treaty, translated it and both the Colonel and native leaders signed it.

In exchange for the promise that native land and livestock would be respected, and their children returned, the band of Navajos would stop raiding and immediately return their Mexican captives. Additionally, the Navajos paid a fine of 300 sheep and 200 mounts to compensate the Americans for the cost of their foray.

In late summer of 1848 and just before the 1st Illinois volunteers left Santa Fe to go home, twelve Mexican captives were returned. Unfortunately, Newby's treaty was never ratified by the American Congress and Navajo children continued to be baptized by their "masters," all over Northern New Mexico.

The following year, Logan learned an influential Navajo leader named Narbona and hundreds of his men concluded another peace treaty with the Army. This time, moments after the treaty was signed and translated to the assembled Navajos. Trouble broke out.

Many of the younger, native men found the terms unacceptable and were upset. Almost simultaneously, a squabble developed between a soldier and a Navajo warrior over a horse. The Army commander reluctantly affirmed his soldier's point of view and the squabble quickly escalated into a fight.

The old man, Narbona wasn't involved in the argument, he nevertheless saw trouble and ran from the ensuing brawl along with most of the Navajo men who were near the soldiers. The Americans were angry and frightened. They began to fire at the Navajos.

Five or six men including Narbonna were killed as they ran from the camp. In a further, stupid and self-defeating act of cruelty, an American soldier used his knife to remove Narbonna's scalp. Hearing the story, young John Logan's opinion of New Mexico was confirmed.

Sixteen years later, at the same time he and Sherman were preparing to burn through Georgia, the Army in New Mexico committed similar destruction of the Navajo heartland. Whereas civilians in Confederate territory were permitted to leave their homes and find refuge where they could, in New Mexico, nearly 10,000 Navajo men women and children were forced to walk across 250 to 400 miles of high desert to a small, ill-equipped reservation on the plains of Eastern New Mexico near Ft Sumner at a place called Bosque Redondo. The land near the Pecos River couldn't support the people. Despair, disease and starvation killed hundreds.

Navajos who managed to avoid the removal and stayed on their homeland were overrun by Ute Indian raiding parties who killed Navajo men and took their surviving families with impunity. In 1868, the Navajo people who had not died of starvation or disease, walked home from Fort Stanton, across the same desert, and resumed life as best they could in what was left to them, of their homeland.

JACKSON COUNTY, ILLINOIS, 1848

John, Doff and Cunningham walked back to Kansas and rode steamers the rest of the way to their homes in Southern Illinois, arriving in Jackson County in the Fall of 1848. They were promptly mustered out of the Army and John went to work with his mother's brother, Alexander Jenkins (after whom John had been given his middle name). Jenkins had served two terms as Illinois' Lieutenant Governor and John was his protégé.

John began as an apprentice attorney. Very soon and through his family's influence, he was appointed deputy clerk in Jackson County, Illinois. Confident that he needn't remain a deputy clerk, John ran and was elected County Clerk in November 1849. Not counting his election to the role of Second Lieutenant, this was John's first public election. He assumed duties as the Jackson County Clerk the following January but he didn't stay in office for long.

He conceived his future as one of a politician and lawyer. He resigned his position as County Clerk early in 1850 and relocated to Kentucky, enrolling in the University of Louisville Law School that Fall. The faculty was composed of only three or four professors. Much of the education involved on-the-job experience in local law practices and courtrooms. John did very well in both and completed his studies in a matter of months

Returning to Egypt in the late Spring of 1851, John was promptly admitted to the bar. He resumed his duties as Jackson County Clerk and shared a law practice with "Uncle Alexander."

His career progressed swiftly. Increasingly ambitious, John was elected to his father's former seat as a state representative within a year. Once at the capitol in his own right, John enhanced both his friendship and his patronage relationship with Illinois senior Senator and Abraham Lincoln's nemesis, Stephen A. Douglas.

Not satisfied merely to campaign for Mr. Douglas or to stay in the background, John found a niche as the primary advocate for enforcement of 1850's Fugitive Slave Act. He insisted that local authorities cooperate with "slave catchers," and return formerly enslaved people to their "owners."

Thoroughly convinced of the superiority of his race and intellect, in 1853, he advocated and successfully passed "Black Laws," preventing free African Americans from moving to, or settling in Illinois.

The same year the Black Laws were passed, John's father died, leaving John both his reputation and his political connections. Young Logan's alliance with Stephen A. Douglas was strengthened and he found common ground with Democrats across the state. Now, a committed, pro-slavery Democrat and with Douglas' help, Logan was elected, at the age of 32, the Representative to the US Congress from Egypt.

Roundly criticized as a loud, profane bully and at a time when politics were personal, Logan had a well-deserved reputation for strong opinions and stronger language. He was as hostile to enemies as he was loyal to friends. In his first speech in Congress, he nearly came to blows with several of Stephen Douglas' opponents but made a loquacious and insincere apology the next day. With ambition fueling his decisions, it was time to get married.

During their service in New Mexico, Logan's friend, Captain Cunningham had often joked that the young Logan would make a good match for his, then 8-year-old, daughter, Mary. In 1855, John's old friend invited him to visit his home, where he met a teenaged Mary Cunningham and was smitten.

Logan visited, corresponded and courted her for several months. By November of the same year Mary became Mary Cunningham Logan. Logan was nearly 30 years old, and Mary was just over 17. Within a month, Mary was pregnant. As effective a political spouse as ever there was, Mary was an energetic partner and advocate of her husband's legacy throughout her long life.

Still a Congressman in 1861, Logan left his wife and child in Illinois when he returned to Washington for a special session of Congress. It had been called to deal with secession and blood had already been shed.

Logan was able to schedule an urgent, but brief, visit to ask Lincoln for a command in the rapidly growing Army. Logan was a "War Democrat," holding a Jacksonian view of the necessity of preserving the Union while remaining perfectly satisfied to preserve slavery in the bargain. Lincoln demurred, asking Logan to wait. His support at home and in Congress would better serve the cause. There was little Logan could say, but he left undeterred.

A few days later, the recently expanded Union Army moved South. The importance of participating in the fight was not lost on Logan. Attired in his civilian clothes and bearing a pass from the War Department, he and a friend accompanied the Army in the direction of the secessionists.

When fighting began, Logan borrowed a rifle and some ammunition. He made a point of being seen in the fight and helping the wounded from the field. The same afternoon, he returned to Washington; well-before the battle had reached its inglorious end. Logan ensured the newspapers and everyone else knew he had selflessly and bravely battled the foe.

With a darker complexion, flowing black hair and a carefully groomed martial moustache, his appearance supported his nickname "Black Jack.[3]"

---

3 In the 1860s, "Black Jack" was not only an easily remembered moniker, but it referred to

President Lincoln knew that it would be devastating to the Union to lose even a part of a Northern state to secession. A former Illinois Congressman himself, Lincoln had first-hand knowledge of the Egyptians' sympathies and fearing a mirror image of Western Virginia's separation from the Old Dominion, Lincoln took a personal interest in the appointment of dozens of "political Generals" throughout the Army, including several from Illinois.

Lincoln also realized the Union cause in Illinois would be better served with John A. Logan happily wearing a blue uniform. The alternative was an unhappy Congressman Logan sporting a frock coat, stalking the hallways of Congress and advocating a quick peace with the seceding states. Indeed, a large company of men, including Logan's brother-in-law crossed into Kentucky, joining the secessionist army and pressing Logan to join their cause.

Granted a commission as a Colonel with permission to raise his own Regiment, Logan set out to gather a thousand men in ten companies. His Regiment would be numbered the 31st Illinois Regiment of Volunteers. John McClernand, a Congressman from a nearby Illinois district was a bit older and better connected than Logan. McClernand succeeded in getting himself appointed as a Brigade Commander (Brigadier General) and Logan would serve under him for nearly two years.

Recruiting wasn't easy at first. Potential volunteers from Egypt shared Logan's commitment to the Union, but they were unwilling to expend any effort on behalf of enslaved people. To overcome their objections, Logan promised his men that he'd bring them home from the war rather than ask them to fight for the "N---s," if it came to that.

By the late summer of 1861, a West Point graduate and down-on-his-luck former soldier, Ulysses S. Grant had been promoted to Brigadier with authority over McClernand. At almost the same time, Grant's little

---

a kind of rum and a pirate flag. Only later did the term become an American substitute for "truncheon." Later still, it became the common name for a card game.

army was on the brink of dissolution. Men who had enlisted for brief terms of service earlier that year, were about to leave. Grant needed them to reenlist and knew his politically experienced subordinates might have more influence with the men than he did. Despite concerns that these anti-abolitionist Congressmen could do more harm than good, Grant allowed McClernand and Logan to speak to the soldiers.

McClernand was uninspiring. His speech went very much as Grant expected, encouraging but not convincing the soldiers.

Then, it was Logan's turn on the podium. Since childhood, Logan had watched, imitated, and practiced passionate persuasion. For the past 15 years, he'd experienced increasing success as an orator and leader. Logan seemed to breath fire. Roaring and gesturing, his passion and ideas inspired the Egyptians. Reenlistments soared and Grant never forgot.

Grant already liked Logan as a fellow-horseman, but now he realized "Black Jack Logan" would become an indispensable subordinate, a superb "political general" and Grant's lifelong friend.

MARION, ILLINOIS, 1858

Mary Cunningham had married Logan at 17 and was immediately pregnant. The Logans named their baby "John" but he died a few weeks after his first birthday in 1857. Desperately lonely and disillusioned by her husband's obvious preference for politics over romance, she often begged him for his attention. By 1858, Mary was pregnant again and her husband was away from home, riding the Illinois legal circuit, campaigning for election, trying cases and strengthening political relationships.

Logan's expectations of marriage were informed by his parents' relationship. His father stayed busy with medicine and politics while his mother bore and raised children. Logan's father spent his time in the company of men and the younger man simply repeated the pattern he'd learned at his father's knee.

Logan's lifetime ambition had been to gain influence, recognition and to become a Congressman. Mary's complaints frustrated and befuddled him. He was a "man's man," who spoke loudly, disputed readily and enjoyed horses and alcohol. "Why was she such a child!"

"Why do you have to go away again on a Sunday?" she lamented. "You only got home yesterday!"

"You know that I have court in Murphysboro on Tuesday," he said with exasperation. "I have to meet with the client on Monday. It will take me all day tomorrow to travel there and get ready for the meeting. I can't ignore my practice," he said with finality, then added glumly, "We need the money to live in Washington when the term begins."

"You promised!" she wailed. "I can't just stay here with the baby all the time! I want to be a wife!"

"Now Mary, you want to bring our little Dollie and go to Washington with me, don't you?"

She sniffed and nodded agreement.

"And you know that you'll need some new clothes because you'll be meeting the President and entertaining Senators and other Congressmen, right?"

She knew where this was going and looked down, tears threatening to fall from the tip of her nose as she blotted them away.

"Now, how do you suppose I can afford your and Dollies' travel, clothing, rent and furnishings if I just sit here in Marion and wait for cases to come to me?"

She'd heard it before and didn't have the energy to plead the importance of his presence to their daughter or the loneliness she felt, cooped-up in their small house while he saw the wide world. With her head lowered, she wept softly and shook her head in silent agreement.

He left his chair and took a seat next to her, wrapping an arm around her shoulder in his best attempt at consolation. "There's a strong girl. You know we'll be together in Washington and we'll have a grand time!" He paused as her sobs diminished. "That's right. You'll be fine."

Her tears hadn't dried when he rose and walked to their bedroom. Without turning to face her, he said, "I'd better pack now. Tomorrow will be an early morning."

She felt defeated. He couldn't wait to leave.

None of this was new. Mary was often frustrated, plaintive and tearful. Her husband had been elected to Congress in 1858 but his term wouldn't begin until 1859. In a letter begging him to return from political responsibilities she wrote, "I have ever looked up to you as a father more than a companion."

Mary found her stride in Washington. She was smitten by the wealth and power she encountered on a daily basis. Basking in the reflected glory of her husband and his patron, Senator Douglas, Mary blossomed as a hostess, socialite and political spouse. She would eventually make her peace with her husband by sharing in his political activities. When the war came, she reveled in his achievements and recognition. She remained a loyal champion of his career to the end of her long life.

GALESBURG, ILLINOIS 1859

The leaden sky of mid-morning was indiscernible from its appearance at dawn. Cold breeze shuddered arching elm branches above the empty, packed earth street. Three tall, sturdy women walked arm-in-arm, and made their slow procession home from the Presbyterian cemetery. All mourned. None cried. They were Mary Ann Bickerdyke, her elder sister Elizabeth and their niece, Rachel.

Late that morning, in the kitchen of Mary Ann's simple, frame house, she sat with her sister at an old table. With half-frozen fingers, Mary Ann traced the scars in its deeply worn top. They heard Rachel in the parlor, reading to Mary Ann's two little boys, Hiram and James. The older women's voices were soft and low.

Last year, after her husband Robert's death, her sweet little Martha and her growing boys occupied her mind and gave her reason to live. the 42-year-old had just buried her treasured, two-year-old daughter Martha, who died from scarlet fever. Elizabeth drew a deep breath and sighed, "The Lord is sending you another, terrible test." Mary Ann didn't look up, hearing her sister's words as both consolation and advice.

Moments passed in silence. Her arms rested on the table and her hands were still. No tears came. Today, she felt as if life had slipped utterly beyond her control. Grief bored deeply into her and she sensed the disintegration of her family. Life threatened to slip away, as it nearly had, in her childhood.

Sitting quietly and aching, Mary Ann was not hopeless. Part of her mind remained aloof, logical and detached. She believed, just as a blacksmith pounds carbon into hot iron to make steel, her pain made her stronger than she would have been had she been simply a victim.

Her past intruded on her thoughts. Death had taken Mary Ann's mother before she was two. Her father couldn't care for the toddler or her four-year-old sister Elizabeth, so Mary Ann's maternal grandparents, the Rodgers, took the girls. Although she was very happy with her grandparents, Mary Ann was forced to return to her father when he remarried. Neither Mary Ann nor her sister adjusted to life with their stepmother, and they were soon sent back to their grandparents. Elizabeth soon married and at 16 Mary Ann was sent to work as a housekeeper. That changed everything.

The housekeeping job began in 1833 at the home of faculty member at the new, Oberlin College[4]. Living in the professor's home, Mary Ann became well-acquainted with Reverend Gale and other leaders of the labor college movement. She absorbed their commitments to abolition, educating women and creating temperate and benevolent communities.

---

4 American religion experienced two "Great Awakenings" in the first half of the 1800s. Passion and social responsibility spurred active temperance, abolition and suffrage movements across Northern states. In 1827, George Washington Gale, a prominent Presbyterian minister established the Oneida Institute of Science and Industry in upstate New York. He believed college students should perform manual labor (in what he called "Labor Colleges") during their free hours. He brought clergy, academics and donors together to establish colleges across the country. The new colleges were unique because they admitted women, blacks and educated their students in social responsibility.

Successful at the Oneida Institute and riding the wave of utopian optimism, Reverend Gale was instrumental in the establishment of Oberlin College in Northern Ohio in 1832 as another of the Labor Colleges. It took Oberlin's founders two or three years to establish their policies, but by 1835, Oberlin admitted black and female students at a time when coeducational institutions were exceptionally rare and integrated colleges didn't exist.

Intensely curious and outspoken, Mary Ann yearned to become a student at the new college. Even so, she couldn't register for classes. In the first place, the college wasn't ready when she arrived. Later, when Oberlin began to admit women, the orphaned housekeeper lacked money for tuition.

Nevertheless, her employer encouraged her to monitor classes and began to include her in academic discussions. Her mind and values were transformed by what she saw, heard and learned. At an age when most young women married, Mary Ann was at a coeducational college learning philosophy and science, discussing abolition, women's rights and temperance. For the rest of her life, she pursued social service and social justice.

Moral responsibility animated her, while diligence characterized her behavior at the college, with her family and in her work. The professor in whose home she served was in his late 30s and the professor's wife was five years younger. Their house was easy to manage and was blessed with surprisingly healthy children. The couple's genuine concern for Mary Ann's welfare and education built Mary Ann's confidence. She was treated with consistent kindness and respect.

It was Mary Ann's deep sense of responsibility that made her invaluable to the young household. Whether it was boiling laundry, baking, cleaning, or any of the countless tasks necessary to keep the home, her energy earned her a reputation for high standards and hard work. Mary Ann was both excited by, and ashamed of the emotions that emerged when the professor instructed her. The stirrings intensified when she was alone and found herself thinking of him.

Her reactions were romantic but not sexual, admiring but not worshipful, distracting but not often disruptive. They were the inevitable excitements of a young woman's heart. Mary Ann's time with the professor's family had to end. Now 20, attractive, curious and idealistic, it was obvious to the professor and particularly to his wife, that Mary Ann needed to marry.

Mary Ann's uncle lived in Cincinnati and her sister Elizabeth's family was nearby. Arriving in Cincinnati to "help" her aging aunt and uncle, it was only a few weeks before Mary Ann began attending the ill and infirm outside the family. Mary Ann's previous education combined with her nursing skills and led her to apply for admission to a traditional (allopathic) medical school in Cincinnati. She soon learned women were not allowed to enroll.

Mary Ann was stubborn, though some preferred to call her "tenacious" or "driven." She soon discovered a less traditional school in Cincinnati. Dr. Hussey and a couple of his friends ran a training school for practitioners of homeopathic medicine.

The "physio-botanic medical school" accepted female students and Mary Ann quickly undertook studies. She shared what she learned with the families for whom she cared. Her growing skill and experience made her a popular alternative to the expensive physicians and surgeons who served the better-off members of the community and although she continued to identify herself as a housekeeper, she was one with special skills in caring for the sick and infirm.

Mary Ann joined the Sixth Presbyterian church near her home in Cincinnati. Jonathan Blanchard, a friend of reverend Gale from Oberlin College, came to Cincinnati and lead her congregation. Sixth Presbyterian of Cincinnati parted from the traditional Presbyterian Church because it refused membership to slave holders, demanded that members abjure slavery and required them to practice complete abstinence from alcohol. These beliefs held Mary Ann's allegiance for the rest of her life.

By 1846, she as nearly 30 years old, and ambivalent about marriage. On one hand, it offered romance and a family of her own. On the other hand, a wrong choice would condemn her to a lifetime of subordinating her thoughts and deeds to some man's.

The few eligible men Mary Ann encountered were attracted by her bright blue eyes, feminine curves and thick, brown hair. Those same men were also intimidated by her height, her obvious physical strength and most of all, by her impatience with frivolity. The frequent deaths and separations of her early life, left her mistrustful of promises of "forever." She had no patience with men who treated women as if they were simple-minded, ornamental or helpless.

That Spring, she attended her friend's wedding reception in their church's garden. A four-piece band played. One of the musicians was an outgoing English widower named Robert Bickerdyke. Like Mary, he was tall, but blonde with bright blue eyes and a distinctive accent. He was struck by an intense feeling of attraction to the tall, confident and unattached brunette.

During an intermission in the music, Robert asked the hostess to introduce him. The hostess was only too happy to try her hand at matchmaking because she perceived Mary Ann's prolonged maidenhood as bordering on spinsterhood. Mary Ann received the introduction and was surprised to find herself looking up at the man.

Robert's accent disarmed Mary Ann's reluctance long enough for him to engage her in a conversation about her church. Always willing to share her passions, Mary Ann found herself telling Robert about her beliefs and concerns. Her eye conceived her heart's desire and her mind came along much later.

Robert was more than a decade older than Mary Ann, but that seemed to make him even more interesting. She realized she'd been talking without interruption for five minutes. With her eyes on Robert, two things reached her awareness. First, he was actually listening to her. This was something she had first experienced with the professor and it inflamed the same part of her soul.

The second thing she noticed was that he looked into her eyes with an expression that warmed her. Her heart opened. Robert was the one.

Walking home after the reception, Mary Ann concluded Robert was even better looking than he had been when she first laid eyes on him. His maturity, his openness, love of music and admiration of Mary Ann's intelligence perfected him.

Robert Bickerdyke was a widower with two pre-adolescent sons. He was as jovial as Mary Ann was reserved. As romantic as Mary Ann was practical and, in a few weeks, he proposed marriage, Reverend Blanchard performed the ceremony and Elizabeth and her family attended.

Used to caring for others' children, Mary Ann readily assumed the role of stepmother to Robert's sons while continuing her medical work part-time. Robert was skilled at faux wood-graining: using paints, brushes and combs to create finishes on indoor walls that mimicked mahogany and other expensive paneling. Although Robert's living came from painting walls, his heart was in making music.

By 1855 Mary Ann was pleased to have borne two healthy boys of her own. She treasured memories of her grandparents' farm and she longed to live in open country. Robert's music career was stagnant and his painting jobs were unreliable. It was clear to both of them that Cincinnati was too crowded and too violent, cut-off from the countryside and increasingly populated by pro-slavery gangs, transients and the unchurched. Robert's older boys were established in the local community and Mary Ann was eager to leave Cincinnati. So, she did.

In the tiny kitchen, Elizabeth put her hand on Mary Ann's, saying, "You're smart and strong and you're so well organized." She paused, then squeezed Mary Ann's hand and added with more hope than confidence "There are a lot of widowers who would count themselves lucky to have you!"

Mary raised her head and looked at her sister with cold determination. Speaking slowly and calmly she said, "I'm 42 years old. Remarriage is no part of my future," her gaze returning to the worn table top she went on,

"With Robert gone and now Martha, I have to do something I'd planned to do later. I want to send the boys to Eddy in Wisconsin. I know he needs help tending his livestock. He'll teach the boys to farm and they'll have plenty to eat and a good school to attend."

In a pleading tone her sister said, "No, they're too young! Send them to me. Jacob and I can look after them." She paused, "Our niece, Rachel doesn't have to go back to school right away. She could stay here and help you. I don't want you to lose James and Hiram too!"

"Elizabeth, you took over for our mother when we were tiny. I wasn't two years old when mother died. Ever since, you've treated me as if I were your daughter. I am so thankful to you." With kindness Mary Ann added, "I would never interrupt Rachel's education. You know how I feel about that." And with soft finality she said, "Hiram and James can go to Eddy's. They'll be happy there. I can manage." Mary Ann kept her boys at home for one more year.

TIFFIN, OHIO, 1860

Rachel's father, Ted Rodgers, was eldest child and only son of a successful farmer in Eastern Ohio. When Ted was about ten, his Uncle Hiram lost his wife and he was left with two little girls in need of a home. Ted's family raised little Elizabeth and Mary Ann. Soon, Ted saw them more as younger sisters than cousins. Ted now had children of his own and Rachel was his older daughter.

Ted inherited a subscription to Heidelberg College from his father who, in return for a significant donation, was granted the right to enroll one student a year. Because Heidelberg was coeducational and Ted's sons had no interest in college, his only daughter, Rachel was allowed to use the subscription.

During the academic year, Rachel stayed in the home of her uncle's friends. The Johnsons, whose home was a long block west of the college near the intersection of Perry and Jefferson Streets, were in their 60s. Their trusting and affectionate natures granted Rachel more liberty than her parents might. Her surrogate grandparents were delighted to have young Rachel in their home, if only to sleep and dine.

One warm, Spring day, Rachel was summoned to the office of the "Ladies' Principal" of Tiffin, Ohio's Heidelberg College. Rachel walked down Perry Street with considerable apprehension toward the single building that housed the college. She suspected her interview had something to do with deportment, but she was unsure which aspect of her behavior had attracted attention.

Leaving Perry Street and following the path to the steps of the college, Rachel found her way into the office of "The Principal of the Female Department," Miss Hartsock: a newly appointed administrator with the quintessentially Victorian task of assuring both a quality academic education and lady-like behavior among the young women of the college.

The furniture in Miss Hartsock's office seemed to have been chosen with the goal of imposing a sense of smallness on visitors. The "Ladies' Principal" pointed to a large, leather-upholstered, barrel back armchair where Rachel should be seated. The sides of the chair were too high for Rachel to rest her arms comfortably and its matching sofa occupied nearly all the remaining space in the office. Rachel folded her hands on her lap and slowly raised her eyes to the matronly, 35-year-old Miss Hartsock.

Holding Rachel's eyes, the black-clad moral guardian began solemnly, "Miss Rodgers," after which she paused dramatically and drew a deep breath. "It has come to our attention that young Mr. Stark of our Sophomore class has been seen in your company on a regular basis. We are especially concerned that your encounters have frequently taken place beyond the grounds of our college and in the absence of a proper chaperone." Having concluded her opening statement, she leaned back, into her chair and eyed Rachel carefully. "You can imagine the risks, not only to your reputation, but to the reputation of the college and of coeducational institutions in general."

Rachel was humiliated and embarrassed. Before she risked a response, her mind raced across as many of her dozens of encounters with Mathan Stark, as she could recall. Had she been indiscreet? Were their alibis inadequate? Had a friend betrayed her confidence? Deciding to concede only to the inevitable and conceal the rest, Rachel answered, "Yes Miss Hartsock. I have spoken with Mr. Stark on several occasions but only in respectable and proper settings."

Sighing and leaning forward on her elbows, the matron replied, "I'm sure that was your intention Miss Rodgers. You must keep in mind the commitments that our college and I personally have made to your parents. The reputations of all our young ladies must remain unblemished. Why, the very fact that your conduct has been questioned should alarm you and renew your commitment to the utmost propriety in your every word and deed." She wrinkled her brow and looked over her glasses making a face that she hoped would express both censure and concern.

"Yes Ma'am," answered Rachel with all the confidence she could muster. "I am quite committed to the standards of the college and I know how gossip can assume a life of its own." She leaned forward in what she hoped would be a convincingly mature demonstration of innocence. "I would very much like to clarify the matter with whomever expressed concern for my welfare and conduct. I am both grateful for their good wishes and alarmed by their misapprehensions."

Miss Hartsock smiled, feeling that she'd made her point and had effectively communicated the jeopardy Rachel might face. "I'm sure that won't be necessary Miss Rodgers, but I'll ask you to be ever-mindful of the disastrous consequences of a violation of our College's standards of personal conduct."

"Thank you, Miss Hartsock. Thank you for your concern. You have no reason to worry about me," said Rachel as she rose from the cavernous chair, waiting to be dismissed.

"You may go now, said Miss Hartsock quietly as she sat back and took up her papers.

As Rachel opened the door, Miss Hartsock added without looking up, "It would be tragic if Reverend Kieffer were required to conduct a similar interview with Mr. Stark."

Rachel nodded at the top of Miss Hartsock's lowered head and closed the door quietly. Rachel felt the trickle of perspiration roll from beneath each arm and she hastened to an empty classroom for a private moment to recompose herself.

Mathan Stark had enrolled at Heidelberg a year before Rachel. During the academic year, he lived in a boarding house at his parents' expense. His roommate was a student of theology and a class ahead of Mathan. On the first day of classes in the Fall of 1860, his roommate introduced Mathan to Rachel Rodgers.

Rachel was taller than most women. Her blue eyes were set beneath a strong brow and highlighted by a creamy European complexion and sandy, blonde hair. Her broad shoulders complimented her feminine curves. Most women quietly admired her appearance. Older men looked at her wistfully and young men competed for her attention.

Rachel and Mathan were surprised by how quickly and intensely they were attracted to one another. Well-matched intellectually, they were inseparable. Long conversations about novels, politics and art were nearly as satisfying as the fulfillment of their romantic impulses.

A few days after Miss Hartsock's admonitions, Rachel awoke to flickers of sunlight crossing her face and dancing on Mathan's arm, where she rested. Breeze stirred the branches above them and she still glowed from the rush of passion that blossomed the moment they embraced in their secret place: a thicket behind the hill.

Now, a few hundred yards closer to the town, she drifted in and out of sleep under a broad maple. The picnic blanket featured not only the dozing lovers, but also a hamper with enough food to convince any curious onlookers that the pair was courting in plain sight.

She reached out to touch Mathan's cheek, gliding a finger across his brow and tucking strands of auburn hair behind his ear. Sighing, he took her hand in both of his and motioned for her to sit up. Now clenching her hand, he faced her and rose to one knee. "You know, you're the most important person in my life. I love you with all my heart and I want to do everything in the world to make your life joyful, fulfilling, and safe." He paused, gathering himself and willing the tears away, his voice trembled as he continued, "Rachel… Rachel, will you marry me?"

She squeezed his hands and trembled, shuddering as she drew breath. A sense of bright light and surging energy blossomed, filling every corner of her body while stopping her thoughts. Holding his eyes, but breathing deeply and struggling to calm herself, she came to her knees and faced him. "Mathan Stark, I would love to be your bride…" and her words hung between them. "but…" then correcting herself she continued, "*and*, I know you're going to go away with the Army and I think we should wait for the wedding until after-"

"Yes!?" he blurted. Nearly crushing her hand, he repeated, "Yes?!"

"Yes Mathan!, Yes, yes, yes!" Tears glistened on her cheeks, "Oh yes! Not right now, but yes! This fighting will only last a little while. Hasn't the Governor said your enlistment is only 90 days? We can get married when this is over, and we'll have even more to celebrate!"

Mathan freed her hand, quickly taking her in his arms, she embraced him and they lost their balance, tumbling over and laughing with happiness and relief, they lay in one-another's arms for several minutes as the moment took root in their souls.

Near the end of the Spring Semester of 1861, Rachel received a letter from her Aunt Mary Ann. She smiled as she absorbed her Aunt's bluntness in asking for help.

Dear Niece,

The fighting has begun and I need (your) help with Hiram and James. I think the Army will create plenty of sickness in our young men and

I intend to help care for them. Our church is gathering medicine and supplies to send to the camps and I need help organizing all that.

When can you arrive, and would you stay for the summer? I've arranged for the boys to go stay with my brother before school starts because I don't want to interfere with your studies in the Fall.

Please greet your parents for me and come as quickly as you can.

Ever Yours,

Aunt Mary Ann

Before finishing the letter, Rachel saw the possibilities. She knew the Mississippi was the key to defeating the rebellion in the West and that Mathan's Regiment was likely to be sent there. She had no better plan for the Summer than the one presented by her Aunt and she decided to tell Mathan and make plans.

GALESBURG, ILLINOIS, 1861

After the semester ended, Elizabeth and Rachel returned to Ohio to help with Mary Ann's boys. It was summertime and Galesburg sweltered.

Mary Ann entered through the back door of Dr. Babcock's combination home-and-medical-office, to prepare for the day's patients. Dr. Babcock looked up from his morning coffee and greeted her before going back to his newspaper.

Mary Ann went from room to room, straightening papers, adjusting furniture and opening windows to circulate the morning air. Vainly hoping to cool it before the day's heat and humidity made the indoors unbearable. She was startled as she opened the front door to see a tall, skinny boy standing only inches from the entrance. Noticing the boy's appearance, she immediately guided him into the examination room.

"Dr. Babcock!" Mary Ann called urgently. "Please come here and look at this boy." She met the doctor at the doorway and whispered softly, "I believe he's got the measles."

The boy was stripped to the waist and seated on a high, wooden stool. He stared, open-mouthed at Dr. Babcock, obviously shocked at the diagnosis. The boy's appearance reminded her of a bird struggling to maintain a perch on a narrow branch. Looking intently at the pale, hollow-chested boy, she kept her eyes on him as she heard Dr. Babcock say, "I see what you mean." With obvious maternal concern and in a gentle voice Mary Ann asked the boy, "How old are you, son?"

Looking up into Mary Ann's eyes, then down at the floor, the teen-ager collected his thoughts. He looked to Dr. Babcock for support he said, "I'm 18." Then turning to Mary Ann, he added quickly, "I came to join the Army with my friends, but I got here too late. The Sergeant says I'll have to wait until the next Company forms in a week or two."

Dr. Babcock's eyes caught Mary Ann's. Mary Ann asked, "How did you know to come here?"

"My mother's friend," the boy said quietly. "I'm staying with her fam-ily and she said pink-eye shouldn't give me sore muscles and a fever at the same time." He added, "I feel alright, but she said I had to come and see you anyway."

Mary Ann walked behind the boy and stopped next to Dr. Babcock. They looked carefully at the boy's skin and the telltale, tiny, red spots on his neck and behind his ears.

"Who are you staying with?" asked Mary Ann.

"Mr. and Mrs. Hitchcock," he said tentatively. "They're near the college."

She looked at Dr. Babcock and said, "I know them from church. They're long-time residents and wonderful, generous people. I should go talk to Mrs. Hitchcock about their family and arrangements."

Dr. Babcock nodded and looked back to the boy. "Son," he said with concern, "You seem to have the measles. You'll need to stay away from people until you're better." Dr. Babcock gave the boy a minute to digest the news. "You're young, you should be fine, but we don't want you around children or older people." Then he asked, "Do Mr. and Mrs. Hitchcock have children?"

"No sir," said Todd, they're all grown and out of the house. That's why they had room for me."

Mary Ann nodded at Dr. Babcock as she picked up her medical case and stepped out the door. She had seen measles many times and knew that when people were crowded with cold food, dirty water, dirty clothing and poor hygiene, the sickness would spread and kill mercilessly. They would try to isolate Todd and watch the Hitchcocks, but the arrival of strangers from all over the state, meant they'd bring their diseases with them.

The Hitchcocks were generous to a fault and Mary Ann was worried about their health. She knew that it could be weeks from one person's illness to the next one's. Although the Hitchcocks were only a decade older than Mary Ann, she looked to them almost as parents and she wanted to protect them.

As Mary arrived, Mrs. Hitchcock was on her way out the front door. "Good morning, Mrs. Hitchcock," said Mary with a smile.

"Well good morning to you Mrs. Bickerdyke!" replied the older woman. "What a pleasure to see you!" she added as she rested a hand on Mary Ann's arm. "What brings you?"

"I'm afraid my visit isn't social," replied Mary Ann, looking past Mrs. Hitchcock toward the house. "Could we sit for just a moment?"

Still holding Mary Ann's arm and guiding her toward the house, Mrs. Hitchcock said, "Of course dear, I was only going our for a few things before the sun got too high… It's Todd isn't it? He's sick, isn't he?" Then she added quickly, "Would it be alright to sit here on the porch? I have some cool water or tea, would you have time join me for some?"

"Oh, no thank you Mrs. Hitchcock." Said Mary looking down, then back into Mrs. Hitchcock's eyes. "The boy, um…Todd… came to Dr. Babcock's this morning. He said he was staying with you."

"Of course!" sighed Mrs. Hitchcock, "Todd is such a sweet boy! His parents are friends of mine and they asked me to put him up while he looked for work here in Galesburg." She paused and added more slowly, "He didn't look well, and I was afraid…" she paused. "Afraid his pink-eye might be something more. I was insistent that he visit you to see what could be done." Then, leaning toward Mary Ann with concern, "What is it?"

Mary Ann thought a direct response would be best. "Yes, Mrs. Hitchcock, we think the boy may have the measles and we want you and your family to take precautions until we're sure." Then, thinking for a moment Mary Ann questioned, "Looking for work, you said?"

"Yes, he was hoping to get on with one of the merchants in town, he said."

"Mrs. Hitchcock," Mary Ann replied in a harder voice than she might have intended, "He told us he was here to enlist in the Army."

Mrs. Hitchcock leaned back in her chair, causing it to creak as she looked thoughtfully down the walk, then back to Mary Ann. "He did, did he? I should have known. He's too young for that you know. Only 15, I think."

"Dr. Babcock and I suspected so. He's certainly not grown into himself yet. He's gangly, more like twelve than eighteen."

"Measles?" asked Mrs. Hitchcock. "Is it bad?"

"Not yet anyway," replied Mary Ann. "It would be better if you kept him in a room by himself, washed his linens separately and kept him away from children." After a moment Mary Ann asked, "Have you and Mr. Hitchcock had the measles?"

"Yes, yes we have, Mrs. Bickerdyke. When we were children."

"Good, then there shouldn't be much to worry about as long as he keeps to himself until a week after the rash starts. Actually, I think it's started today. He won't feel very well anyway. Watch him closely for trouble with breathing or anything severe. We'll come if you need us." Then she added, "It's good that he came down with it before he got to the Army. Measles can run through those camps like a wildfire. A lot of the boys get deathly ill."

Mrs. Hitchcock said, "Of course we'll take good care of him. And, when he's well, my husband will be taking him straight back to his parents with the whole story. I wouldn't want my boy in the Army before he was ready!" Then she paused, and said thoughtfully, "After what I hear happened in Virginia last week, I'm afraid this war could last long enough for Todd to grow into it."

Mary Ann decided to take a short detour and visit Mary Allen West in her cramped closet-of-an-office at their church. The church was built in 1837, when the town was founded, and materials were scarce. Mary Allen West was the first child born in the new town. Mary Allen entered Knox College at 13, graduated at 17 and became a whirlwind of social advocacy for the rest of her life. The smartest child most had ever met was somehow aware that her time on earth was short and her tasks were countless.

Mary Allen admired Mary Ann's outspoken tenacity while sorrowing that the older woman had been denied the education that would have refined her native intelligence, curiosity, and organizational skill. They complimented one another: youth and experience, education and practical skills, common sense and aspirations. Together, they were a powerful force and had advocated, organized, and prepared at the state and local levels. Army volunteers from their community must be supported in every way possible and Mary Allen and Mary Ann were just the two to see to the task.

Seeing her friend making entries in a ledger, Mary Ann cleared her throat and Mary Allen looked up and smiling at her friend, she said, "I was just thinking about you!"

"You were?" asked Mary Ann. "And why would that be?"

"Well!" said Mary Allen picking up a letter from the corner of her desk, "President Lincoln signed the act creating the United States Sanitary Commission. It's going to work with the War Department but be independent and mostly staffed by volunteers. It's similar to our Soldiers' Aid Society and it's what we've been waiting for. We're not just 'women of the church' anymore, we're a Federal Agency!"

Mary Ann stepped forward and took the paper from Mary Allen for a closer look. Having read a few paragraphs while her friend waited, Mary Ann returned the letter and said, "What does this mean for the supplies we're sending to Cairo next week?"

"It means that before long, we'll be coordinating our work with Societies all over the state and that we'll be able to raise money for more than just bandages, bedding and simple supplies. They plan to provide help for the wounded when they come home, and for the widows of the ones who don't."

A few days later it was Mary Allen West who blew into the room like a cannonball (which was also a reminder of her general appearance and demeanor). "The supplies are ready and I want to put your name forward as our representative. I want you to be the one who looks after our boys and makes sure the supplies reach them and that no one derails them for other purposes."

Mary Ann half smiled and held Mary Allen's eyes for a moment before answering, "Certainly. I'd planned to go somehow, and now that you're making a formal offer, I'm only too happy to agree. When shall I plan to go?"

"In a week or maybe two. The regiment they formed from our boys is only committed to serve for 90 days, so I expect they'll move South pretty quickly. The Army hasn't had much time to prepare for them, so heaven knows where the boys will sleep, how they'll clean themselves or even if there will be enough to eat. Heaven knows there's little enough been done if any of them gets sick."

Mary Ann replied, "They're going down to Cairo. I hear there are tents and a warehouse to receive supplies, but I want to see that with my own eyes. I want to be there as soon after they arrive as possible, a week later, at most." Mary Ann smiled. Although neither of them said it, both saw the war as a fight for abolition. They knew women had an essential role to play. They also knew that powerful men opposed their ideas vehemently.

In early August 1861 and two weeks after visiting Mary Allen West at church, Mary Ann was on her way over 300 miles south from Galesburg to Cairo. The little train jolted and bucked down the rails toward the confluence of the Ohio and Mississippi Rivers. Cairo was booming with the Army and expansion of Fort Defiance at the tip of the state. Mary Ann alternated between opening the window to allow a breeze to cool the sweltering interior of the rail car and closing it against the cascades of cinders from the locomotive. It took two days and a couple of changes to roll the 300 miles from Galesburg through Egypt, to Cairo, Illinois.

CAIRO, ILLINOIS 1861

Cairo, Illinois, at the extreme southern tip of the state, was the site of Fort Defiance and the starting point for Union troops battling for control of Missouri, Kentucky and the Mississippi River. Southern Illinois forms a triangle, like the tip of an arrow embedded between the states of Kentucky and Missouri. Cairo was the same latitude as North Carolina and nearly as far south as the Northern border of New Mexico and Arizona. Egypt's politics were conservative, and abolition was widely unpopular. Nevertheless, politicians who wouldn't lift a finger in support of emancipation enthusiastically supported the preservation of the Union, referring to themselves as "War Democrats" or "Jacksonians."

Ladies from the church met Mary Ann at the station and walked her to the church where there was a small sleeping space for volunteers. As they walked the few blocks to the church, they pointed down the road that led a mile to the fort, where the supplies from Galesburg would arrive.

Churches in Cairo strongly supported the soldiers who gathered in their community and one of the churches offered Mary Ann lodging. She worked with other volunteers to manage the distribution of extra clothing, pickled foods, patent medicines and packages from soldiers' families. Mary Ann supervised the reception and distribution of those shipments. She stayed with them until all the crates were delivered to the Illinois Brigade's quartermaster. She learned where the supplies would be stored and how she could access them,

A couple of weeks later, Mary Ann returned from the Fort to find three women waiting for her at the church. The obvious leader of the trio was white, in middle age, tall and imposing. Mary Ann recognized her as the well-dressed wife of an Elder in Cairo's Presbyterian Church. Impatient to begin speaking, she was clearly on a mission. Mary Ann noticed the other two women wore traveling clothes. Each carried a case. The younger white woman was barely five feet tall. Her back was straight, and she looked squarely at Mary while waiting for the Elder's wife to speak. A black woman of about 30, of average height and whose hands revealed a history of hard work watched the elder's wife. Mary Ann noticed the way she stood between the other women and met Mary Ann's eyes without apology or challenge.

"Mrs. Bickerdyke?" asked the elder's wife.

"Yes," replied Mary Ann, allowing the others time to introduce themselves.

As you probably know, I'm Mrs. Stewart. Indicating the shorter woman, she said, "This is Mrs. Turnby, just here from Ohio. Finally placing a hand on the third woman's arm she said, "And this is Mrs. Allen. She's traveling with Mrs. Turnby and we're here to ask your assistance."

"Please, how can I help?" asked Mary Ann without moving.

"To get straight to the point," said Mrs. Stewart with the tone of a lady never questioned, "Mrs. Allen is here to find work. Her husband is employed by a Regiment of Ohio volunteers who expect to be sent here in the near future. She needs work." Then, turning from Mary Ann she added, "Mrs. Turnby will explain."

The younger woman smiled at Mary Ann, who smiled back. "Mrs. Allen is a dear friend of mine. She was born in Canada and came to Ohio. She has always been free. She has her papers and I carry a copy for safekeeping." With that, Mary Ann looked to Mrs. Allen and said, "I'm Mary Ann Bickerdyke and I am pleased to meet you. I will do all I can to help you."

Mrs. Turnby relaxed noticeably, and she went on, "Her husband, Reverend Alexander Allen is a Methodist-Episcopal clergyman and had a congregation in Tiffin and when the war began, he wanted to enlist. As you know, there are no colored troops from Ohio. He chose the next-best thing and is under contract to the quartermaster as a blacksmith and wheelwright. He helps the waggoneers maintain their equipment. They're scheduled to come to Fort Defiance and Mrs. Allen would like to have a place for him when he arrives."

Mary Ann turned to Mrs. Allen, ""Your husband is a pastor, Mrs. Allen?"

"Yes, Mrs. Bickerdyke, he is. He was torn between ministering to our people at home and joining the Army. He believes too many politicians won't help us with freedom because our people haven't *earned* it."

"Earning a God-given right?"

Mrs. Allen nodded and sighed. "They don't see it that way. He wants to set an example and to help the cause. She added wistfully, "Who knows what will come of it."

"Well, there are certainly many here who would benefit from his ministry-and even more who would support him…" she paused. "I want to hear more about both of you, but for now, have you ever cooked for large groups of people?"

Mrs. Allen nodded hopefully.

"Have you cooked for over 100 people?"

Mrs. Allen paused. "With help, I don't know if I could prepare and cook meals for one hundred all by myself."

"You'd have help Mrs. Allen. Can you manage a laundry for 100?"

"Yes Ma'am. I can do that."

"Can you read?"

"Yes."

"Do sums?"

"I am comfortable with algebra and geometry. I was educated in Canada."

"I apologize Mrs. Allen. I need your help very much," said Mary Ann taking both of Mrs. Allen's hands now and ignoring Mrs. Stewart and Mrs. Turnby.

Mary Ann continued, "The military surgeon with temporary charge of our medical facilities is a quite a challenge. When soldiers are detailed to assist us in establishing, maintaining and operating our hospitals, they're usually called back to their units without concern for the disruption caused by their departure. It seems the only ones they leave us are the sick, lame and lazy. We need help running our hospitals and that means, cleaning, cooking, baking, laundry, nursing and all the administrative details that come with ordering, receiving and distributing supplies.

Now addressing all the ladies present she went on, "Dr. Brinton, our 'Temporary Surgeon,' sees the women who have sought work here as, in his words, 'dilettantes, whose concern for the troops might be better expressed in financial donations than in nursing the sick.' He's doubly upset that so many of our volunteers live at the dangerous margins of life. They come seeking work, lodging and meals in return for whatever task we might set them to."

"That Dr. Brinton has even described our volunteers as, '…helpless, irritable, unhappy, fussy and intent on notoriety and glorifying (their) good works.' Makes me furious! I overheard him ask a friend, 'Can you fancy half a dozen old hags … surrounding a surgeon insisting on their, little wants?'

"But no matter how much he fusses, he can't run the hospitals without women's help. He's called on Roman Catholic Sisters in hopes they'll replace all of us. He values chastity and submissiveness highly and finds those things in the Catholic sisters. If he must employ women, he wants nuns."

Mary Ann smiled. "But it was all over once he acknowledged that the Sisters could nurse. If a Roman Catholic woman could nurse, so could good Presbyterians, Methodists and Congregationalists! I doubt he'll ever let go of his bad attitude towards women, but I believe the US Sanitary Commission's weight will match his."

Mrs. Stewart and Mrs. Turnby appeared to be troubled by Mary Ann's story, but Mrs. Allen was smiling. "I'm very familiar with your Dr. Brinton's type, Mrs. Bickerdyke. I've run into lots of people with his attitude all my life. And I don't imagine I've been underestimated for the last time."

"Indeed!" said Mary Ann. I made the same mistake myself when I met you and I am very, very sorry."

"Thank you, Mrs. Bickerdyke." said Mrs. Allen brightly. I heard about you from people who knew you in Cincinnati. I'm pleased to meet you and proud to work with you."

"Then you know that I have no patience with anyone who was more interested in recognition than contribution or whose priorities are selfish!"

"Of course, Ma'am."

Mary Ann turned to the other two ladies. "Thank you both, very much for introducing Mrs. Allen to me." Looking at Mrs. Allen she said, "If I show you to a place where you can stay and keep your things safe, are you ready to begin work today?"

Mary Ann led Mrs. Allen to a medium sized room adjacent to the hospital where narrow, wooden bed frames were built into the walls and stacked two high. "Mrs. Allen, would you be alright here? It's not full, but you'll be sharing space with several other ladies who've joined us to help with our work."

That night, after finishing with her first long day at the hospital, Mrs. Allen came to Mary Ann's tiny office. "Ma'am, I have something to ask."

"Yes, Mrs. Allen," said Mary Ann, lowering her pen and sitting back in her chair. "What's on your mind?"

"Mrs. Bickerdyke, I have been led to understand that you are sensitive to the needs of fugitives." She paused, letting her question blossom.

Mary Ann set her pen to the side and leaned forward on her forearms, holding Mrs. Allen's eyes. "I am deeply concerned about the needs of fugitives. Why do you ask?"

Leaning forward to match Mary Ann's posture, Mrs. Allen said, "Because Cairo has the potential to assist so many people on their way to freedom. Will you help me?"

Mary Ann took Mrs. Allen's hand again. "Mrs. Allen. Nothing in my life could be more important to me than helping people find their way to freedom." With equal intensity she added, "We must be able to trust each other and to be wise in our decisions. I know people who will help us."

"Revered Blanchard told me to find you and now, I understand why."

In the late August 1861, Mary Ann returned to Galesburg to say good-bye to her boys. Rachel heard the train whistle signal its arrival and stood on the porch, waiting for her aunt to appear. She thought better of taking Hiram and James to the station. It was difficult enough to keep track of them near home. A visit to the railroad depot could result in her spending a day hunting for her two, young cousins.

"There you are!" Called Mary Ann as she turned the corner and saw Rachel on the porch.

Rachel smiled, took the two steps to the garden path and strode toward her aunt with both delight and relief. "I'm so glad you're back home!" she said, hugging Mary Ann and holding on for a moment longer than Mary Ann expected.

Returning the long embrace, then holding Rachel at arms' length, Mary Ann smiled, tipped her head and looked up mischievously asking, "Boys keeping you busy?"

Rachel's straying hair, wrinkled apron and fatigued expression answered before she did. "They've been fine," she answered unconvincingly. "They're healthy and are ready to go back to school."

"Let's talk about that, Rachel," said Mary, picking up her suitcase and taking Rachel's arm with her left hand.

During the 45 minutes before the boys returned from their adventures, Mary Ann told Rachel about the conditions and work at Cairo, the need for more supplies, and finally, gave Rachel details of her plans to send the boys to Wisconsin and return to Cairo for the duration of the war.

"You'll be able to start the Fall semester with your class, Rachel. I know how important your education is to you and it's every bit as important to me."

"I'm of two minds, Aunt Mary Ann," began Rachel quickly. "I don't want to spend the war in a classroom while everyone else is helping." Looking into her aunt's eyes she went on, "Someday, I want to complete my education, I want to teach other women and to make it normal for women to go to college."

"I know you do. It's what you *should* do," said Mary Ann, attempting to settle the matter before Rachel could offer an alternative. It didn't work.

Rachel straightened her back, "Mathan and almost all of the young men from Heidelberg have enlisted in a Regiment from down by Zanesville. I don't want to just sit in class and wait for him to come home, I want to help too." Then she added the words Mary Ann hoped not to hear, "Can I come with you?"

Mary Ann knew enough to answer slowly, although she had the answer in mind weeks ago. An Army camp was no place for an attractive single woman like Rachel, no matter how determined she was. She began, "There's certainly more work to do than we have hands to do it. You're so smart and so willing to work…."

"But?" Rachel interrupted her suspiciously.

"But," Mary Ann said, "We require all nurses to be at least 30 years old. Besides that, we're supposed to be plain looking." Smiling at Rachel she added, "You can wear black, you can pull your hair into a knot and you can leave your pretty things with your mother. But you can't be 30, no matter how hard you try."

"If those boys at the recruiting meetings are all 18, I'm *at least* thirty!"

Looking down to hide her smile, Mary Ann shook her head. Then looked up and into her niece's eyes, "I love you as if you were my own daughter. I know you want to help, and I think you should. College will be there next year or whenever this war ends. But being at an Army camp isn't the right place. Stay here and help Mary Allen if you want. Or go back to Tiffin or even Zanesville and work with the US Sanitary Commission there. But stay near friends and other ladies. There is so much to do!"

Rachel admired her Aunt and knew that arguing with Mary Ann was like trying to make water run up hill. She recognized that Mary Ann's attachment to Mary Allen revealed an understanding of, and appreciation for, energetic young women. Rachel realized, the better she understood her Aunt, the better they could work together. She also intuited that when another person knows your history and your feelings about it, they're much more likely to view you as a peer and ally than as a dependent or student.

Rachel nodded and leaned over to hug her Aunt. I've already made stew for supper. The bread should be done any time now."

Following the scents into the little house, the women were soon joined by the boys. The question of Rachel's service remained open until after dinner, when the boys were asleep and Rachel decided to try another approach. "Aunt Mary Ann, tell me how you came to Galesburg and how you decided to go to Cairo and the Army."

"Rachel, that's all, old news and I suspect you know most of it. I'm tired now and would like to go to bed."

"I hate to insist, but I'm calling-in a favor: the boys are a joy, and they take some work. If I understand how things got to where they are, I think I'd have a better idea about how my being here, fits in."

"Alright, but I'll keep it short." Mary Ann leaned back and began her story. "You see this town is called Galesburg after Reverend Gale. The Reverend was a friend of the family I worked for when I was your age. In about 1836, just before I left for Cincinnati, Reverend Gale also left Oberlin to come up here and start Knox College. He was here with the Hitchcocks, the parents of Mary Allen West and several others. The little town that grew up by the college needed a name, so they called it Galesburg, after the Reverend."

But you didn't come here all that time ago, did you? I mean, didn't you meet Robert in Cincinnati?" asked Rachel, trying to get more from her aunt.

"Well, yes. In about 1847, long after I'd settled in Cincinnati, the college needed a new president. Reverend Gale was also a friend of my pastor at that time. He convinced Reverend Blanchard to leave our Church there in Cincinnati to become the president of Reverend Gale's college."

Rachel nodded and waited, knowing the Mary Ann was likelier to tell the whole story if she wasn't prodded too often.

"Well," sighed Mary Ann, "Robert and I kept up a correspondence with Reverend Blanchard. It was more frequent at first, but eventually we only exchanged a couple of letters each year."

"Did he invite you to come here?"

"Not really. He told us about the town and college. But with the boys and the babies, we were busy and pretty well-rooted there in Cincinnati."

"So, what made the difference?"

"A few things. I had finished my homoeopathic studies. A certain Dr. Babcock was a colleague of my mentor, Dr. Hussey and Dr. Babcock was the only homeopathic physician in Galesburg. Reverend Blanchard asked whether we were acquainted but we weren't. Dr. Hussey's letter of introduction made it possible to ask him about relocating here."

"Well, it was a surprise, but Dr. Babcock invited us right away. He said my skills would be most welcome. That made us think, and once we started thinking more seriously about getting away from Cincinnati … You know how the crime and violence are there, President Blanchard also wrote that Galesburg had room for a music instructor. Right up Robert's alley. To make our decision even easier, he also offered to hire Robert to help paint new college buildings."

Rachel nodded and thought about it. Cincinnati was close to family, but the river traffic and trade with the Northwest had turned it into a large city. Tiffin, where Rachel went to college must be more like the Cincinnati Mary Ann first encountered. "Was it difficult to convince Robert?" Rachel asked.

"Getting Robert to agree to move here wasn't difficult, Mary Ann said with a heavy smile. "He was always such a romantic!" He let me make most of the practical decisions and, when the chance to play and teach music came up, he was more than willing to try something new. To tell the truth, it was more difficult for me to say good-bye to our family and the church than it was for him."

"He let me handle the details of our move and I guess it was about Springtime of '56 when I said good-bye to your Aunt Elizabeth and we left the older boys, pretty much on their own by then. We packed up a couple of trunks and the two little boys and came here. It wasn't long after that our little Martha arrived."

Pausing as she remembered the baby and her Aunt's grief at her death she went on, "So, I that's how you got here, why did you decide to go to Cairo?"

Mary Ann realized it would be easier to tell the rest of the story now instead of going back to the beginning the next time the questions arose. "I've asked myself the same thing! There are so many connections. I really think God has his hands in it." Now, Mary was more reflective and telling a story she seemed to have told more than once.

"Reverend Gale had long ago preached the very first sermon at our Second Presbyterian Church here in Galesburg. His encouragement was all it took for us to join that congregation when we arrived. That's when I met Mary Allen West."

Taking a deep breath she went on, "Stay with me here: Reverend Gale brought Reverend Blanchard. Reverend Blanchard brought us. Then Reverend Gale helped us find a church and that's where I met Mary Allen West. And she's a remarkable woman, about your age, too!"

Rachel had met Mary Allen at a Women's Community Service gathering, but they hadn't become friends.

Mary Ann went on enthusiastically, "Mary Allen was not only been the first child born here in Galesburg, but she is also the daughter of two founders of Knox College. You can understand why she's always been a favorite of Reverend Gale's. That young woman is a prodigy. She taught at the college beginning at the age of 13 and graduated from college when she was just 17."

"I have always envied and admired her education and we've been friends in spite of the difference in our ages. You see, I think that she saw something in my medical work and maybe some of my more practical skills. But the real bond between us is our commitment to Christ, abolition, temperance and women's rights." Mary Ann sat back, looking into Rachel's eyes for her reaction.

For her part, Rachel leaned forward saying, "Oh! I agree, I agree completely; I'd like to talk to her again."

"Well, we've become good friends. I help Mary Allen with her practical skills and I have to say, Mary Allen helped me develop a more … diplomatic approach… To dealing with men." She leaned forward, smiling sardonically, "Men who think they know everything because, well, because they were born male!"

"What about President Lincoln?" asked Rachel. "Didn't you meet him when he came here for the debate?"

Mary Ann's eyes lit up and she leaned back, smiling. "In October of '58, the fifth time Damned-Douglas and President Lincoln were debating. Well, he wasn't president yet, but his words and ideas stunned me!

"I was standing in the crowd, right there in front of the college and I was just appalled at Douglas' attitude towards abolition. Ooh, how that little man went on! And I've always thought Mr. Lincoln didn't go far enough in challenging him.

"I wasn't alone in that. Lots of us thought he should just speak for abolition no matter the cost. Douglas didn't want abolition. He even wanted us to help capture runaways from the South and make them go back. Can you imagine!"

She went on with rising anger, "Those damned Copperheads! They think the problem will just go away if we let it go on!" Well, we were plenty fired-up but Robert saw it a different way. He was very pragmatic.

"Robert saw that there were twice as many people in town for the debate as were usually here and he made the most of it! Oh my, did he entertain them! He became sort of a local celebrity and was busy all the time. He stopped painting altogether and just taught and played music."

Rachel realized her Aunt Mary Ann moved amidst a circle of influential people. President Blanchard's wife, Isabella was Harriet Beecher Stowe's dear friend. Harriet was famous for her recent book, *Uncle Tom's Cabin*.

Harriet's father was the famous abolitionist preacher, Lyman Beecher. Together Isabella and Harriet influenced Harriet's brother, Edward, to join them in Galesburg. Now she was working in Cairo with at least three different Generals who were former Congressmen.

Mary Ann was tired and it was late. "Those long days teaching music and longer nights playing for all kinds of audiences took their toll on Robert's health. He wasn't young anymore. The next year, at the end of March, the 29th it was, Robert just fell over. I don't know if he fell because he was ill or was ill because he fell. Either way, he never woke up again and he died quickly." She paused and smiled sadly.

"I'm so sorry Aunt Mary Ann. That must have been terrible!"

Mary Ann nodded thoughtfully, then looked up. "Back then, I had little Martha and the boys. The whole town got together and put on a concert to raise some money to help us with expenses and to celebrate him." She looked as if she were finished, and Rachel put her hand on her Aunt's.

"Aunt Elizabeth and I were here after that, when Little Martha got sick."

Mary Ann looked up and nodded. "So, here's the end of the story," she said with resignation.

"A few weeks after Robert's death, I left the Presbyterian church and joined the First Congregational Church where Reverend Beecher... Remember, I told you about the connections between his sister and President Blanchard? Well Mary Allen West and I were in complete agreement with Reverend Beecher's views and they were so kind to take me in and to allow me to join them in work resettling fugitives and like that."

"Is that where you got involved with the Sanitary Commission, Aunt Mary Ann?" asked Rachel quietly.

"Yes, a while later. It's their work that's taking me to Cairo," she said rising and holding Rachel's hand. "Now let's get some sleep and talk about your future in the morning."

COLUMBUS, OHIO, MAY 1861

Congressman Clement Valandingham was an Ohio representative who knew both that he was very persuasive and very good looking. He was also an outspoken critic of the war and a strong advocate for making peace with the seceded states. Opponents referred to politicians like him as "Copperheads," and viewed them as virtual traitors.

Seated across from the Governor of Ohio, legs sprawled and smirking at the angry politician behind the big desk, Valandingham had just finished reciting his denunciation of Governor Dennison's refusal to cooperate with the Fugitive Slave Act. He loudly demanded both government officials and citizens return fugitives to those who claimed "ownership."

Dennison had an entirely different opinion. "Damn you!" he sputtered. "I'll raise 100,000 men if I must! We have no more to discuss! Good day!"

"Governor," said Valandingham dripping with sarcasm, "You'll lose next year's election and you're saddling our people with a debt that will cost thousands of our boys' lives and yield only widows and grieving families." He stood and leaned into Denison and spoke softly. "For what, Willie? For what?"

Now taking his own seat and assuming a calm tone, Governor Dennison replied, "We're finished now. Go." Looking down at his papers he added, "You and I have nothing to discuss."

Vallandingham smiled to himself, turned and walked out of the Governor's office. He passed several men in frock coats, standing in the waiting room. As he passed them, their downcast eyes and discomfort with his presence told him they'd overheard the meeting.

Mortimer Leggett was an experienced lawyer who was also the superintendent of schools in Zanesville, Ohio. He and four others filed into the room and stood before the Governor's desk. All were Whigs, or members of the new, Republican Party. All agreed with the Governor's point of view and all were either college administrators, lawyers or both.

Governor Denison began, "You see what we're up against. This war will be about more than states' rights. The future of Ohio, our people and our economy are at stake." His small group of supporters nodded gravely and a few murmured agreement.

"You men are not only servants of our youth, but you're all leaders in your communities. I need your help. This war is small now, but it could become a test like our revolution, with consequences to match.

The South is led by wealthy men. They earn their fortunes by forcing others to do their work and keeping the fruit of their labor for themselves. The plantation owner controls the local government at his pleasure: using it to favor his businesses and to perpetuate his feudal system."

"And they mean to press this unholy form of government right up to the banks of the Ohio and across the continent!" His speech was well-rehearsed but the feeling behind it was sincere.

He leaned back in his seat and looked from face to face as he went on, "I've asked you here because you indicated your willingness to raise Regiments for the State. I assume that has not changed?"

They nodded and murmured their agreement. Each would raise the ten companies of 100 that would make up a volunteer infantry Regiment.

The governor nodded in gratitude. "I'll appoint each of you a Colonel of the Ohio Volunteers and a commander of the Regiment you raise. We'll provide your uniforms, arms and equipment. We're building camps for training. You'll appoint quartermasters, men with some experience in keeping accounts and merchandising to assist you. I've also identified over 50 healthy veterans of the Mexican War to assist you with training. I'll appoint them to Regiments near their homes, with your consent. Aside from those men, you can choose your own officers or allow your volunteers to elect them."

The governor was used to giving long lists of instructions to attentive audiences and went on, "I have someone who will help you with details and will share what he knows about the most effective recruiting and training practices. He'll be here momentarily to get each of you started. Do you have any questions?"

There were none. The governor stood and the four men before him also came to their feet. A slender man with a ruddy complexion and wearing a Brigadier General's uniform entered from behind them and placed five Bibles on the governor's desk, one in front of each man. The governor led their oaths of office; afterward, he congratulated each man.

Finally, Governor Denison said, "This is General Sherman, Senator Sherman's brother. He's here in Columbus on his way to a new command in Louisville." They all shook hands. Standing behind him was a shorter man in a similar uniform.

"This is General McClellan. He's the commander of Ohio Volunteers. He'll be leaving us soon for duty in Virginia, but I wanted you to meet him." Turning to Leggett he added, "Colonel Leggett, I believe you're familiar with General McClellan. He's asked that I assign you to his staff before you raise your Regiment. Is that still alright with you?"

"It is sir," said Leggett shaking the governor's hand and turned to McClellan with a smile.

"Gentlemen," said Sherman broke in confidently, "Please follow me."

A couple of weeks later, Leggett crossed the Ohio with McClellan's little army and gained valuable experience in leadership, logistics and combat tactics. Before McClellan was called to senior command in Washington, Leggett went back to Zanesville.

Mathan Stark had come from Heidelberg College with several other students, to join the 78th Ohio Volunteers in Zanesville. He did not seek a leadership role, beginning his service as a private soldier, but within a week of training, the first elections were held, and Mathan was selected the First Lieutenant to his company commander, Captain Z. M. Chandler. Within a month, Colonel Leggett took Mathan as his administrative assistant and Captain Chandler replaced Mathan with 35-year-old, Lieutenant Greenbury F. Wiles. Wiles would eventually command the 78th.

There, in the parlor of his home, Leggett held a series of meetings with his new staff officers and Company[5] commanders. "Lieutenant Stark," said Colonel Leggett, looking up from his desk at the sturdy young man who'd been on his staff for only a couple of weeks. "I understand you volunteered to go ahead of the Regiment to Illinois?"

"Yes sir, I did." Answered Mathan with some trepidation.

"Tell me about your decision to request this duty," said Leggett leaning back in his chair and looking up patiently at Mathan.

"Well, sir," he began slowly, "I know we're being assigned there, and I thought I'd like to go ahead of the rest of the Regiment and make sure things were ready." He thought for a moment and added hopefully, "To make a smooth transition."

---

5 Usually a Company of volunteers came from communities in or near the Regimental commander's home. At the beginning of the war, the hundred or so men of a company might elect their Captain, Lieutenants and Sergeants but field grade officers (Majors, Lieutenant Colonels and Colonels) were appointed. As the war progressed, field grade officers more often appointed their subordinate officers.

Leggett looked down at the papers in front of him and nodded, then looked back to Mathan quizzically. "It has nothing to do with any particular young woman?"

Mathan swallowed and dropped his eyes from his commander's. Not knowing what to say, he didn't answer.

"Lieutenant," continued Colonel Leggett calmly. "I was a young man once and I've heard that you're engaged and that your intended is a remarkable young woman: one certainly worthy of your attention. But I can't have you distracted by other priorities or preoccupied when important matters are in your hands."

"I understand sir..." but before he could finish his thought, Leggett continued over him.

"I know about Miss Rodgers joining her aunt in Illinois. When I was with McClellan in Virginia, he told me about his cousin, Doctor Brinton. Turns out Brinton's being assigned as our Division's surgeon and the Doctor has already had a run-in..." He rephrased himself, "An *encounter* with Mrs. Bickerdyke. Your Miss Rodgers' Aunt, I believe?" A few of my friends from the faculty at Heidelberg were talking about Miss Rodgers' departure and they attributed that departure to as much to your decision to join the Regiment as to her aunt's invitation," he said with a parent's sincere concern.

He concluded, "I wouldn't have agreed to discuss the matter with you if I thought you couldn't manage your duties and your personal life at the same time."

Then he smiled at Mathan. "We'll be part of one of the Illinois Divisions under Congressman," he corrected himself, "General Lewis Wallace. Another Brigadier named Grant is in Cairo, Illinois. We'll eventually be assigned to his Division. His staff will tell you where you should go to make arrangements for our arrival. You'll stay in close contact with us. The 78th should arrive sometime in January." Still smiling he added, "Acceptable to you?"

Mathan tried to stifle his own smile but couldn't. "Yes sir, thank you. I'll keep first things first and stay in close contact."

"See that you do Lieutenant. Please give my best regards to Miss Rodgers when you see her." Going back to his papers he added with a quiet smile, "You're dismissed."

CAIRO, ILLINOIS, 1861

Mathan arrived at Cairo with all his possessions in a small trunk. He traveled in uniform because it made it easier to obtain transportation and he was less likely to be challenged by local authorities. He was quickly directed to the Safford's Bank Building that served as Grant's headquarters. There he found several Lieutenant Colonels in a waiting room where they were engaged in casual conversation. When Mathan entered, the circle of older men stopped talking and appraised Mathan with cool amusement.

"What can we do for you, Lieutenant?" asked one of them with a hint of sarcasm.

"I'm reporting here on behalf of the 78th Ohio Volunteer Infantry. My Regiment." He said, extending his orders tentatively. We're being sent to Cairo and I'm here to coordinate their arrival with the Division's staff.

"Lots of Regiments headed this way, Lieutenant," said one of them doubtfully. "Are you sure you're assigned to this Brigade?"

"No sir, I'm not. I only had orders to report here and go to General Wallace's headquarters or wherever I'm sent."

Just then, the office door opened and an older man wearing a Major's golden oak leaves said, "Colonel White, General McClernand and Colonel Logan would like to see you now."

Turning to Mathan, the Major said, "Did I hear you say, 78th Ohio?"

"Yes sir," said Mathan with some relief.

"Well, you're in the wrong place. Your Regiment will be assigned to General Lew Wallace's Brigade alright, but they're establishing a liaison with our headquarters about a mile up the road from here. They're not ready for anyone yet. Maybe we can put you to work. Sit down over there and wait until I come get you."

The Major motioned Lieutenant Colonel White to enter a tiny room behind the waiting area. The other officers quickly departed, leaving Mathan alone in the empty room for nearly an hour. He could hear the men's voices but not what they were saying. He felt perspiration run down his neck and back.

When the office door finally opened, one of the two Generals was shaking hands with a dark-haired Colonel while the taller, thin General looked on. "Thank you again for your help, Logan," said General Grant as he turned to face the taller General. "John, what you two did has strengthened us immeasurably. You have my thanks!" The Major stood behind the three officers and watched with a relaxed smile.

Following the other men into the waiting area, Grant looked into the ante room and asked, "Who's this?" as he sized-up Mathan, standing at attention and staring straight ahead.

The Major said, "He's one of those liaison officers from Ohio. Said each Regiment would send one, but Lew's not ready for anything like this yet. He doesn't want them, just wants to receive the Regiments at his camp in the order they arrive." All three officers nodded in understanding and stared at Mathan.

"Looks like you don't have a job … Lieutenant?" paused Grant smiling at Mathan and waiting for his name.

"Lieutenant Stark, Sir" replied Mathan without moving his eyes.

"Stand at ease, Lieutenant Stark," said Grant turning to the other officers. "Do either of you need an extra hand? If not, we could put him to work or send him home."

McClernand and Logan said they had enough help and declined to take the young officer. General Grant said, "Good then, Lieutenant Stark, please go with Major Webster, here. He's my Chief of Staff: takes care of everything, so I can concentrate on ... so I can concentrate on other things. He'll get you set up with quarters and explain what you'll be doing here with us. No sense sending you back to Ohio. They'd probably turn you around and send you here again!"

Major Joseph Webster was not only Grant's Chief of Staff, but he was also a civil engineer and a veteran of the Mexican War. He explained that Mathan would be added to the General's staff, performing whatever duties were assigned, until the 78th arrived and retrieved him. Until then, Mathan was under Webster's command.

"By the way, Stark," added Major Webster, reaching into a desk drawer and stirring through the contents. "Here they are," he said extending a set of black colored shoulder tabs with silver Captains Bars. "You're a Captain now, Stark," said Webster. "These will make your job easier. I'll take care of the paperwork with you in the morning."

"Sir?" said Mathan with a doubtful look, "I'm only here temporarily."

"Listen Captain," said Webster adopting the tone of a professor. "Rank is a tool." Then he went on, "Think of your rank as a hammer. When you're a Lieutenant, we give you little, tiny tacks and a little, tiny hammer. If you can drive the tacks quickly and straight enough, we may give you more tacks. Succeed again and we'll give you bigger tacks. Eventually we give you nails and for those, you'll need a new hammer. Bigger nails, bigger hammer. General Scott has the biggest hammer of all because he has the biggest spikes." Mathan nodded.

"Now here's the most important part." Webster had Mathan's attention and held his eyes, "When you get a promotion you've been given a bigger hammer. It's rewarding, but it's not a reward. It grants you authority, and you can delegate authority. You can't delegate your responsibility. Bigger hammer, bigger jobs, more authority. Rank is not an affirmation of your value as a man or as a soldier. Your conduct determines those things. When you're done with the job, you give the hammer and the rank back. All you keep is your character and you can keep that forever. Understand?"

Mathan nodded again and gestured at the shoulder tabs. "I'll return these when I go back to the 78th," he said softly.

"Not so fast, Stark," said Webster. If and when you go back to the 78th, you'll switch back to blue tabs, but the decision about your rank is your commander's, not yours. Your Colonel may need a Captain or a Major with your experience. It can be difficult to get much done outside a Company when you're a Lieutenant."

Mathan said, "Yes Sir."

Webster picked up a sheaf of papers and said, "Come with me now. I'll show you to your quarters and your mess."

At nine the next morning, Mary Ann entered the quartermaster's office. A uniformed man was engrossed in copying receipts into a ledger. She didn't wait for him to look up but said firmly, "Corporal, where is the Supply Sergeant?"

Since the voice obviously belonged to a woman, the Corporal didn't look up and replied, "Don't know." He went on copying.

Neither surprised nor tolerant, Mary Ann stepped around the counter, strode past the Corporal and passed through the door that led to the warehouse. This got the Corporal's attention.

"You can't go in there!" he said loudly and turning in his chair. Before he could rise, Mary Ann had pulled the door closed behind her and the Corporal heard her calling, "Sergeant Dawes! Ser-geant Dawes!"

Before the Corporal was through the door behind her, he heard his Sergeant's weary voice answer, "Yes Mrs. Bickerdyke. What can I do for you?" Shaking his head, the Corporal released the doorknob and quietly returned to his desk, relieved that it was the Sergeant and not he, who had to deal with the lady today.

"I want you to release 100 sets of sheets and the same number of sets of undergarments for the men in our hospital. We need them immediately and your Corporal seems to believe that accounting takes precedence."

Resting his hands on a bale of blankets, the Sergeant leaned forward and said, "We've discussed this and…"

"And here's your requisition!" she interrupted holding a folded page out to him. "General Grant's staff has authorized me to collect these supplies immediately."

Shaking his lowered head and sighing in resignation, the Sergeant held out his hand and took the form. He read it more carefully than was necessary. Raising his eyes to her without raising his head he said, "When can you take them, Mrs. Bickerdyke?"

"Put them in my wagon, out front. It's the one with only two mules." She paused, looking around the room. "I'll need four more mules as well. Can you give me those?"

Hefting a bundle of clothing he said, "No Ma'am, you'll have to get those from the Sergeant at the livery. Afraid I can't help you there."

Mary Ann nodded as the blankets and clothing were placed in the bed of her wagon. She offered her polite thanks to the quartermaster Sergeant and reminded him she'd see him again soon, when she needed more supplies. He was more than relieved to see her go.

Pastor Alexander Allen had arrived in Cairo a few weeks following his wife's arrival. Mary Ann arranged for him to work under the auspices of the US Sanitary Commission. This, she hoped, would grant her some influence, if not control, over his assignments and keep husband and wife together. Pastor Allen was driving the wagon and Mary Ann placed her hand on his forearm. "Would you take us by the greengrocer's on the way back? We're nearly through our vegetables and this is a good time to restore our supply." As they waited for a line of wagons to pass the camp's exit, Mathan saw Mary Ann and walked to the wagon where she sat.

"Good morning, Ma'am," he said raising his hat slightly. "Did you get everything you need?"

"Yes, I did Captain," she said, pausing. "Well, not everything. As you can see, I could use a could use two brace of mules. Can you help us with that?"

"I'll look into it, Ma'am. I think I can have an answer by tomorrow. Would that meet your needs?"

"That would be very helpful, thank you Captain," answered Mary Ann as she turned to Pastor Allen. Mathan was staring at the driver but couldn't place him when he heard a very familiar voice.

"Aunt Mary Ann, Aunt Mary Ann!" called a young woman. "Is it too late to requisition some uniforms for the patients?"

She ran to the side of the wagon, breathlessly adding, "Some few of them are likely to be returned to their Regiments tomorrow."

Mathan saw Rachel across the wagon, holding a paper past the driver, toward Mary Ann. Their eyes met and he felt energy surge through his body. Rachel's cheeks flushed and she froze with her arm extended towards Mary Ann but with her eyes on Mathan. Mary Ann knew this was the young man with whom her niece had studied and whose marriage proposal she accepted and then, deferred.

The pause lingered and when Mary Ann sensed one of them was about to speak, she said, "Rachel, get up in the wagon. We're going to the grocer's. Captain, you may call on us at the Methodist Church. It's on Eighth Street and Walnut. We'll be there at half past four this evening and there will be time then." Without waiting for his reply, she added, "Let's go Pastor Allen."

As the wagon carried Rachel away from him, Mathan stood, staring after them until they were around the corner and beyond his sight.

When he returned to the office, Mathan ran into Major Webster who asked impatiently, "Where the heck have you been, Captain?"

"Sir, I was taking a requisition to Mrs. Bickerdyke. She's one of the ladies from the northern part of the state who brings supplies. She also volunteers as a nurse at one of the hospitals."

Mathan was surprised when Webster's demeanor changed. "Those ladies are indispensable and they'll be even more so when we have a serious fight." He paused as the two men passed through the doors and into Webster's office.

"Have you ever really thought about how important sanitation and nursing are to an army?" Webster began another lecture for his apprentice.

"Most of our towns have populations of only a few hundred up to a couple of thousand. Only nine of our cities have over 100,000 people. Their capitol of Richmond is their biggest city and it doesn't even have 40,000 people. We have about 25 towns that size and we'll build armies that are twice that size if we have to, to win this war. Now, think about something Stark, what do you think is killing our soldiers right now?"

"Well, I guess it's sickness, sir."

"Damned right, and that's only going to get worse when we crowd into the camps and forts this winter!" We have to have clean water when we bring all those people together. The air that rises from the camps makes people sick, too. You can smell it and it kills them."

Major Webster went on, matter-of-factly, "We started fighting in Charleston Harbor last April and not one person on either side was killed until after the firing ended. All last Spring, we only fought small engagements. Altogether, only a few hundred were wounded and it wasn't until the Battle at Bull Run that we had a lot of wounded at once. That day, over 1,500 were wounded and that's when we realized there was no way to care for all of them. If it hadn't been for volunteers, most of those soldiers would have just died on the side of the road or in some tent, waiting for... Waiting for Army doctors and nurses who would never come.

"And that's only when we fight. Do you realize that every single day, a camp with just 15,000 men and 4,000 horses and mules will generate thousands of gallons of human urine and tons of human waste? Besides that, our livestock will generate at least 60 tons of dung, every single day! Any lapse in waste management can be catastrophic. Cholera, typhoid, liver cholic, flux and other diseases rage every time we forget s--t."

"Our surgeon, Doctor..." Webster paused, considering. Then he gave Mathan a knowing glance as he rephrased the name and went on, "*Major*, Doctor Brinton is from back East. He told us about the British in the Crimea and how careful sanitation cut their deaths in half."[6]

He paused. "Our people are going to get sick. There are going to be wounded at the same time. This fight is about to become bigger than

------

6 The "germ theory" of disease and sterile surgical techniques were unknown to the medical community until the 1870s. Instead, medical professionals and the public believed that "miasma" or a poison that floated in foul air, caused disease. The theory guided some useful approaches to public health, like waste disposal and washing. It neglected others. Tens of thousands of young men, raised in the relative isolation of local farms, were brought together in camps. Their childhood isolation exposed them to relatively few viruses and left them vulnerable to diseases common in other communities. Moreover, childhood diseases like measles and mumps caused far more severe symptoms among adults. Inadequate management of tons of sewage cost even more lives. During the Civil War, for every soldier killed in battle, more than two died of disease.
Because disease (not battle) killed thousands of American soldiers, Congress passed, and President Lincoln signed, an act creating the US Sanitary Commission (USSC). The USSC was an extra-governmental agency attached to the War Department. Its purpose was to coordinate the acquisition, distribution and use of medical supplies, hospitals and nursing care for the benefit of Union Soldiers and sailors. It also educated Army leaders on matters of sanitation and public health.
By October 1861, the Chicago Branch of the USSC opened. Within weeks, Galesburg's "Soldiers' Aid Society" became the Galesburg Chapter of the US Sanitary Commission. Mary Allen West led the local chapter and Mary Ann was their agent in the field.

anyone ever imagined, and those Sanitation Commission ladies are just about our only hope right now. So whatever it takes to help them to help us, the General is going to give them, no matter what Major Brinton says. Understand?"

"I do," said Mathan meekly. "Thanks for telling me. I guess I was more concerned about getting better rifles and more training instead of keeping the men healthy."

"Remember, you're on the staff now. Everything is our responsibility. Rifles and training for sure, but transportation, pay, roads, railroads, boats, contracts, tents, housing, fuel, ammunition, livestock, food, medicine, tools and supplies too." He paused. "Politics, it's all ours." He paused again, "And tons of raw sewage. It's all ours to manage. We don't have the luxury of worrying about just one thing and criticizing the army about everything else. We work for the General and it's all our business."

CAIRO, ILLINOIS, SEPTEMBER 1861

Cairo was a new town. Most of the buildings had gone up in the last ten years. The war was bringing money and soldiers. In rapid succession, transportation, construction, entertainment, government, schools, churches, residences, hospitals and all the other elements of a small city were in place. Levees kept the Mississippi and Ohio at bay during high water, but they also kept the town hot, humid and airless.

It was a short walk from headquarters to the church. Mathan could see a spire where he supposed the Methodist Church stood and crossed the street in that direction, skirting some muddy, standing water. He sensed her before he heard her voice.

"Mathan!" came her voice from behind him. He turned and saw her nearly running toward him along the boardwalk. "Mathan!" She fell into his arms and they embraced without kissing: arms pulling one-another as close as they could. He was strong and made it difficult for her to breathe but she said nothing. Both of them were overwhelmed, each absorbed by the presence of the other. He pressed his cheek against the side of her face and inhaled the scent of her hair. She felt the sweet roughness of his stubble and held back her tears.

Slowly they relaxed their embrace and parted enough to look into one another's eyes, faces and then to scan their figures. The excitement of reunion momentarily pushed any embarrassment from their thoughts.

Impulsively, Mathan wrapped his arms around her waist, pulled her toward him and lifted her off her feet, turning in a full circle, delighted beyond speech at her presence.

Modesty intruded on Rachel before it reached Mathan. "Put me down!" she said, looking about with emerging embarrassment. "I've missed you! Are you well? How much time do you have?"

Mathan beamed and held her face in his gaze, "All the time." He said almost as if praying. "All the time, until you have to go." The sun was low. It would be dark too soon.

Rachel reached down from his shoulder and took his hand, smiling at him. "Let's walk," she said, pointing toward the East with her chin. "Over past the railroad station on the levee."

Mathan did his best to appear calm, authoritative and comfortable, as if they walked together every day. He turned her elbow into the bend of his left arm so she would be nearer when they walked. He intentionally shortened his steps as well as his slowing pace.

Her scent displaced any thoughts he might have had a moment before, filling him with the sense of her presence. Her touch, the occasional press of her breast against his arm and the rhythm of their steps made him tremble. Flushed, exhilarated and intoxicated, he wanted to take her some-place beautiful, private and away. Anywhere, and away.

Rachel felt all the restraint imposed by her aunt, her mother, her church and the deferred wedding date. Even so, her fears slipped silently beneath the waves of excitement that pulsed from the deepest parts of her body. Yearning flashed from her core to the surface of her skin. To inhale his breath, absorb him and bring his essence into herself. She would find a way to see him, alone and soon.

MISSISSIPPI RIVER,
NOVEMBER 6, 1861

Men and their animals clomped aboard the steamboats. Sergeants shouted directions, sending men, beasts and equipment to their places while engines rumbled and cinders sprinkled the decks. Despite several rehearsals of boarding and transporting infantry, gunboats and cavalry it was still 4:00PM when the last of the men had boarded in Cairo, only a few minutes before sunset. While the sky was still glowing, a line of six steamers backed away from the landing and crossed the river where two boats boarded cavalry, artillery and two more Regiments under the command Colonel Dougherty. Completely loaded by 6:00, the additional steamboats left the bank and slowly glided into line.

By now, it was dark and there was less than a quarter-moon rising, making it difficult for pilots to avoid hazards. Not surprisingly, one of the boats ran aground, requiring several other boats to attach cables and pull the heavily laden transport from a submerged bar. Finally underway at around 9:00, the six steamers and two gunboats moved at a walking pace, sliding a scant few miles downriver before pointing their bows at the bank and tying-up for the night.

The recently promoted Brigadier General Grant was no stranger to this part of the country. He knew the secessionists' camps, their fortifications and most of their roads. He knew they were watching his small flotilla. To distract and confuse his enemy's defensive planning, he'd sent several small armies across Missouri and Western Kentucky to cause alarm and distract their forces. There had only been limited skirmishing because neither side was ready for more.

Map of Western Tennessee and Kentucky

Grant was also keenly aware of Southern leadership and their locations. Knowing that an effective feint might freeze them, Grant's small flotilla stopped on the Eastern (Kentucky) shore, North of Columbus, only an hour or so after beginning the trip. Grant's intended target was a few miles downriver on the Western bank.

His camp was secure by 11:00 PM. The Mississippi lapped softly at the boats' sterns. Most of the men remained aboard where they quietly fought tension, imagined sleep and counted the minutes before dawn.

Columbus, Kentucky was on elevated land overlooking the river and was home to the greatest concentration of secessionist military force in the area. Confederate General Leonidas Polk concentrated his artillery and troops to block Federal passage down the Mississippi.

Just after midnight, when secessionist leaders received reports of the landing, they concluded that the soldiers on the boats would join forces with a small army already in Kentucky and attack the fortress at Columbus, only five or six miles South of the loading.

Before midnight, Grant's small staff of adjutants, administrators and clerks worked under lamplight at a long, narrow table against the wall of the "Ladies Cabin" on the *Belle Memphis*. This was a quiet, carpeted salon where Grant and his staff could plan and communicate with the leaders of their Division. Few spoke and when they did, their words were few and their voices, soft. Navy Commander Walke tipped his chair back against the far wall, carefully reading a packet of loose papers.

Grant sprawled comfortably in a low-backed armchair. He was alone next to a large, round table. Unadorned, unassuming, and easy to over-look. His legs stretched before him, toes pointed to the ceiling, the soles of his boots facing the salon's entry. Average height, average weight, aver-age build, untrimmed brown hair. His appearance was matched by a soft voice, calm expression, and unassuming attitude. Wearing a soldier's sin-gle-breasted, blue wool jacket with a plain hat on the table, "Sam" Grant was a well-worn version of the soldiers he led. He glanced up calmly when he heard thumping footsteps, laughter and jumbled conversation coming along the deck.

Grant knew them. They were noisy. Guffaws, laughter and back-slap-ping masked their shared tension. The six men who blustered into the room were all politically connected and most had been elected to some public office. Grant knew none had commanded soldiers under fire, although a couple had participated in the Blackhawk or the Mexican Wars. Only Grant was an experienced combat commander.

The new commanders' joking and laughter became louder as they piled into the now-crowded "Ladies' Cabin," continuing their conversations and taking seats at Grant's table without waiting to be asked. Five wore the new uniform of a Regimental commander (Colonels). One was a Brigade commander (a Brigadier General) and he seemed to preen, even when he sat still. Mindful of their inevitable competitiveness, Grant would focus their attention on leading their own men and cooperating with one another.

By November of 1861, Congressman John McClernand was the senior of two brigade commanders under Grant. Logan's 31st Illinois, Buford's 27th Ohio and Fouke's 30th Ohio made up McClernand's Brigade. The other Brigade commander was Colonel Dougherty, commanding both the 27th Illinois and 7th Iowa under Colonel Jacob Lauman.

"General McClernand. Colonel Dougherty, Colonel Logan, Colonel Buford, Colonel Fouke. I'm glad you're here. You all know Colonel Lauman from Iowa and our naval commander, Commander Walke, Commander Rodger's replacement," said Grant calmly as men stopped their side-conversations and shook hands all around.

"As you know, Commander Walke has made several visits to this part of the river and exchanged some iron with the people at Columbus. Members of our staff accompanied him and have prepared your maps. Early tomorrow morning, Commander Walke will take us to our landing on the Missouri side of the river. He has agreed to engage their big guns on the bluffs across from our objective while we're busy. Once we've done what we came to do, Commander Walke and the steamboats will carry us home again." Grant turned to the Commander, "Hank, do you have anything you'd like to add?"

Walke was tall and had a resonant voice. Unlike the politicians, Walke was a career officer with a well-deserved reputation for recognizing opportunities and taking prompt, effective action. If permission wasn't available in a crisis, he might seek it after the fact. Grant trusted him.

"General Grant," Walke paused and looked at the clutch of blue-clad politicians, "Gentlemen, the guns at Columbus are numerous and formidable. They'll probably be able to reach us if they like, but we've chosen a landing beyond their view. Trees and terrain should mask us and make their fire ineffective. The transports will remain at the landing all day, while I take Commander Stembel's *Lexington* and my *Taylor* far enough down river to draw fire from their long-range guns. I'll stay as long as I can, but they'll eventually get our range and I'll have to withdraw. As you return after tomorrow's action, we'll be nearby, covering your embarkation."

Grant nodded and added, "Polk has most of his men in and around Columbus and I think he's expecting us to attack him there. We'll cross the river to the Missouri side at first light, unload the boats and assemble the men in marching order. We'll send a cavalry screen well-ahead of the column to keep the way clear and to report their movement. When we find a suitable place, we'll deploy into a line of battle, chase-off their skirmishers and engage their garrison. I intend to destroy the Rebel camp on our side of the river and to disrupt their ability to move men and supplies into Missouri. We'll go back to our transports before dark and return directly to Cairo."

He paused and looked at each man in turn, then added, "An orderly disembarkation and a rapid march to the point of attack is important. Once we're in line, you'll receive further orders." He paused, waiting for questions, but none came.

"Commander Walke, last we spoke, you said we'd put in at Hunter's Landing. Still good for us?"

Walke nodded.

Grant asked, "Are you still able to disembark us in the order we discussed?"

"Yes Sir," Walke answered calmly. "Hunter's Landing is out of sight of their guns, but they'll know we're there. You'll be three miles above their camp near Belmont when you disembark."

"That's fine," said Grant, nodding at Walke. "Close, but not too close." Grant paused and looked at the map, then raised his eyes to the circle of inexperienced commanders.

"Gentlemen," Grant rose, leaning forward and resting his knuckles on the table while looking into each politician's eyes, "We'll leave here at first light and cross the river quickly."

He waited for a nod or sign of understanding and agreement from each. "Unload quickly. Here's your order of march." Grant turned his head and nodded at Mathan, who had been sitting against the wall with Major Webster and two other officers. Mathan rose and walked to the table, placing a map and two pieces of paper on the left of each of the seated officers.

Mathan finished and stepped back with his eyes on Grant who said, "One set for each of you and a copy for your Lieutenant Colonels." Grant paused briefly and looked at Colonel Buford, then around the room as he spoke. "The 22nd will leave five companies near the landing to form the rear guard and to secure our hospital. Each Regiment will send a company of skirmishers to their fronts. You can recall them when the fighting gets hot." Still, there were no questions.

"Colonel Buford, get the 27th off the boats as quickly as you can. Once the rear guard is on the road, you'll move further down the road, pushing their pickets back and preparing the way for the rest of the column.

"The 27th will be followed, by the 30th and then the 31st in that order. Colonel Dougherty, you'll command both your own Regiment and your Brigade. You'll follow the 7th. Your 22nd, less the rear guard, will be the final regiment in the line."

Looking to a staff officer seated against the far wall of the cabin, Grant added, "Major Brinton, you'll establish your hospital with the rear guard. Move forward as the day progresses to whatever place you think practicable. Remember, we aren't staying here, so choose a place from which you can withdraw easily and quickly." Brinton nodded in understanding.

McClernand looked to Dr. Brinton. "You're General George McClellan's cousin aren't you, Brinton?"

"I am sir," answered Brinton brightly.

"Well, any friend and family member of the Commanding General of the United States Army is welcome here! Pleased to meet you, Brinton!"

Grant looked at Logan. Logan dropped his eyes to some papers and Grant went on, "General McClernand will assume overall command if anything should happen to me. I'll either visit you myself or send a member of my staff with instructions as the day progresses. Stay in close contact with the Regiments on your flanks unless you get orders to the contrary." He paused again. "Questions?"

Colonel Dougherty asked, "Do we know how many they are, sir?"

"Not exactly sure, Colonel." Said Grant calmly. "I suspect they'll see us moving but won't commit reinforcements across the river until it's too late for them. Commander Walke's gunboats will make it difficult for them to ferry their men anywhere near us."

"Anything else?" Grant looked from one man to the next as the newly minted Brigadier General McClernand rose, dripping with self-importance.

Having stood and surveyed the faces of each of the officers around the table, McClernand let the silence continue. Just as he sensed someone was about to speak their own thoughts, he began in his deepest (albeit tenor) voice, a recently prepared oration. "On this eve of a great struggle, we stand poised to reclaim the Mississippi River, the great economic artery of the West! The wealth of our nation arises from its banks and flows through its tributaries. This battle will reopen our natural access to all the markets of the great, wide world! A free nexus between our honorable farms and factories and every port across the globe."

Another pause to ensure the faces of his captive audience were suitably grave. "The Secessionists would pierce the heart of our homeland's providence, dividing the mighty Mississippi into antagonistic parts!" His voice rising with each phrase, he reached a crescendo, shaking the cabin walls and bellowing "Never! Never shall we permit such tergiversation!"

Grant lowered his head and almost managed to hide his amusement.

McClernand paused again. This time, to absorb the admiration, respect and awe he assumed he would see in the faces of those who, "craved his perspicacity."

He continued, "Our cause…" he paused for a moment for dramatic effect. "is just."

Another pause gave the small audience time to return the nods and grunts of assent that would propel the train of his speech even further down the tracks. "Our men are eager to join battle. On the morrow, the enemy will shudder at the thunder of our guns and bleed from the bite of our steel!" McClernand paused again, seeking his audience' approval.

Grant seized the moment and rose. McClernand looked at Grant with a smile. He assumed this was the beginning of an ovation by his Commanding General.

As McClernand stood in anticipation of applause, Grant smiled warmly and extended his hand. McClernand looked at the hand, fearing the disruption of his oration. Grant continued to smile with both respect and confidence, his hand suspended in the center of McClernand's vision. In the manner of all politicians who see an open hand, the stunned Congressman took it.

Grant held McClernand's hand tightly, continuing to smile warmly as he said, "General McClernand, thank you for your insights and encouraging thoughts."

Still holding his subordinate's hand and maintaining a warm smile Grant turned to the others he said, "We will adjourn now. I shall see you here at half six. We leave at first light."

"But," McClernand sputtered as he considered whether to retrieve his hand from Grant. "I hadn't completed …"

Grant gave McClernand's hand a final pump, saying, "Fine sentiments, much appreciated." Followed instantly by, "Rest well, General McClernand." He repeated the last praise twice as the taller man made a feeble, final attempt to resume his speech. Only when McClernand's eyes dropped to the floor and he rolled his shoulders in submission did Grant release his grip.

Sputtering like a wick at the end of its fuel, McClernand made the best of it, repeatedly mumbling, "Ah, yes, yes." The others rose and began to move to the door.

McClernand partially recovered saying, "A privilege and a pleasure General Grant! I bid you a good night!"

Mathan and the other staff officers exchanged glances, turning toward the walls to hide their smiles. As the last of the commanders left the cabin, McClernand remained, standing and looking slowly around the room, as if waiting for something.

Grant murmured, "Good then, General. Get some rest. I'll see you very soon."

McClernand blinked as Grant resumed his seat, picked-up some papers and began to study them. Looking at the backs of the busy staff, then down at the preoccupied Grant, McClernand closed his mouth. He took a step backward, then turned and walked slowly out of the cabin and down the corridor. Grant knew that his second-in-command would be much more difficult to quiet in the future.

Mist hovered cold and damp above the black water as the stars on the Eastern horizon began begun to fade. The steamers' boilers built towards full pressure and twelve tall stacks ejected rolling plumes of black smoke high into the early morning air.

The last perimeter guards re-boarded in silence under the eyes of a small detachment of cavalry who screened the departure. The boat's crews drew in the stages. Except for muffled commands, no one spoke.

At nautical twilight, with the sky brightening behind the eastern bluffs, the last of the lines holding the steamboats to the shore were drawn in. First one, then in a roar, all the paddle wheels splashed, then churned, dragging the boats away from Kentucky.

Grant's little army had slept fitfully but were now wide-awake. A few spoke, but only in soft murmurs to those near them. Looking back at the bank, they noticed the treetops had brightened. Moving across the river at first light, their feint succeeded in keeping southern troops awake, behind their earthen fortifications on the high ground around Columbus.

The splashing of the sternwheels was the only sound on the turgid, gray water. Protected by their gunboats, each of the six steamers pirouetted away from the Kentucky shore and began their short dash across the Mississippi to Missouri. In minutes, all six turned their bows into the low spot on the Missouri bank called Hunter's Landing.

Crews cast lines, tied-up to trees and dropped stages. Within several minutes of reaching the bank, men, horses, mules and equipment unloaded quietly. Guides met each boat, escorting commanders and their men to their places. The air was cool but not cold. The sun rose a few minutes before seven peeking over the trees a few minutes later. As the sky shed its pink ribbons, it revealed a broad, blue expanse. Sounds rose to meet the day.

Cavalry went forward with scouts who'd been at the landing overnight. They cleared the road South, enabling a rapid march to engage the enemy. By 9:00 AM, the head of the column, Buford's 27th Illinois Volunteer Infantry, was already a mile south of the boats. Logan led his 31st Illinois in line, a quarter of a mile behind Buford and only 20 yards behind the last Company of the 30th Illinois.

Logan's tall, black gelding was anxious, sensing the rider's tension as he repeatedly twisted his body and shifted his weight. The entire small army snaked down the road for more than half a mile. Here and there were bulges in the line where men on horseback conferred. Murmurs rose and fell above the thumping of soldiers' brogans and the sharper clops of iron-shod horses. Logan's hand rose, calling his long column of men to a shuffling stop.

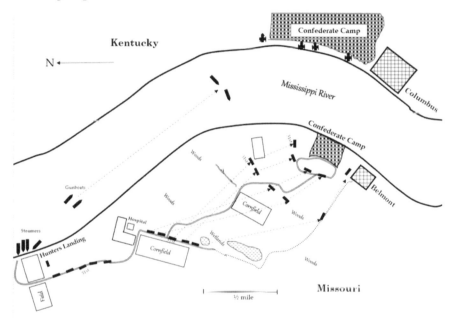

Map of Belmont Battlefield, November 7, 1861

Mathan rode down the column on a cavalry mount, covering ground faster than most men could run and maintaining a steady posting gait. He reined-up just in front of Logan, raised his right hand in salute and held it at the brim of his hat, awaiting Logan's acknowledgement, which came quickly.

"Captain Stark," said Logan expectantly, permitting Mathan to begin.

"Sir, General Grant asks that you follow Colonel Fouke's 30th past the vidette[7] and past the cornfield. Just beyond that field, turn right onto the road between the field and the woods," said Mathan in a formal tone. "General Grant asks that you immediately send a company of skirmishers into the woods and form your battle line beginning on the left of the 30th." Mathan added, "After the 22nd is up on the far left, General Grant will send further orders." Mathan settled back in his saddle and waited for acknowledgement or questions.

"Thank you, Captain. I understand," said Logan firmly but calmly.

Mathan saluted briskly. The moment Logan returned the formality, Mathan dropped his hand to his reins, nodded and prodded his mount, posting past the 31st and moving quickly to the next commander.

Logan turned to his second in command, Lieutenant Colonel White, and asked, "Would you call the Company commanders?" White turned to the drummer and ordered, "Call the Company commanders!" The drummer quickly beat the brief cadence, repeating it three times.

In under a minute, the ten Company commanders turned their men over to Lieutenants and jogged up the column toward their commander. Saving considerable time and effort for the trailing commanders, Logan rode back to the middle of his column. Looking down from his tall, twitching, black horse, Logan repeated the orders and asked for questions. There were none. Logan returned to the head of the column and with a hand in the air, signaled his column to resume the march.

It took only ten minutes for the now-silent soldiers to pass a small house on their left where two wagons stood with mules in harness. This was the field hospital. A dozen or more medical orderlies were unloading supplies. Surgeon Brinton was mounted on a tall, black horse and had trouble controlling the beast. It turned and bit at the reins while he tried to face it towards the passing column. The men smiled but didn't know their

---

7 A few cavalrymen on look-out or sentry duty.

surgeon well enough to shout mock encouragement. A few yards further, they passed between two, stubble-filled fields. The only sounds were the thumps of brogans on packed earth and the clink of tin against steel. Light poured through nearly bare branches on that early November morning. It was bright, cool and comfortable.

Turning right, the "road" onto which they had been directed, revealed itself as little more than a wagon track with weeds rising between shallow ruts. Logan's Regiment took their place in line, standing silently with a field of dry corn stalks behind them and second-growth woods to their front. The silence was broken when Logan swept his arm toward the trees and shouted the command, "Skirmishers! ... Forward!" In an instant, eighty-five men from Company A spread themselves into a long line extending the width of the remaining nine companies. At their Captain's command they stepped briskly into the woods with their rifles ready. The rest of the Regiment continued to spread themselves along the road to the left of the 31st. Two rows deep. One man in front, the next man a pace behind him, both facing the woods.

They had rehearsed the movements many times in training, but none had ever walked toward an unseen enemy with life at risk. Skirmishers would lead the advance toward the Secessionist camp, chasing any enemy troops away, towards their own lines. Skirmishers warned the main body of troops if they encountered obstacles, artillery or anything unexpected. Logan turned to check his troops and to assure himself that they were in line. When he looked to the front, his skirmishers had been swallowed by the woods.

Faces glowed in the sunlight. Steel sparkled. Buckles glinted. Eyes gleamed. Hearts pounded. The straight road was long and level enough to give General Grant's 2,300 men a chance to draw strength from the sight of one another. They sensed an additional 700 men who had either been left to protect the landing or had already advanced.

This was the first time Grant commanded a division-sized battle. He knew future success would require his men to have confidence that can only be gained through successful combat.

The skirmishers were still about 100 yards ahead of the line and under cover in the woods when they heard the Division's drums. Reassured and guided by their Captains, Lieutenants and Sergeants, the long line of skirmishers moved deeper into the woods that lay in the mile between them and their enemy. The rest of the Regiments would follow behind in a long row, two ranks deep and stretching half a mile from end to end.

Mathan gazed to his right and then to his left. The main line of troops was almost completely still. The tension of the moment built. Skirmishers were engaged with secessionist pickets well in front of them. Rebels darted like deer between trees and other cover. Mathan watched crows rise from the woods as the skirmishers flushed them. For a moment, he was absorbed in their rising, turning flight and their sharp silhouettes against the blue sky.

Mathan ducked his head before the sound of the gunshot registered in his mind. His horse stepped to the side then steadied but continued to flick its ears. As Mathan searched the woods for movement, the sound drums all along the line took up the roll, tap, tap-tap-tap, roll, tap, tap-tap-tap, "Ad-vance!"

After a minute that seemed to be an hour, raised his own sword, rotated it and pointed to the front and he rode into the trees followed by the 31st Illinois Volunteer Infantry. It quickly became obvious that the low brush, fallen timber and uneven ground would make it difficult to maintain the straight lines so often rehearsed on the parade grounds and open fields near Cairo.

Well ahead of the advancing 31st, the first sounds of musket fire rose. For nearly an hour, the men moved forward as best they could. Logan's skirmishers fired back at puffs of smoke that rose from trees and bushes two hundred yards to their front when suddenly, the pace of firing increased. Logan's companies advanced and drove the gray men from their cover and back towards their camp, other Regiments moved forward and did the same.

When their enemies reached their first lines of defense and began to fire at the approaching Union skirmishers in earnest, their firing became steady. Federal skirmishers ducked behind trees or sought shallow depressions for cover. The main body of Federal soldiers behind them in the woods, continued to move forward, together. Toward the sound of gunfire.

Logan stared into the woods, trying to see what could not be seen but only imagined. Mathan appeared suddenly at his side but did not salute. He waited only until Logan's eyes were on him when he said, "Colonel Logan, General Grant asks that you and Colonel Fouke maintain alignment and take the left flank of the advance."

This order meant two Regiments on his left, the 22nd and the 7th would wait until he passed, then move behind him and to his right. It also meant that Logan and the 31st would be nearest the river and potentially the first to encounter the main body of the Confederates. They would be nearest to the huge enemy guns on the bluffs across barely a half-mile of water.

Mathan continued, "Colonels Dougherty and Lauman will be on your right with the 7th Iowa and 22nd Illinois. Colonel Buford will take the 27th around the marsh on our far right. Artillery will cover your advance."

Logan understood that Grant, and perhaps McClernand, were trusting him to prevent an attack on the vulnerable left flank. Grant had personally scouted the area a couple of weeks before and had sent cavalry scouts again this morning. "Thank you, Captain Stark. We are ready," said Logan, loudly enough for his small staff of officers and messengers to hear. Mathan turned his horse and rode to the knot of men and horses that marked General Grant's location.

Posting back to his position behind the Generals, Mathan glanced down at the buttons on the short, blue wool jacket he'd been given at Cairo.

Although he was an infantry officer, he'd be in the saddle most of the day and a short coat made it easier to mount and ride. Unfortunately, this jacket was a bit too small, and it pressed against his shoulders and across his chest. Once he took his place and settled his mount, he saw his buttons shudder. He realized they were bouncing in synchrony with his pounding heart. For an instant, he remembered Rachel's last embrace and lingering goodbye kiss. The memory flew as quickly as it had arrived.

Logan didn't recognize fear or dread. But he was familiar with rage and his was boiling. Keeping his eyes forward, he raised his saber and bellowed, "Advance under cover and hold your fire!" allowing his men to adjust their almost-straight lines and take advantage of the trees and other cover offered by the woods.

Logan's seat atop his horse gave him a better view and he sent Lieutenant Colonel White to the left end of his line to keep an eye on progress there. Their horses allowed them to move among their line much faster than if they were afoot. Branches dropped on them from above, cut by Confederate rounds passing high overhead. Logan had advanced nearly 100 yards into the woods when he was startled to see three soldiers emerge from the brush almost directly in front of him, moving hastily towards the rear. "What happened to him?" asked Logan of the Private nearest him.

Without stopping, the soldier looked over his shoulder and said, "Caught it in his ankle sir. Maybe they can fix him up." The wounded soldier couldn't have been 18. His face was blanched where it was not smudged black by powder, his eyes were red and they glistened with tears, his face twisting in torment with each step. Logan was mildly surprised he had no reaction to the sight of the boy's dangling, bloody foot.

"Give him to the first orderlies you see, then get back to your Company. If you can't find your Company quickly, join another one," said Logan firmly as he looked away from the wounded man and to the woods.

The advance seemed uneventful for another ten minutes. Keeping lines organized while stepping through undergrowth was complicated enough. Doing it while anticipating the arrival of hostile fire complicated matters immeasurably.

The unmistakable sound of a cannon in the near distance startled his men. "Keep moving!" he exhorted them. His Captains immediately repeated the direction and the line resumed its advance.

Two hours or more, had passed. Firing at the front was frequent but remained at some distance. It seemed the secessionist pickets were willing to give ground rather than contest control of the woods. A crack! every second or two, sometimes several almost at once but always from different directions.

Further along, Logan saw a soldier in blue, seated with his back to the safer side of a large tree. As he rode nearer, he saw more clearly that the man's chin sagged to his chest. His arms lay unmoving at his sides and his hands were purple with blood. The man's breast was wet and black.

As Logan stared at the dead man, the sound of hummingbird wings passed rapidly overhead. He looked up, almost as if he might see the bullet that was instantly far behind him. "You don't hear the one that gets you," he reminded himself and resumed his movement forward, conscious that his men could see him.

He was not surprised when a Sergeant from the Company of skirmishers jogged towards him. "Sir, Captain Somerville says we've reached the far edge of the woods. There's a cornfield and another stand of woods beyond."

"Thank you, Sergeant." Logan was pleased that his voice sounded so much calmer than he felt. "Tell Captain Somerville to advance about 100 yards into the next woods and stop. The rest of us will hold at the beginning of the woods while the 22nd and 7th pass behind us. I'll send orders after that."

The Sergeant saluted, turned and without waiting for the Colonel's reply, jogged back along the same trail he'd used a moment before.

Logan turned to his staff. "Lieutenant Patterson, tell the Company commanders…" his voice trailing off as he composed his orders. "Tell them to hold at the edge of the cornfields until we're all up. Tell Company G to be sure to stay aligned with the 30th on our right. Don't leave any space between our Regiment and Colonel Fouke's."

Lieutenant William Patterson looked up at Colonel Logan, and was momentarily distracted by his commander's flowing, walrus moustache, long, black hair and glinting, nearly black eyes. The slap of a lead ball against a nearby tree trunk startled him and he felt a burst of energy and pride as he sprinted down the line to communicate Colonel Logan's orders.

When the 31st reached the cornfield beyond the first section of woods, he checked to be sure his men were protected. Looking to his left, he saw two Regiments on angling behind him in a compact column.

Grant wisely insisted that politically appointed commanders have a veteran at their sides. Logan liked and admired his Lieutenant Colonel, an old friend who had been a Sergeant Major with Logan in the Mexican War. Lieutenant Colonel White had taken responsibility for drilling and preparing their Regiment for its first combat. In the meantime, Logan lobbied for equipment and worked the politics of keeping Egypt aligned with the Union.

"Colonel White," said Logan without looking at his second in command. "Would you move to our left again? You'll have the companies on our left flank. If you can, stay in cover and keep an eye out for our artillery. Getting those guns through this mess will take a long time if they make it at all. Since there's a path on the left of the next cornfield, I expect you may have at least a couple of them to support."

Logan knew the extreme left flank would benefit from White's leadership and experience, especially if the big guns opened on them. With White on the flank, Logan would be free to go wherever he was needed.

After a brief pause, Logan rode to his right and met Colonel Fouke who was talking to General McClernand. Several staff officers were behind them, on the road. McClernand said, "Jack, as soon as the 22nd and 7th are in place on Fouke's right, we'll advance through these woods. They're not that deep and they front on cleared land. Nothing from there to the river but our enemies." Looking to their left, Jack pointed to the path on the left of the cornfield they'd just crossed.

"Sir, that road leads to the Secessionist camp. It will be the fastest path for our guns to come up." Logan paused to allow time for the image of artillery to settle into his Brigade commander's mind. Then he added, "If we guide to the left a bit, we'll keep our line anchored on the road until the artillery arrives and by moving to our left, we'll shorten the path for the 22nd and the 7th."

Fouke nodded and McClernand looked from one of his Regimental commanders to the other considering the alternatives. He decided. "Good thought, Jack. Please do that."

Firing had picked up all along the front and Logan sent for Captain Somerville to bring his skirmishers back to align with the rest of the Regiment. It was good that Logan brought his skirmishers in. They would have been overmatched by the number of Confederate fighters whose lines closed-up as they inched back. Like a funnel, as the fight came closer to the Confederate lines, the two opposing lines compressed, and firing became much more intense.

Just after 10:30, Logan raised his saber and pointed to the woods ordering another advance. The drummer beat the cadence and the line entered the second stand of woods in surprisingly good order. Firing picked up quickly. Most men kept their places in line and refrained from unnecessary stops.

Logan was absorbed by the fight. He heard the whirring sounds of bullets passing overhead. He registered a sound like a hammer striking hard-packed soil when a ball found a soldier. He noticed cries of pain and he saw two wounded soldiers writhing near the feet of his horse, their hands clutching wounds.

Rage rose within him, but no fear. Seeing suffering, he felt no compassion. Logan was possessed by outrage and bellowing his fury. Roaring at his men to aim low, reload, advance, and make them pay for the dead, for the wounded, for making this damned war.

The 31st's advance was steady. The line moved forward ten or twenty yards, took firing positions and opened on any target they thought they could see. Firing continued until Logan was satisfied the enemy had withdrawn sufficiently. Only then did he order another advance. The wounded who were able, moved to the rear, Logan eying each one briefly, promising himself and anyone who could hear him that he'd shoot the first uninjured man he saw withdraw from the line. There was no need.

After an hour of fighting and advancing, the forest thinned abruptly and gave way to open land. Ten yards from the beginning of open ground, he ordered a halt. Junior officers echoed his order down the line in both directions. He directed his men stay behind cover or to lie down. He didn't have to tell them twice. Looking to his right, he saw that Fouke was lined-up with him. Further to the right, he saw Lauman and Dougherty had also reached the edge of the woods.

The Confederate defenses were in clear sight with nothing between the line of woods and their abatis.[8] Well behind the pits, Logan could see a Confederate flag atop a pole, marking the Confederate camp.

Now reorganized and facing their enemy, Logan commanded, "Commence firing!" Immediately the drummer began: thump-thump-thump-thump-thump, tap-tap-tap, tap followed instantly by the sound of nearly a thousand muskets exploding together. "Give it to 'em men!" he roared, riding a few steps behind the line of men, and pointing at the smoky lines not 200 yards away. "Fire! Aim low and fire!" he shouted with a passion that blocked sound and sensation.

---

8 Rows of trees with sharpened branches facing the front) before mounds of earth. Behind the mounded soil were firing pits (short trenches).

Logan rode to Lieutenant Colonel White. "Colonel," shouted Logan over the roaring gunfire, "Have you seen our artillery? Is it coming?"

"Sir," replied Lieutenant Colonel White with enough volume to be heard, "They're a couple of hundred yards back, but they're coming. Their Lieutenant told me they'd unlimber[9] on our left."

"Damn! They should be here! Lord I hope we don't get orders to attack those lines until the artillery breaks them up some!" Logan was grateful for White's calm confidence, and it strengthen him.

Turning toward the center of his line and riding a hundred yards, Logan heard tree limbs crack along with the sound of a dozen hammers striking tree trunks. An instant later, he heard the roar the cannons that had sent grapeshot,[10] every ball with enough power to shatter several men.

More artillery followed the grapeshot. It was well-aimed and struck the 30th's right and the center of the 7th Iowa's lines. What began as a simultaneous roar became a series of blasts as the Confederate gun crews sponged, reloaded and fired at different rates. Union troops exposed to artillery, sheltered in the nearest cover and few returned fire. The Confederate artillery stopped and for a moment, the field was almost quiet.

The moment ended with the scream of two entire Regiments of Tennesseans, rising from behind their cover and advancing in line toward the Union lines where the cannons had just smashed Federal troops. If the Rebels made it to the woods in front of them, they would break through the line and cause a rout, a disorganized dash to the boats and the capture of much of Grant's Division.

Reigning his horse to his right, Logan came quickly to Captain Sommerville's Company. Just beyond them he saw the men of the 30th. Confederates rose from their rifle pits 300 yards away and were following

---

9 To separate a cannon from the animals pulling it, then preparing it to fire.

10 A can of small iron or lead balls fired from a cannon and used primarily as an antipersonnel weapon.

the aim-points of the artillery, pouring across open land and directly towards Foulke's and Lauman's men. The wave of Confederates screamed in a hellish chorus as they approached the two Regiments of Iowans and Illinoisans.

Logan bellowed at his men to fire on the advancing enemy from their places far to the right of the rapidly approaching Rebel soldiers. In seconds, the advancing Rebels accelerated to a steady jog and were rapidly closing on the Union lines.

The screaming Southerners were barely 100 yards from the Union soldiers and seemed to be gaining speed. Suddenly, the entire Union line facing the onrushing men exploded with the simultaneous volley of a thousand or more muskets. The line of running men slowed, many fell, and others looked behind as if to measure the distance back to the trenches they'd just abandoned. Even so, they rose to resume their progress towards the Regiments that recently moved to Logan's right.

The Union guns had arrived late, but not too late to meet the Confederate charge. Before the Rebels had taken three steps, a thunder of artillery rose from Union lines. The Union's first volley of explosive shells silenced the confederate artillery. Splinters, dust and smoke engulfed the distant cannons and they didn't fire again.

Mathan was behind the artillery. The union battery unlimbered in sight of the Confederates who knew they had to reach the guns before they could be fired at them. A Company of Logan's inexperienced Union soldiers charged with protecting the cannons spread out about fifty yards in front of the guns and to the sides of their line of fire. The "green" troops realized the guns were a magnet for enemy fire and they sensed they were now on the hottest part of the field. When they saw hundreds of screaming Rebels dashing toward them, the sounds of bullets striking nearby, the cries of wounded friends and the bodies of people they knew became too much and they began to back away from the fight.

The crescendo of the oncoming rebel yell was met with the first volley of fire from the Union cannons. Mathan saw the gush of fire and the clouds of smoke explode in the direction of the on-rushing rebels. He had barely steadied himself after the thunder of the guns before the rebel screams were renewed and Mathan saw the horde of men rising from their cover and seeming to be coming straight at him.

Mathan resolved to stand with the defenders and protect the guns. As he dismounted, he noticed a few men who were leaving the line. They were soon joined by others and in less than a minute, he saw over half the company had left the line and were hurrying to escape the on-rushing rebels. Mathan remounted and rode quickly to confront the fleeing soldiers.

"Turn the hell around!" he bellowed. "Turn around, God damn it! Get back to your Company!"

As he shouted, he drew his infantry sword and pointed it at the nearest man. Seeing more men skirting him and making for the rear, Mathan reigned his horse and cut them off, like a man herding cattle. Waving the sword over his head and turning his mount from side to side he shouted at the top of his lungs, "Turn around, damn you!" Seeing their commander, Captain Somerville, he shouted, "Somerville, control your men!" Get back to the guns, get back!"

The Union guns roared again. Mathan couldn't hear Somerville's reply.

A second volley from Union guns poured grapeshot into the onrushing Rebels, stopping their attack and causing the Tennesseans to look over their shoulders once again, to the comparative safety of their own lines. This time, they retreated, running headlong away from the Federal guns.

Despite the Rebel retreat, firing from Union troops hadn't completely stopped. Logan rode to the boundary between his right and the 30th's left where he found Mathan, nearly a hundred yards to the rear, turning his mount one way, and then the other while obviously arguing with another officer on foot. The two were bracketed by nearly a hundred union soldiers watching the exchange.

Logan galloped to them. Reining his mount to a skittering stop between the two young officers he demanded, "What the hell is going on here!"

As the infantry Captain turned and opened his mouth to explain, Mathan shouted, "They pulled back from the battery! Left them exposed!"

In an instant, Logan grasped what had happened: As Logan's rightmost company felt the pressure of the on-rushing wave of Confederates, the artillery had arrived and unlimbered. Mathan encountered a Company of soldiers backing away from the fight, leaving the artillery exposed and vulnerable. Mathan was arguing with the Company Commander, shouting that there were no orders to fall back and telling him to return to the front and protect the guns.

Logan exploded. "By God, you sons-of-bitches had better turn yourselves around and follow me back up there before I blow your f-ing heads off your damned skinny shoulders!" Without waiting for a response, he reached down and grabbed the Company commander by the collar and reined his mount toward the fight, dragging the staggering Captain at his side. The men of the Company saw this, looked at Mathan, then at Logan and realized their Sergeants were running ahead of Logan. The entire Company followed immediately with Mathan watching as he caught his breath.

After a few seconds, Mathan, still mounted, followed at a walk, ensuring there were no stragglers. Logan's rage was infectious and a glare from Mathan was all it took for the last couple of uncertain young men to follow their leaders to the front.

As the chastened Company resumed their places and saw that the Confederates were backing toward their trenches, Logan turned to Mathan, "Damned good thing you stopped them! Well-done!" Turning away, leaning forward in his saddle and scanning the battlefield, Logan looked back at Mathan. "Captain Stark, can you keep an eye on this part of the line and report to me?"

"Sir, my last orders were to tell you to advance with the 27th and the 7th when General Grant signals the advance. It should come any minute. He didn't tell me when to return."

"Fine, Captain. I need you here. I'll talk to the Generals later. See to it that we stay aligned with the 30th. I'm going to our left." With that Logan turned his back on Mathan and rode to the left of the Union line and out of Mathan's sight.

Mathan noticed busy artillerymen a few yards to his right. They labored with cans of grapeshot and he was surprised to see them load two cans, instead of one, into each gun. There were still some Confederates just over a hundred yards ahead and there was sporadic musketry from both sides. As quickly as the cannons were loaded, they thundered. Before he regained control of his now-dancing horse, two more fired, then the last three, at nearly the same instant.

The breeze quickly drew aside the curtain of black-powder smoke. Where the Rebel charge had been well-along, Logan now saw swaths of dead and dying men covering the ground. A moment later, he saw the last of the enemy who were previously on the ground rise and sprint away from the Union lines. The Confederate infantry realized they may only have 15 or 20 seconds before the guns fired again.

The enemy charge broken, a cheer rose all along the Union line, even from the Company Mathan was shepherding. They had faced a terrifying combination of artillery and on-rushing infantry. Even if they had lost their resolve, they had returned to the fight.

As the cheer ebbed, Mathan saw Grant, on his mount, trotting behind the lines of troops. Suddenly Grant's horse stumbled and fell to its knees, throwing the commander over the horse's head, Grant was launched over his mount's head, feet first.

Mathan froze. What happened next took only a few seconds and seemed to happen in silence. The General landed on his feet and staggered a couple of steps to regain balance. Turning, he stepped quietly to his horse's wounded side. As he ran his hands over the horse's forelock he bent to the horse's ear.

Then, Grant rose and faced a nearby soldier. He said something and pointed to the horse with his chin. Then the General stepped aside and lowered his head. The soldier raised his rifle and fired. The horse rolled to its side and dropped its head.

Grant faced the horse with his head bowed for a few seconds. Raising his head as if finishing a prayer, he turned and accepted the reins of a new mount.

Mathan saw an explosion of smoke from the distant side of the Rebel camp, followed by the clap of simultaneous discharges of over 700 muskets. The 27th had flanked the Confederate's left rear, placing the Rebels at a terrible disadvantage and boxing them in on three sides. He saw the enemy abandon their rifle pits and dash toward the camp that lay between the pits and the riverbank.

Suddenly, McClernand appeared behind Logan. "Jack, begin your advance through the obstructions and stop when you occupy the rifle pits." He paused looking at Logan. "Please repeat the instruction so that I know it was clear."

Logan shouted so that his men could hear and so that McClernand would have no doubt the orders were understood, "Form your Companies! Reload! Advance through the abatis and occupy the rifle pits. Hold, when you've taken the pits!"

In the distance, they saw Confederate soldiers leaving their positions. "Advance! Advance!" Logan shouted over the sound of distant firing. Captains took up the order and Logan heard Sergeants all up and down his line ordering the men to move forward. Logan saw the men rise and move forward, under his command. He felt he might burst with pride.

Logan then turned to McClernand and saluted. McClernand retuned the salute, reigning his mount to his right. Only then did Logan notice McClernand was mounted on such a small horse, that his long legs nearly drug along the ground.

The 31st advanced in good order, this time, obeying their Captains and Sergeants with enthusiasm. There was almost no enemy opposition as the Regiment cleared and occupied the rifle pits. When the few remaining occupants saw the long blue lines jogging towards them, they threw their weapons aside, raised their hands and stood at the back of their trenches hoping for the best. Nearly a dozen Confederate stragglers were rounded up without resistance.

"Company C!" shouted Logan at the Captain nearest him. "Detail two squads to take those prisoners and the wounded men to the rear!"

"Yes sir!" came the immediate response.

"Tell your men to turn the prisoners over to the commander at the landing and have them stay there and make themselves useful until we return. I don't want anyone getting lost going back and forth."

Logan's 31st Illinois was on one of the three sides of the Confederate position, facing inward toward their camp and firing into the retreating mass. Logan rode the length of his line exhorting his men to maintain their fire. For nearly 15 minutes, his men reloaded and fired round after round until the Union cannon joined them and roared again. This time, dropping explosive shells into the middle of the Confederate camp, not two hundred yards in front of Logan's men. He looked to his right and saw the captured Confederate guns being wheeled to join the Union battery, nearly doubling their potential firepower.

The next round of explosions obliterated the center of the Rebel camp. Sensing the moment his men could rush the camp and rout the enemy, Logan turned his horse back to the center of his line and dashed the hundred yards to Lieutenant Colonel White. Logan ordered his men to charge the camp just as a third series of explosions shook the air and filled it with dense white smoke. Clumps of soil fell like hail into the holes just created by Union guns.

Logan and White were together when they heard a cheer rise from the entire line of Union soldiers. He saw the backs of hundreds of Rebels running towards the river, hopping over the embankment and disappearing.

Grant's entire force surged forward, pursuing the fleeing enemy. The routed Southerners who had disappeared over the levees kept running North or South along the river. The moment Union soldiers reached the Rebel camp, they stopped chasing the fleeing enemy.

Cooking fires still burned. Nearly every tent contained personal possessions. Some sheltered Rebel wounded. All of this attracted the curiosity and avarice of the victorious and inexperienced army. Discipline evaporated like rain pelting a campfire. Federal troops looted the camp.

McClernand didn't recognize the loss of discipline but saw an opportunity to make an impression. And a speech.

Within minutes, Brigadier General John Alexander McClernand, called for the band to assemble under the flagpole of the newly-liberated Camp Johnston. While soldiers were in the midst of looting, McClernand climbed atop a trestle-table, ordered the band to play and as soon as a sufficient crowd had gathered at his feet, began a victory speech. But it didn't last long.

It was just past two in the afternoon. The disorganized but invisible Confederate Army hadn't quit. From their vantage points less than a mile away, Confederate artillery commanders noticed their flag no longer flew over the camp. Riverbanks had blocked their view of the fight but seeing remnants of the Southern forces abandon the field they realized there was no danger of injuring their own troops when they fired.

Grant placed videttes all around the newly-taken camp. He also sent word to the landing, three miles away, to be prepared for Confederate stragglers and to anticipate the return of the Union Army.

The General was dismayed by his Division's dissipation. This discomfort was dramatically compounded when a messenger informed him that secessionist ferries had landed about 1,500 enemy infantry a half mile south of the camp. Just then, Dr. Brinton appeared on his, now more docile, mount to reinforce the messenger's report and to point out the movement of the fresh Confederate troops. Making matters worse, some of the escaping Confederates reformed behind the Federal troops, blocking their escape to Hunter's landing, where the transports were waiting.

Grant immediately found Logan and a couple of the other Regimental commanders. He ordered them to call their men into ranks immediately, sending the same word to McClernand and all the other commanders. Before the drums began to call for assembly, Grant ordered his cavalry to set fire to the entire camp and its supplies, pausing only to remove prisoners and the artillery they'd overrun. Horribly, several wounded men were left to die in blazing tents.

In a matter of ten minutes Grant's Regiments were nearly all in place while smoke billowed across the camp. On the bluffs above Columbus, Confederate artillerymen opened fire, dropping explosives on the camp and inducing the Union Regiments to depart at a run.

The army that had marched three miles, fought a pitched battle and looted a camp still had the energy to double-time back up the road from which they'd arrived. Having been on the far left of the fight and being nearest the road at the end of the fight, Logan's 31st Illinois led the return march. Once beyond the danger of the guns across the river, they slowed from the nearly six miles an hour of double-time to the still-brisk, four miles per hour of quick-time, closely followed by the rest of the army.

It had only been an hour since the Confederates clambered over the bank and ran for cover. The celebration, speeches and looting had lasted only twenty or thirty minutes before it became clear to Grant that a counterattack was imminent.

The quick reassembly of the small army and its rapid departure was a testimony as much to the leadership of Grant and his commanders as it was to the impetus provided by the Confederate guns across the river.

Returning by the same road that led them to their prize, cavalry dashed to the head of the returning column. They returned to Logan and described a strong line of Confederates astride the road to Hunter's Landing, only several hundred yards ahead.

Simultaneously, the sound of steady musketry broke out at the back of the column, half a mile to their rear. The last units to leave Camp Johnston got the worst of the Confederate artillery from across the river and were now trading fire with newcomers from Kentucky.

The Second Brigade commander, Colonel Dougherty, suffered a shattered leg that would soon be amputated. Lieutenant Colonel Harrison Hart assumed command of the 22nd and had help from Colonel Jacob Lauman, leading the similarly battered 7th Iowa Volunteers. Together, they were holding off the 1,500 fresh Confederate troops.

Confident that the rear of his formation would hold for a time, Grant posted to the front of the column where Logan and McClernand were waiting to meet him. Grant pulled a new cigar from his coat pocket and raised it to his lips, not lighting it, but holding it between his teeth for a moment before he spoke. "What do you have, Logan?" asked Grant, not looking at McClernand.

"They're across the road up there, sir. I'd like to hit them as quickly as possible. They have to be as tired as we are." Logan's inner fire flared as he watched for Grant's reaction."

"Well," Grant paused, looking calmly at Logan, "We cut our way in." Then looking over Logan's shoulder and up the road they'd have to follow, "We'll have to cut our way out." He eyed Logan, waiting for his reaction but knowing the words had been exactly the ones the young Colonel wanted to hear.

Smiling and backing his horse, Logan saluted with a half-smile and replied, "Yes Sir!"

Grant smiled and looked down at his reins while Logan turned his horse and spurred it to the head of his column at a gallop. General McClernand turned to Colonel Fouke and said, "Please assist Colonel Logan with the attack." And Fouke saluted, trotting back to his command without a word. McClernand watched all this with a tightly clenched jaw.

Logan called to his drummer, "Sound officers, come for orders!" The boy beat the short rhythm several times and within a minute, the leaders of each company and Logan's staff gathered around him. "Captain Somerville, keep your men in a skirmish line and move out immediately. Get close enough to fire with effect. Hold their men where they are and give us a few minutes to form up." Logan leaned down from his mount and put his hand on Somerville's shoulder. "Have you got that? Repeat it." He said firmly.

"Skirmish line, get close enough to hold the enemy in place for a few minutes, Sir." Somerville was tired and uncertain. By force of will, Logan was sending his own fire into the young man. He held Somerville's shoulder for an extra moment, staring into the young man's eyes.

"Have you got it!" Logan asked again.

This time Somerville was firm, "Yes Sir!"

"Now go!" said Logan firmly as he turned to the others. "Company A, align with the woods on the left side of the road, 2 ranks deep. Company B, right side of the road, 2 deep." Checking for acknowledgement, each repeated the order aloud.

"Good!" he said looking now at the other Company commanders. "The rest of you alternating sides, same alignment, ten paces behind each other.

"Make sure bayonets are firmly fixed. We're going to advance on the double quick. I'll signal the advance and a volley. Don't fire until you're within a hundred yards. Then, just the one volley and charge immediately. Keep your lines in good order."

He sat back in his saddle and said, "When we break through, Companies on the left of the road, wheel left and press to the left, for only 50 yards, to good firing positions. Then hold there. Companies on the right, do the same, press ahead, wheel right, take firing positions and keep the road clear." He paused looking from one young man to the next.

"Questions?" Logan asked intently, his eyes glowing. He looked to each for their commitment. "Those are the bastards we just whipped. They're scared to death of us and we're gonna give them another dose!"

"Form your Companies!" he shouted, and the drums rolled. The soldiers filed left and right into the brush they'd beaten down on their way in that morning. Colonel Fouke's 30th was poised to flow through the gap the 31st would open. They would get to the clearing on the far side of the Confederate line and hold the way open for the rest of the column.

The plan worked just as Logan hoped. The Confederate troops were the ones who'd fled the camp. They were low on ammunition and intimidated by the massed men who bore down on them. Moreover, the Confederates had been disorganized by the retreat and they hadn't the time or space to reorganize. Fighting as Companies or mixed clusters under a temporary command, they were disorganized and melted away from the 31st's determined assault.

Logan's men kept the road wide open. Remaining Regiments flowed toward the ferry landing. The two big gun boats that had distracted Columbus's guns during the earlier fighting had withdrawn upriver to cover Grant's men. Now they focused their devastating, large guns on the concentrations of Confederate soldiers who dared to come near Hunter's landing.

A rear guard allowed Logan and his men to follow the column to the landing and Grant was there to greet them. It took nearly two hours to board the troops and load the wounded, many of the dead, the guns, wagons, horses and prisoners. Throughout the embarkation, Confederate troops scattered in the distant woods kept shooting, but with little effect. Mathan was aboard with Grant's staff, slumped in a chair, smelling the black gunpowder smoke on his clothes. And remembering the fight. But he couldn't remember the faces of the dead. Something in his heart hardened.

As darkness neared, the last of the rear guard was withdrawn and only some cavalry remained to screen the departure of the steamers. These, last cavalry would ride north, along the river and be picked up early the next morning.

But first, the cavalry had to redirect Dr. Brinton. It seems that he had become lost between the withdrawal from the camp and the point of re-embarkation. Riding briskly but aimlessly through the woods a mile inland, he was nearly captured but fled toward the Union troopers who redirected him.

Brinton got lost again and this time, was reoriented by an enslaved man to a hastily improvised collection point for stragglers, a half mile north of Hunter's Landing. The Doctor was one of the last men aboard a steamer that was detailed to collect the delayed and disoriented[11].

Nearly all the Federal soldiers were aboard. They lined the rails of each steamer and fired at anything that looked like it might be a Rebel soldier. A couple of cannon were rolled onto the deck and joined in. All this kept Confederates well-back.

Grant would not board the steamers until he was confident no one was left behind. He rode alone, toward what he thought was his rear-most position. Ignorant that the last cavalry vidette had already been withdrawn, he trotted down the road toward what he thought were his cavalrymen. They were actually the leading element of Confederate reinforcements.

A superb horseman since his youth, riding was effortless, and he focused on his surroundings. In the field, Grant wore a Private's uniform

---

11 Despite of his misfortune, he wrote in his autobiography that, "I acquired some little credit as a valiant doctor." In any case, he was a very fortunate one.

and a battered hat. As he neared what he supposed were his men, he realized they were, instead, Rebels.

Pausing, Grant did his best imitation of an unconcerned scout. He looked for a moment, slowly turned his mount and rode casually away. Once out of range, he galloped to the landing.

The ship's Captain was anxious to leave, and smoke belched from the stacks as the engines rumbled below. Men swarmed over the decks, watching the last rider approach.

There was a single wooden plank connecting the boat to the riverbank. Grant coaxed his mount across the narrow board and onto the deck amidst roars of approval. Confederate marksmen fired helplessly from the distance as the steamer backed into the channel and turned upstream.

As darkness fell, the line of boats arrived at Cairo, but it was four in the morning before the last of the guns was unloaded and the commanders could fall into their beds.

CAIRO, ILLINOIS, NOVEMBER 8, 1861

Next morning, Mathan was shaken awake by Major Webster. "Come on Stark, you need to learn this," said the fifty-year-old Major. "Get your boots on and meet me at the *Belle Memphis* in twenty minutes. I have a sidearm for you and there's food aboard. Let's go."

Having had only a few hours' sleep, Mathan was bleary-eyed. He pulled himself to his feet, staggered to the privy behind his room and began to revive in the brisk morning air. Pulling his coat over his shirt and buttoning himself clumsily he finished dressing with a splash of water across his face.

The walk to headquarters was a blur. He revived slightly when he took a cup of coffee from a Sergeant at the entrance to the headquarters. Picking up a hard roll from a street vendor outside the Hotel St. Charles, he was mostly awake when he reached the landing

The steamer belched a thick fog of black smoke from its twin stacks as Mathan clomped aboard. He was surprised to see sixty or seventy Confederates under blankets on the deck surrounded by a dozen drowsy guards. Two medical officers chatted quietly at the edge of the cluster of prisoners.

Twenty minutes later, Major Webster arrived with a small entourage. The boat drew away from the landing and turned downriver, gliding back towards Belmont, this time under a large white flag. Passing yesterday's landing spot, they stopped just beyond the range of Columbus' guns where they met a smaller steamer, also flying a white flag and coming upriver to meet them.

Mathan watched with the other staff and medical officers as Major Webster and a Confederate Captain talked quietly. Webster turned back to his officers and said quietly, "They'll let our burial party go ashore and take care of the dead. They've already searched the field and have taken our wounded across the river to Columbus. They're keeping them along with the other prisoners." He paused, turning to the surgeon nearest him.

"Doc, would you supervise the transfer of the wounded Confederates to the other boat?"

"Certainly," said the doctor, tapping his colleague on the shoulder and moving to the gangway.

Webster turned and said, "Captain Stark, I need you to go ashore with the burial party and assist the chaplains with their work. I'm sending half a Company of men we brought from the garrison at Cairo, to help. They're fresh and they probably aren't acquainted with the ones you'll bury."

Mathan nodded his understanding. He noticed two young Confederate officers standing some distance behind Major Webster. Webster caught his glance. "You'll also have two escorts from General Polk's staff, in case anyone over here thinks we're looking for trouble. Keep good notes on the locations of the burials. Some family will probably want to collect the remains."

"Yes Sir," Mathan replied softly. "When shall we be back aboard?"

"When you're finished or half an hour before sunset, whichever comes first. I'll stay aboard, in case you need anything."

Within minutes, the Confederate boat chuffed downriver with its load of wounded. Mathan's boat tied up just below Hunter's landing where they had disembarked the day before.

Within minutes the burial party identified a suitable site for the first mass grave. Half the recovery party set about opening a trench while the remaining soldiers took their wagon in search of bodies. When they found a dead soldier, the chaplains were careful to search them for identification, valuables, papers and objects that could be important to a family.

Once the chaplain approved the remains for burial, soldiers placed the body on a stretcher and moved it to the nearest trench. When the trench was full or there were no more bodies nearby, the party conducted a brief service, closed the trench, marked it and moved closer to abandoned Confederate camp, to repeat the process.

Mathan and most of the burial party were heartsick. It was cold and the bodies were stiff: easier to move, but retaining their postures of death, even as they were lowered into the burial trench.

"Captain," called one of the chaplains. "I need your permission to send a couple of soldiers back aboard the steamer."

"What is it Pastor?" asked Mathan quietly.

The chaplain took Mathan aside and spoke softly. "They're suffering from what they've seen. A few minutes ago, two of them found one that was still warm. Must have crawled under cover and suffered alone all night before he died. When they lifted him, his wound opened and, well, you can imagine."

Mathan looked down, then back at the chaplain and beyond him to the line of woods. He remembered yesterday's fight. Today's broken trees, wagon ruts and the chuffing sounds of digging mingled with memories of shouts, smoke, musketry, cannons and the shrieks of wounded men and animals.

"Captain?" asked the chaplain again.

"Thank you, Pastor," said Mathan with a nod. "We'll take them off the retrieval squad and have them trade duties with some of the diggers." Before the chaplain could restate his concern Mathan added, "I think it's better if they finish the job with their friends. If they leave now, that man will be all they remember. If they help us honor the dead, maybe it will be easier later. What do you think?"

The chaplain lowered his eyes in thought, then met Mathan's eyes. The chaplain's eyes were wet and his cheeks were flushed. "You're probably right, Captain," said the chaplain looking down, then turning away to hide his tears. "This is damnably painful work. I detest it!"

Mathan didn't ask whether the chaplain referred to the burial detail or the war. As he squeezed the chaplain's upper arm and turned from him, he knew the answer was both.

When they finished for the day, Mathan took roll twice, to ensure he had everyone aboard. He was quiet during the short trip to Cairo. Disembarking first, he made it a point to wait at the pier, thanking each soldier as they left the boat and following the last one back to camp. He found their Company commander and handed him a letter commending each soldier for his performance of very difficult duties.

Walking back to his room, he tried to think of Rachel but was haunted by memories of the past 36 hours. Opening the door, he tossed his coat aside, kicked off his boots, offered an incoherent prayer for strength and rolled himself in his blanket. Falling back into his bed, he lay immobile for twelve hours.

The next evening, Mathan excused himself quietly from the mess to take a walk. The others suspected he was meeting someone, but didn't ask. He walked slowly down Commercial Avenue to Seventh Street and to the small, rented room he'd taken behind a general store. Rachel was already there.

"I have to be back in an hour," she said quietly locking the door and turning to face him. She saw his faint smile and knew something was wrong. She sat next to him on the edge of the bed and put her arm around his back, resting her head on his shoulder, she asked, "What is it?"

132

His mood was gloomy and his eyes were unfocused, but he could feel her warmth and gentle encouragement. She ran her hand across his back and asked, "What is it?"

"Nothing," he said turning to her with a half-smile and moving his hand over hers.

She took his face in her hands and turned him towards her. "Yes, there is. You just got back from fighting." She looked into his eyes for permission to ask, "Can you tell me what happened?"

It had only been four days since they were last alone. "I ... don't want to think about it." He took her hands from his face and held them to his chest. "I slept last night for the first time in days. When I woke up this morning, all I could think of was you."

The small, quiet room relaxed them. He kissed her slowly while her arms enfolded him, pressing her body to his. They relaxed onto the bed. Their bodies silenced their memories.

Entwined, he held her gently. Silent tears rolled down his cheeks and he struggled for self-control. Then Rachel wept and Mathan's resolve failed. Her breath on his cheek and the depth of her concern overcame him. He also broke into sobs. Compassion replaced passion and they cried in one another's arms. They cried for love, for relief and for sorrow. They cried for time and its passing. They cried for their past and for their future.

"Rachel, I don't want to wait until the war is over. I want to marry you right now." I want you to be my wife. I want to know I'm coming home to our house, to us!" Rachel looked at him without answering.

Rachel sighed, "I'll marry you, Mathan. It's what I want most in this world." She took a slow breath and looked down before continuing, "But, not yet."

"Why not!?" he was pleading.

"This war will end soon, Mathan. We'll go home. I want my family and friends to be at my wedding. I want my pastor, not some chaplain I've never met, at I church I've never attended, marrying us in front of a handful of strangers, only to watch you go off, heaven knows where, while I wait behind you! No thanks. We can wait."

Mathan lacked the energy and the words to argue. He rested his head on her breast and moaned; defeated and still.

Too soon, Mathan walked her to within a block of her hospital and watched her go. He was emotionally and physically spent. He walked slowly back to the room and lay down on their bed, inhaling her scent and welcoming numbing sleep when it came at last.

Rachel was not so fortunate. She met her aunt just inside the doors of the hospital. "I'm glad you're back," said Mary Ann busily. Rachel's expression stopped her.

"Something's happened," said Mary Ann, not asking.

"Nothing." Replied Rachel looking down, then avoiding Mary Ann's eyes and looking furtively to the ward of wounded men beyond.

Mary Ann took Rachel's hand and led her to a small room where Mary kept a writing desk. She seated Rachel behind the desk and leaned across it to face her. "I'm glad you saw your young man. Is he alright?" she asked with genuine concern.

"Yes," said Rachel quietly. "And no," she added looking up. He had to go back to the battlefield yesterday, they made him collect bodies that were left behind and bury them. It sounded terrible," she went on, reexperiencing the pain she felt so recently in his arms.

"He told you about it?" Mary Ann asked.

"Yes, some of it," said Rachel softly. "I just let him tell me what he wanted to."

"That was a gift he may never appreciate," said her aunt firmly. "But you can't carry it for him. You have to let it go like he did, or it will crush you." Then she looked down the corridor toward the rows of beds. "There's more than enough here for you to do without carrying his or anyone else's burdens."

Looking up at her aunt, Rachel replied, "I know. I'll be alright. I promise."

"I accept your promise," replied Mary Ann leaning close to Rachel's forehead. "The only way to deal with these things is with friends and faith. We'll get through this and we'll talk to God about it too." As Rachel nodded to herself, Mary Ann finished, "Now come with me. I'm going to put you to work with the sick boys. No need to deal with wounded ones for a few days. There will be plenty more. Eventually, you'll get used to it. But not today."

Mathan and Rachel had no free time for days. On the fourth day after the battle, Mathan was back on the steamer, *Aleck Scott*. This time, he was with Grant, Logan, two dozen staff members and nearly 50 captured Confederate soldiers. They planned to meet the Confederate commander on the river to discuss additional prisoner exchanges. Grant left the deck so he could speak to Major Webster and Lieutenant Colonel Rawlins in a private cabin.

Logan remained in the salon and leaned across a card table and spoke with authority to the rest of the staff, "Let me tell you about Polk. He's their commander at Columbus and you should know something about him before we meet."

Assured he had everyone's attention, Logan leaned back, then held forth. "General! Bishop! Master!" he said, with an extra pause for effect. "Leonidas Polk! His credentials are many. His primary personal achievement was to graduate from West Point in the same class as the secessionists' 'President', who seems to regard him as a special friend."

Glowing with his audience's attention he continued, "It seems old Polk resigned his commission a couple of months after graduation because he didn't relish the thought of frontier duty, although he said it was because he wanted to become an Episcopal priest. He had a desire to run plantations and profitable businesses while at the same time, performing holy service to Our Lord. Seems the young Polk's inherited wealth was insufficient for a future aristocrat so *Lieutenant* Polk became *Reverend* Polk and a rich man at that."

"He gathered up hundreds of slaves, expanded his plantations, and eventually had himself anointed the Bishop of the Episcopal Church in Louisiana! This last elevation in rank required him to withdraw his congregations from association with the rest of the Episcopal church on account of their political distaste for his manner of earning a living. You know Southern Episcopals advocate slavery as an article of faith." Logan took a deep breath and smiled.

"He's down here trying to hold onto Kentucky and reporting to their General Johnston. Johnston, now, is as fine a general as they have..." Just then, Grant returned. He smiled at the gathered staff and apologized to Logan for interrupting him. Then sat in the chair next to Logan's.

"Introducing the men to the Bishop's history, sir," said Logan with a smile.

Grant smiled to himself and looked up. "Quite a story he has." After a brief pause he went on, "Seems, there will be a slight change of plans," continued Grant in his usual soft manner. "Last night, General Polk returned from Memphis where he met some important people from their side. After he was finished there, he took a train back up here to Columbus and had his supper."

"The General's men wanted to show-off one of their big, new Dahlgren[12], a ten-incher pointed in our direction and named after the General's wife: the 'Lady Polk,' they said."

Grant took a deep breath, then resumed, "That gun fires a shell weighing as much as 128 pounds! They were going to show him the range

---

12 A very large cannon designed for ship-board use and too large to relocate quickly on the ground. Ironically, they were especially designed to resist the very kind of accident Grant related.

and impress him with their ability to keep our shipping far from their shores. Unfortunately for General Polk, the demonstration went wrong. It seems, when they attempted to fire the monster, it just … exploded. The blast carried all the general's clothes away, burned him pretty badly and left him senseless. He's bed-ridden just now. In no condition to meet us."

A few of the men murmured, "Too bad," or "Sad to hear it."

We'll be meeting with his subordinate, General Cheatham. General Cheatham and I were acquainted in Mexico, and you may recall that we renewed our acquaintance on the field a few days ago." After Grant finished, there were a few comments and trivial questions, but nothing that changed any understandings or plans.

Within the hour, the *Scott* met the *Prince* and crews lashed the ships together. Negotiations were respectful. Officers of both armies dined at the same table and chatted. More meetings followed, the wounded Confederates went ashore and several other prisoners were exchanged. After dark, Grant and his staff retired to Cairo.

The next time Grant's army left Illinois, two and a half months later, they would bring ten times the number who fought at Belmont and everything would change.

The day after they returned from their meetings on the river, Grant and Logan wanted to visit their men at a couple of the seven military hospitals in and around Cairo. Major Webster had arranged for Acting Chief Surgeon, Brinton to meet the General inside the entrance of the largest surgical hospital.

Busy with his patients and intolerant of distractions, Brinton was on good terms with General Grant, but not happy to be assigned to the task of escorting visitors. Before the General and his staff arrived Brinton said, "Orderly, I want you to get over to Wards five, six and seven. Tell the surgeons there to ensure that any of the patients who have passed are immediately removed from the ward and their beds remade. Have them administer an extra dose of morphine to any of the patients who are loud, deranged or agitated."

The young orderly had been scolded enough times to know not to ask questions, but to do his best to fulfill the chief surgeon's orders immediately. Sliding around the corner of entrance to Ward five, he nearly careened into Mrs. Bickerdyke. "Mother B" had earned near-universal respect.

"Carful Private! You nearly knocked me over! What's the hurry?"

"Ma'am," he said gulping, Doctor Brinton's on his way here with General Grant and a bunch of other officers!" As he scanned the ward for one of the other surgeons he added, "Doctor Brinton says to give all the patients extra morphine to keep them quiet!" Not seeing a surgeon, he added quickly, "I have to go to the sixth and seventh wards to tell them!"

"Go on back to your duties, Private," said Mary Ann calmly. "I'll talk to the other wards and see that we have things ready for the General when he arrives."

"Yes Ma'am, I will," said the private nodding rapidly. "I sure will," he paused then looked at Mary Ann adding, "but if Doctor Brinton…" Mary Ann's sharp glance cut him off.

"Leave Doctor Brinton to me. You've passed his instructions to all three wards. Now, go make yourself useful." She smiled to herself as he scuttled out the door on the far end of the floor.

Mary Ann called two of the other nurses to her side. "There are some Generals coming to check on our patients. Try to stay with the visitors and answer their questions as best you can. If you don't know the answer, just say so and check with me. I'll be nearby."

The younger women nodded and thanked "Mother B" for the early warning. They would be sure to be available when the visitors arrived. Mary repeated the message to all seven wards and returned as Surgeon

Brinton was explaining details of a surgery he'd done to stabilize a soldier's fractured jaw. The young man lay still and silent on his bed, recovering from the chloroform that enabled Surgeon Brinton to do his job.

Looking up from the patient, Grant saw Mary Ann at the back of the clutch of visitors. "Mrs. Bickerdyke!" Grant said brightly. "It's good to see you again!" He stepped around his surgeon and staff (including Mathan) to greet Mary Ann.

Mary Ann smiled confidently and extended her hand. "General Grant, thank you for visiting the boys. Your visit means so much to them."

Shaking her hand and smiling, he placed his left hand on hers as he turned over his shoulder. "Logan, this is Mrs. Bickerdyke. Mrs. Bickerdyke, this is Colonel Logan, one of my finest Regimental commanders." He paused. "I suppose you already know him?"

Mary Ann knew of him. And what she knew filled her with disgust. Author of the "Black Laws," outspoken advocate of the Fugitive Slave Act and Senator Douglas' pet attack dog. "Yes, General Grant, Colonel Logan's reputation certainly precedes him," she said calmly. Logan's political nature emerged immediately.

Half-bowing he said, "Mrs. Bickerdyke! It's my pleasure to meet you. I've already heard so much of what you've done for our men. On behalf of my men and their families, I thank you."

Having discussed Mary Ann's politics with Rachel, Mathan could barely restrain a smile as he waited for Mary Ann's reaction.

"I'm pleased to help where I can, Colonel," she said without meeting Logan's eyes. Then turning to Surgeon Brinton, she added, "Much of what you see here is a direct result of Surgeon Brinton's tireless devotion." This time she held Brinton's eyes. He seemed uncertain whether she was issuing a compliment or a condemnation.

Grant added, "I spoke to Mrs. Bickerdyke just yesterday!" Turning to Brinton he added, "I'm sorry I didn't speak to you earlier, doctor." Grant said pausing to sort out the look that passed between the surgeon and Mary Ann. "We've made Mrs. Bickerdyke the Matron of this hospital. I've issued her and a couple of other ladies, passes to the camp so they can come and go as necessary to care for our men."

"Sir!" sputtered Brinton, "I'm somewhat surprised that…"

Grant raised a hand to silence the pending objection, "I know you're not sure about having women with any authority in our hospitals, but Mrs. Bickerdyke has shown us something different. Doctor, she's part quartermaster, part nurse, part cook and every bit the most strenuous advocate for our sick and wounded that I've met in 20 years!" Grant was smiling and Logan was nodding in agreement. Then he added, "I know you and Mrs. Bickerdyke will work out the details, Brinton. Just tell me whatever it is you need." Then he added, "My congratulations to your cousin! General McClellan has a big job and I'm sure he's up to the challenge."

Mary Ann looked at Grant but felt the surgeon's glare. It was not the first time Brinton had visited her hospital and nor the first time he had expressed criticism of her. She knew it would not be the last.

Mary Ann understood that Brinton wanted Grant to create a medical branch composed not only of surgeons and contract doctors, but of enlisted men who would be under Brinton's direct authority[13]. Grant wanted to preserve his manpower for fighting and logistics. By supporting Mary Ann's presence with her staff of female volunteers Grant saved hundreds of men for other duties and frustrated Brinton's plans for a robust medical corps.

Logan spoke up, "If I may, Ma'am."

"Colonel, my name is Mrs. Bickerdyke."

---

13 Brinton would return to Maryland and establish a "Pathological Museum:" a task better suited to his pedantic predilection. When his cousin, General George McClellan fell out of favor politically, Brinton was relieved of duty at the museum.

"I'm sorry, Mrs. Bickerdyke," pausing and looking into her eyes. "I only wanted to compliment you on the cleanliness of the wards and the attention you've given out men."

"That's nice of you to notice, Colonel Logan, but I didn't attend to your soldiers." Looking across the room she raised her hand to indicate two Black women carrying bundles of soiled laundry. "They took care of those boys."

Logan looked at the women, now half-way across the ward. "Of course, Mrs. Bickerdyke." He thought a moment and added, "With your permission, I'd like to thank them myself."

"Colonel, you don't need permission to speak to them anymore than they require *permission* to speak to you."

Logan felt his back straighten slightly, despite his intention to make a friend of this tough woman. "You're certainly right about that, Mrs. Bickerdyke."

Logan strode across the room in time to catch the ladies as they neared the exit. He shook their hands and to Mary Ann's surprise, he seemed to be *listening* to them.

Mary Ann noticed Grant's obvious discomfort with soldiers who were bleeding and his preference for those who were alert and comfortable. Mathan stood behind Grant and appreciated how quickly Mary Ann's concern for the sick and wounded was expanded to include concern for Grant's distress.

She guided the rest of his visit to soldiers with whom Grant could interact more comfortably. Those conversations appeared to uplift both the soldiers and their commander. When it was clear that Grant was ready to leave, Mary Ann leaned close to him and said, "You're doing a world of good for these boys, thank you."

Then, for the benefit of the other officers present, she straightened her back and in a full voice asked, "General Grant, may I take your Captain

Stark for a moment? I'm curious about your young Captain; we're both from Ohio and I believe we have mutual acquaintances. May I take him aside for a bit?"

Logan looked surprised. He wondered what Stark had to do with Mrs. Bickerdyke.

"Of course, Mrs. Bickerdyke," said Grant cordially. "Stark, we'll see you when you're finished here. Don't hurry." He shook hands all around and left with Logan, who looked back, over his shoulder, at Mathan. Webster and the others trailing behind.

When Brinton turned to look for Mary Ann, she was already leaving the ward through a side-door with Mathan behind her. Brinton growled to himself and paced back to the surgery. He'd deal with her later.

Taking a seat behind her small desk she began gently, "You've been spending some time with Rachel?"

"Yes Ma'am," replied Mathan, holding her eyes. "I'm very fond of Rachel. We studied together at Heidelberg College before the war." The redness rising in his cheeks betrayed the confidence he hoped to convey.

"There are things I know and there are things I suspect," she was more direct now. "I know how much Rachel would suffer if she had a 'problem,' so early in your relationship. I *suspect* that you are as concerned as I that Rachel suffer no problems?"

Mathan blushed even more brightly as he struggled to keep his eyes on Mary Ann. He repeated, "I am especially fond of Rachel." After a pause he added, "As you know, I asked for her hand while we were still in Ohio and she said yes, but wants to wait. She wanted to join you, here."

"I understand that's the case," said Mary Ann calmly. "And I am glad that you two are still courting. Unfortunately, I am her only family in Illinois, and I must see to her best interest."

Mathan dropped his eyes briefly and steadied himself. "Yes ma'am. I know she cares very much for you, too. And she's deeply grateful for your guidance and support."

"I'm quite sure she is," said Mary Ann resuming her calmer voice. "I have spoken to her about avoiding problems, particularly here in Cairo. She will need your help." Mary Ann looked into Mathan's eyes, seeking evidence of comprehension.

Understanding flashed across his face. Mathan knew Mary Ann was both a homeopath and a nurse. He also knew about her practicality and impatience with negligence. Looking into Mary Ann's eyes he said, "We are," pausing to gather his thoughts, he changed his tack, "I am very concerned about Rachel's safety and welfare. I am also very grateful for your help."

"You are essential to her safety. Both now and I suspect, in the future." She reached for Mathan's hand and took it gently in both of hers. "Let's agree to cooperate," she said softly. "Each of us loves her and each of us wants the best for her."

Mathan squeezed Mary Ann's hand and nodded. "Yes Ma'am."

"She's at the church this morning," added Mary Ann gently, releasing Mathan's hand and gaze. "She's sorting a shipment of food and personal items down from Galesville. I imagine she could use your help. I think the General could spare you until after lunch?"

Mathan brightened and thanked her before backing out of her small office. He'd walk the few blocks to the church as quickly as he could and make the most of a brief visit with Rachel. As he left, Mary Ann looked over his shoulder in the direction of the surgery. She imagined her next encounter with Surgeon Brinton and sighed. Stepping back onto the ward with her hands on her hips, she surveyed her patients and decided there was no need to check on her nurses before visiting the kitchen.

In the following weeks, General Grant prepared for his next action. He was under the authority of General Halleck who was both scholarly and cautious. While the President and most of his advisors agreed that Kentucky and Tennessee must be removed from Confederate control, General Halleck's political self-importance, posturing and risk-aversion resulted in muddled planning and delayed action. Politicians in Congress and the President's Cabinet also dabbled in military strategy, further complicating, delaying and politicizing Grant's plans.

Mathan had remained at Cairo under Major Webster on Grant's staff. One afternoon in January, Mathan received word his original Regiment, the 78th Ohio, was mustered into active service and would move to Cincinnati under General Lewis Wallace, a politician from Indiana. Mathan's position had been filled in his absence and the 78th did not need him to return. Mathan was now Major Webster's to assign.

The problem was resolved the next morning when Lieutenant Colonel White, Logan's second in command, went to headquarters to ask General McClernand for administrative assistance. Of course, General McClernand was away on a political errand and the request went to Major Webster's desk in the form of a note from McClernand's chief of staff.

Webster read the note and thought for a minute. He and Mathan had a close relationship, owing to months of collaboration and Logan had commented on Mathan's performance at Belmont, further enhancing his reputation. "Hey, Stark!" he called. "Come in here for a minute, will you?"

Mathan said, "Yes sir, what's up?"

"We have those political commanders you know: McClernand and Logan? Well, they're both away on business and their staffs are short-handed. How would you feel about spending some time with Colonel

Logan? We'd be in close contact and you'd see a different level of command. Might make you that much more useful when your Regiment calls in their chips and makes us give you back."

Realizing he could give no other answer, he said, "Certainly sir."

"I'll write the orders and give them to you in the morning. You can finish up here and report to Lieutenant Colonel White at the end of the day tomorrow, said Webster returning to his work." Logan's headquarters was in the same building and Mathan was acquainted with Lieutenant Colonel White, who'd be Mathan's boss.

That evening, Mathan visited Mary Ann and Rachel at their new boarding house. When Mathan told them about his transfer to Colonel Logan's staff. Rachel's eyes widened a bit, but Mary Ann nearly spat her tea onto the floor.

"Who!?" she demanded.

"Colonel Logan," answered Mathan with eyes on Rachel, appealing for support.

"I don't know what to make of that man," groaned Mary Ann. "He is as hostile to black people as any overseer on the worst plantation! He was Stephen Douglas' lackey and now that he's in Congress, he's setting himself up to replace Douglas or heaven knows what!" She was nearly shouting when she leaned toward Mathan and added menacingly, "Don't you dare let that politician infect you with his ideas, do you understand!"

Mathan looked down and smiled to himself, then gathered his thoughts and answered. "I agree that his politics contradict much of what I believe. That said, we agree on a few things: That we have to fight to preserve the Union. It will take a war to save it and, this is more important than any other political issue since the Revolution."

Mary Ann glared at him. Rachel looked at him with understated but genuine admiration and support.

Mathan added, "I've seen him fight. His men admire him and will follow him anywhere. He was the most effective officer at Belmont. General Grant relied on him for every important part of that fight and he will count on him again the next time. Maybe you can give him a chance, Mrs. Bickerdyke?"

"You'll be with him, won't you Mathan?" asked Rachel sadly.

"Yes, I think I will. I'll be on his staff at least until the 78th wants me back or Major Webster sends me somewhere else. I'd like to go back to Colonel Leggett."

"That's better," said Mary Ann definitively. "He's not one of those Copperheads, is he?"

"No Ma'am," said Mathan with some relief. "I suspect he thinks like you do."

The conversation slowed for a few minutes and Mathan excused himself. It was late and it had become very cold. "Early day tomorrow. Thank you for a very interesting evening, ladies," he said with genuine warmth. "I'll see you again, very soon."

Mary Ann did not reply but turned her attention to a book. She ignored Rachel's departure with Mathan. The couple found an unobserved space just inside the door of the boarding house, there was time for an embrace and a lingering kiss good-bye.

The plans for an invasion of the South were well under way and Mathan was looking forward to getting away from the monotony of the camps. He'd seen Rachel frequently enough that the thought of a separation for a campaign didn't seem too daunting. He didn't realize that General Grant was about to lead his army into a series of battles that wouldn't end for over three years.

Logan used the time between late November 1861 and mid-January 1862 to go East, in pursuit of political support, equipment and better weapons for his men. The Union's industrial output was growing but hadn't approached its potential. Amidst conflicting priorities for limited resources, the constant attention of politically connected officers increased the chances their Regiments and Brigades would be quickly and effectively supplied. One such visit by Logan was to a cloth mill in New York run by a "Mister Stoff."

Stoff sat still and stared blankly at Logan. In his attempt to remain expressionless, he revealed that he knew exactly why Logan was there.

"Mr. Stoff," Logan began. "I know you were delighted to receive the contract for uniforms from the War Department. You may know that my friends in Congress are very interested in the welfare of our troops and the honesty of our contractors. I've checked a shipment your people were preparing for my men in Illinois. Now, there seems to be a small problem." Stoff nodded almost imperceptibly.

Logan continued, "As you know, our contracts specified wool uniforms, but not the manner of cloth used in their construction. It seems some of our suppliers have turned to that English technique of grinding scraps of old woolen cloth with huge, toothed rollers. Can you believe it?" He asked with feigned incredulity.

"Then, they treat the globs of pulverized threads with chemicals, dyes and they squash it into something like rolled felt! My quartermaster said they call the fabric 'shoddy.' At only 10% of the cost of new woolen cloth, I can see why contractors love it." Logan paused to give Stoff time to think about this and to wonder how much more Logan knew about his business.

"But, Mr. Stoff, here's my concern. Shoddy's durability matches its price! 10% as costly and 10% as durable!" Logan sat back and smiled. "I'm sure there will be no shoddy used in any of the shipments to us in Cairo! Am I correct?"

Both men knew that cutting corners was nothing new in government contracts. Stoff also knew that coats made of shoddy were warm enough, but virtually melted in a heavy rain. He knew that Logan was a Congressman and had friends in Washington.

Soon thereafter, Stoff was tripping over himself, hurrying to change goods scheduled for delivery to Illinois and replacing them with more expensive (and durable) coats. He would deliver Logan's original "shoddy coats" under some other contract but at least, he'd avoid this particular Congressman's ire. Logan knew exactly what Stoff would do, but was satisfied with obtaining the best supplies possible for his own men. He couldn't change human nature or the spoils system of government contracting, but he would take care of his soldiers.

Satisfied with his success at the clothing manufacturer's, Logan renewed his pursuit of quality rifles for his Regiment. With remarkable ease, he succeeded in acquiring nearly 1,000 new .58 caliber rifles. Instead of firing lead balls that were nearly ¾ of an inch in diameter and prone to spinning away from their intended targets, the rifled muskets fired a longer but somewhat narrower, conical bullet. The grooved barrels of his new rifles spun those bullets around their long axis, increasing both their range and accuracy.

Compared to old, smoothbore muskets, the 31st's new rifles were lethal at half a mile and (after some training and practice) were about as accurate at a quarter mile as old muskets were at 100 yards. This was especially important in a pitched battle when an oncoming enemy could cover 100 yards in half a minute. Extra range allowed extra time. Soldiers with rifled muskets could fire four times as many "aimed rounds" as soldiers with old "smoothbores."

Early that winter, orders came that Grant interpreted as providing the direction and permissions he wanted. The invasion of Tennessee would begin on the first of February. Logan returned to Illinois in late January of 1862. Within days, he was leading the 31st Illinois (and Mathan) into the first, decisive battle in the Western Theater of the Civil War.

FORT HENRY, TENNESSEE, FEBRUARY 12, 1862

Lifting himself into his saddle, Mathan saw the sun peek above the tree line to the East. The early morning air had only a light chill, despite the cloudless sky. The rising sun was welcome. It would be hours before the 31st took their place in the long line that snaked East, along the Ridge Road towards the enemy fort on the Cumberland River. In the meantime, it was Mathan's job to keep track of the rest of the units that were loading their cooked rations and taking the earlier places in the line of march. His saddle creaked less as it warmed beneath him and he rocked with the motion of his mount.

He smiled to himself at the irony of their long wait at Fort Henry. He recalled his youthful assumption that armies just got up and walked from one place to another whenever they needed to relocate. In reality, roads were narrow and countless starts and stops caused "accordioning" of the line. Although it was only the 12th of February, the weather felt like the first of May. Still riding near camp at ten in the morning, Mathan removed his coat and enjoyed the Spring-like weather.

Major "Doff" Ozburn was the 31st's quartermaster. His job was to work with the Brigade and Division quartermasters to obtain, manage and distribute the ammunition, supply and logistical support for the Regiment. "Hey, Stark!" called Ozburn to Mathan as he rode past a couple of wagons.

"Yes Sir?" asked Mathan as he turned his mount back to where Ozburn stood.

"These wagons are pretty heavy, and I imagine the roads will be terrible by the time we get going. I'd like to redistribute the loads. I want you to go to Ogelsby's headquarters and see if we can get a couple of empty wagons with teams."

"If I can get them, do you want them here or over nearer the road?" asked Mathan as he calculated the time it would take to find the Brigade quartermaster, then get permission, find the wagons and lead them here. Ozburn should have taken care of this long before now.

"Bring 'em here so we can transfer some of the extra ammunition and supplies. Maybe they have a couple of ambulances that aren't full. If the quartermaster can't help you, go check with the surgeon," said Ozburn turning away and not giving Mathan the opportunity to object.

Mathan reached the Brigade's supply area and tied his mount to a nearby tree. He was distressed to see the quartermaster's tent swirling with activity and it took Mathan ten minutes of asking just to find the Lieutenant in charge of the wagon park.

"You're kidding me, right?" asked the incredulous Lieutenant. "We're not taking wagons on the march. They'll come up later, after the men are in place. Why do you think you have orders to carry 40 rounds of ammunition and two days of rations?!"

The Lieutenant was older than Mathan and not at all impressed by Mathan's rank. He had work to do. "We allocated all the wagons and teams days ago. We made a few adjustments yesterday, but everything's accounted for by now. I'm sorry, but half the Brigade is already on the road and you guys should be on the road in half an hour. I have to get back to Headquarters and report our status. Good luck Captain. I don't know what else to tell you." The Lieutenant disappeared while Mathan was scanning the area for ambulances.

As he rode to the hospital tent, Mathan encountered Lieutenant Colonel White coming from the Brigade headquarters tent on foot. Looking up at Mathan he asked, "Why aren't you with Colonel Logan and the Regiment? Is there a problem?"

Mathan explained his errand and Major Ozburn's direction that he seek an ambulance wagon as an alternative.

"The hell you say!" blustered White. "I'll deal with Ozburn, he should have taken care of this yesterday! Damn, sending you on a fool's errand. We need to get on the road now!"

"Yes, Sir," said Mathan calmly. "Shall I tell the Major we can't obtain a wagon?"

"Sure, sure. Tell him I said there are no wagons and no time to hunt for them. Have him get his men into line immediately."

Mathan returned to the Regimental staging area and found Major Ozburn chatting with his friend, Colonel Logan. "Sirs!" said Mathan saluting and looking to Logan who returned a casual salute. "Quartermaster has allocated all the wagons and Colonel White says there are no ambulances available."

"Ambulances?" asked Logan incredulously.

Mathan's eyes moved to Ozburn who replied impatiently, "That's just fine, Captain. I doubted that you'd find us any help." He glanced at Logan with a smile then turned to Mathan. "You can go now Captain. Better luck next time."

Mathan saluted and rode to the cluster of Company commanders who were making last-minute agreements about the line of march and what the men would carry and what they'd leave behind. "You guys need anything before we fall in?" asked Mathan.

"Nope," answered Captain Somerville, who had become a friend of Mathan's after the fight at Belmont. "We're ready." The others grunted in agreement.

Mathan rode back to Logan and passed the Company Commanders' report. A rider arrived from the Brigade and told Colonel Logan he should be ready to begin the march in five minutes.

It was just over an hour before noon when the order came. The men fell in, most taking extra care with the new Enfield rifles Logan had procured and that they'd been issued as they boarded the boat for Tennessee. Today was their first-ever march in warm weather and Company commanders allowed soldiers to leave coats and blankets in a wagon if they chose to, confident they could retrieve them at the end of the day's march.

Cavalry scouts cleared the way ahead. Engineers went with scouts to identify water sources, campsites and places for new bridges. The army frequently employed fugitives from slavery to precede the columns and improve roads. They filled holes, cleared obstacles and lay stones or small tree trunks across the worst sections of road.

Soldiers who left the line between scheduled breaks to answer the call of nature, to gather fruit or tend blisters, disrupted the smooth movement of an army. Small delays accumulated and could spread a single Regiment over miles of road. Eventually Regiments overlapped and mixed, so that sorting the men out at the end of the march could present an significant challenge.

Complicating every march was the inevitable deterioration of dirt roads. A brief shower could make a road slippery and a steady rain created a shoe-sucking quagmire with bogs as deep as a horse's belly and totally impassable to heavy wagons and artillery. Only couriers moved swiftly. But making way for them could also delay a march.

By 3:30 that afternoon, the column was nearing Fort Donelson and nearly every man was in light clothing. Tired, they trusted the supply wagons at the back end of the column, to deliver their overcoats and blankets before they were needed. At one brief stop along the road, several men made a careful pile of their coats and shelter-halves, marking it with their Regiment's name.

They trusted the weather to remain fair. As the sun began to set that night, the wisdom of their decision came into question. By nightfall, fewer than half the men had collected their overcoats, tent-halves or blankets.

Logan's men made camp on a spot where they had been directed, just right of the center of the Union lines. They had to camp in the open. The slow pace of the march delayed their supply wagons. Large tents (and the coats packed with them) couldn't arrive until late the next day. The night was chilly, but manageable and fires warmed their coffee and their feet.

"I don't care which Regimental surgeon sent you! We're not moving from here!" Said Mary Ann, fists balled up and pressed to her hips as she leaned toward the young doctor, intimidating him with her tone, her posture and her gaze.

"Well, Ma'am, I don't know what to tell you, I have orders..." But he didn't have time to finish.

"Just bring your things over here and send word to your Regiment where they can find you. I don't have time to argue and you don't have the authority to overrule General Grant. Now, let's agree that you'll attend the boys who arrive here and I'll have things ready when they start to come in." She didn't wait for a reply but turned on her heel, nodded to several black ladies who were there to help and entered the house she had prepared as a surgery.

"Ladies, she said brightly, "Let's hope that's the last of that. Would you take the big kettles from the first wagon and set them over coals behind the house? I want one with boiling water and we'll use the other to stew that awful pork they sent us. I think we also brought some greens and potatoes. At least we can have something warm to feed the ones we get here."

A small group of soldiers had just finished unloading the ambulances and stood around waiting for someone to tell them what to do next.

They had been sent to help with medical supplies because they were too old or too lame to march and fight. Mary Ann said, "You'll stay here at the hospital. You'll be a great help to us and I want you to start by clearing out space in the barn over there. No fires! That barn is much too old and dirty for fires."

Pointing to the cooking fires that were smoking in the farmyard she continued, "I want you to make a big pile of bricks or brick-size stones over by those cooking fires. We'll heat them and wrap them in old cloth. Later, we'll tuck them in with the wounded. It will help keep them warm in that old barn."

Some seemed to understand, but none moved or said anything. They just looked at her with blank expressions. "Get to it!" she snapped. We have no idea when things will happen, and we don't want to fail because we didn't prepare! Now get to work!" So they did.

OUTSIDE FORT DONELSON, FEBRUARY 13, 1862

The next morning, Mathan arose well before dawn to check on the recently posted pickets[14]. He decided to wear his pistol although he had only fired it twice, for practice. He checked with the sentry watching at the edge of the camp who directed him to the reserve position behind the pickets. Before leaving the cover of the camp, he looked back for campfires and the moon. Lieutenant Colonel White had warned him not to silhouette himself when moving in the dark.

Mathan neared the picket line and rehearsed the sign and counter-sign that would identify him as a member of the 31st. As he reached the spot where he expected to find one of his sentries, he heard the click of a drawn hammer and hushed voice emerge from behind a tree whispering, "Dirty!"

Mathan looked to his right and saw the barrel of a new Enfield, only twenty feet away and aimed directly at him. Staring at the muzzle and absolutely still he replied in a shaky voice, "First."

"Proceed," was all he heard. Mathan waited for muzzle to lower before he moved a muscle. The muzzle disappeared and Mathan heard a click as the hammer was decocked. He drew a deep breath before he

---

14 Pickets were individual or small groups of soldiers placed in advance of body of troops to observe enemy movement and to warn the main body of danger.

continued along the path. Not far beyond the sentry he found the reserve position where part of the Company (about fifty men who weren't presently on the picket line) clustered in small groups behind a small rise. A couple of Sergeants and their Lieutenant chatted quietly and kept their eyes toward the front.

Fifty yards beyond them and centered on an imaginary line about 200 yards across and parallel to the Confederate lines were the Union pickets: squads of a few men clustered every fifty feet or so, depending on available cover. Their job was to prevent any Confederates from sneaking across the space between the armies to gather information. Pickets would also warn the rest of the Regiment of any advance by the enemy. Usually, they would have been placed much further forward, but the soldiers were new to this kind of fighting, it was dark and the enemy lines were relatively close. No one wanted to be so far in front of their own lines that someone could creep up and capture them.

Stepping quietly from one picket to the next, across the front, Mathan assured himself that all of them were in place and alert. Twenty minutes later, when he returned to the supporting company, he saw Major Ozburn talking to the Lieutenants and Sergeants. "Colonel Logan wants to know what you've seen tonight. I'll give him your report," he said in a voice louder than it needed to be.

Before the Lieutenants could answer, Mathan approached them and said, "Sir," paused and waited for Ozburn to speak.

"What are you doing here, Stark?" asked Ozburn dismissively.

"Sir, I was just checking on the pickets."

Ozburn puffed himself up before asking, "Who asked you to do that?"

Mathan was ready for his question because he'd considered it before he left camp. "Lieutenant Colonel White told me I should take a look, Sir."

Ozburn paused and looked to the front where the sky revealed the first evidence of dawn. "What did you see?"

"Sir, the men were all in place, alert and none reported seeing anything."

Ozburn turned to the Lieutenants. "And you two. Did you see anything tonight?"

They shook their heads without saying a word and looked from the Major to the Captain and back.

"OK then," said Ozburn with finality. "I'll report to Colonel Logan. Stark, what are you supposed to be doing now?"

"Staff meeting at first light, sir."

"I'll see you there. No need for you to bother the Commander. I'll give him your report." Then looking to the front he said, "Better come back with me now," as he turned back to the camp and began to walk.

Mathan looked at the Lieutenants as if to say good-bye and they raised their eyebrows and smiled, looking at Ozburn's back. Mathan nodded and followed through the brush and back to camp.

Dawn of the thirteenth of February broke with a clear sky and hope that rations would soon reach the front. Yesterday, after the last troops had begun the eight-mile march from the river to Fort Donelson, the wagon trains followed. They carried ammunition, food, tents and other supplies. Wagon parks were set out in the rear of the Divisions where Brigades and their subordinate Regiments could collect necessities. Frequently, Brigades established smaller depots for important supplies and Regiments brought wagon loads of food and ammunition to their camps to ensure access in a crisis.

The force Grant brought to Fort Donelson was more than eight times the size of the little army at Belmont. The larger army required a different organization and McClernand had been promoted to the command of a Division. McClernand's Division was divided into three Brigades including Ogelsby's. Colonel (Uncle Dick) Oglesby was a colleague of Logan's in the Illinois State Legislature and the 31st Illinois was assigned to him. Years later, Ogelsby served as the governor of Illinois and would lose a campaign against Logan for a seat in the US Senate.

This morning, the process of resupply was still incomplete and nothing had reached the Regiment. The men had only the food, clothing and ammunition they'd carried from Fort Henry. As they milled around cooking fires, Mathan soaked his hardtack in a cup of steaming coffee. He was careful to withdraw it when it was soft enough to chew but not so soft that it disintegrated. A few bites of cold pork completed his meal.

Colonel Logan called the Company commanders and his small staff together to share what he'd learned at Headquarters earlier that morning. The secessionists at Fort Donelson had received thousands of reinforcements from Fort Henry, that Federal Gunboats had captured the week before.

This morning, the 31st Illinois Volunteer Infantry would move down the Winn's Ferry Road with the rest of their Brigade. Engineers from Division Headquarters would guide Ogelsby's Brigade (including the 31st) and allow Colonel Ogelsby's staff to post them opposite the enemy's left. There, they would prepare to attack the fort.

Logan decided Lieutenant Colonel White would arrange the 31st's Companies under whatever cover the terrain allowed. Men would be ready for battle and keep their weapons at hand. Orders would come when they came. Logan didn't offer a guess as to when that might happen. As the meeting broke up and men gathered personal equipment, the sound of heavy artillery reached his camp from the Northwest.

The fine weather that made yesterday's march so comfortable blew away by the afternoon of the 13th. In its place came a heavy afternoon rain and a steady decline in temperature. By dark, the rain turned to sleet. The sleet gave way to snow, and by that night, a few inches of snow covered. Men, still without tents and most without blankets or overcoats, were freezing.

The night of the 13th to 14th was absolutely miserable. Rain, sleet, snow and wind took turns assaulting the soldiers and making it difficult to walk or hear. Fires weren't permitted on the front because it provided light for snipers and targets for artillery. Soldiers huddled together or rested with their weapons. Few slept except when exhaustion overtook them for a moment. The fortunate ones had their overcoats. The unlucky ones shared blankets or wrapped themselves in anything they could find to keep the frost from their skin.

Before dawn, Lieutenant Colonel White called, "Come on Stark! There's some fighting and Colonel Logan wants us to keep an eye on it. At their distance, they couldn't see what was happening. What the trees didn't obscure, the terrain did. They tried to discern the pattern of the fight, but the wind confused them and neither White nor Mathan could draw a conclusion about who was winning. After 90 minutes, they rode back, behind the lines toward the 31st's camp.

There was indeed, fighting a mile and a half West of Logan's position that morning. General Smith tested the fort's outer defenses. An attack by armor-clad steamboats on the fort also failed and the boats had to return to Illinois for repairs. Still later, an attack on the center of the Confederate failed at the expense of dozens more casualties. The last fight took place within half a mile of the 31st. The familiar sound of spent bullets striking the ground brought back memories of Belmont.

Half-way back, they rode past a small home with a tight cluster of ambulances parked under a tree. White told Mathan this was one of the houses Doctor Brinton had designated to serve as a casualty collection point and field hospital. "Our boys will probably be brought to this one if there's much fighting."

"Isn't this pretty close to the lines?" asked Mathan, who was imagining stray artillery reaching this far.

"It is," acknowledged White, "but it has to be. See the roads leading back West and North? Ambulances will take the wounded to the river. The boats will take them upriver to hospitals at Cairo, Mound City or wherever Doc Brinton sends 'em." They returned to their camp by just before dark and found the men deployed into a loose formation at the edge of their camp, facing the Confederate lines over a mile away.

Very late the night before, and as the rain turned to sleet, Mary Ann had called to two of her medical attendants to join her. "We're going to get some of those wounded men who are still out there from today's fighting. Bring up one of the ambulances and two stretchers. We'll leave in ten minutes."

The men looked at each other and thought better of asking questions. All of them walked quietly to the barn to collect four mules. They passed one of the ladies who tended the fires, cooked and washed. "Here's the milk punch[15] you asked for Ma'am, said the lady, passing a bundle to Mary Ann. "I heated it extra hot and wrapped the jug in a blanket to keep the warmth as long as we can."

"Thank you, Miss Allen. I'm grateful. I know the boys we find will be, too." Then looking to the small porch in front of the cabin she raised her voice and said. "Doctor, we'll be back soon. I expect we'll have some men in need of your attention."

The young surgeon looked back and said nothing. Mary Ann saw the ambulance coming, picked up her lantern and the jug of milk punch and took a last look at the surgeon who was just reentering the small house.

She passed a couple clusters of soldiers on the bone-chilling and sodden half-mile ride to the first line of troops on the Winn's Ferry Road. Mary Ann's reputation preceded her and when her driver shouted through the rain that the lady on the seat was Mrs. Bickerdyke, the sentries recognized

15 A beverage made of hot milk, sugar, vanilla (when available) and some hard liquor.

her and allowed her to pass. She had the attendants pull the wagon up near the line of horses tied behind one of the Regimental headquarters areas. As it turned out, she was only several hundred yards west of Mathan's regiment.

Pointing to the stretchers she told the men to bring just one. She took a lantern in one hand and a medical bag in the other and stalked toward the last sentry behind the picket company. "We're going forward to where the fighting and the fires were this afternoon. There may still be men out there who need us."

Just then, a tall man appeared, leading a horse and rider out of the darkness from the direction of the picket line. The man held the leg of a soldier who was slumped in the saddle and groaning softly. The soldier's clothes were singed and he was shivering.

The sentry looked at the soldier in the saddle, then at the tall man. "Hello Chaplain, did you find another one?"

"Yes, I did. There are at least five more out there." He looked at Mary Ann, then saw the men with the stretcher. "The Brigade said they retrieved all the wounded they could, but the pickets heard calls for help and I went to find them."

"Where are the others Chaplain?" asked Mary Ann with concern.

"About a hundred yards, past the only clump of trees I could see, then down a little stream bed. I think they crawled in there to escape the fighting." He paused and looked down. "I found a couple of them who must have burned to death when the brush around them caught fire."

"I understand," said Mary Ann with concern. "I think we can bring five of them out. Do you need to take some rest?"

"There must be others, but I can't just blunder through the woods to find them. I walk behind our lines, as close to the front as I can get and listen for them to call. Or the sentries and pickets tell me where they heard or saw someone." I brought in a rebel earlier today. He was wounded and all mixed up. He ran into our lines, then decided to hide until dark. It got cold and his wounds got the better of him. He couldn't walk and decided to call for help."

"That was the right thing to do Chaplain."

"Yes Ma'am. You're Mother Bickerdyke, is that right?"

"It's what some of them call me, that's right."

"Well, Mother. Please be careful. This is going to get a lot worse before it gets better and we can't spare you."

"Nor can we spare you Pastor. Please be careful." Hearing a faint call for help she looked to the front. "I have to go now," she said as she stepped past the sentry and into the gloom.

Following the sounds, she realized there were at least two voices in the distance. Sleet was turning to snow and the wind slackened. Now, it was easier to hear. After walking several hundred feet beyond the last picket, she heard a southern accent call out, "Who's there!"

Mary Ann turned to the two attendants who accompanied her and "shushed" them. She turned to the direction of the voice and said, "Sanitary Commission, we're here to retrieve wounded men." The pause before the Confederate picket's reply was unnerving. Then she heard whispering.

"You stay right there, hear?"

"We heard men calling for help, we need to find them."

"You just wait."

"Young man, if it were your friend, would you want us to wait?" The sentry didn't answer but she heard more whispering, then another voice.

"This is Lieutenant James of the Beauregard Rifles. We have half a dozen muskets aimed at you. Why are you here?"

"I told your friend, we're here to retrieve wounded men. We heard voices from this direction and we're looking for them."

"Ma'am, I can tell you're not from around here, so I'm guessing you're with those boys across the way. Any of your people who were down between here and our lines are either dead or captured. None of your people alive around here." He paused, then added, "But about a hundred yards behind you and to your right is a low spot. My men think you might find some wounded there."

"Would you mind very much if we went to check on them?" she asked with a hint of sarcasm.

"We'd appreciate it Ma'am," he answered brightly. "They've been making noise all night and it makes it hard for my men to sleep!"

Mary Ann didn't reply but turned toward the place the Lieutenant had indicated and led her attendants away. It took a couple of minutes to find the place. It was even colder by then and snow had settled on the two men she found. One had already died. The other looked at her with tears welling in his eyes.

"You came!" he said, choking back a sob.

"How are you hurt son?" she asked, setting her lantern on the ground and brushing snow from his hair. "What's your name?"

"I'm Daniel. It's my knee. My leg hurts so bad." He was shivering, teeth chattering as he spoke.

"Daniel, we have to move you and I'm afraid it could hurt worse than getting shot. Be strong." She nodded to the attendants who lay the stretcher on even ground just above Daniel. One moved to his shoulders and the other moved to the side with his good leg.

"We're going to lift you onto the stretcher and get your bad leg fixed-up," he said. "One, two, lift!"

Daniel's scream of pain startled even Mary Ann. "Don't stop moving him!" she ordered. "It won't get easier if you stop, just get him on the stretcher and let's go."

Daniel groaned with each step toward the ambulance. It was snowing steadily and they had trouble finding their way to the wagon, striking the road a hundred yards from the picket Company where they'd left it.

When they placed Daniel in the wagon, they were surprised to see two men already there, who were bloody, dirty and shivering.

"Ma'am, when we realized who you were, we went looking again," said the Lieutenant. "These are the only ones we found that you can help. The rest out there are dead already."

"These boys aren't going to die," she said firmly. "Thank you for bringing them to us." She mounted the wagon with one of the attendants while the other moved to the rear of the wagon to keep an eye on the wounded soldiers. Looking back at the Lieutenant, Mary Ann said, "Would you please tell the Regiment West of you that we'll be back in half an hour to collect casualties? I don't want anyone mistaking us for targets."

Thirty minutes later, she was at the next Regiment's front line. This time she was recognized and welcomed. One unconscious soldier was loaded into her ambulance and she took the attendants to check on a small group of men who may have been near one another when artillery struck them.

Again, they were in the no-man's-land between the pickets. By now, the ground was freezing and she and her attendants had to break the men free when their blood froze and bound them to the ground. All were dead. She repeated the journey to the front of a third Regiment where she met others doing the same work but coming from the next field hospital. She took three more men back to her hospital.

There she was met by a Sergeant wearing a heavy woolen coat. "Ma'am, I'm Sergeant Billings. I've been asked to bring you to General McClernand's headquarters."

"I'm needed here Sergeant. I'll come when I'm able. Or General McClernand can come here at his leisure." Mary Ann began to enter the small house where the surgeon was amputating the unconscious Daniel's leg.

"Ma'am, I hate to insist, but my orders don't leave me any room. I'm to come back with a squad and force you to come to the headquarters if you won't come willingly."

Turning in the doorway and glaring at him she said, "That's just fine Sergeant. Just fine!" How far is it? She asked.

"It's not far Ma'am. We can walk."

And they did, arriving amidst scattered snowflakes. They passed men without coats, sharing a blanket or running in place to prevent frost-bite. The house commandeered for McClernand's headquarters was slightly larger than Mary Ann's hospital-house and had a raging fire surrounded by dripping wet staff officers.

"Wait here Ma'am." Said the Sergeant disappearing into the back of the house. Surgeon Brinton appeared in the doorway in the company of a middle-aged man in civilian clothes, still wearing a wool scarf around his neck and glaring at Mary Ann.

"Surgeon Brinton," said Mary Ann with a wry smile. "It's very late. What's on your mind?"

Hands behind his back, Brinton half-smiled and said, "Mr. Culbertson here, says he saw you pilfering bodies on the battlefield this evening and he wants you arrested. Mr. Culbertson looked at Brinton, then back at Mary Ann and nodded vigorously as he glared at her.

"That's absurd!" she said disdainfully. "We brought back half a dozen boys who'd been left out there, wounded and about to freeze to death!" Then stepping up to face Mr. Culbertson she said bitterly, "No one has time for this nonsense!" Keeping her eyes on Culbertson, she half turned to Brinton and said with vehemence, "You gave credence to this man's criticism?"

"One can never know, Mrs. Bickerdyke. Perhaps we've overlooked a problem here."

Mary Ann didn't answer but turned on her heel. Half-blind with indignation and rage she walked right into Colonel Logan's chest. Nearly as tall as Logan she recognized him immediately and shook her head, attempting to push past him, when she saw he was followed by one of his assistants: Mathan.

Logan placed his hands on her shoulders as much to steady himself as to slow her departure. "Mrs. Bickerdyke!" he said brightly, "It's good to see you." He looked up and read the faces of Brinton and Culberson, then looked at Mary Ann and said, "What's the misunderstanding here?"

Not wanting to answer but feeling the need for some support she backed away from his hands and answered first, "These two …" she paused, deciding not to call them fools, idiots or worse. "These two, *gentlemen* have accused me of pilfering the pockets of our dead!"

Startled, Logan looked from Mary Ann to the two men who met his eyes only briefly, then looked down at the same time. "Mrs. Bickerdyke, I know there has been a terrible mistake. Please go back to the hospital with my aide here. I'll talk to Colonel Ogelsby and General McClernand to ensure there is nothing more to this. Turning to Mathan he said, "Escort Mrs. Bickerdyke to her hospital and get back to me here, right away."

Logan walked between Brinton and Culberson. He paused long enough to give each of them a withering glare. Then he shook his head with resignation and entered the parlor where McClernand was surrounded by senior officers. Mary Ann was gone before Brinton and Culbertson looked back toward the front door.

She declined the offer of Mathan's arm as she marched back towards the hospital. He was intimidated and said nothing. After a hundred steps, the cold air settled Mary Ann's temper enough for her to open the conversation.

"I'm very glad to see you Mathan. Are you alright?"

"I am, Ma'am," he said with more confidence than he'd shown the first time they met. "and you?"

"Frankly, Mathan, I'm sleepy. And I imagine you are too." He nodded as they walked on. Reaching the hospital in a matter of minutes she turned to him, "I'll be fine from here. Please go back to your Colonel. Tomorrow will be much worse than today, and you need at least some sleep and food."

"It was good to see you," said Mathan with a smile. Mary Ann put her hand on his shoulder and smiled warmly.

"God bless and watch over you, Mathan. I'm not the only one who's praying for you tonight." He turned and she watched him walk away, into the swirling snow and darkness.

As Mathan made his way back to Logan, Major General Lew Wallace arrived on the field with strong reinforcements.

McClernand knew his right flank was exposed. Although he doubted anything serious would happen overnight, he sent to Grant for help. Grant responded with a small Brigade of three Regiments from General Smith's Division arrived late on the 14th and went to the extreme right of the Union line. They marched three miles in the cold and dark to reach their assigned positions. They didn't have the time to develop a strong defensive line. Then all hell broke loose.

The Brigade Commander of the three Regiments who arrived so late that night, was Colonel John McArthur. He had been raised in lowland Scotland where he became a blacksmith. After emigrating to Chicago in 1849 he became a trusted and respected leader of the immigrant community. When the war came, he was elected to lead a Regiment of volunteers who referred to themselves as Scotsmen and Highlanders, going into battle wearing tam o' shanters. By February 1862, he was appointed to command of the entire Brigade.

Astronomical twilight, when the stars begin to fade but before the sky appears to brighten, brought ominous sounds to McArthur's poorly placed outposts. Less than half a mile to their left, Logan's 31st rested in the middle of a Union line that would receive the strongest attack the Confederates could make. The 31st Illinois were freezing and clustered together for shelter and warmth. Lucky ones sipped steaming coffee brought from well-behind the front line. Most of their uniforms were whitened by the snow and many were stiff with frost or even ice. Every man's breath condensed as he exhaled.

A few minutes later, the foremost pickets of McArthur's 12th Illinois noticed birds rising from trees in the Lick Creek drainage to their right. As the first hint of gray touched the Eastern horizon, Mathan and the men around him heard firing in the distance. First a few pops, but the sound quickly rose to the crackle of an obvious skirmish, then the roar of a fight.

Confederates had slipped out of their fort in hopes of opening a path of escape but first, they had to push the lines of Union troops away from the roads. Eleven Confederate Regiments moved quietly to the extreme right of the Federal lines in hopes of surprising and overwhelming McArthur's cold and sleepy men. Waves of The Rebels knew that failure meant capture or death; that day or the next.

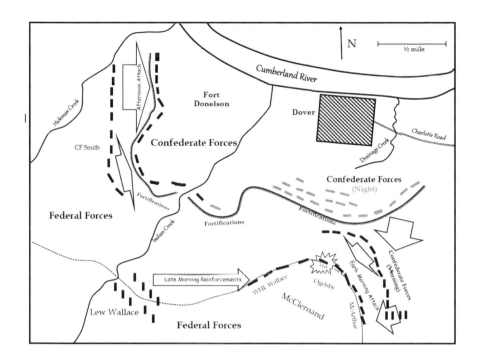

Map of Fort Donelson Battlefield, February 15, 1862

It took ten minutes for messengers from McArthur's headquarters to reach Logan and the other Regiments of Ogelsby's Brigade with shocking news. Thousands of Confederates were moving towards them, up the slopes of a ravine. Immediately, the drummers' "long roll" echoed for over a mile down the line as each Regiment was called to take their fighting positions.

The Confederate advance had been screened by cavalry under Lieutenant Colonel Forest. His horsemen gave the impression they were merely looking to capture a few prisoners and harass Union pickets while they were actually marking the route for the bulk of Fort Donelson's soldiers to mass in front of the right of the Union's long line. The Confederates chose to make their attack at the extreme end of the line because it enabled overwhelming numbers to attack the Federal Regiments one at a time. The maneuver was called "turning the flank."

As the light enabled the first assault to begin, their overwhelming force crashed against the outnumbered and inexperienced defenders from Chicago. Pickets tried to slow the advance enough for the rest of the 12th, 41st and 9th Illinois Volunteer Infantry Regiments to get into line. They failed. The attack was overwhelming. Dozens of Illinoisans were killed within minutes. After half an hour, it was clear that the mismatch was forcing the sequential withdrawal of each Federal Regiment.

A second messenger from McArthur arrived at McClernand's headquarters less than 20 minutes after the attack began. McArthur couldn't hold and would soon be forced to withdraw or be annihilated.

Warm in his headquarters, McClernand doubted the severity of the attack, clinging to his belief the main attack would come from behind the Confederate defenses, straight into his waiting lines. He concluded McArthur was overreacting and the attack on the right was a ruse to get McClernand to shift forces away from the center of his lines. He would not move men away from what would (in his mind) be the primary point of attack. Consequently, the right end of McClernand's line, McArthur's Brigade, was shattered, one Regiment at a time.

It took only 15-30 minutes for the onslaught to overcome each Regiment. By about 8:00 AM, more Confederate troops arrived and spread across the entire front of McClernand's Division, holding them in place and preventing McClernand from reinforcing his right. Ogelsby's and W.H.L. Wallace's[16] Brigades were unable to maneuver to help McArthur. The assault overwhelmed the Union line from its right toward its left. The 31st was half-way down that line.

With the first news of the attack, Mathan dashed to collect his and Logan's mounts. The snowy ground caused Mathan to slip repeatedly as he ran to the horses. Moments later, Lieutenant Colonel White and other staff officers saw Mathan riding forward, leading five horses as Logan shouted,

---

16 Brigadier General William Hervey Lamme Wallace: known as "WHL" to distinguish him from others named Wallace, including his superior, Major General Lew Wallace.

"Colonel White! See to the organization of our line! Ozburn! See what you can do about bringing up extra ammunition and any food that's already prepared. Sergeant Wharton! Get to the nearest hospital and bring up a couple of ambulances and some orderlies if you can."

Lieutenant Colonel White mounted his horse and faced Logan. "Jack, if the right doesn't hold, we'll be getting it from two directions. I want to adjust the line in case we need to defend our right."

"Do it!" shouted Logan as White nodded and reined his mount toward the on-rushing tide of Confederates. Logan knew he had a half-hour and took Mathan and a Sergeant toward McClernand's headquarters. They hadn't ridden a hundred yards when they ran into Lieutenant Colonel Ransom, the commander of the 11th Illinois, the Regiment immediately to Logan's left.

Ransom seemed calm and said, "Colonel Logan, we've been told to hold our positions. Here's a copy of the order for you. McClernand has sent a request to General (Lew) Wallace to bring his entire Division to our assistance. They marched in from Fort Henry yesterday and they're a couple of miles back, near Grant's headquarters. If they get here in time, we should be alright."

Logan looked behind Ransom to the distant cluster of men at McClernand's headquarters. The orders were clear and Logan didn't want to waste time listening to McClernand make speeches. Instead, he turned his horse to parallel Ransom's.

"Colonel Ransom, if all goes well, we'll keep our alignment and protect your right, but if our right becomes exposed, we may have to change our front. If that happens, I'll let you know, but it will be essential that your men understand. They must understand the movement they'll see is my Regiment, refusing the right, not advancing Rebels."

"I understand, Colonel," answered Ransom with confidence. The 11th will be prepared to join you on the right if we're turned." Ransom watched as Logan spurred his horse and Mathan galloped after him toward the 31st and the growing crash of musketry.

Uneven ground was disguised by frost and snow. Near the lines, Logan's horse lost its footing and tumbled onto its right side with Logan still in the saddle and his boot locked into the stirrup. He couldn't roll away from the crushing weight of the falling horse. His boot was stuck and the horse's ribs came down on his ankle. As quickly as it fell, the horse rolled to its left and tried to regain its feet with Logan's foot still trapped and Logan sagging to the right.

Mathan was off his mount in an instant, taking the reins of Logan's horse in an attempt to control it. Logan grunted and managed to kick his right leg free. With one hand in the ground, he drew his left leg over the saddle and used it to kick away from the horse. He fell on his back, rolled, and did his best to stand up immediately. But Logan was in obvious pain.

"Damn!" he shouted as he tried to weight his right foot. "God Damn it!" he shouted as he hopped toward his horse, taking the reins from Mathan and moving as quickly as he could around the front of the horse to its left side while Mathan backed away, prepared to catch Logan if he lost his balance. "Twisted my damned ankle! Don't think I'll be able to walk, but I can stay in the saddle. Stay close Stark!"

They rode the last fifty yards to the center of the 31st's line. It was about 8 AM and the sound of passing bullets was so frequent that it became part of the background and Mathan didn't notice. Confederates facing the 31st across a shallow ravine surged forward and Logan's men met them with steady fire, repulsing each attempt to advance while the Confederates continued to roll-up Regiments far to the 31st's right.

Men fired, then rolled behind a tree or stump and reloaded: tearing a paper cartridge, pouring the powder down the barrel and poking the flat end of a bullet into the muzzle with their trembling fingers. As quickly as they could, each soldier drew his ramrod from beneath the barrel and forced the bullet (and with it, the powder) to the rear of the barrel. They replaced the rod and dropped a hand to a second, smaller pouch on their belts. From there they took a pea-sized copper pip filled with mercury fulminate and placed it atop the nipple (tip of the tube that would carry a spark from the cap to the powder charge inside the rifle). When they drew back the hammer and were ready to fire.

All this took at least twenty seconds but could take nearly a minute if the soldier's hands were cold, wet, trembling or all three. It also took longer if the soldier was seated or reclining, because he had to pour powder down a near-horizontal barrel. Loaded and capped, the soldier still had to take a firing posture and when possible, aim before firing.

Each man carried forty rounds into the fight. A lack of targets and lulls in fighting meant that those forty rounds might last well over an hour, but soldiers couldn't sustain a fight of this intensity for an entire morning without more ammunition. The 31st desperately needed cartridges and caps. Ozburn had been hunting for them.

Not much later, Ozburn ran forward, leading two soldiers who were carrying a wooden case of ammunition. They dropped it on the ground near Logan's feet. "I could only get four of these, Jack!" shouted Ozburn.

"Damn-it Doff!" cursed the enraged Logan. "That's not 20 rounds per man! Go back! Get more!"

Bullets came very close. Ozburn ducked at the sound of a round whizzed above his head. Logan heard it too, but the sound came from below him. Men around them fell in agony, or silence.

Mathan heard Logan curse loudly, "Damn! Damn! DAMN!" Logan's hand was clutching his right thigh and Mathan saw blood rising between Logan's gloved fingers. Mathan dismounted and ran to his side, looking up at Logan and offering help.

Ozburn crouched and shouted back, "I'll try, Jack. But there was only one ammunition wagon at Brigade and the others swarmed over it like ants at a picnic. I'll have to go further back but the roads are clogged, and they'll probably be pretty stingy!"

"Just go! And don't come back empty handed! Understand?" shouted Logan as he spurred himself to the right of the column.

As Mathan and Logan reached the lines, Logan shouted the name he'd used to stir the men to action, "Come on you bastard Dirty First! Make 'em pay for every step they take!" He rode to the extreme right of his line and glared at his enemy. He saw them carefully moving across the brush-filled terrain, towards his men.

Suddenly, Logan's left hip seemed to explode and he grunted loudly. Again, Mathan dismounted and ran to Logan's side where he saw the butt of Logan's pistol was shattered and the left side of his uniform was torn in several places. Logan clutched at his ribs. "I'm OK! Ball must have hit my pistol and broke up." Logan ungloved his right hand and ran it along his trousers and inside his blouse. Glancing at his hand he said, "No blood! I'm fine!" Pulling on his glove he said, "Get back on your damned horse, Stark. I'm OK! Now, go find White and bring him to me!"

Mathan didn't ask any questions but remounted and rode quickly to the left, looking for Logan's second-in command. He found him with a Company commander, pointing toward the front. Mathan heard him saying something about the most likely lines of attack across some open ground and helping him align his Company. "Sir!" Mathan said loudly. "Colonel Logan asks you to meet him immediately. McArthur's Brigade is in trouble, he's leaving us in the air!"

White nodded calmly, slapped the Company Commander on his shoulder and followed Mathan back to where Logan was mounted. Logan shouted, "Neither of us can see the entire Regiment. I want you to see to the refusal of our right with three Companies. I'll stay to the left and see to our front. Have the men scavenge ammunition from the dead and wounded." In obvious pain from his leg wound and the serious bruises on his other thigh, hip and ribs, Logan was every bit as intense as he had been all morning, but his voice wasn't as loud and he labored to breathe.

"I have it, Jack," said White confidently. "I'll see you when all this settles down." Turning to Mathan he added, "Stick close to the Colonel. He'll likely need your legs before this is over." With that, White trotted his horse toward the right. Logan reigned his horse to the left, where the sound of fighting was more intense. Mathan followed Logan to the left end of their line.

Passing an opening in the trees, Mathan could clearly see the puffs of smoke rising from brush and trees two or three hundred yards ahead, in the direction of the Confederate works. A man screamed, rolling across the ground, clutching his thigh. An ounce of solid lead, moving five hundred miles an hour had shattered the man's kneecap and exploded his knee joint. He bled heavily. Other men from the 31st had been hit and were under cover and behind the line. Still others had been taken to the hospital.

Mathan saw only three dead men. Their faces were calm but their eyes were glassy. He didn't look long enough to see how they died, noticing only the contrast of their blood with melting snow. A few yards further along, he saw young McIlrath, one of the volunteers from Egypt, with his weapon to the side. The boy bowed over a soldier's body.

Logan bellowed at the kneeling figure, "Private! Get up! Get in the fight!"

As the 17-year-old boy slowly turned to face his commander. Tears streaked his smoke-blacked cheeks. Mathan recognized the boy's father on the ground. The elder James McIlrath's forehead was smashed by grapeshot, lifeless on the muddy ground. Forty-seven-year-old McIlrath had joined the Army to watch over his nineteen-year-old son, Robert. Now, Robert said good-bye to his father for the last time.

"Damn you!" shouted Logan again, just as he grunted and grabbed his side. He turned from the McIlraths to look further to the right where White was organizing the line.

A Sergeant emerged from the trees from White's direction. He was running at full speed towards Logan and waving. He arrived quickly and shouted, "Colonel! Colonel McArthur's Brigade is gone and we're falling back.

"Who the hell are you?" demanded Logan.

"29th Sir! We're taking fire from the right and front! Colonel Reardon says we can't hold and told us to withdraw. We're almost out of ammunition!" he didn't wait for Logan to reply, but turned to run back the way he'd come. He looked back over his shoulder and shouted, "Wants you to be ready!"

"Stark, go tell Reardon we're low on ammunition too, but can hold while they withdraw. He can join on our right or behind us if he must. Now go!"

Mathan, on horseback, crashed ahead of the running Sergeant and behind the "bent-back" line of the 31st's right. He was nearly to a clump of officers marking the remains of the Colonel Reardon's 29th when he recognized one of Reardon's men, Lieutenant Brayman running towards him. The terrified Lieutenant shouted, "We're pulling back, tell your commander he's about to get hit hard!"

Mathan froze for a moment as he saw men backing away from cover, a hundred yards beyond him. Although some of the soldiers fired as they backed away, most maintained a rough line and turned their backs to the enemy, jogging towards the rear. It was too late to reach Colonel Reardon. Knowing the 31st was next. Mathan spurred his mount and covered the ground back to Logan in under a minute.

He reached Logan and breathlessly interrupted Logan's shouts of encouragement. "Sir, the 29th is broken and pulling back. The Secesh will be on our flank in a few minutes!" Although they were in the middle of the 31st's position, they were shocked to see the enemy moving in the near distance to their front and to their right.

"Find White and get him back here!" said Logan to Mathan.

Mathan asked, "Will you be alright sir?"

Logan's enraged glare settled the question without words.

Mathan rode as quickly as he could to the right where he last saw White on his horse. Mathan could make out Union soldiers running to the right and rear of the newly formed right angle created by "refusing" a third of the Regiment. Firing on the right slackened. Getting closer, Mathan caught a glimpse of White entering a blossoming cloud of smoke. But White didn't emerge. Mathan rode the last 100 yards to where he found White's obviously dead body beneath his lifeless horse. Just like that, John White was dead and Mathan felt the white-hot stab of rage, banishing fear.

A Company commander was seated against a nearby tree with a bandage on his leg. He was still and looked to Mathan who said, "Jake, you have to hold them. I'll be back in a few minutes."

Mathan dashed back to Logan who moved his horse to a space with a clearer view of the approaching enemy. Any mounted man drew extra fire but Mathan's arrival added a second target and made the pair even more attractive to sharpshooters. Within seconds, Mathan recognized the sound of several near misses. Before he could report White's death, tree branches snapped off and splinters of wood, dislodged by artillery, spun through the air. Logan turned to Mathan and began to speak but fell backward off his horse. Mathan saw Logan fall limply to the ground, clutching his left shoulder.

Off his mount yet again, Mathan rushed to Logan's side where he saw a small hole in Logan's uniform, on his upper, left shoulder. Logan sat up, dazed, a Sergeant bellowed for the assistant surgeon. Within a minute, a young man with bloody sleeves and no coat ran to Logan's side. He pulled Logan's coat open and pushed his shirt to the side, revealing a round, red hole just below his left collar bone. Blood flowed slowly from the wound. Pulling Logan forward, the assistant looked at his back for an exit wound.

Logan grunted in pain as Mathan scanned for immediate danger. Nearby men were watching. "Keep your eyes and muzzles forward men! He said as firmly as he could. "Colonel will be alright. Aim low!"

The assistant surgeon reached into his pocket and drew a small bandage to pack the wound on both sides. The medic said, "Colonel, the bullet passed through you cleanly. I don't think it hit bone."

"S—t!" grunted Logan. "That's the good news?"

"Yes sir. We have to take you back!" The Assistant Surgeon looked around for help moving their commander.

"The hell!" shouted Logan in a hoarse voice. He rolled to all-fours and began to rise. "Take my horse!" he said to Mathan. Logan managed to stand as Mathan took Logan's horse aside. His ankle made walking impossible.

Looking to the men around him Logan said, "We have to hold." Then he shouted, as loudly as he could, "We'll hold this damned line! Hold!" as he stood behind his still fighting men.

Mathan leaned forward and shouted into his ear, "Sir, I'm sorry. Colonel White is killed." Logan's face was already pale, but the muscles sagged as they had not before. Logan explored Mathan's face even as his eyes welled. Mathan went on, "The 29th is disengaging and the Rebels are coming on our right.

A few minutes later, as Logan remounted, one of Colonel Ransom's staff officers arrived from the next Regiment in line. "Sir," said the Lieutenant awaiting Logan's acknowledgement. Logan glared at the young man without saying a word. "Sir, Colonel Ransom said to tell you he is retiring from the field, and he wants you to do the same. General Wallace is on the Winn's Ferry Road, less than a mile back with a full Division and coming this way. We're to form a new line on their right. Reinforcements are arriving soon, sir!"

"Logan looked down and then along the line to his right and nodded slowly. "Tell Colonel Ransom I can hold for ten minutes, then we'll retire as well."

Mathan stayed close to Logan for the next thirty minutes, feeling the weight of responsibility settle on him. As the units on the left and right of Logan's "Dirty First" retired, the Confederates slowed their advance. Perhaps to reorganize for a final push and destruction of the remaining Union line.

Logan realized he must withdraw or lose everyone. He passed the order to send all wounded back immediately. Reeling in his saddle from loss of blood he waited until he saw what he believed were the last of the wounded moving away from the fight. Major Kuykendall was now the ranking officer in the Regiment after Logan. Logan leaned down from his mount to order Kuykendall to disengage in five minutes and withdraw to the left-rear. He added with bitterness, "When you get near the rear, have the men hold their empty cartridge boxes up in the air. I want those idiot quartermasters to know they left us high and dry."

Moments later, Logan fell forward, onto his horse's neck and began to slide from the saddle. Mathan reached for him and a nearby soldier caught him before he fell. Two Sergeants carried him unconscious, to the rear. The 31st disengaged from the fight in good order: many men, forced to rely on bayonets because they had no bullets. Mathan left the fight with them. He had aged a decade in a day.

The attack had begun on the right-most flank of the Union Army and had rolled up one Regiment after another until they reached the 31st. Logan's "Dirty First" was the last Regiment to withdraw from the line. They'd fought for nearly four hours with nearly one in three men becoming casualties: almost 10 percent killed or missing and twice as many wounded. None of the Regiments from the 31st to the furthest on the right were able to resume the fight after withdrawing.

The 31st was relocated to the rear of the main body and camped on a snow-covered hillside. Far enough from the threats of fighting, Colonel

Ogelsby permitted the men to light fires. They had hot food for the first time in three days.

Major Kuykendall took command when Logan went to the rear. Kuykendall was Logan's age and had been a colleague of Logan's in the State Legislature, sharing Logan's devotion to Stephen A. Douglas. At the campfire that night, Kuykendall was talking to Major Ozburn when the pair saw Mathan enter the firelight. "How are you Stark?" asked Major Kuykendall warmly.

Mathan stopped and looked toward the voice. His eyes adjusted and he recognized Kuykendall and Ozburn. "I'm alright Sir," sighed Mathan with obvious exhaustion in his voice. "I could use a rest, though."

"Come up here for a minute, could you?" asked Kuykendall. Mathan noticed Ozburn's eyes on him as he approached the fire. "Any news about Colonel Logan?" asked Mathan.

"Don't know much. He was still at the field hospital last I heard," said Kuykendall. "But they said they'd take him to Grant's steamboat as soon as he can move." Kuykendall looked from Mathan and into the fire. "Doc wants to take his arm off." Then looking back to Mathan and chuckling he added, "I talked to the nurse at the hospital and she said Logan told the doctor to go to hell!"

Kuykendall's eyes went back to the fire. "She's not sure they can save his arm."

Ozburn leaned toward Mathan and nodded in the direction of Fort Donelson. "Your old friends from the 78th Ohio arrived today. Too late for the fight but not too late to guard prisoners, I guess," he said smirking. He waited a minute, but Mathan didn't react. "They're going to need you back. I want you to find them tomorrow. Ogelsby's staff will give you orders. No need to check back with General Grant's staff. They won't care."

Mathan said nothing and looked to Major Kuykendall who noticed the question in Mathan's eyes. "We're pretty beat-up, Stark," he began. "We really have enough officers for now. Besides, I'm going back to Illinois as soon as I can. Ozburn, here will take command for now."

Mathan looked back at Ozburn who smiled at him and snorted, "You can get back with your Ohio folks. I think you'll find their politics match yours better than ours." Major Kuykendall looked sharply at Ozburn who didn't take his eyes off Mathan.

Mathan knew how sensitive politics were to Regiments from Southern Illinois. Ozburn suspected Mathan was a Republican and that he supported abolition, but when he learned of Mathan's friendship with Mrs. Bickerdyke, he was certain. The presence of the 78th Ohio at Fort Donelson gave Ozburn the excuse he needed to dismiss Mathan.

Because the 31st held, every other Regiment to their left could disengage safely, reform in the rear, and join the afternoon's decisive counterattack. The Confederate forces surrendered the next day.

A day later, on the afternoon of February 15th, fighting had slackened but the surgery stayed busy. Surgeons were inundated with wounded men. On the table near a window, two of them sedated men and amputated limbs. Of every four men who entered the surgery three had an arm or leg removed. Half the surgical patients died from the shock of surgery or infections that inevitably followed. Although chloroform and ether were available, no one understood sterile technique.

Mary Ann's task was to meet the ambulances and sort arrivals into groups: The ones who could be saved with prompt attention went to the front of the line. The ones who required attention but could wait were set down close to the hospital. The ones who had superficial problems went to the orderlies who patched, sewed or soothed the injuries, cleaned them up, fed them and sent them back to their Regiments. Finally, there were the ones beyond help. Mary Ann did what she could to keep them comfortable until their time came. Sometimes it was quick, sometimes it took days.

Logan felt terrible nausea. He lay flat on his back, cold, wet and trembling. His eyes traced contours of what he saw but his mind didn't focus. He was disoriented and he didn't comprehend speech. Arriving at the Brigade hospital before noon, Mary Ann was so busy with the other men in his ambulance, she didn't look at Logan. By the time she returned from moving others to the hospital, an orderly saw Logan had stopped bleeding and decided he could wait.

An hour later, when Logan attempted to sit up, he succeeded only in vomiting on himself. An orderly who noticed, attempted to turn him on his side but when the orderly pulled on Logan's bad shoulder the Colonel roared with pain and his eyes filled with tears. Fortunately for Logan, the movement uncovered the eagles on his shoulder straps. The orderly gulped when he realized he had a Colonel waiting for treatment and two Sergeants ready to tear him apart for hurting their commander.

"Mrs. Bickerdyke! There's a Colonel in the bunch they brought in before noon!" wheezed the breathless, middle-aged orderly. "He's got it in his chest and leg. Maybe more."

"Is he bleeding again?" She asked with a raised eyebrow.

"No Ma'am, he's been patched, sort of."

"Is he breathing regularly?"

"Yes Ma'am. Had enough breath to scream at me when I kept him from drowning in his own spew."

"Can he walk?"

"Don't think so Ma'am. Ankle looks like it's tryin' to bust out his boot and he's pretty chilled.

Mary Ann looked back at the cabin. "Surgeon's got a few more amputations he's going to do now. I'll tell the surgeon we're bringing a Colonel in after that." She paused and looked across the garden where most of the wounded lay. "Where is he?"

"Over there," said the orderly pointing at the tree. "On a tent half."

"Thank you. Now, fetch a mucket of milk punch and a blanket and bring it to us there. As Mary Ann approached the prone figure beneath a single blanket, she recognized the walrus moustache and dark eyes of Jack Logan. His complexion was waxy green and he moaned with each breath.

Kneeling next to him, Mary Ann covered his brow with her hand, reassuring him while assessing his temperature. "Can you hear me Colonel Logan?" she asked softly. His eyes opened as slits and he turned his head toward her voice.

He nodded slowly. "Mrs. Uh, Mrs." His head rolled and he was unconscious. The orderly arrived with the blanket and punch. Mary said, "He's not able to drink anything just now. Cover him with an extra blanket and let's warm him up. Get a hand and take him into the barn. Bring a couple of those heated stones too. We'll put him with the others until he goes to the surgeons."

Along with the orderly, the two Sergeants were able to lift Logan onto a stretcher, cover him with both blankets and carry him to Mary Ann's makeshift ward in the old barn. The Sergeants insisted on staying with him. They'd sent a report to the Brigade and stopped orderlies and attendants to ensure Logan wasn't forgotten. Mrs. Allen met them at the door of the barn where it was twenty degrees warmer than outside.

Looking to the orderly, the black woman who was in charge of the barn said to the orderly, "I'm Mrs. Allen. I work for Mrs. Bickerdyke. She doesn't want anyone except the hurt soldiers to use this place. Did she send this bunch to us?" She paused waiting for confirmation. The orderly nodded quickly while both Sergeants eyed Mrs. Allen suspiciously as they waited to be told where to place their Colonel.

The orderly tried again. "He's hurt Mrs. Allen. He's shot and heaven knows what else." Mrs. B told me she'd come for him pretty soon. Looking around the room the orderly asked, "Can you and the ladies clean him up and have him ready for the surgeon?"

Mrs. Allen surveyed three rows of men spread across the floor of the barn. "Yes," she answered, "we still have warm water, bandages and enough blankets to get him ready for the doctor. Go back and be sure Mrs. B knows where he is."

"Thank you, Mrs. Allen. I know he'll appreciate it," said the orderly as he left the barn. The Sergeants looked at each other and at Mrs. Allen.

"You two could help the Colonel and me if you want to," she said matter-of-factly.

The Sergeants' eyes met. They were doubtful about entrusting their Commander to a black person. The older Sergeant answered, "We're glad to help, but when's the surgeon coming?"

"He'll call for your Colonel very soon, I imagine. Is this Colonel Logan? Mrs. Bickerdyke told me about him before we even arrived here. She won't do more for him than she'll do for the other boys, but she'll worry more and I suppose that's something."

Logan awoke to a pounding headache and a tongue dry as shoe leather. Everything hurt. His boots and uniform were gone. His stretcher was suspended between a pair of sawhorses and some man wearing blood-stained coat poked his shoulder, causing agonizing pain.

"Bullet went all the way through. Bleeding has pretty much stopped."

When the surgeon removed his bloody fingers from the bullet hole, Logan dropped back onto the stretcher. "Damn!" he groaned. "Damn, that hurts!"

"Colonel Logan, I'm Surgeon Brinton. Do you remember me?"

Logan's eyes widened with recognition as he nodded in silence.

"Good. You seem to be doing pretty well. Your right ankle looks like it was broken or at least, badly sprained. You've got quite a bruise from your left side to your left hip, but nothing seems to be broken there. Spent bullet?"

"Hit the butt of my pistol. Blew it all to hell," said Logan quietly.

"Lucky, that," said Brinton with a sympathetic smile. "The crease on your other leg is superficial. I sewed it up, but it may hurt to walk for a while. It's that wound in your shoulder that has me worried." He paused, staring as if Logan knew what he was asking.

"You see, Colonel Logan, the bullet passed through your shoulder and I believe I've collected all the dirt and fragments of cloth from the wound. I doubt the bone was fractured, but the muscles and tendons are another story. You're blessedly fortunate, I'd say." He smiled and watched for Logan's reaction.

Logan looked at him blankly but said, "Let it be, Surgeon. No cutting." He took a breath and collected as much authority as he could, adding. "Understand?"

"Well, Colonel," soothed Brinton. "We'll see later. For now, we need to rebuild your strength. We'll watch the wound and decide in the morning." Brinton nodded at Logan and left. There were other important patients and complicated cases to manage. Fighting was starting up on the left, nearer Grant's headquarters and Brinton wanted to be there to supervise his medics.

Before Brinton left, he paused in front of Mary Ann saying, "Logan is one of Grant's favorites. Take good care of him."

"Thank you for that reminder, Doctor. Colonel Logan is a strong man. I'm sure he'll survive your attempts to treat him."

Brinton grunted and decided not to reply. He pulled on his gloves and mounted a more docile beast than the one who tried to kill him at Belmont.

Half an hour later as darkness began to fall, Logan raised his head and looked to the Sergeants. "You two, get something to eat and go back to the Regiment. I know the people here. I'll be fine.

The older of the two said, "Sir, Captain Stark and Major Kuykendall said one of us could stay with you all the time." The younger Sergeant nodded several times in affirmation.

Logan closed his eyes and let go. He fell into unconsciousness more than sleep. The younger Sergeant said, "I'm going to get the nurse. They can't leave him alone here like this."

The elder Sergeant kept his eyes on Logan and said, "Good. Go."

It was dark the next time Logan awoke. He was jostled and jounced as he slowly gathered his senses. The ambulance bucked and squeaked on its new springs. Recognizing the clomping of two horses and the tinkle of their tack, he knew they were taking him somewhere. Dimness hid their faces but Logan sensed a man on a stretcher next to him. At his feet were two seated figures. Beyond them were several shadowy forms appearing to walk but coming no nearer.

"How are you doing Colonel?" Logan recognized the voice of the older Sergeant.

"I'm alright, Sergeant," he said with more of a groan than he intended. "Where are we?"

"Taking you and Colonel Ransom to General Grant's boat, Sir."

"Tom?" Logan asked the figure next to him. "Is that you?"

"How are you holding up, Jack?"

"I've had better days. Looks like you got cross-ways with something too."

"Shoulder. How about you?"

"Me too." Logan was in pain and struggled not to reveal it. "Did you manage to disengage alright?"

"We didn't get away clean," Ransom began quietly. "When you went down and your Regiment withdrew, we moved into your position for a while. Then their cavalry got behind us. Last I heard, we lost over 300."

There was silence for a moment as Logan felt additional grief on top of anguish over the loss of his own men. "I'm so sorry Tom."

"Yeah. It was bad for all of us," he said consolingly. "Pushed 'em all the way back into their trenches this afternoon, though. I hear Smith broke into their works on the left."

Logan felt his composure slipping. Tears rolled from his eyes as he lay quietly, no longer resisting the movement of the wagon. He squeezed his eyes closed and fell back into oblivion.

He next awoke in a bed, noticing warmth and daylight. Sunbeams lit the opposite wall. He recognized Colonel Ransom sitting up in the bed across the small cabin. "Where?" asked Logan.

"We're on Grant's boat. It's called the *New Uncle Sam*," answered Ransom, smiling. He was only 26, good-looking and well-spoken. He was one of those young men who attract followers but never resentment. "They said you lost an awful lot of blood. How are you feeling, Jack?"

"Like I was trampled. Everything hurts."

"I'll bet. Doc Brinton came in with another surgeon this morning. You didn't even wake up when they looked you over, I guess. They said you were lucky to be alive."

"Feels like I'd have to get well to die," said Logan ironically.

"I believe you," mused Ransom. "I'm leaving as soon as I can. I need to get back to the 11th."

Logan looked at him with envy. "If you see my boys…" he said, pausing as waves of emotion washed over him. He welled in spite of himself, "Tell them I'm fine and I'll be back in no time."

"Will do, Jack."

Logan sagged into his pillow, realizing he wasn't going anywhere for a long time.

Images of McIlrath and his son filled Logan's memory. Smears and puddles of blood on the snow. His friend, John White's face, as he turned his horse to the onslaught on the right. So many men sprawled on the ground. Exhausted soldiers dragging broken bodies to the rear. Smoke, whirring bullets, grapeshot and fragments. The punch in his side and the hot-iron stab through his shoulder. The cold. Faces, noise, cries, bodies, hordes of Rebels charging towards him in endless rows. Pressing his eyes closed, he yearned to escape the memories; to wake up and find it was all a bad dream and he was home. Instead, he felt his body tremble. Every wound ached. He couldn't allow himself to cry, but the tears kept coming. Struggling to face the memories, it was too much for his body to bear and he lost consciousness.

He awoke much later, to the sound of a woman's soft voice. "Colonel Logan? Are you awake?" asked Mrs. Allen, the black woman who'd been with him at the first hospital yesterday. "Mrs. Bickerdyke said I'm to stay with you until we get you back to Cairo or wherever we're going. Can I get you anything?"

Jack looked at her blankly. A personal nurse. A black, personal nurse. Mary Ann's favorite assistant. "I just need some privacy Mrs. Allen," he said weakly. He needed to urinate.

"Nature?" she asked gently.

He nodded once and attempted to sit up but couldn't. Mrs. Allen moved to the side of his bed and slid her arm behind his back, helping him. He gasped. Pain stabbed him in the ribs and shoulder.

"I think you're going to want to try this on your own, aren't you?" she asked, smiling warmly.

"I think so," he said through his teeth.

"Here's a towel and the pot. Water in the pitcher is still warm. I'll pour some in the basin for you." She handed him the towel, filled the basin and went to the door of the small cabin. Before she left, she said, "Rap on the wall when you're ready for me to come back. If I don't hear your knock, I'll come in after five minutes, anyway." Nodding, she pulled the door closed behind her.

He'd never felt so helpless. Trembling with the effort of maintaining a posture that enabled him to relieve himself. He was grateful for the towel and the basin. He did his best to clean his hands and leg. With all his strength exhausted, he fell back, onto the bed, lacking strength even to draw covers across himself.

Mrs. Allen returned as she said she would. Placing a tray nearby on a low table, she arranged his body on the narrow bed, covered him, and tucked the blankets against the draft. Seeing he was too weak to feed himself, she fed him.

As Mrs. Allen brought each spoonful of broth to his lips, he felt something moving in his mind. He was unused to needing care and he was even more unused to being cared for. But, his helplessness was undeniable and likely to worsen.

"You're having a rough time of it, Colonel," she said softly as he took the broth.

Logan had never depended on a black person before. He looked at her as he sipped. He sensed her genuine concern for both his comfort and his welfare. This was new. "How is it out there?" he asked in a whisper.

"They surrendered, Colonel. You and the others gave them more than they could handle, and they sent out white flags this morning. It seems to be over."

Jack felt his body relax. He sank deeper into the pillows and drifted. Mrs. Allen blotted his face with a warm, damp cloth and straightened his bedding. She pressed her hand to his forehead. No one had touched him this way since he was a child. Not in New Mexico when he had measles, not his wife. Confused and afraid, he drifted back into oblivion, feeling still more tears cross his cheek.

"Hey, Jack, you awake?" asked Doff Ozburn as he shook Jack's good shoulder.

Opening his eyes slowly, Jack recognized Doff's face leaning over him with an expectant look. "Yeah. I'm awake." Then he looked more closely at his old friend. "You alright?"

"I am Jack," he said rocking back on his heels and smiling down at the pale figure on the bed. "You were on the killed list, you know?" he added with an amused tone.

Jack thought for a moment, then felt a jolt of concern. "You have to tell Mary I'm alright!" He looked into Ozburn's eyes. "Have to get word to her right-away. Now!"

"Done!" said Ozburn, pleased with himself. "We sent a message with the first boat back to Cairo."

"Good," Logan sagged. "Thank you."

"Hey, General Grant will be here in a few minutes. He had you brought here so Doc Brinton could keep an eye on you."

"Nice of him. What about our men? How many?"

"Not sure yet. Lots. White, Captain Williamson, Lieutenant Hale, Tom Grant, Sergeant Short from Company A. Milligan too. All killed. Lieutenant Youngblood and Riley[17] are hurt pretty bad but there's lots more. About two hundred, I guess. Some still missing."

Seeing the pain cross Logan's face, Ozburn changed the subject. "I got rid of that n---er nurse who was in here. Got you one of those Catholic nuns that came down from Indiana, I think."

Logan opened his eyes and stared at his friend. "What did you do with her?" he asked anxiously.

---

17 These men were all casualties at Fort Donelson along with James McIlrath and others.

"The black one? Should have sent her down river, but that 'Bickerdoodle' woman from the hospital said she was some sort of special helper. I can't believe she sent that n---er to take care of you!"

"Bickerdyke, Doff, her name is Bickerdyke. She's from Galesburg." Jack felt disgust and even revulsion towards Doff. It surprised him as it welled from some deep place in his mind. "That was Mrs. Allen. She did alright, Doff. I was glad for her help."

Ozburn snorted but otherwise ignored the comment. "Ogelsby said I should take the Regiment while you're recovering. Kuykendall doesn't want it. Wants to go home as soon as his time's up."

Jack nodded, "Congratulations."

"Sent your boy, Stark back where he came from, too. His friends from Ohio are here now. Their Colonel is a Republican. That Lew Wallace from Indiana has them assigned to the Fort, guarding prisoners and stuff. Looks like they may leave us here for a while too."

There was a knock on the door and General Grant came in, followed by McClernand.

"You look terrible, Logan!" said Grant with a smile, gently taking Logan's right hand. "But a lot better than you might."

Before McClernand could speak, Logan said, "Thank you sirs. I'm grateful for your concern."

"We'll send you home soon, but for now, Doc Brinton wants to keep an eye on you. We sent for your bride last night. Turns out you were on a list of the killed. Well, we can't let her think her Jack is worse off than he actually is!"

"Sir, don't let them take-off my arm," asked Logan, almost pleading.

"I think you and Mrs. Logan will convince the Surgeon better than I could. Don't worry. Just get your strength back. You did exceptionally well Saturday. You and Ransom held the line while Wallace came up. Smith smashed them on our left and we rolled them back on the right.

Surrendered! Fourteen thousand prisoners. Some slipped upriver with their Generals overnight."

"I'm glad to hear that, General."

"Just get well. I have lots for you to do when you're better. For now, just rest easy."

Jack nodded and lay back in his bed. As the Generals left, McClernand looked back with a wordless glare.

Now that the room was cleared, Ozburn stepped back in. "I have to go too. I'll check on you. Mary should be here soon."

"Thanks, Doff," Logan said softly; glad to see his old friend leave.

Mary Logan used her husband's connections to get a berth on one of the boats returning from Cairo to Fort Donelson. She went directly from her steamer to the *New Uncle Sam* and found her way to Logan's small cabin.

"John!" she asked breathlessly as she burst in. "Are you alright?"

"I am," he said softly, smiling and extending his good arm to her.

She took his hand and kissed it, pressed it to her cheek and carefully leaned down to kiss him first on the forehead, then on the lips. Her tears flowed freely as she stifled sobs of relief. "I was so afraid!" she said in a rush. "They came to the door and they showed me the newspaper that said you'd been killed, and I was shattered and I couldn't believe it at the same time and, and," she paused gathering herself to go on, "They told me they had reports you were killed and then they just left! And Mamma and the Pastor were there. Oh, Jack! I'm so glad you're alright!"

"How did you learn my name was on the wrong list?"

"Well," she began, "the next morning I boarded the train to Cairo. I was coming to get... to get..." she said with sobs interrupting her, "And that was the worst day of my life! I thought you-" She stopped. "Then I got off the train at Cairo and asked where General McClernand's headquarters was."

"But when I walked in, it was as if they'd been waiting for me!" Her eyes rose to him and a broad smile crossed her face, "They said there was a mistake. There was a corrected list and you were only wounded! What a relief that was! It was as if the sun came out after a tornado had passed!" Tears ran freely down her cheeks. "They didn't say how badly you were hurt and I thought the worst and..." she paused to blot her eyes and blow her nose. "Oh Jack, is Doff alright? We haven't heard from him."

"He's fine. Not a scratch. Checked on me," said Jack, sagging into his pillow with a low groan.

"Are you in pain? What's wrong with you? What happened?"

He opened his eyes and began slowly, "Started when my horse slipped and fell on my ankle. The fight got pretty hot. A piece of shot cut me on the thigh. It's mending alright. A bullet hit my sidearm and just splattered all over my side. That one bruised me up, alright. And this one," he said pointing to his left shoulder with his chin, "this one went all the way through. We can't allow the surgeons to take it off like they want to. I've got the fever, but at least it's oozing plenty of pus and Doc Brinton says that's a good sign."

Logan was fragile and exhausted. The adrenaline rush of their reunion ebbed. His ability to focus sank with his energy. Mary Logan kept talking, but her husband lost consciousness, falling into a deep sleep. He dreamed an old dream. A dream of a family of black people. A mother wailing for her children, a father bound, unable to help.

Mary Logan wept without restraint. "Oh, my Dear John! Oh, that's terrible. I'm so, so sorry! Oh..." Her weeping brought one of the nurses from the corridor, a Catholic Sister entered quietly. "Is everything alright, Miss?"

Mary snuffled, then corrected the nun, "Mrs. Logan."

"Of course, Mrs. Logan. I'm sorry. How is the Colonel just now?"

"He's tired, Sister. I'm afraid for him."

"Of course you are." She said with the same tone she'd used for her first apology. "Surgeon Brinton comes by every day. He's the best physician in the Army and he's watching the Colonel very closely. He believes the next few days will tell the tale."

Mary's eyes welled as she looked from the nun to her husband. "He can't … he can't!"

"We're doing everything we can for him. The most important thing for you to do is keep up his spirits and help him with his needs. He's not very comfortable with our assistance," the nun added as she looked down demurely.

It took a moment for Mary to catch the nun's meaning. Despite her own discomfort at the thought of helping her independent husband with basic activities, she pulled herself together and tried to sound convincing when she replied, "Of course Sister. That will be no," she paused to choose the right word, "no difficulty at all."

"That's good," said the nun sympathetically. She added before closing the door, "I'll have meals brought for you and we'll make-up the other berth as well."

Mary turned her eyes to the perspiring man with shaggy black hair and walrus moustache. He looked smaller and infinitely weaker than he had before he left.

From among her wounded soldiers, Mary Ann and the Surgeons chose those who could safely return to Cairo and Mound City on the boats. Many died in Tennessee: too badly wounded, even to make the trip and die among family. Even so, the hope of getting home to recover with family filled every deck with wounded.

Mrs. Allen was back at the Brigade hospital, caring for the dying and transferring the others. The barn was nearly empty. "Mrs. Bickerdyke," asked Mrs. Allen during a pause in their rounds. "May I ask a favor of you?"

"Certainly Mrs. Allen. What can I do?"

"Mrs. B, it's my husband. He's working with some teamsters and they're taking the wagons back to the boats now that there aren't so many wounded."

"Yes?"

"Well, I'm afraid to have him down here in Tennessee for too long. Those slave-catchers will keep their distance from the Army here at Fort Donelson, but some of the wagon trains are going back to Fort Henry. Some of them have been taken by raiders. I'm so afraid he might be taken if he's on one of those trains!"

"You're right Mrs. Allen. Of course, I'll help." Mary Ann looked around the makeshift hospital. "Where is Mr. Allen now?"

"I think he's down at the fort, by the Confederate warehouses. They're moving some things today or tomorrow." Her eyes widened and filled with tears. "I wouldn't have asked, but I learned he was down here just this morning and I'm so afraid for him."

Mary Ann saw the Commissary Sergeant coming in her direction. "Sergeant Johnson, I was just looking for you!" she said brightly.

"Yes Ma'am?" he said politely. "I was coming to ask something of you as well."

"Please go ahead, Sergeant Johnson." Mary Ann listened to hear how her need might be compatible with his.

"Ma'am, Major Ozburn wants to know how many of our boys can we send home this afternoon on the next hospital boat?" After a breath, he went on, "And whether you can use a few crates of canned meat and pickles that he can send you."

Mary Ann thought for a moment. "We have a broken wagon here, Sergeant and no teamster to drive it back with our wounded for the ship. There's a particular man from the 78th Ohio. They're part of the garrison at Dover now. He's supposed to work for the US Sanitary Commission and he knows how we do things. I want you to bring him to us with a wheelwright to look at our wagon. Can you do that?" Then she added, "If you do, I have at least four men I can transport home today."

Sergeant Johnson nodded and smiled. I'll go and check with Colonel Leggett. He's the commander at Dover and he's responsible for that, now."

Turning to Mrs. Allen, Mary Ann said, "Please go now and get the four men we were going to send home first, as long as they're not burning up with fever."

Stepping into Leggett's tent across the creek from the little town of Dover, Tennessee, where Fort Donelson was situated, Mathan said, "Hello Sir, I've been sent back to the 78th."

"Hello Stark!" shouted Colonel Leggett warmly as he rose from his camp desk and strode to Mathan with his hand extended. It's good to see you!" Leggett cocked his head to one side as he looked Mathan up and down. "None the worse for wear I see. Grab a cracker box and have a seat. If you have some time, I'd like to catch up with you!"

"Yes Sir, it's good to see you too."

"Let's start with how the fight went for you. I hear you were with Ogelsby's Brigade? Sounds pretty rough."

"It was, Sir. We lost nearly 200 killed, wounded and missing. Colonel Logan was hit three times and I understand General Grant has him on his steamer." Mathan reviewed events up to Major Ozburn's decision to send him back to the 78th. "So, I'm here and ready to help," concluded Mathan.

Leggett paused and smiled, then picked up a roster of names. "We've filled all the positions for Company commanders and quarter master. I have an adjutant, so for now, I'd like to assign you as his deputy." He saw Mathan's face fall a bit. "Don't worry, we'll have plenty for you to do. We've been assigned to stay at Fort Donelson and I'll command the garrison. Your friends from the 31st Illinois will be here too."

"The quartermasters have dozens of fugitives. They need work and we can use them. If you're up to it, I want you to make sure they're employed at productive work, treated fairly, fed, housed and safe."

"Are we going to take them North?"

"Not now. Maybe sometime later, but Halleck's General Orders say we can't allow fugitives into our lines. Grant said not to return them to the people who claim to 'own' them, so for now, we'll put them to work. I imagine some of those unfortunate people will find a way North," said Leggett thoughtfully.

Musing, Leggett added, "Six years ago, the good people of Dover perceived some kind of conspiracy among the slaves. They thought the slaves would revolt, steal white women and run North. The sheriff and townsmen tortured some until they got confessions to that effect, and hung twenty or thirty men, right there in the town square." Leggett shook his head in disgust. "When they finished that, they cut the heads off some and stuck them up on poles. I imagine the locals are no better disposed toward black people now than they were then."

Then Leggett sat back and added, "According to General Hallek's orders, we must not allow escaped slaves to enter Union lines on any account." He looked down and smiled, "But no matter how hard I try, I can't prevent some from slipping through when I'm occupied with other pressing duties." Looking up at Mathan's open face he finished, "Do you understand me Stark?"

"Yes sir, I do." Mathan thought a moment. Mary Ann. She would have connections if anyone did. And she was committed to abolition.

"Sir, there's a busy hospital that's taken care of a lot of the wounded from Ogelsby's Brigade. Could I assign some of the refugees to the Matron there? She can house and feed them, and I'll keep tabs on them."

"Sure, Stark, take women. You'll need the men for heavier work at the fort and with supplies. Start there. Tell me how that goes."

Mathan walked up the hill from the camp on the East side of the little town of Dover, then to the fort, bordering the town on the west. He asked where he could find the quartermaster and requisition a wagon and a driver. A Private on guard duty pointed with his chin toward a dirt track. "Couple hundred yards down that way, last I saw, sir."

Mathan nodded and set off briskly. The Private was correct. When Mathan arrived, there was considerable activity and no clear sign marking the senior quartermaster. Mathan saw several men clustered around a wagon, remounting a wheel. He approached them and waited for one to look up.

A large man with huge forearms was watching the others work and made eye contact with Mathan. "Sergeant," asked Mathan, "Can you direct me to the quartermaster."

"Ja, I can do," said the big man. He looked vaguely familiar to Mathan. "I think he's down that way," he added, pointing at the only permanent building in the area.

"Would you know whether there's a wagon I could requisition for a day?"

"Who would like that wagon, Captain?" asked the Sergeant.

"I'm Captain Stark, 78th Ohio. Colonel Leggett sent me."

The big man stared at Mathan, reaching into his past. "Stark, you say? I remember a Stark. Stark means 'strong' in German and I remember a boy named Stark."

Mathan recognized the voice. "Are you a wheelwright?"

"Ja, I am."

"Did you have a shop on the river at home?"

"Ja!' shouted the big man. "Did you try to drown yourself about ten years ago on a tiny raft?"

"Mathan beamed and held out his hand, "Yes sir! That was me! You saved my life!"

"Hey, Allen!" shouted the big man. "Allen, come over here, there's someone here who owes you a favor!" From behind one of the tents came a tall, black man carrying a hammer and tongs. "Hey Allen, you remember about ten years ago you pulled that kid out of the river and swam back to the bank on my boat."

Mr. Allen thought for a moment. "Sure! Sure do!" Then he looked at Mathan, "Is that…?"

Mathan extended his hand, beaming and said "Yes, sir, you two saved my life!"

"Well how 'bout that!" said the big man with enthusiasm. "I'm Sergeant Himmelstoss and this is Pastor Allen. He's part of our quarter-masters. You must be the Lieutenant they sent to Cairo last year to get things ready for us!"

"Turns out they had little use for me, said Mathan modestly."

"Well, we never did go to Cairo anyway. They put us with General Lew Wallace and we didn't even get here until the day of the big fight. By the time we were ready, everything was over. Looks like we'll just hang around and guard the place in case they try to come take it back!"

"Sergeant Himmelstoss, Pastor Allen, it's a pleasure to meet you again. I'll to buy you dinner as soon as we find ourselves somewhere a good dinner can be had!" said Mathan, still glowing with surprise and enthusiasm.

Himmelstoss and the pastor stood side-by-side and beamed at him. "How can we help you…" asked the Sergeant pausing before adding with a smile, "this time?"

Mathan smiled back warmly. "I need a wagon to take some people and supplies to one of the hospitals."

And with that, Allen's eyes lit up. "Sir, may I ask you which hospital?"

"Of course, it's Ogelsby's Brigade Hospital. Mrs. Bickerdyke's the matron."

Allen suddenly seemed electric with tension that Mathan didn't comprehend.

Himmelstoss said, "That's the lady Mrs. Allen works for!" He leaned forward, Adding, "When we thought we were going to Cairo, Mrs. Allen went ahead and found work. She was going to be there when the 78th and Pastor Allen, here, arrived. He was working with Mrs. Allen when one of the Sergeants took him from her and assigned him to us."

Mathan was delighted at the coincidence and the opportunity to reunite the couple. "Pastor Allen, do you have your papers with you? I hate to ask, but it might make things a lot easier if we're challenged."

"Yes sir, I do, and Colonel Leggett has a copy in a safe place."

"That's fine, Pastor. Sergeant Himmelstoss, what's the best way to get you two assigned to the wagon and me for the day?"

"Come sir, I'll take care of it."

As Mathan and Himmelstoss walked toward the quartermaster's tent, Sergeant Johnson from the 31st was walking toward them. "Hello Captain Stark!" said Johnson with a smile. "Surprised to see you here!"

"Hello Sgt Johnson," said Mathan shaking hands with the 31st's quartermaster Sergeant. I'm back with the 78th Ohio now. Our Colonel Leggett is also the garrison commander and he sent me here to fetch a wagon."

"Me too!" said Johnson. "I need a wagon and a wheelwright for a job at the Brigade Hospital. Have to bring them some supplies and take back some patients. I'll need the wagoner to stay with the wagon because we need it for a trip back to Fort Henry this afternoon."

"I'm going to the hospital anyway. Mind if I take those supplies off your hands and move the patients for you? Sergeant Himmelstoss and this man Allen are wheelwrights and can probably fix anything that's wrong with the hospital's wagon. I also have several contrabands to take there for work."

"Alright by me, Captain. I know you'll do what you say, but if Major Ozburn asks…"

Mathan smiled. "Sergeant Johnson, I order you to transfer your cargo to my care. I will deliver it for you and collect the wounded for transport and deliver them to the landing. I'll get the wagon back to you before two this afternoon. Any questions?"

Smiling and extending his hand, Johnson said, "No Sir, thank you Captain. Be safe."

With that, Pastor Allen went back to work with the others and Himmelstoss visited the quartermaster's office to sign out the wagon for their delivery. To make doubly sure, Himmelstoss explained things to the 78th's quartermaster Sergeant Bigelow. Bigelow would come along to ensure all went well.

Soon, Bigelow and Himmelstoss were at the hospital and in less than an hour, the others arrived. They led a wagon loaded with three large crates of supplies. Four young women rode atop the cargo. They knew each other well and were very happy to help when they were promised they'd be inside Federal lines and would only be away from their friends for a couple of days.

Bigelow had been listening to Mary Ann explain her needs. She stopped speaking as the wagon, passengers and soldiers arrived. "Mrs. Bickerdyke, this here's Sergeant Himmelstoss," continued Sergeant Bigelow with a smile. He's your wheelwright. He'll help you out." Turning he pointed saying, "Is this the Mr. Allen, you asked about?"

Mary Ann said, "Yes that's *Pastor* Allen. Thank you. And, who are these ladies?"

Mathan stepped forward saying, Mrs. Bickerdyke, Colonel Leggett said we could assign these ladies to help you here at the hospital if you could house and feed them for a couple of days before sending them on to their families near Cairo. We're not allowed to take them North, but we can protect them as long as they're within our lines."

Mary Ann nodded, "Of course we need their help, but you know, very soon, we'll close this hospital. Then?"

"Not sure, Ma'am," said Mathan looking down. "We'll need to get them together with their own people pretty quickly."

"Yes, Mathan, yes we will."

Sergeant Bigelow interrupted her, "Ma'am, when the wagon's unloaded, you can use it to send some of the wounded men to the river for transport. After that, we need the wagon to move supplies back to Fort Henry. I'd appreciate it if you'd make sure the wagon gets back to me before supper. Lots still to do."

Before answering, Mary Ann turned to Mrs. Allen. "Would you please take this man—" She pointed at Pastor Allen. "and prepare four wounded men for transport?

Allen waited until they were out of sight before he plucked his wife into his arms, twirled in a circle and kissed her deeply.

While Bigelow walked back to the Fort, Mathan told Mary Ann the story of his reunion with Pastor Allen and Sergeant Himmelstoss. She was pleased that her need to transport patients and special cargo meshed so neatly with their reunion.

Mathan explained Pastor Allen's vulnerability if he were separated from the 78th with whom he was recently serving as a free man. "Mrs. Bickerdyke, I know he used to work with you and that the pastor has his papers. Colonel Leggett has a copy. The Colonel is very sympathetic but has to follow Army orders."

Before Mathan could make a plan, Mary Ann assumed responsibility for protecting the couple, saying, "I have a copy of Mrs. Allen's as well." Just then, Mrs. Allen arrived to say the four patients were ready.

Mary Ann said to both Himmelstoss and Pastor Allen, "Now this is essential. I have three large boxes of personal possessions. All three must be kept upright and not be tipped, dropped or frozen. I want you to mark these containers very carefully and be sure to keep them from being forgotten. They must be transported on the first boat and delivered to the Presbyterian Church in Cairo, immediately. Get those crates delivered in less than a day. Do you understand?"

Himmelstoss looked from side to side to see whether anyone was watching. He made an exaggerated wink and nodded towards Mary Ann, saying slowly and loudly, "Ja, Mrs. B. I understand!" Then Himmelstoss turned to Allen and asked. "Allen, do you understand?"

Allen looked to his wife in the distance, then to Mary Ann and smiled, shaking his head, saying softly, "Yes Alex, I understand."

The men led the wagon into the barn and gently loaded three large crates into its bed. Next, they drove it to the front of the hospital where four stretcher patients were laid across the tops of the crates. The stretchers were carefully secured to the wagon and the patients to the stretchers. When they were ready to leave, Mary Ann called to Mrs. Allen. "Send me that walking-wounded fellow we got this morning. The one with the bumped head"

Within moments, a tall, rail-thin private in a tattered uniform ambled out of the barn.

"You're the one who came in last night, is that right?"

"Yes Ma'am. They brought me here 'cause of my head."

"Bad bump, wasn't it?" Mary Ann asked with warmth.

"Yes Ma'am. My Company was marching this way from Fort Henry a few days ago when the weather was nice. Of a sudden, out of the woods pops a bunch of secesh cavalry! Caught us from the side and we backed away to the other side of the road as fast as we could. I guess I was running when I tripped and fell pretty far down the side of a hill and hit my head. When I came to, it was snowing like everything. Wandered 'til I found a house and the people there said they'd keep me safe until they could get someone to come and get me. I was pretty sick and sore and my head wasn't right, so they just left me on some straw in the corner of their cabin and gave me something to eat."

"Next morning I pretended to be asleep and I heard 'em talking. It was pretty clear to me, they were waiting for some of those same secesh cavalry boys to come fetch me and I didn't think I wanted any part of that. Pretended to wake up and said I had to go to the privy and headed off towards what I thought was where we started, but it took me a couple of days to find my way here."

"Quite a story Private," said Mary Ann blankly. "You want to go back to your Regiment?"

He smiled broadly, "Yes Ma'am, I surely do!"

Well, Sergeant Himmelstoss is going to put you on a wagon that's going back to Fort Henry and from there you can bring the wagon back to the fort and rejoin your friends. Would that suit you?"

"Yes Ma'am, that would be fine!"

Then Himmelstoss leaned towards Mary Ann. "I have some family heirlooms in those boxes that I have to get to Cairo and protect. I'd better keep an eye on them all the way back, don't you think? Our Sergeant Bigelow says I should go back to Cairo with 'em."

Mary Ann smirked and looked at the ground for a moment before turning to the thin man. She asked, "What's your name rank and unit?"

"Private Wilson, 12th Iowa Volunteers. With Colonel Cook's Brigade Ma'am."

"Sergeant Himmelstoss will show you where you're to go with this wagon."

Turning to Pastor Allen, Mary Ann said, "I'm afraid I can't allow you to return to the landing with your Sergeant Himmelstoss. Private Wilson, here, will replace you. I must insist that you accompany Mrs. Allen and me as we take the next boatload of wounded back to our hospital in Cairo. Do you understand? You're assigned to my hospital now!"

Finally, turning to Himmelstoss she said. You have Private Wilson to replace Mr. Allen, correct?"

The big man nodded, smiling.

"I have no idea why you're smiling, and I don't want anyone else to wonder either, so wipe that off your face and get to work!"

His face fell abruptly as she watched Pastor Allen guide the wagon to collect the stretcher patients. Later as Himmelstoss walked next to the wagon, he looked back over his shoulder, smiling at Mary Ann. But when he caught sight of her glare, he turned his head quickly, looking as solemn as he could.

Mathan walked beside the wagon as they left the hospital. Mary Ann called after them, "Remember Sergeant, the crates go to Miss Rachel Rodgers at the Presbyterian Church. Can you remember that?"

As Allen watched from his wife's side. Himmelstoss shouted back, "Rachel Rodgers. Yes Ma'am." Mathan smiled. He could remember the name.

That night at Fort Donelson, Mathan was assigned responsibility for the camp sentries. Unlike other camps, the sentries at the Fort Donelson encampment faced both outward and inward. Donelson was cold, wet and muddy. Some men were moved into wooden huts left by the (now imprisoned) Confederate troops. Many Union soldiers were still under canvas.

Mathan had two Sergeants to help him keep an eye on the sentries this night. Sergeants would move the sentries every two hours and replace them every four hours throughout the night.

The most hated place on the camp perimeter was the Confederate burial ground. It occupied low land, probably because it was near their hospital and the soil was soft and easy to open. The burial detail seems to have been rushed, or maybe they hit the water table. Either way, the graves were very shallow. In many places, the Southerners buried the remains under less than a foot of soil. Run-off from higher terrain crossed the burial ground on its way to the river uncovering the decomposing remains of dozens of soldiers. The stench of death hung in the air despite an occasional breeze and the cold air. It was a terrible place to stand guard and Mathan didn't leave anyone there for long and he ensured no one ever had a second watch at that place.

Even so, Mathan didn't mind asking a man to use skills that he lacked, but he knew it was bad leadership to ask a soldier to do something, merely because he was a subordinate. He remembered advice Webster had given him in Cairo, "A subordinate never forgets the difference between his rank and his superior's. A good superior never considers it." Mathan took a second watch at the pit, so another soldier didn't have to.

Mathan made it a point to perform every undesirable job at least once. When he had time, he looked for men doing the dirty, thankless jobs necessary to maintain an Army and he helped them. He helped dig latrines, he mucked stalls and burned refuse. He buried the dead and wrote letters to their families.

Tonight, was cold and Mathan was lonely. Standing in the dark at the edge of the burial ground his eyes moved from one gruesome image to another. His eyes rose to the black surface of the river, moving Westward. He knew the water reached the Mississippi and eventually, the Gulf. He wondered how far down the river he would go.

Standing on the edge of this pit, he had no fear, but he hurt deeply. He imagined his "old self," the one from just last Summer. Like a furnace, the war melted his old form, leaving him shapeless and, waiting to be cast into something different. For now, he was a soldier—an officer. He was still amidst the flames.

He looked up at the night sky. Behind the clouds, he knew was the inconceivable expanse. The moon, planets, stars. He didn't know what form his future would take, but he knew he could not recover the person he had been. He was changing.

Above him was Colonel Leggett, above Leggett was Wallace. Above Wallace was Halleck. Above Halleck was McClellan and above McClellan was President Lincoln. Who was above President Lincoln? Mathan smiled to himself; Mrs. Lincoln?

He had never asked himself these questions, but neither had he encountered so much death, so often and so intimately. He wondered if there was anything left beneath the surface of his public self. Beneath his uniform, his education, his acquaintances, friends, loves? What was behind his faith? He stared at the ghostly arm, thoughtlessly dumped into the muddy ground. Hidden below the shallow covering of mud (for now) was a body. A couple of days ago, it had been a man. Maybe his age. Maybe a young husband.

Melancholy gripped him. He realized he couldn't recall the feelings of being safe, happy, loved, warm or secure. Loneliness possessed him and he yearned to be home.

Home sickness, like other sicknesses, develops over time. The first symptoms are discomfort and gloom accompanied by yearning for familiar surroundings. It progresses by stages into feelings of distance from new people and a longing to be with people who know and understood you. Mathan's "symptoms" lurked somewhere just below conscious thought. Other times, his sickness was intense, like a spiking fever. Sometimes it took the form of abject despair rising from the depths of his soul.

When it was bad, he feared no one and nothing would (or even could) relieve feelings that his life meant nothing and he would be forever alone. When he was in that mind, no one's concern or attention made any difference. At best, their efforts to "cheer him up," were annoying. At worst, they made him very angry and he frequently felt like punching someone. He'd tried alcohol, but when he drank enough to forget, he just vomited and had an awful hang-over.

He thought about battles. About the intensity of combat, the immediacy of a fight and his brotherhood with the others. There was no homesickness in a fight. But afterwards, it returned. Almost always, his war-fever broke. Sleep helped when he could achieve it. Hard work distracted him.

His relief arrived at dawn and he could return to his tent and lie down. He slept deeply until that afternoon. As he left his tent, the warmth of the afternoon sun and the sound of birds soothed his heart. Looking at the passing clouds, Mathan had a thought. He considered that if a thing were worth dying for, it could be worth living for.

A couple of days later, Himmelstoss returned, reporting, "Miss Rodgers was right there at the church and took charge of our cargo. She made me wait and then asked an awful lot of questions about you." He reached inside his coat and added, "She gave me these letters for you. Said she misses you."

Mail was special. Reading from paper she had held, seeing her thoughts expressed in her handwriting. Descriptions of her days, reminiscences about their courtship in Ohio, news of friends and a closing promise to wait for him were worth reading over and over. They brought her close.

It was late March and he hadn't seen Rachel for weeks. Busy days pushed his melancholy into the background and there was no time to get back to Cairo for a visit.

About that time, at a meeting of the officers of the 78th, Leggett began, "Gentlemen, we're being reassigned to the Third Brigade, Third Division under Colonel Whittelsey and General Wallace. We're boarding boats and could be aboard for a day or two. Company Commanders, get your men ready: make sure they have rations and ammunition. This will be big." Looking from one young man to the next, he saw no questions and dismissed them. They would join General Buell's Army and drive into Mississippi.

A couple of days later, they boarded a steamer at Dover and began their trip to Crumps Landing, 100 river-miles South. Men occupied every inch of space on the decks while their wagons and mules were loaded onto another boat. During the boat ride, they heard the occasional whiz of a bullet. They knew there were snipers in the hills and sometimes, along the banks. Fortunately, the river ran high, allowing boats to keep a safe distance from snipers and none of the men of the 78th were hurt.

In the gray light of a chilly, early Spring evening, they clomped across the stages, got into line and followed a troop of cavalry West from the river, to their first, rough camp. There were Rebels at Purdy, a town a couple of miles further to the West so the next morning, after breakfast, the 78th Ohio marched five miles further inland to Adamsville. It was a small crossroads town where they established a long defensive line guarding the approach to Crumps Landing, where most of the troops and supplies were disembarking.

Two days after General Wallace and his three Brigades secured Crump's landing, Grant established his headquarters on the East bank at Savannah, in Mr. Cherry's big house overlooking the Tennessee River,

The rest of his headquarters spread from Mr. Cherry's house down into the small town of Savannah. Mary Ann brought her hospital on one of the 90 steamers that came from Cairo, Fort Henry and Fort Donelson. Mathan didn't know Mary Ann had Rachel with her.

SPRINGFIELD, ILLINOIS
APRIL 1862

Logan recovered steadily at home. Mary was deeply involved in her husband's political life and things were about to change dramatically.

"Mary?" Logan asked calmly. "Would you mind bringing me those letters over there. I'm expecting something from Grant."

"Here they are," she said, reading the envelopes as she crossed the room. "Several from the Army." She stopped short of the couch where he reclined. "Is this about the promotion?" she asked brightening.

"May be." He raised his hand expectantly. She shuffled through the last two letters to satisfy herself before presenting them to her husband. He sorted through them quickly until he found the one he wanted. "From Grant!" He kept his eyes lowered as he read carefully. A smile crossed his face, then he beamed and looked up at Mary. "It came. I'm promoted!" Their eyes met in shared delight. "I'll have a Brigade, maybe even a Division!"

"Oh, that's wonderful! I'm so proud of you!" she giggled as she leaned over to share an embrace.

He smiled and leaned back onto the mound of pillows that supported him. His face became more serious. "You know, this means I have to resign from Congress."

"You what!?" she asked incredulously.

"There's too much pressure to turn my military service into a political mission. That's why you can't be a General and an elected official at the same time. The men need me to focus on just one thing. Even McClernand resigned when he was promoted."

"Oh," said Mary flatly. "I know Washington's not the same anymore, but I don't want to lose my friends."

Logan said, "Maybe we'll go back after the war, Mary. Right now, the war is the most important thing." Even during his time in Santa Fe, Logan had never felt anything like this burning commitment to his soldiers: His men.

"Well," she sighed, considering what this meant for her role in his career, "the newspapers are full of your service."

"And just as many want to give the credit for what happened to other people. The Democratic troublemakers keep saying I'm an abolitionist!"

"Oh! Those editors! They ought to put down their pens and pick up a rifle!" Mary added indignantly. She loved being the wife of an influential politician. As a temporary substitute for Congressman Logan's wife, the title of "General Logan's Wife" might be satisfying.

He turned it over in his mind, recalling his own hostility to abolitionists. And now, his duty and passion were focused on the war. That's what mattered. Putting down the rebellion. Restoring the Union. Expanding the territories under a single rule of law. If that required the end of slavery, well, that was an economic problem the country could manage.

"Mary, you know it's always like that. Editors want to sell more papers so they can charge more for advertising. The more scandalous the story, the more copies they sell. You think there's really a market for simple facts and calm analysis? If there is, it's a small one."

"But calling you an abolitionist is just destructive and wrong! After you resign, you're going to have to overcome all this negative press when you run for office again."

"They'll forget most of it," said Logan calmly. "They'll remember who did them a favor and who is most likely to help them with their next investment. Emotional and moral objections don't make much difference once the next scandal makes the headlines."

"They make a difference if the subject is important enough! What about some of the terrible things they said about President Jackson and that Margaret Eaton, or General Sickles and his wife?" argued Mary. "The papers ruined those women!"

Jack sighed. "I've always said, 'A bad news story won't turn your friends against you. A good news story won't turn your enemies toward you and, frankly, no one else remembers.'"

Mary, now asserting her preferred role as Logan's advocate and protector said, "If the paper convinces people in Egypt that you're an abolitionist, you may never get elected again. Your law practice might even dry up!"

"I've been at this a while, Mary. I've met plenty of abolitionists. Most of them are good people. They even agreed with me about the problems that sudden emancipation of all those uneducated people would cause. And the financial consequences for the southern economy!"

"Exactly," said Mary, pausing and looking at him suspiciously. "So, what are you thinking now?"

"One thing is different from before. We have to win this war. If we don't, there's nothing to keep our country from chopping itself into a dozen confederacies, kingdoms and confusions. We'll become just like Europe and we'll be at war forever. It can't happen. In my mind Mary, everything is secondary to winning this war and preserving the Union. Even Lincoln understands that. I know he's an abolitionist at heart, but you heard him when he was here. He won't touch slavery if he can end this war without abolition."

"I suppose Egypt is likely to stay the way it is. The press could hurt me if I run down here. I think about that. But I'm going to fight this war to the end. When it's over, if the Union is broken, I'll get ready for the next war. Mexico will side with the South and we'll have to fight the Mexican War all over again or England will get involved and reach for the gold in California the way they've done in Australia. God knows…"

"But if we win… If we win and I decide to go back into politics, I'm going to run for a state-wide seat. I'll run for a Senate seat. Douglas taught me that. At the dinner table and the city council, arguments are all-or-nothing. But you remember our time in Washington? Everything there is about horse-trading, deals, promises and exchanges. The further you get from a single town or a single county, the more important compromise becomes. The higher the office, the more room there is for an opinion that one small town or another doesn't like."

Mary challenged Logan again, "The Copperheads are after you to make a clear statement. They want you to lay down your marker for now and for always. If you don't, they'll keep saying you're an abolitionist."

"I know, I know." Jack looked down at his promotion papers. "Mary, I can't do anything about this abolitionist thing. I have to get back to the Army. The men I promised to lead are counting on me and I may be able to get out from under McClernand and work more closely with Grant. That man is remarkable. He'd make a terrible politician, but what a commander!"

"You haven't answered my question, Jack." she said with some petulance, "What do I tell people?"

Logan had had enough of Mary's interrogation. He was feeling annoyed. "Tell them I'm a soldier and I'm devoted to preserving the Union. Tell them that what matters now, is supporting the soldiers, taking care of their families, and winning this war." He looked up with some anger in his tone. "Mary, do you understand what I'm telling you? *That's* what we tell them."

She nodded and took the promotion papers from his hand. Her imagination stirred, "Mrs. General Logan!" she said proudly. This is what Mr. Washburne told me about! He said that between General Grant's praises and the support from people here at home, he thought the President would appoint you. And he came through!"

Logan smiled to himself. Although he was proud of his recognition, he also knew his appointment had more to do with the inertia of past events. His father's decision to come to the frontier made it likely, as the town's only doctor, to ascend to local prominence. His father's status was easily transferred to his oldest son and namesake. Introductions that followed inevitably led to an apprenticeship inside the Democratic Party. The apprenticeship introduced him to people who recognized his talent for hard work and public speaking. He voiced their priorities consistently and seemed untroubled by philosophical contradictions. He worked hard for Douglas and was rewarded with a seat in Congress. Being a Congressman made him a Colonel. Being in the right place at Belmont and avoiding failure resulted in his role at Fort Donelson.

Now, the Army was growing so rapidly, the number of Generals was bound to grow proportionally. He was near the front of the line for promotion. He was swept along by a flood of events he neither initiated nor controlled. His only choice was where to position himself within the flood. To choose the risks he would take and which he'd try to avoid. Logan decided to risk combat to preserve the Union. He would risk being shot by rebels, but he would avoid the question of abolition. Sharpshooters with pens were more dangerous to his career plans than sharpshooters with lead.

Mary left the room. And Logan sat quietly, reflecting on his return to combat. A shadow crossed Logan's mind. Images more than thoughts came to him. Young McIlrath's face as he kneeled by his father. One of his men, decapitated by a cannonball and spouting blood from the neck, staggering a step before collapsing. Mrs. Allen's gentle hand on his forehead. The days he sensed and feared his own death. His absolute helplessness.

Feelings of helplessness brought images from New Mexico. The faces of the Navajo children in the towns. The anguish of the cantina owner in Taos.

He got hold of himself. He told himself he had to choose a course and follow it. "Focus!" he told himself. "Choose a path and follow it. No dithering!"

His thoughts turned immediately to his men. The power of their affection and trust soothed him and it energized him. He loved them. No ambiguity, no doubt. Win the fight. That was the right path, the natural path. The certainty of his next step restored his confidence and enthusiasm. He had to go back to his men. It wasn't politics, or promotion or war. It was the men, his men. He had to go now.

SAVANNAH, TENNESSEE, APRIL 1862

General Grant's superior was General Halleck. Known as "Old Brains," Halleck was very smart, very cautious, and very, very jealous. Particularly of Grant's victory at Fort Donelson: the first major victory of a Union Army in the Civil War. After a polite, but intense disagreement, and with Lincoln's full support, Grant was given command of the Army of the Tennessee.

Mary Ann marveled at the size of the flotilla (over 90 steamers) that delivered much of the Army and her hospital to Savannah, Tennessee. It was Rachel's first time away from Cairo and the size of the flotilla and Army camps stunned her. As they disembarked, their escort pointed to the sharp Western bend in the river saying, "General Wallace's Third Division is just up that way a mile or so at Crump's Landing. They're breaking up railroads over there." Rachel looked to Mary Ann for permission to ask a question, but Mary Ann ignored the escort's comment.

"Sergeant, where's the hospital?"

The escort knew better than to question Mrs. B and pointed to a cluster of tents on a low hill. "There, Ma'am. That's most of it."

"Let's go there now, said Mary Ann to the escort. "Rachel, join me as soon as the Allens collect the wagon and a team. You'll bring our first load of supplies and we'll get things in order. In the meantime, I have to find the Surgeon and anyone else who's working here."

The temporary hospital was set up in a field outside town. The stench from the place reached Mary Ann a quarter of a mile before she got to the entrance. Encountering a pair of sentries posted there, Mary Ann asked, "Where can I find the surgeon in charge of this place?"

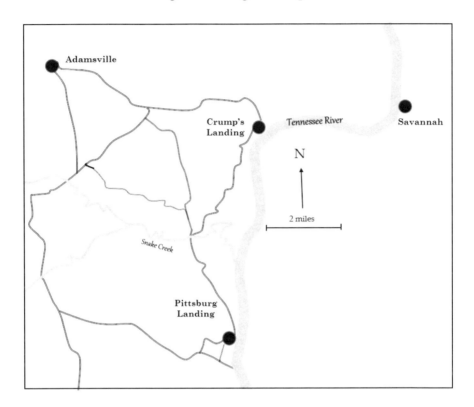

Map of Towns Around Shiloh Battlefield in April 1862

"No idea Ma'am." The first sentry paused, challenging Mary Ann with his glare. "Ma'am, women aren't allowed into the camp."

Unfazed, Mary Ann smiled politely. "I understand your concern Private. Here's my pass."

The sentry handed the pass to the second sentry with some embarrassment saying, "It'll be easier for him to read it."

The younger of the two whistled in admiration. "My oh my!" he said, looking up at Mary Ann. "You have General Grant's signature himself! Says you can go where you want, when you want and that we should help you however you want!"

"Thank you Private," said Mary Ann taking the pass back from the sentry. We'll be on our way." She stepped into the compound with her escort and poked her head into the first tent she saw. She was sickened.

There were ten men in a tent designed for eight. They smelled of vomit, feces and sweat. Their bedding was stained and the men lay still.

Disgusted, she went to the next tent where things were nearly as bad. On her way to the third tent, a young man in an open shirt strode toward her, demanding, "Madam! What are you doing in this hospital? You have no business here!"

"And who might you be, young man?" asked Mary Ann, smiling, but prepared to do battle.

"I'm Deputy Surgeon Brinton's assistant. Who are you?"

"I'm Mrs. Bickerdyke. I'm the representative of the US Sanitary Commission and this is, or will very soon be, my hospital." She didn't wait for a reply but glared and held General Grant's pass towards the man.

Reading, then refolding the pass and returning it, the young man said with barely concealed resentment, "Of course, Mrs. Bickerdyke. We heard you were on your way." Then, with mock subservience he said, "We are at your disposal."

"Well, Doctor, the only disposal that interests me just now is you disposing of the filthy linens in this hospital! Do you have a functioning laundry here?"

Momentarily taken aback by her tone, the young surgeon replied, "I, I don't really know, Ma'am."

Consciously permitting some of her outrage to surface she leaned toward him and scowled, "You don't know!? Well, you'd better find out!"

She looked beyond the assistant surgeon and saw a middle-aged man with short legs and a round belly whose suspenders made smudged arcs across his sweat-stained undershirt. "Who are you, sir?"

The older man glanced at the Assistant Surgeon before answering, "I, madam, am Private Xenos Dunbridge, Medical Attendant, Office of the Surgeon, Army of the Ohio, at your service."

"Private Dunbridge, you say?"

"Yes Madam. Dunbridge, of the Columbus, Ohio Dunbridges. How may I assist you?"

"You can take me on a tour of this pestilent hole!" Turning to the surgeon she said, "Please tell Surgeon Brinton that I would be grateful for his attention following my tour of this place. I'm sure he'll be able to find me."

With that, Mary Ann turned back to Private Dunbridge who smiled at her and led her on a tour of dozens of tents, scattered haphazardly in clusters of five to ten, across an open field that was crossed by a couple of dirt paths and was centered on a corral holding a dozen mules. There was a larger tent nearby, with one side rolled up. Inside, sat a man furiously writing at a desk. He looked up.

Aging quickly but apparently still in his forties, the man had a large, straight nose and bags under his eyes. His hair was frizzed over his ears in the style of the previous decade. His chin receded a bit and he was carefully preparing a requisition.

As Mary Ann entered, she looked at the uniform coat draped across a camp chair. It bore Major's leaves. "Dr. Murray?" She asked. He looked up, over the rims of his reading glasses. "I am Mrs. Bickerdyke from the US Sanitary Commission. General Grant has directed me to organize a hospital here in Savannah. I've brought cooks, laundresses, teamsters and a few attendants. We have nearly an entire shipload of supplies and equipment being unloaded as we speak."

Dr. Murray slowly lay down his pen and raised his head without otherwise altering his posture. "Mrs. Bickerdyke? Yes. I was told a representative of the Commission would arrive with General Grant. I am General Buell's Surgeon as you must know. It seems we are to collaborate."

"Indeed sir. I have visited the medical facility. I understand that you already have eight hundred men in sick beds. Is that right?"

"Something like that. Actually, almost all of them are yours!"

Mary Ann didn't care whose they were. "I am most concerned for their welfare. They are filthy and poorly fed. I must find permanent structures to house these men. I saw a row of warehouses that I assume are used for cotton or other produce, near the river?"

Murray brought himself slowly to his feet and, without acknowledging Mary Ann's request, poked one arm and then the other, through the sleeves of his coat. He ceremoniously buttoned himself and wrapped his green sash about his waist. He took up his hat, and using both hands, placed it squarely on his head. Then he faced Mary Ann.

"You have grievously intimidated my young assistant and," he added with a sad smile, "accurately assessed the condition of our hospital." He paused, holding her eyes. "My staff is at your disposal for now. I will see to the preparation of our surgeons and our Brigade facilities." He smiled knowingly and added, "Your General Grant's Army seems to have arrived and to have brought most of the State of Illinois in his ships. Your Doctor Brinton has also arrived and will be involved, I'm sure. General Buell's Army should be here in the coming week." He looked at her with a collaborative smile. "Can we agree to meet tomorrow before supper to compare notes?"

"That will be lovely, Major. Shall I meet you here?"

Murray nodded and, without saying good-bye, collected his papers and tucked them into a leather satchel. He smiled at her once more, before turning to walk calmly away.

Three men remained in the tent, looking expectantly at Mary Ann. "My niece will arrive momentarily. She is my assistant. Let's begin by arranging to take possession of those warehouses."

Rachel's wagon approached the row of long, low warehouses above the river. They were weathered and many had open sides, but their roofs appeared sound and fresh water was nearby. Wood smoke rose from long trenches filled with low flames and glowing embers. Above the fires hung a series of kettles, many boiling. A few women stepped quietly from one kettle to the next, carrying their long paddles to add, retrieve or stir boiling laundry. On a green field adjacent to the warehouses was spread more than an acre of freshly washed clothing and sheets, drying in the sun.

Rachel sat up front, next to the driver and jolted in the seat. She was in the first of nearly a dozen wagons delivering food and medical supplies to the temporary hospital. Mary Ann met the wagons and directed them to buildings she'd chosen for surgery, wards, kitchens, administration, storage and housing for her staff. After a brief but warm greeting, Mary Ann went back to giving direction to the orderlies and nurses.

Pointing to the smallest warehouse, near the entrance, Mary Ann asked Mrs. Allen to check on the quarters of their female staff. The administrative offices would occupy a small part of the space. As soon as the sick soldiers were moved into the new warehouses, their tents would be aired out. The best of them would house male orderlies. Rachel noticed a couple of men digging what must be latrine trenches, downhill and downstream, away from the tents and fires.

Before Mrs. Allen was out of earshot, Mary Ann added, "Mrs. Allen, as soon as the ladies find their places, would you please get the cooks to work, prepare meals for tonight and tomorrow morning. Let's get the bread started while the men build and fire-up the ovens."

"Rachel, the moment the rest of our orderlies arrive, have them wash and dress the patients in clean hospital clothes. Change the bedding while the occupants are being washed. Remember to sort the dirty clothes into piles of things we can salvage and set the rest aside to burn.

"Pastor Allen, would you take a few men and clean out the warehouses, as each tent is cleared, we'll move the men into fresh beds. Let's try to get as many as we can into the warehouses tonight and move the rest in the morning." Then muttering to herself she said, "Better get moving, it will be even busier soon."

As the hospital took shape on one side of the village of Savannah, Grant and his staff established headquarters at the Cherry House. Other administrative functions were set up in the town. The river was choked with boats delivering soldiers, equipment and supplies and it was almost dark when Dr. Murray entered the medical compound. The sentries pointed out Mary Ann at the "turn-around" where wagons off-loaded cargo or patients before returning to their starting points.

Plain looking, with his crumpled round hat, deep set eyes and prominent nose, the lanky, Dr. Robert Murray began brightly, "There you are Mrs. Bickerdyke! I'm glad I found you. I'd like a few minutes of your time if I may."

"Hello, Doctor Murray. I'd hoped to see you earlier today. Can we speak here, or would you rather we found a quieter place?" she asked calmly.

"Hmmm," he thought for a moment as he looked around the still-busy hospital. "I must say, the aroma of your fresh bread reaches all the way to the headquarters building! I wonder if you might have a bit to spare for the staff?"

"We can check, Doctor. Can you tell me whether there's anything we need to discuss first?"

Bringing his eyes back to her, then lowering his head as he gathered himself. "Shall we walk?" he said, sweeping his right arm in the direction of the cooking fires up a small rise. Mary Ann said nothing but walked next to him and waited.

"Mrs. Bickerdyke, I've spoken with your Dr. Brinton." Mary Ann cast a sidewise glance but Murray gave no sign of concern. "He assured me that you are a remarkable woman and quite in control of your hospitals. He lauded your concern for the men." Taking a few more steps he added, "Described your strong relationship with his leaders. Yes, he did."

"That was very kind of him to say." Mary Ann continued her walk.

"Well, the thing is, Mrs. Bickerdyke," Murray paused to gather his thoughts. "The thing is, General Buell has never met you and seems to share some of Dr. Brinton's views about females in camp."

"I see," mused Mary Ann. "Do you foresee difficulties?"

"No, perhaps not. I wonder, Mrs. B., I wonder if you might acquaint my surgeons and myself with your hospital? One of the Brigade Surgeons who'll be arriving soon is something of a young hero." Murray paused and faced Mary Ann, adding, "His name is Irwin and he is rather opinionated. It would be best if the surgeons who are here when he arrives, have a established positive opinion of our operation. He may absorb their opinions by a sort of 'collegial osmosis' and be better disposed to cooperate."

Murray stopped and added, "You see, we anticipate a rather large engagement in the next few weeks. It will probably be upriver, near Corinth. Your hospital may be needed to receive the wounded prior to their return to hospitals at home. Good relationships with our Brigade surgeons can only smooth the way for our patients."

She stood facing him. "I understand Dr. Murray. Some of the surgeons we've encountered cherish an eighteenth-century view of women's roles. I've found that most will come around. The rest are able to grasp General Grant's opinions on our role here." She placed her hand on Murray's forearm and guided him toward the rows of ovens. "Remind me of the name of this young surgeon, in case he arrives before you're able to, um, prepare him."

"His name is Captain Irwin, Ma'am. Doctor Bernard John Dowling Irwin and he likes to use all his names. Assigned to 'Bull' Nelson's Brigade—General Nelson, I suppose. Those two are as loyal a pair of friends as I've ever met. If you earn the cooperation of one, you'll have both. Alienate one and you've alienated both."

As they reached the bread ovens, Mary Ann asked one of the cooks, "Miss Elizabeth, could you bring me two of those loaves please? Two of the cooler ones?"

Elizabeth handed two loaves to Mary Ann with a smile. After thanking Elizabeth for the bread, Mary Ann turned back to Murray. "These are for you and the other doctors to sample. We are not in the practice of taking what few, healthy foods are available to the sick and wounded and offering them to officers, merely because they feel a sense of entitlement." She held his gaze until his eyes dropped again. "I'm glad you understand. Is there anything else?"

Murray shook his head as his eyes wandered across the row of warehouses, lit by lanterns and busy with the relocation of patients.

"Thank you for your visit, Doctor. I look forward to meeting your Captain Doctor Owling Derwin." Said Mary Ann with a sense of finality.

Under his breath, Murray said, "Oh dear." Then he added with a tone of entreaty, "Bernard, John, Dowling, *Irwin*."

Two days later, a solitary rider cantered past the sentries without stopping and reined up his horse in the middle of the hospital courtyard. His uniform was clean and well-tailored, his complexion was ruddy, with rusty-red hair. His beard was trimmed short. The sentry reached him to complain that he hadn't stopped at the entrance.

Brigade Surgeon Bernard John Dowling Irwin scowled, turning the man away with his icy glare. Although unannounced, he remained rigidly upright in his saddle, seeming to expect a formal reception. He waited impatiently, surveying the hospital with the irritated eye of a superior being. Rolling up to the entrance were three heavily laden ambulances.

Their drivers were accompanied by a sentry as they moved quietly into the courtyard. An occasional, low moan emerged from a passenger.

When the sentry reached him, Irwin didn't look down, instead scanning the row of lantern-lit warehouses he demanded, "Where is the surgeon in charge!"

"No idea, Captain. In one of the wards, I suppose," mused the sentry looking up at the rider with more curiosity than deference.

"Well, send someone to find him and tell him the 4th Division Surgeon, Army of the Ohio is here and must see him!" Irwin's eyes returned to the sentry in mid-sentence, but only for an instant. Then he resumed his appraisal of the buildings and grounds.

Puzzled, the sentry called to a pair of men, standing outside one of the wards, unloading tools from a wheelbarrow. "Hey, Spider!" the sentry shouted with more volume than necessary. "The Captain here is looking for Major Murray, Doctor Brinton or one of the surgeons. Go find one of 'em would you?"

Spider looked at the sentry with some annoyance, then caught the young surgeon's glare and nodded without another word. As he jogged toward the next warehouse, he looked back over his shoulder to ensure he wasn't being pursued.

After five minutes of impatient and disapproving grumbling, Doctor Irwin's eyes registered two people walking toward him from the far side of the compound. One appeared to be a surgeon of some sort and the other was a young woman.

Irwin remained mounted as Rachel and an Assistant Surgeon approached. He ignored the surgeon and focused on Rachel, first taking in her height, then her complexion and her confidence. As she strode nearer, he saw past the severe hairstyle and formless black dress to the beauty beneath. He dismounted immediately and half-bowed to her, introducing himself with all the charm he'd acquired in his prep school, university and military experience.

"I'm pleased to meet you Doctor Irwin," said Rachel calmly as she watched him with some amusement. "This is Assistant Surgeon Tomkins. How can we help you?"

"Miss Rodgers, I have men in need of care. I understand this is the Headquarters Hospital? Can you take these men?"

"Yes, Doctor Irwin, that's why we're here," she replied as she turned to Tomkins. "Steven, would you look at the patients and send the drivers to the appropriate wards?"

Tomkins nodded and stepped to the first wagon. Irwin ignored him, focusing on Rachel. She was experienced enough to recognize a charm offensive but young enough to enjoy it. Would you like to accompany your patients and see our hospital, or shall we take them from here?"

Irwin inclined his head slightly toward her and smiled. "May I ask you to conduct me on a tour?"

"Certainly Doctor. Shall we follow the wagons?" As the ambulances rolled on, Irwin took his reins in his hand and led his mount while walking beside Rachel.

Spider and the sentry grinned at each other, rolled their eyes and shook their heads. Irwin's chivalrous approach to Miss Rodgers wasn't the first flirtation they'd seen but it was the most elegant. They were surprised she hadn't turned her back on him immediately as she usually did.

That afternoon, Dr. Brinton and Dr. Murray sat side by side on a small bench beneath a large willow outside the Cherry Mansion where Grant stayed. The large home rested atop an ancient mound built by pre-Columbian natives, overlooking the Tennessee River and adjacent to Savannah. Buell's Army of the Ohio was delayed but would soon arrive. This would be one of the last quiet days for a very long time.

Like many men, Brinton was comfortable with peers and truly deserved the favorable professional reputation that preceded him. His regard for women predated his education and emerged unbidden, and sometimes, destructively.

Turning from their discussion of inadequate lodging, Brinton complained, "It seems we have hundreds here with disease, but very few combat wounds. That Bickerdyke woman manages the hospital adequately and I despair of being rid of her. She employs contrabands, freemen and a platoon of volunteers from home to operate the place."

Murray nodded. He liked Mary Ann and had a more positive opinion. "I understand she has the General's support?" he asked mildly.

"Oh! Yes, indeed! She made an impression in Cairo and again after Belmont. Taking care of Grant's friends at Donelson, that really did it!" added Brinton with disdain. "At least she's efficient at moving the wounded from hospitals to steamers and getting them settled without worsening their condition too much. At any rate, I leave tomorrow for St Louis. We're desperately short of medicine and supplies. Grant authorized me to speak for him in St Louis. I expect to return as soon as my business there is concluded."

Murray looked across the river and grunted in acknowledgement. He looked up to see Mr. Cherry, the owner of the house and a man sympathetic to their cause, standing next to them. "Gentlemen, Mrs. Cherry asked me to invite you upstairs to General Smith's room. She is most concerned about him."

The men rose. As they followed Mr. Cherry toward the house, Irwin strode up to them. "Doctor Murray!" announced Irwin with his hand extended. "I've just dropped our seriously ill at the local hospital and..." He caught Brinton's indignant look and apologized. "I beg your pardon, sir." Irwin extended his hand saying, "Irwin, Army of the Ohio, Fourth Division Surgeon." And he waited for Brinton's reply.

Slowly extending his hand he said, "Brinton, Deputy Surgeon, Army of Tennessee," then waited for the difference in rank to settle onto Irwin. It didn't.

Murray smiled at Brinton saying, "Dr. Irwin is something of a legend! 500 Apaches had 60 of our finest surrounded in the Arizona Territory just last year. Irwin here, took about fifteen troopers, all that were left at the fort, sneaked-up on the Indians and commenced to fire on them from every different direction. Well, the Apaches thought they were under attack from an entire Brigade and just ran off! Irwin here, brought out all the survivors without another scratch!" Nodding towards Irwin whose smiling face watched Brinton for a reaction, Murray concluded, "Very close to his Major General Bull Nelson, too!"

Brinton nodded. "An incredible story," he said calmly, letting both meanings of the word hang in the air for a moment. "We must follow Mr. Cherry up to General Smith's room. He's been suffering. Would you like to join us Doctor Irwin?"

The three men crossed the lawn, passing Grant's command tents. Entering the home, they climbed a long flight of stairs to the room allocated to General Smith.

Brinton began, "Smith was Grant's commandant at West Point, you know. Just before we arrived here, Halleck replaced Grant with Smith. Well, General Smith badly scraped his lower leg during a transfer from a steamboat to a yawl. About that time, Halleck reconsidered and swapped Grant for General Smith again."

As he reached General Smith's door, Brinton concluded, "General Smith's leg injury seemed of little concern at first, but the wound has become prurient and he's developed a fever. The General's bowels seem to have become uncooperative as well." As the physicians entered Smith's room, they could see the older man was in pain. Even so, he preserved his dignity during their examination.

The physicians stepped back into the hallway where Murray and Irwin listened to Brinton's diagnosis and recommendations. All agreed and Brinton returned to Smith's room to reassure him. Irwin turned to Murray saying, "Are you acquainted with Miss Rodgers from the hospital? Quite a remarkable young woman!"

Murray was disappointed that Irwin's first thought after seeing General Smith involved romance. "I'd be careful," began Murray slowly. "Miss Rodgers is Mrs. Bickerdyke's niece. More like her daughter, actually. She watches that young woman the same way a bear watches her cubs. I suspect any approach by a young man will elicit an unabashedly ursine response." He paused and held Irwin's eyes. "The young lady is rumored to have a fiancé in Lew Wallace' Division. They're just across the river at Crump's Landing. Haven't met him."

"I assure you, Doctor. My intentions are completely honorable. I simply appreciate beauty when I encounter it."

Murray grunted as Brinton returned. The three physicians quietly wished one another well and went their separate ways. Brinton to pack for his trip to St. Louis, Murray to dine with Grant's staff and Irwin in search of an excuse to see Rachel.

In the coming days, Irwin frequently "found" Rachel. Under the guise of coordinating supplies and patient transfers, he'd spent several hours with her. For her part, Rachel experienced the sort of attraction that men with good looks, self-confidence and a history of success so often provoke. Uncertainty and self-criticism were strangers to him and his substitution of attentiveness and charm for the usual, clumsy flattery held Rachel's attention.

"Watch out for that Dr. Irwin," warned Mary Ann as they returned from the supply building. "He has no reason to spend so much time here. His intentions can't be good."

"Oh, Aunt Mary Ann! He's just flirting. I can handle that! And I'm learning a great deal from him about medicine and taking care of the wounded."

Mary Ann grunted dismissively as Rachel went on, "He's very concerned about the number of men who bleed to death on their way from the brigade hospitals to surgery. He's also unhappy with the number of men he believes would be better served if they didn't have to be moved at all.

"Rachel, he may have a fine medical mind, but he's a wealthy, single man with more on his mind than medicine. You have your reputation and your fiancé to think about, remember?"

The sharp look from Rachel surprised Mary Ann. "I'm no fool, Auntie. I know exactly what he's thinking. I've probably thought along those lines myself. I know what's important and what's fantasy. I know he's not the sort of man I'd ever want for a husband." She paused and smiled. "I'd have to spend my life thinking of new ways to praise him and when he got tired of that, I'd have to organize a Captain Doctor Bernard Irwin Admiration and Praise Society! No thanks."

Mary Ann clucked dismissively.

"But he *is* a fine-looking man," said Rachel as they entered the administration building.

ADAMSVILLE, TENNESSEE, APRIL 6, 1862

The 78th Ohio was part of the vanguard for the Army of the Tennessee. They'd arrived three weeks before and secured Crumps Landing, across from Savannah. The bulk of the Army would land five or six miles further South at Pittsburg Landing where they would protect the next suitable landing up the river (the Tennessee flows North here).

Mathan's Regiment was part of Whittelsey's Brigade and was several miles West of Crumps Landing at Adamsville, stretched North to South, facing the town of Purdy, a couple of miles further West.

Mathan stirred some sugar into the muddy, black coffee he'd acquired at Colonel Leggett's tent. It had been warm the day before, but this morning, clouds appeared and it was surprisingly cool. Colonel Leggett had just returned from a pre-dawn staff meeting at Crumps Landing where General Wallace had his headquarters. He called Mathan to his portable desk and eyed him with concern. "Mathan, I'd like you to take word to the Company Commanders. It's simple: 'Be ready to march by eight AM.'"

Leggett went on, "When you return, I'm going to ask you to go back to the landing for me. There may be mail for us and I don't want to leave it in the hands of the Division and hope it catches up with us later. There may be something more going on."

Mathan nodded and began his walk along a mile of road to the North of the town. He visited each of the Company commanders and none seemed surprised. Mathan's walk was familiar by now, and pleasant. The dim light of earliest dawn cast gray light over fruit blossoms, early bulbs. The landscape blushed in soft shades of gray-green. He passed, small clusters of men standing at fires, eating breakfast, their bacon scenting the air downwind for a hundred yards. Behind the lines, supply wagons were in good order, mules were content, it was quiet.

As Mathan delivered the orders to the final Company commander, a breeze brought the far-away sound of thunder. Going to Crump's Landing to collect mail, Mathan rode through camps and wagon-parks. The ride took fifteen minutes. During the ride, Mathan realized the sounds were not thunder, but were distant artillery. When he reached the landing, there was considerable excitement at the river's edge.

Mathan dismounted and tied his horse to a rope line. Ensuring it was secure, he made his way to the Postal Service Tent where he signed for a canvas bag of mail for his Regiment.

Stepping outside into the early morning light, he saw Grant's boat, *The Tigress* under full steam, nearing the landing from the direction of Savannah. Mathan recognized General Wallace hurrying from headquarters to the landing. Wallace was followed closely by a skittering clutch of senior officers.

The Tigress didn't land or quell its engine, it simply tied up to Wallace's boat. Mathan recognized Grant at the rail, speaking hurriedly to Wallace. Mathan was much too far away to hear what was said but he recognized unfamiliar urgency in Grant's demeanor.

Grant's uncharacteristic tension was more than matched by Wallace's remarkable deference. After only a couple of minutes, Grant's boat pulled away. Wallace saluted his commander and turned immediately to his own staff. After speaking a few words, they scattered like pheasants flushed by a hungry dog.

One of the Majors hurried from the landing to the quartermaster's tent. Mathan recognized him. "James!" Mathan called as he jogged to the older Major. "I'm going back to my Regiment with mail. Can you tell me what's going on?"

James looked around like he was trapped. He stared into Mathan's eyes, then put his hand on Mathan's shoulder. "This is for you, only! If we start rumors, it'll only confuse the real orders when they come. I don't know exactly what they'll be, but I can tell you there's big fight beyond Pittsburg Landing. Been going on since before dawn and we're likely to move that way."

Mathan nodded and thanked his friend, threw the mail bag over his shoulder and leaped into the saddle. He raced back to Colonel Leggett who stepped through the tent-flap as Mathan dismounted. Mathan repeated the Major's warnings but before he could finish his report, a runner from Colonel Whittelsey's headquarters arrived with a paper in hand.

Opening the order carefully, Leggett looked at Mathan and said, "We're moving South to join on Sherman. Our Regiment is the third of three in line with the Brigade. The 56th Ohio is pulling back to Crumps as the rear guard. We'll be the last in the order of march. We need to be ready to fall into line by 9:00 AM."

Others were listening and Leggett repeated the orders, then sent Mathan on the same rounds he'd made in the early morning, only this time telling each Company commander to be ready by 8:45. The meeting dispersed suddenly with men hurrying in different directions. Despite their experience, chaos reigned.

The 78th Ohio stored their gear in wagons and packed rations for the day, only to wait hours to begin the march. They waited all morning as thousands of men passed them. The head of the Brigade marched West, then South and their passing took the entire morning. About noon, the column stopped in its tracks. Mathan and the others could see their place at end of the line and were ready to fall in. But the column just stood there, seemingly frozen for two hours.

Leggett's men watched in confusion. Thirty minutes after the line stopped, a rider came down the column with orders to get off the road, but to stay in line. Ninety minutes later, the first Regiment that passed them in the morning reappeared, now marching back the way they had come.

Days later, Mathan learned General Wallace misunderstood Grant's intentions. Instead of following the road to the rear of Grant's position at Pittsburg Landing, Wallace undertook what he thought would be a more direct route to the fighting. Going to the far right, next to Sherman's Division.

Only when messengers reached Wallace to tell him Sherman had been pushed back over a mile and Wallace was marching into danger, did Wallace decide to "Countermarch," instead of just facing everyone in the opposite direction and saving time.

A countermarch required Wallace's column of 5,000 men to reverse course, like a snake reversing direction along the same path it had just followed. When the line was completely reversed, it was well after 2:00 PM. Only then, was there space at the end of the line for the Third Brigade to fall into line with Mathan's Regiment the last one to join.

The road they followed had been softened by rain, but the passage of ten thousand men, their animals, wagons and artillery churned the road into a mushy stew. It became even worse as they picked up the road from Crumps to Pittsburg Landing. Men, mules and horses slogged through an ankle-deep quagmire of mud, animal droppings and gravel. Frequently, goo filled the soldiers' shoes. Too often, the muck held their shoes fast. Men walked right out of them, forcing the barefoot, muddy, exhausted soldiers to retrieve, empty and replace their brogans.

In rapidly fading light, Lew Wallace's men were still two miles from their destination and it was raining lightly. Hundreds of dead animals and human bodies were scattered along the road and beyond. The column encountered countless stragglers and wandering gaggles of soldiers, all separated from their officers.

Not long after full darkness, as rain came down in sheets, the 78th reached their stopping place. In soaking darkness, they took their places on the far right of the Army, far to the west of the day's heaviest fighting. Campfires were banned. The men were given permission to "sleep" in the open with their rifles at their sides.

Near Shiloh Church and further South, Federal forces had taken a beating. As they backed away from the pressure of the Rebel Army, their lines constricted around Pittsburg Landing. Mathan's mentor, Webster, organized an immense collection of artillery. It stopped the Rebel Army and keeping them at bay overnight. Buell's Army arrived and took their places alongside Grant's Army. Grant had no thought of withdrawal; the next day would be different.

NEAR SHILOH CHURCH,
APRIL 7, 1862

Predawn was cold, wet and very dark. Mathan shivered as he followed the long row of men organizing themselves into a battle line on the edge of a field. Colonel Whittelsey's Brigade was still the very last in line and they looked anxiously even further to the West, remembering Fort Donelson and fearing the arrival of a force on their unprotected flank. With dawn, their attention moved to the East, where the crackle of firing rose quickly and became steady, accentuated by roaring artillery.

Mathan struggled to stifle his trembling as he stood quietly behind Leggett and the other bone-chilled staff officers. There were eight Companies across their front and two more directly behind them as a reserve. The men kept their weapons in hand but were allowed to kneel or sit where they were aligned.

Nothing happened at dawn. The noise of fighting from their left roared and didn't abate all morning. The men of the 78th were anxious to join the fight and their discontented muttering caught Mathan's attention.

Mathan was quiet. Belmont and Donelson merged into a single memory. Loneliness crept into his mind. Nothing was happening. No riders came. No enemy appeared. As the others groused about their exclusion from yet another fight, Mathan remained tense and alert.

Hours passed as Mathan felt himself begin to sag under the burden of delay, hunger, cold and memory. He was acutely aware of being the only one who had seen a big fight. Had seen fresh wounds, painful death and pooled blood. He remembered the cat-like wailing of attacking Southerners. He told himself to remain ready. This was Colonel Leggett's fight to lead, if it came to that.

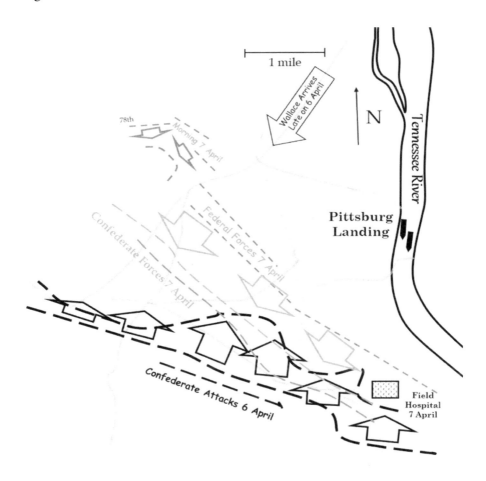

Map of Shiloh Battlefield , April 6-7, 1862

Before noon, a rider arrived with orders. The rows of men watched expectantly as Colonel Leggett listened, nodded and looked to his left, where the courier pointed. A moment later, instructions rippled down the line. The men faced left and followed. Mathan learned they were to align themselves with Colonel Thayer's Brigade a few hundred yards in front of their position. They marched through wet grass, still attentive to firing in the distance, but also hearing an occasional spent bullet whizzing overhead or plopping into the soil. In a few minutes, they were in place. They presented themselves to the enemy, over half a mile away. Nothing happened. They waited for drums and bugles to signal their advance but still, nothing happened. After an hour of standing there, they were ordered to withdraw. They began to march in the direction from which they'd just come.

The men's grumbling quieted abruptly when they heard firing in the direction they were marching. They moved faster, looping behind some woods before coming to the front at the edge of some woods, facing south across the large open field.

There were several snipers in the trees across an open field in front of the Ohio men, but they were too far away to hurt anyone. Mathan was satisfied with marching or waiting in preference to fighting but the men of the 78th wanted a fight. To their disappointment, the sharpshooters withdrew when they realized more than a thousand men were coming to get them. As the last snipers fled, orders arrived for the 78th.

They were, once more, ordered to march to their left and line up behind the 20th Ohio. Colonel Leggett turned command over to Lieutenant Colonel Woods, while Leggett went forward to speak to the new commander of the 20th, Colonel Force. Leggett knew Force, as both were lawyers from the Southeastern part of the state. They chatted amiably for several minutes while their men watched.

When Leggett returned, tension rose. There was a battery of Confederate artillery in the woods across the way and the 78th were going to follow the 24th Indiana and 20th Ohio who would cross the open field and capture the guns. While the younger men of the 78th were very disappointed to be, again, in a supporting role, Mathan had no wish to run toward artillery.

The 78th Ohio watched as the men of the other two Regiments entered the field ahead of them. They had progressed only a hundred yards when cannons, still hundreds of yards distant, belched fire at them. Each gun firing a sack of steel balls, like a giant shotgun. The balls bounced into men, shattering limbs or smashing ribs and skulls.

The two advance Regiments stopped and lay down, firing toward the guns. The men of the 78th hadn't moved yet but were also down. No need to expose themselves to an enemy their rifles couldn't reach.

Mathan heard a man grunt as if he'd been kicked. Fifty yards to his right, Mathan saw another soldier he didn't recognize, raise a hand to his head. The wounded man struggled to his feet, staggered a few steps to the rear, then collapsed. A couple of men from the reserve companies ran forward to carry the limp soldier away.

For an hour, the men of the 78th crouched or lay in lines, inside the edge of the woods. They watched as other men from Ohio and Indiana continued to fire at the distant artillery. Past two in the afternoon, a Lieutenant with the red tabs of an artillery officer appeared next to Leggett.

"Colonel Leggett?" asked Lieutenant Thurber.

"You have guns with you?" asked Leggett without exchanging pleasantries.

"Battery of five, sir."

"Well, I think you have targets across the field there."

Raising his field glasses, the Lieutenant grunted in disappointment.

"Problem, Lieutenant?" asked Leggett with his eyes searching the distance.

"Must have seen us arrive. They're limbered and about to ride off. I won't be able to get a shot at 'em."

"Are you unlimbering?"

"Just among those trees there, sir."

"Clear that field in front of us, won't you?"

Lieutenant Thurber smiled and saluted Leggett. "Pleased to sir!"

Within five minutes, there was a simultaneous explosion of all five pieces. Each gun fired a few times as Lieutenant Thurber's men sent round after round into the woods across the field.

The last of the big guns fired and it became very quiet for five minutes. Men in the field from Indiana and Ohio rose. Colonel Whittlesey sent word to advance across the ground just vacated by the Confederate battery. Resistance disappeared. By three that afternoon, the entire Brigade had advanced nearly two miles. The only Rebels they saw for the rest of the day were dead, wounded or captured.

When the advance came to a well-used dirt road and stopped, the 78th was aligned between her sister Regiments of Whittlesey's Third Brigade. It was eerily quiet on this part of the field. And despite low rumblings to the South, the 78th was finished for the day. Leggett turned to Mathan and asked, "One killed and a handful wounded?"

"Yes sir. As far as we know now. No one is missing."

"Less action than I'd expected."

"Yes sir." Mathan was waiting for Colonel Leggett to speak.

"You still have friends with Grant's Staff?"

"Yes sir, I believe there are still several there."

"Let's have you take a message to a friend of mine on the staff. I appreciate what you brought back this morning with the mail and I want you to keep your eyes and ears open. I want to know what's happening with the Army. I'm sure Colonel Whittlesey and General Wallace will fill us in, but I'm happy for another perspective. Can you get to Pittsburg Landing and find us again before ten or eleven tonight?"

"Yes sir. I'll see what I can learn. Anything in particular you'd like to know?"

"No, I don't want to focus you on the wrong things. Just find out what they determine from today's activities. We didn't see much, but as far as we advanced and as much firing as we heard, I imagine tomorrow will be important."

That afternoon, Mary Ann stood below Rachel's perch on the edge of the bluff. Breeze rustled Rachel's skirt as she strained to see movement in the distance. "Rachel, do you see anything?"

"You mean besides all those boats headed back down river with our wounded? No, all I see is smoke rising from the woods. Less of that now than when we looked this morning."

"If I'm right, we'll be receiving wounded from across the river for a long time. It's going to be even busier." Mary Ann paused, then added. "I received a message from Dr. Irwin at about noon today."

Stepping down from her perch to the road, Rachel tried to appear unconcerned, but there was tension in her voice when she said, "And?"

"He said he's taken possession of Colonel Stuart's old camp near the river. Said he wants to make it a hospital and asked for all his Brigade's supplies and anything else we can offer. Said he has over 100 tents and room for at least 300 men. Wants everything: bandages, clothing, food and most of all, he wants people."

"Can we help him?"

"I want to stay here or across the river at Pittsburg Landing to supervise loading the boats. If we're careful when we put them aboard, they're much more likely to survive the trip. I want you to talk to the Allens and send enough people to operate a laundry and kitchen for 250. I'll check on you later. But listen to me," she added with her hand on Rachel's to ensure her full attention, "You are not to cross that river unless and until I've spoken to General Grant's headquarters and I'm sure it's safe, understand?"

"I understand. Is Doctor Murray going over?"

"I haven't spoken to him, but I suspect he'll stay at our hospital. It's closer to headquarters and the landings. Too busy for him to go across right now, but maybe later."

Rachel found Pastor Allen at the warehouse, "Pastor, can you load the Fourth Brigade's medical supplies in a few of their wagons and get two more for extra food and supplies?"

"Yes, Miss Rodgers. How soon would you like them ready?"

"Doctor Irwin has asked that we send them across the river immediately. How quickly do you suppose you can be ready to take them?"

"Maybe an hour?"

"I'll see you right here, with the wagons in two hours. Thank you!"

Pastor Allen nodded and Rachel set off to find Mrs. Allen who was at the laundry.

"Mrs. Allen, can you get together enough cooks and laundresses to serve two hundred fifty men without ruining our operation here?"

"What do you need?" Mrs. Allen asked incredulously. "Why do we need that?"

"Doctor Irwin is moving his medical supplies across the river to a camp he's using someplace over there. He said he's short of orderlies and help."

"Will they be safe?" asked Mrs. Allen anxiously.

If we get Doctor Irwin's support, we'll have General Nelson's support and if Bull Nelson wants our Black attendants to be safe, they'll be safe."

Mrs. Allen looked into Rachels' face and asked gently, "So you're thinking *you* have the best chance of getting Doctor Irwin's support?"

"I do, Mrs. Allen. I know the kind of man he is.

They loaded their supplies and helpers on one of the smaller boats shuttling across the river to collect and transfer wounded soldiers. With help from Grant's headquarters, Rachel, Mrs. Allen and their supplies were guided behind Union lines and parallel to the river. They found Doctor Irwin's hospital a couple of miles South, in a clearing near three good, fresh-water springs.

The camp quickly became the first field hospital ever operated by the US Army. Wounded soldiers came directly from the field and stayed until they were well enough to tolerate the ambulance ride to the landing and at least 48 hours aboard ships.

Three days later, early on the morning of the 10th of April, Mary Ann arrived with the first of the Assistant Surgeons who had accompanied wounded to Cairo and returned to the battlefield. She showed up at Doctor Irwin's hospital with a squad of soldiers.

Climbing briskly down from the ambulance, Mary Ann took three long strides with her hand extended to Doctor Irwin. Not waiting for pleasantries, she began, "Dr. Irwin, I've met with Dr. Murray. Have you heard from him?"

"I spoke to him last evening, Mrs. Bickerdyke. What's on your mind?"

Mary Ann saw Rachel appear from the command tent, walking toward the conversation, but stopping behind Irwin as she brushed her skirt smooth.

Mary Ann sensed that Rachel was, just for a moment, embarrassed. "I've learned General Halleck will replace General Grant tomorrow. General Buell's and General Grant's staffs will function under General Hallek's command. Doctor Brinton won't be back for a while, so Doctor Charles McDougall is the Medical Director for the Army here."

"I've heard that," said Doctor Irwin patiently. "What can I do for you Mrs. Bickerdyke?"

"I'll be moving our operation to Pittsburg Landing from Savannah. I understand we have at least three large tent-hospitals like yours here, is that correct?"

"It is."

"Doctor Brinton sent us more ambulances and a handful of men to take care of our collection of ambulances and their mules. Doctor McDougall wants to centralize ambulances to coordinate transfers from the hospitals to the hospital ships. The fighting isn't over and we're getting more sickness each day.

"I've seen that too, Mrs. Bickerdyke. It seems that as quickly as I empty the bed of a wounded soldier, it's occupied by a sick one." Irwin paused and looked back at Rachel but spoke to Mary Ann. "Miss Rodgers and her staff have been invaluable to us here. I hope we can continue to count on her support?"

Mary Ann gave Rachel a hard glance, then replied to Irwin, "Of course Doctor. She's very important to the entire operation. I'll leave her with you as long as possible, but I recommend that you and she plan for a replacement in the coming week. I need her help at Cairo, coordinating the arrival and distribution of supplies and the attendants who will stay with them."

Without looking at Rachel, Irwin nodded at Mary Ann, who spoke again.

"I'd like to introduce you to Sergeant Himmelstoss and his men." They'll be at the landing with me, and they'll take charge of dispatching, maintaining, and repairing the ambulances. They'll keep teams available as well. Rachel, would you have Pastor Allen show him around?"

Irwin then looked to Rachel and said "Miss Rodgers, would you please see to the Sergeant? Also, we'll be sending ten ambulances to the landing right after breakfast. Could you be sure those who are leaving have fresh bandages and all their possessions before they go?" He turned back to Mary Ann and smiled. Will there be anything else I can do? Would you like to tour our hospital?"

"Thank you, not today, Doctor. I hope to return tomorrow if our work allows it. I'd enjoy a tour then if it's convenient."

Mary Ann shook Doctor Irwin's hand again and watched for a moment as he turned toward Rachel. Mary Ann was surprised to see Rachel step quickly away from Irwin.

Pastor Allen walked toward Rachel, wiping his hands with a rag. As she turned to introduce Sergeant Himmelstoss her friend shouted, "Axel!" as he rushed to his old friend.

"Alex!" beamed Himmelstoss as he stepped close enough to Pastor Allen to embrace him. "You're here!"

"I am. What brings you?"

"Mrs. Bickerdyke saw to it that I was detailed to headquarters. We have a Lieutenant, and we manage the ambulances for the whole Army in Tennessee. I'm supposed to see to the hospital."

Rachel was surprised by their familiarity and waited to begin the tour.

"Miss Rodgers," said Pastor Allen confidently. "The Sergeant is a great friend from home in Ohio! I can show him the hospital if that's alright?" Rachel assented quickly and watched with some surprise as the two men walked together in the direction of the ambulances, both were gesturing and talking loudly.

As Mary Ann, who was not surprised at the reunion of old friends, rode away, Irwin turned to Rachel saying, "Perhaps we can continue our discussion some other time," he paused briefly, smiled and added, "Soon." And he walked back to his tent.

Rachel checked the people still near enough to have heard, fearful they'd recognized his veiled reference. Her cheeks glowed for a moment and she hurried to her work.

"Axel! How did you get here?" Asked Pastor Allen with a big smile.

"You won't be surprised Alex," began the big Sergeant. "Our Mrs. Bickerdyke has been sending lots of your people up North with the patients. She knows that transportation from the lines where they come in, to the rear is the most important time for them. She knows people who'll help them on their way. Lots of your people too."

"Since we have plenty of work for the women at the hospitals, she wanted to make sure we get the right people in the right places." He smiled at Allen adding, "Ambulances can go anywhere, just about any time and no one asks questions. Makes it easier to check on people and let them know what's next."

Allen nodded with approval, "Good thought, Axel."

"Glad you think so. Mrs. Bickerdyke said I'm to bring you and Mrs. Allen back to Pittsburg landing with me. She says you're essential people and she wants to keep you close."

"I'm happy to go back with you but it might not be so easy with Mrs. Allen. She's worried about Miss Rodgers."

Himmelstoss looked back over his shoulder in time to see Rachel go around the corner of one of the supply tents. "What's that about?"

"You remember that young Captain after Fort Donelson? The one who brought the wagon we loaded with three special crates?"

"Sure! Captain Stark! What about him?"

Mr. Allen looked at his friend and smiled.

Himmelstoss looked back at where Rachel had been. Then looked at Alexander. It took a few seconds. "Ohhh!" he said. "The Captain and that one?"

Allen nodded, sadly.

Himmelstoss thought for a moment, remembering Doctor Irwin's demeanor and Rachel's emergence from his tent. "Ohhh," he repeated in a concerned tone. "That's not good."

Mrs. Allen thinks Miss Rodgers has been careful so far, but my wife is very fond of Miss Rodgers and very protective. She's heard rumors about that Doctor. Was a hero in the Indian fighting before we got him, and he seems to think he's never had a bad idea in his life."

"I see," said Axel thoughtfully. "Maybe you want to stay with Mrs. Allen until we can get all three of you back?"

"That's a tough choice. Miss Rodgers has a plan but let me talk to her and we can decide when you come back tomorrow."

They finished their tour, the Allens said their good-byes and Himmelstoss drove his ambulance out of the compound without seeing Rachel or Doctor Irwin again.

Newly-promoted, Brigadier General John A. Logan stood on the steps of the Cherry Mansion, looking West, across the river. Major General Lew Wallace faced the same view but stood at the bottom of the steps.

"General Wallace?" asked Logan from above.

Turning to the sound of the voice and shielding his eyes from the sun, Wallace answered, "Yes, I am, but I can't see you for the sun."

Logan came down the steps to stand on Wallace's left. "I'm sorry, General. We've met before. I'm John Logan, Illinois."

"Of course! Black Jack! So good to see you again." He paused, looking back across the river. "Terrible thing about HL (General WHL Wallace). Smith's not doing well either, I'm afraid."

Logan grunted. "Terrible."

They stood side-by-side without speaking for several minutes. Logan looked at (Major General Lew) Wallace with concern. "More on your mind than that, I think?"

Looking sharply at Logan, Wallace said, "Really? What have you heard?"

Logan decided not to be coy, but also, not to judge the man. "I heard there was confusion getting your Division into the fight and that you did very well the second day." He waited for a change in Wallace's demeanor, but it didn't come, so he added, "I hear you may be moved to the reserve with McClernand."

"Where did you hear that?" demanded Wallace with his face beginning to reveal anger.

Logan looked at him and waited.

"Grant told you, didn't he?"

Logan nodded as Wallace returned his gaze to the river.

"I have a little whiskey. Can I offer you some?" asked Logan consolingly.

"I think so, Jack." Wallace sized up the newly minted General Logan. Then he asked, "Shall we walk?" After a few steps he added "Would you mind calling me Lew when the men aren't about? Not feeling 'the General' just now."

The men walked toward Savannah, stopping at a small inn that had been transformed into sort of an "Officers' Club." They found a quiet corner and Logan produced a flask, called for service and stood a glass of beer on either side of his flask. He poured a long draft of whiskey into each beer and picked his up. "To Union!"

Wallace clinked his glass against Logan's and made eye contact, "To Union!" Wallace drank his beer in a single draft and held up the mug for more. When the owner returned with a full mug, Logan enriched it again. Wallace took it a bit more slowly the second time. "Hell of a birthday Jack," said Wallace, looking into his beer glass.

"Your birthday? Congratulations on …" Logan paused, reconsidering his words. "How old today Lew?"

"Today, I am thirty-five years old. Old enough to be president."

"What's got you?"

Wallace looked at Logan briefly, then stared into the distance. "You talked to Grant. He's been set aside by Halleck. Surprised he's not here drinking with us," added Wallace glumly.

"I spoke to Grant just before I saw you on the steps. Sober as can be. Disappointed, *and* sober."

"Deserves it! At Donelson, he was off the field when Ogelsby was about to be overrun, but," Wallace paused and looked at Logan for a reaction, "you were there. You know that my counter-attack saved him from disaster. And then, Monday, the same thing. He's up here at Savannah when all hell breaks loose at Pittsburg and he comes to tell me I have to do it again, only this time, he forgets to tell me Sherman has been pushed all the way back." Wallace shook his head and looked down. "Got there too late to make a difference on Sunday. Buell gets credit for Monday. My Division mostly watched at a distance."

Logan nodded in understanding more than agreement. "You really saved my Regiment at Donelson. We were out of ammunition and hanging in the air. If you hadn't come up, you'd have to share your beer with someone else. I owe you."

"I'm thirty-five years old today. I'm the youngest Major General in the Army. And I'm about to be returned to the Reserve and relegated because Grant needs someone to blame for Sunday's mistakes."

"You figure your war's over, Lew?"

"This part sure is. Halleck sacked Grant and Grant took me down with him."

"You have any plans?"

Wallace sat back and looked gloomily at Logan. "John, I know you're no abolitionist. And I know just as firmly, you're a Unionist and a hell of a fighter."

Logan lowered his head and nodded gently.

"When I was a boy, I read about the Algerine pirates and what they did to the Europeans they captured. To the whites. To the women and children. Did you ever read about that?"

Logan shook his head and looked at Wallace. "Heard about it a little. I thought we finished that nearly fifty years ago. Never thought much about it."

"No, John. They're still at it. Not Englishmen and Americans, but white Europeans and anyone they can get their hands on, for that matter. When I was a boy and I read about that, it didn't take much for me to realize we do the exact same thing to Blacks. I won't ignore that."

"It's not the same, Lew." Said Logan, sensing the irrationality of his statement even as he spoke it. Trying to recover his position he said, "We're Christians."

Wallace rolled his eyes, then looked at Logan for a long moment. Out the window, both men noticed three black women carrying huge bundles of laundry in the direction of the hospital.

The younger General lowered his head and shook it, saying softly, "He sent me to proclaim freedom for the prisoners, recovery of sight for the blind and to set the oppressed free." He looked into Logan's eyes and asked, "Are you blind, John? Don't you see the humanity?"

Logan's mind was still on the captive Europeans. His first thought was that he'd die fighting before he allowed himself to be taken as a slave. Next, he felt outrage as he imagined Mary's vulnerability. He recalled Mrs. Allen's hand on his forehead. Her kindness and concern. Her eyes. He remembered his father's concern for Black families.

Logan looked to Wallace. "You recited Luke. I've always held Luke 12 in mind, 'For unto whomsoever much is given, of him shall also, much be required; and to whom men have committed much, of him they will ask the more.'"

Wallace put his hand on Logan's arm. "In that Chapter of Luke, Christ was warning us against complacency. But you've seen slavery. You know what it means, what it does. You know better. I know you can't ignore that."

Logan returned his arm to his side and looked out the window. He didn't want to think about this. He didn't answer but sat for a few moments.

Wallace recognized the risk of saying more. "You were badly hurt at Donelson?"

"Not that badly. Bruises mostly, and a hole in my shoulder that's about healed by now. I'm ready to get back into it."

"I'm glad you're here. What will you be doing?"

Logan smiled and sat back. "Sounds like we'll be working pretty closely. I'm taking the First Brigade in McClernand's Division of Reserves."

"Who will you have, Logan?"

I'll have the 31st Ohio, my old Regiment. Doff Ozburn has taken my place there. Lawler and his guys from the 18th Illinois, Dennis and his from the 30th. Quinn from the 12th Michigan. Looks like 'Old Brains' has a plan for us to build trenches from here to Corinth. Couldn't be more different from Grant."

Wallace nodded in silent agreement. He finished his second fortified beer and placed the mug on the table solemnly. "I have to go Logan. It was good to see you. I'm looking forward to the next time, whenever that will be."

Logan rose and took Wallace's hand. "Likewise, Lew. This could be a long war. I'll see you again."

They left together, but Logan returned to the Cherry Mansion and Wallace went to his headquarters, across the river.

Mary Ann was leaving the building as Logan returned. "Mrs. Bickerdyke!" he called her name as she came down the steps.

"Colonel ... General Logan!" she said extending her hand. "You are back with us and looking quite well," she said, looking at him, then back at the upstairs of the Cherry Mansion.

Logan followed her eyes. "General Smith?" He asked with concern.

"He passed. Such a shame. General Grant is shaken," she added sadly.

"Smith was Grant's professor at West Point, was in charge here, at the beginning. He was the General's friend." Logan waited.

"So it would seem," she added. "Dr. Brinton was with him as he passed."

Logan expressed surprise, "Doctor Brinton!"

"In the flesh. Seems he's going to remain to 'help us' with the next phase of the campaign."

"Your plans?" Logan asked solicitously.

"We'll take our hospitals and follow the Army South. I suspect we'll stay near the river for the most part." She thought to test him. "There are so many fugitives and contrabands. I can employ many of them, but not all. Most I have to send North. General Logan, you know General Grant was amenable to the movements, but General Halleck is taking over from Grant and I wonder whether you know his sympathies."

"Mrs. Bickerdyke, I believe General Halleck has little interest in or sympathy for the problem, except to ensure it does not interfere with his operations."

"And you General Logan?" asked Mary Ann with genuine interest. "How are your thoughts progressing on this subject?"

"Mrs. Bickerdyke, I am here to preserve the Union. I would do nearly anything to preserve it. My time with you and Mrs. Allen has made me think about things. I am still, no abolitionist, but I must admit, I am no friend to the slaveholder."

"General, you must know that slavery is pure evil. It was a mistake not to get rid of it when we became independent. The Mexican War may have been a dastardly appropriation of another nation's land, but slavery is the theft and scourge of countless souls, and in that, it is profoundly craven."

"You have some strong opinions Mrs. Bickerdyke. I'm sure lots of your friends share them." Logan paused and looked at the gathering of General

Officers, come to acknowledge Smith's death. "Thank you very much, for the care and concern you and Mrs. Allen showed me at Fort Donelson. I am ever in your debt." He paused gravely. "Now, I really must go."

Mary Ann shook his hand and looked into his eyes. "Think about it General. Pray," she added gravely, "about emancipation."

Logan did not shrug off her words. Those words and his experiences were changing Logan's heart and, soon, would change his mind.

A couple of days later, Leggett returned to the 78th's camp on the West side of the battlefield. The wounded were in hospitals or had been shipped home. The bodies were nearly all buried but there was still disease and many more men from the 78th were stricken by disease at Shiloh than had been injured in combat. The Colonel called his officers to a meeting before supper.

Mathan was there with twenty officers, waiting for Leggett beneath a large tree on the edge of their camp. A few men had camp stools, but most stood and waited.

Leggett arrived and began to speak immediately. "I've returned from Savannah where I met with most of the Regimental Commanders under Generals McClernand and Wallace. The 78th will remain aligned as we are, in the Third Division, Third Brigade under General Wallace and Colonel Whittelsey. We will move South behind the center of three columns converging on Corinth. We are part of an Army of 120,000 men."

"You'll hear about this anyway, so I'm about to tell you what really happened. I don't want you to fall prey to rumors. It's simply this: This morning, General Halleck arrived. He has taken command of the entire operation and he's made General Grant his deputy." A few of the younger officers drew breath audibly. "You'll also hear something of what General Halleck said. He said that the combined Armies of Ohio and Tennessee won a decisive victory. He said our success has opened the road to Corinth, the heart of the South and that we will divide the Eastern and Western halves of the Confederacy. He said we'd be moving South. He also had some strong words about the first day of fighting." At this, the officers murmured among themselves.

"General Halleck was clear in his opinions, and you should know them because they reveal a difference between General Halleck and General Grant. General Halleck attributed our problems on the first day to a lack of preparation, a failure to construct field defenses and a lack of a clear focus for our Army." The men were surprised by the harsh assessment of Grant, a man they universally admired and respected.

"Let me say this as well. General Grant accepted his commander's appraisal without the slightest expression of disagreement or rancor. He will serve as General Halleck's second-in-command and will oversee operations to maintain our lines of supply."

Leggett lowered his voice and went on. "Men, here's the difference, as I see it, between how General Halleck and General Grant differ in their approach to the war. General Halleck believes in constructing defenses as part of every single movement the Army makes. We will reinforce our positions every time we stop. Trenches, dug-outs, header logs and rifle pits will be part of every encampment, every day. He moves very slowly and carefully.

"Now, here's my opinion, and I assure you, only my opinion about the difference between our two Generals. General Halleck believes the war will be won when we take their capitols, their railroads and their ports. He will concentrate our efforts on those objectives. The Confederate army is of interest only as an impediment to his ends."

"On the other hand, General Grant views the objective as the destruction of the Confederate Army. Once it is destroyed, he believes resistance to Union will cease. Simple difference. We'll attack cities or we'll attack Armies. Either way, we'll attack and I need you to be prepared to do that.

For now, we will equip and provision ourselves in anticipation of movements to begin in about a week."

Leggett looked into the faces of his officers. "Questions?" The young men looked to one another for questions, but none spoke or signaled. "Very Well. You are dismissed, except for Captain Stark and Lieutenant Peterson."

The other of the officers left Leggett, Peterson and Mathan alone. Leggett continued, "Lieutenant Peterson, I will ask you to become my assistant, is that alright with you?" Then he added, "Stark will be leaving us."

"Y-Yes Sir," stammered Peterson, looking at Mathan.

"Good, you can begin in the morning, after breakfast. You may go now, Peterson."

Mathan felt his heart sink. He had no idea what was coming next, but trusted Leggett.

"Stark, I ran into General Logan. Yes, *General* Logan. He's taking a Reserve Brigade as well, under McClernand again and you know how he feels about McClernand?"

"I have a good idea Sir."

"Well, I believe all of us would be better served if you were back on his Logan's staff. I've arranged for you to report to him tomorrow. McClernand's First Division, First Brigade. Alright?"

Mathan paused, trying to read Colonel Leggett's face.

"Mathan, I'm not likely to stay with the Regiment much longer. The Army is expanding, and our experience makes us valuable at the next levels of command."

"Sir, do you happen to know whether General Logan's Brigade includes the 31st Illinois? His former Regiment?"

Leggett smiled and looked at the ground between them, then looked up at Mathan. "Ozburn?" He asked.

"Well, yes, sir. Major Ozburn had little use or respect for me, and…"

"Wait Mathan. First of all, it's Colonel Ozburn now. He commands the 31st Illinois." Leggett watched Mathan's face fall. "Second, I discussed the very thing with General Logan and he knows the kind of man Ozburn is and understands his reactions to you as jealousy. Logan believes that Ozburn will be too busy with the Regiment, and too full of himself to be threatened by a young Major."

"A Major, Sir?"

"Yes. You'll be promoted when you arrive. Back into the black tabs, I believe. Congratulations!"

"Thank you, Sir," said Mathan softly. "I'll miss you very much Sir, and the rest of the Regiment."

"Don't worry, Stark. I suspect the 78th will see more of General Logan in the future. I can't say more for now, but I'll see you again."

SOUTHERN TENNESSEE, LATE APRIL 1862

120,000 soldiers clustered near the landings of Savannah, Pittsburg and Crump along the upper Tennessee River. The soldiers were visited by countless merchants who followed the Army with wagons and tents, selling whatever the soldiers would buy. There were also reporters, curiosity seekers and camp followers. Roads were crowded and strangers seemed to roam freely.

Irwin's hospital was an oasis amidst the squalor. The terrain stood above marshy ground. Latrines drained away from the springs. Roads led to and from important places. Supplies were abundant. There were enough helpers.

Following the carnage around Shiloh Church and Pittsburg Landing, Doctor Irwin's field hospital was busy. As wounded men recuperated sufficiently to travel, Irwin approved their movement and Rachel ensured the men were clean, fed and escorted to their ships. The amputees' places were taken by victims of every disease that thrives on an encamped and sweat-soaked Army.

Mary Ann was preoccupied with the hospital ships and ensuring the men aboard were well cared-for from the battlefield to their destinations further North. Rachel was on her own in the war for the first time. At night, on her cot, the weight of death was suffocating. Images of shattered men kept her from sleep just as it had Mathan and Logan. When exhaustion forced unconsciousness upon her, the images haunted her dreams. Echoes of screams, anguish, grief and despair came unbidden and often. Profound helplessness froze her, and she wept silently. These times came, went, and always came back again.

She awoke too early, then worked feverishly before the day began. When she wasn't busy with administration and paperwork, she helped nurses tend to the weakest and sickest. Sometimes, she relieved a laundress, taking her long paddle and stirring the boiling pots at a distance. Other times, she carried waste from tents.

It wasn't long before she had nearly exhausted her health. Rachel had no idea that anguish and passion were obverse and reverse. One intensified the other while both misled and possessed her. There was no rest, but there was John Irwin. In him, Rachel saw the traits she doubted in herself: Competence, confidence, strength and hope. He was gentle with her and he was obviously attracted to her.

Rachel sensed Irwin's lingering eyes often enough to know he wanted her to see him looking. For the past several days, he seemed to find any excuse to chat, and to extend conversations. One afternoon, she was helping him check a wounded soldier's sutures. Rachel felt him pressing his side against hers. This time, Rachel pretended not to notice. She became aware that she looked forward to his attention, to seeing him. To "bumping into" him.

The next day, Irwin slipped under the flaps and into her tent. This time, he didn't speak. He moved slowly towards her. Looking at him expectantly, Rachel felt her heart speed and her breath become shallow and quick. Irwin took her hands and stepped so close she could smell his body and feel its warmth. The impulse to step back was smothered by excitement. She was drawn to him as softly as a snowflake might tumble from the sky. F

She sensed he would kiss her, and she would let him. Even so, Rachel was surprised to find herself fervently returning his kiss. Without conscious thought, she pressed her body to his, aligned her arms and her hips with his. There was no time, only experience. Feelings of isolation, hopelessness and grief were outside. At last, her nightmares had competition.

It didn't end there.

As days passed, Rachel's sensuality arose involuntary and was increasingly welcomed. When work was routine and repetitious, her mind drifted to Irwin. Desire, draped beneath a gauzy fabric of romance, soon progressed to yearning. The tide of her emotions drowned concern about consequences. The shattered boys, the cries of the hopelessly ill and relentless administrative demands made time irrelevant. Time evaporated: and somehow, her guilt over betraying Mathan was pressed down under layers of emotion. Guilt was no match for the seductive mixture of pain, longing, and ardor.

Irwin was utterly ignorant that Rachel saw others' suffering as something she should share. He knew she was distressed, but couldn't understand, nor did he care, that she felt overwhelmed. He sensed only that she sought relief in romance, and he took full advantage of her feelings.

Irwin saw sickness and injury merely as problems to be solved. Some problems were simple. Others, complex. Some worthy of his effort, others futile. The greater his success in solving medical problems, the more certain he became of his competence, value and superiority.

He saw women in much the same way. They were creatures to be enjoyed. Some were simple, others complex. Some worthy of effort, others unrewarding. The greater his success in achieving their favor, the more certain he was of his desirability, charm and superiority. He developed an almost infinite capacity to absorb both knowledge and praise.

Although Irwin carefully ingratiated himself to her anxieties, he bore no sense of responsibility for Rachel's feelings. He accepted her admiration as his natural right and reassured her that she was dear to him. When he managed to be alone with her, he wrapped her in his arms and spoke tenderly. He praised her mind, expressed awe at her character, kissed her deeply and explored her body with insistent curiosity. She couldn't recognize his lack of commitment, unconcern for her feelings and shame-lessness. His were thoroughly disguised acts of prurience and self-indul-gence. Then Mathan arrived.

"Miss Rodgers," called Mrs. Allen rushing to intercept Mathan before he reached Rachel's tent, "There's a Major here to see you!"

Rachel froze for a moment, excited at the thought Doctor Irwin was there to see her. She rose quickly, brushed her hair back and straightened her apron. The tent flap rose and Mathan was framed by the morning light.

Rachel didn't move. She expected to see Irwin and failed to recog-nize Mathan immediately. As recognition dawned and she sensed warmth and joy. Her smile grew. At that moment, Irwin appeared behind Mathan, then pushed past him.

"There you are Rachel!" said Irwin brightly, "I've missed you this morning!" He saw Rachel's eyes on Mathan and thought little of it at first. But, Mathan recognized a tone in Irwin's greeting that told him more than he wanted to know.

The three were momentarily silent. Irwin was unused to waiting for Rachel to return his greeting and he followed Rachel's eyes to Mathan with curiosity. Irwin broke the quiet, asking Rachel, "Who's this?" his tone dismissive.

Mathan glanced from Rachel to Irwin, then back. When his eyes met hers, the delay in her response revealed her unease.

Her unease revealed the truth. It was not lost on Mathan, who looked back at Irwin, but said nothing.

Rachel did not introduce Mathan as quickly as someone usually introduces their fiancé. In fact, Rachel was overwhelmed.

Irwin resolved the confusion in his own mind by assuming the young visitor was an acquaintance at best, perhaps merely there on an errand. "I'm Doctor John Irwin, Division Surgeon. This is my hospital, and you are?" Irwin paused without extending his hand but edging nearer Rachel.

Mathan held Rachel's eyes and he replied without looking at Irwin, "I'm Captain, um, Major Stark. General Logan's staff."

She looked back silently, pleading without words. Trembling. Feeling tears fill her eyes.

Mathan was shaken, saying, "You're..." he paused but she said nothing. "Busy. I'll call again later." He didn't wait for her reply, turning his back on the pair and leaving them alone in the tent. It was that or beat the smarmy SOB to death on the spot.

Mathan strode away from the tent, blind to his surroundings and beyond the reach of words.

Mrs. Allen ran after Mathan who walked quickly, away from the hospital. "Major Stark!" she called to him in desperation.

He didn't stop so she scurried past him and turned, stepping directly in front of him, blocking his way. She put her hands on his shoulders. He stopped but looked over her head.

"Major Stark," Mrs. Allen nearly shouted, "You have to understand!"

He tried to go around her. One way, she blocked him. The other, again she stepped in front of him. She pressed her hands on his forearms even as he pulled away from her.

His eyes welled and he attempted once again, to step around her, but she cut him off and shook his forearms. "She's at the end of her rope. She didn't know you were here!"

"I - am - here!" he said through his teeth, fighting for self-control.

"Give her a chance to explain! That girl loves you!"

Mathan jerked his arms away from Mrs. Allen and looked away, this time blinking away tears of rage. "It didn't look that way to me!" he grunted, then strode away.

He passed ten thousand soldiers but saw no one and said nothing. Consumed by feelings of abandonment, jealousy, grief and rage, his heart hammered and his body trembled. He marched over two miles, past Shiloh

Church to Logan's headquarters without slowing and without recovering his composure. His soul blazed and his thoughts convulsed. As he reached his camp he paused.

Still for a moment, he scanned the camp spread before him. Unready to resume his duties, Mathan turned on his heel and started back to Rachel. He had taken but a few steps when he heard Logan's Adjutant, Major Hotaling call him, "Major Stark! Major Stark! The General wants to meet with us immediately!" The Adjutant didn't wait for Mathan to acknowledge him, instead hurrying on, presumably in search of other wayward staff officers.

Now that he had decided to confront Rachel and the Doctor, it strained every nerve to follow his order and relinquish his plans. Despite his heartache, he lowered his head and returned to the Headquarters area. The two-hour wait before the last of Logan's staff arrived was more torturous than any wait he'd endured before battle.

Logan came out of his tent and stood beneath a magnolia tree with arms folded. He told his staff to "Circle up!" The Regimental Commanders stood nearest their new Brigade Commander; their staffs mingled with Logan's on the periphery.

"We're moving tomorrow morning." He paused to make eye contact with each officer present. "We'll get marching orders later tonight, but our role is in the reserve. When something happens, we'll move directly to the hottest part of the fight. Until then, General Halleck will have us in close order, staying in place until advance fortifications are ready to receive us. Or, we leap-frog and build advanced camps for others, each night.

We will move slowly, or I suppose I should use the General's term, 'Deliberately.' He plans to entrench every night until we reach Corinth. And, when I say entrench," Logan paused for effect, "I mean we'll dig a twenty-mile-long line of trenches. We'll live behind them and in them." Logan paused and smiled sadly. "Questions?"

Not surprisingly, there were several questions about roads, supplies, sequences and timing. Logan or Hotaling answered each briefly and directly, obviously wanting to end the meeting. When the first "What-if," question was asked, Mathan's heart sank.

"What-if" questions are based on assumptions and require long answers filled with even more assumptions. Every new assumption provoked additional "What-ifs," eventually exhausting the patience of all but the most committed worriers. Mathan felt the choking urgency of speaking to Rachel. He knew he might not see her for a long time, once the Brigade broke camp.

To Mathan's surprise, Logan interrupted the third, "What if..."

"Men," began Logan with authority. "I don't like being in meetings with people who like being in meetings. I've never liked them and truly detest the long ones. They waste time, accomplish little and are dominated by the ones among us, who enjoy them! So, this one is over. If you have additional questions, check with your commanders."

Mathan tried to stay out of Logan's line of sight, lest he receive some task that would interfere with his return to Rachel. He stood behind a copse of trees, deciding it was safer to wait for the crowd to thin before exposing himself to questions. He was startled when a Sergeant appeared asking, "Alright if we strike your tent before breakfast tomorrow, Sir? We want to get the headquarters onto the wagons first thing."

Mathan considered his few, loose possessions, knowing he could toss them into his travel chest that night. He straightened his cap and answered, "I'm fine with that, but you'll have to tell the other officers I share with. I'll be away on an errand." The Sergeant grimaced, knowing he'd have to make a second visit and any problems the next morning would be attributed to his failure, not Mathan's.

"Yes Sir. I will." He turned and moved to the next tent.

The sun would set soon, and Mathan had to hurry. He cut through a stand of woods, hurrying the two miles Southeast, to the hospital as quickly as he could. Everyone and everything was in motion.

Mathan found a worn path through a wood lot before he caught sight of Rachel's hospital. Beginning to jog, he found his way to her tent without difficulty. He didn't notice how quiet the hospital seemed, or that there were no ambulances or wagons nearby. Breathing heavily and standing outside her tent he called, "Rachel! It's Mathan, Rachel!" There was no answer. He took a step nearer. He couldn't wait and pulled back the flap. The inside of her tent was very dim. And it was empty.

Halleck had seen one day of combat in the Mexican War, was a primary author of the California State Constitution and succeeded in that new state as an exceptionally successful land speculator while serving as an officer in the Regular Army. His nickname was "Old Brains," because at the age of just thirty, he had written, *Elements of Military Art and Science,* read by every cadet at West Point after 1846. A favorite of the ancient (seventy-five-year-old) and venerable (General of the Army) Winfield Scott, Halleck had a reputation for intelligence and organizational skill.

Now 47 years old and affirmed by General Scott's successor, George McClellan, Halleck reveled in control of the Army that won at Shiloh.

With a characteristic abundance of caution, he increased the size of his army by tens of thousands, eventually fielding over 100,000 men. He delighted in applying his long-held theories during a ten-day, eighteen-mile, mud-soaked crawl toward Corinth, Mississippi: the critical railroad hub in the region. Every day, men began by moving a mile or two, establishing a new camp with fortifications, only then breaking the old one.

The long respite after Shiloh allowed the Confederate Armies to rest, reorganize and reequip. Referring to the snail-paced advance, Logan wrote to Mary that his commander was, "Recklessly over-cautious." Later, disgusted by Halleck's lack of aggressiveness, Logan also wrote, "My men will never dig another ditch for Halleck except to bury him."

Long before Halleck's Army inched close enough to consider an attack on the railroad hub linking Memphis and Vickburg with the rest of the Confederacy, Halleck's scouts observed Corinth from a distance. They returned with reports of countless railroad trains arriving both day and night. Each arriving train was met with band music and cheering. Halleck concluded the trains were loaded with hordes of fresh reinforcements, harbingers of a titanic and imminent battle.

At the same time Halleck prepared for a cataclysmic engagement, Logan's experienced railroaders pressed their ears to tracks leading to Corinth and listened. They could tell the arriving trains were empty, but the departing trains were heavily laden. Their reports, at odds with Halleck's plans, were disregarded.

On the last day of May, with Halleck finally prepared to storm Corinth, a startling report arrived. The only thing Halleck's enormous army faced were abandoned defenses and empty buildings. Quaker guns (tree trunks on wheels, painted black and meant to look like cannons at a distance) guarded heaps of smoldering supplies amidst a vacant town. In his excitement, Halleck wrote to his wife, "I have won the victory without the battle!"

Unfortunately for his troops, General Halleck's caution cost his army the initiative. Taking the town meant little because the Confederate Army was resting, reorganizing, and re-equipping. Halleck's men would have to fight them again. Halleck controlled the railroad intersection but left others to fight the battles of Iuka and Corinth before the Rebel Army disengaged and crossed Tennessee into Kentucky where they seriously threatened Ohio. And Rachel.

A week after Halleck's army occupied Corinth, and ninety miles West, a handful of Union and Confederate steamboats met on the river in front of Memphis. The heavier and better armed Union ships sank or captured all but one Confederate vessel, receiving the city's surrender before lunchtime. Western Tennessee quickly came under the domination of Grant's Army.

With the fall of Memphis, Logan's Brigade was reinforced by a new Regiment: Mortimer Leggett's 78th Ohio Volunteers. Logan and his large Brigade were sent to Jackson Tennessee (between Corinth and Memphis) with orders to protect transportation routes in all directions.

Rachel stayed with the Army of the Ohio and with them, she waited for the well-rested Rebel Army to attack.

NEAR JACKSON, TENNESSEE, JUNE 1862

The cotton-town of Jackson, Tennessee was home to an essential railroad junction, connecting Nashville, Memphis, and Northern Mississippi. Grant hoped to reach Vicksburg from the East, after first moving South from Tennessee into Mississippi, then West, eventually assaulting Vicksburg from its vulnerable, Eastern side. Railroads were essential to supply his Army. While cotton and geography drew railroads to Jackson, the railroad drew Logan. His job was to protect Grant's supply lines.

Logan's march from Corinth back to Jackson was slowed by rain that swept the countryside every couple of days. The heat and humidity fostered hordes of every sort biting, stinging and swarming insect. While the insects fed on the Brigade, locals fled the thousands of approaching Federal troops. Cavalry scouts had little trouble keeping the route clear from Corinth to Jackson.

Mathan was riding behind Logan when the General turned over his shoulder and said, "Ride up here next to me, Stark. You're a friend of that Mrs. Bickerdyke and I have a question for you."

Mathan quickly reached Logan's side. "Yes Sir?" he asked quietly

They rode on for a few minutes while Logan considered how to approach the younger man. "Stark, I've heard you're a good friend of abolitionism. Is that right?"

Mathan paused, looking at Logan for some clue as to the reason for his question, but the General rode quietly and maintained a blank expression. "Well, yes, Sir. I am," and he said no more.

"Tell me why, Stark. I want to know why you think that way."

"Sir?"

"Stark, how did you come to the conclusion that we should be fighting for abolition instead of Union."

"May I speak freely Sir?"

"Damned well better!"

"Well Sir, I don't think it's an either-or question. I think the first thing is Union. If we fail, slavery will continue or get worse. Feelings will harden between North and South and we'll be at it again in the West, in Texas, Mexico and heaven knows where, but I think this whole war is about slavery."

Logan turned his head and watched as their horses took a dozen steps. "What about States' Rights?"

"Sir, that's important, but we can't have a Federal Government if states can ignore the Federal Government any time they want, and the South uses that argument mostly to preserve and expand slavery."

"So, you're thinking abolition is a political necessity?"

"It may be, Sir, but in my mind, it's a moral certainty.

"Certainty, huh? You sound like those Lovejoy brothers. You know what happened to them, don't you?"

"A little. Isn't Owen Lovejoy a Congressman?"

"He is. He's a raging abolitionist and his brother was killed when he got crossways with people who losing money because of his ideas and decided to get rid of his printing press for the third time. I've known Lovejoy since we were in the State House, and he got tied up with the Republicans. He's a Lincoln man, through and through."

"Sir, when I was in college I read 'The Liberator,' and other aboli-tionist publications. I don't agree with Mr. Garrison's rejection of the Constitution, but his religious argument about the essential equivalence of all men is based in scripture. And … I agree with the abolitionists. God made people to be free and everything I've seen and read, everything we've seen since we came south. The beatings, whippings and tearing families apart. Abusing women and depriving them all of education. Sir, I could go on, but the reason it sickens me is because it's poisonous."

"So, you're here as an abolitionist?"

"Sir, I'm here because I volunteered to become a soldier. It's not easy, but my political opinions, and I suppose most of my moral opinions, take second place to being the best soldier I can."

"So, let me get this straight, you're an abolitionist and you believe slavery is a sin and must be ended. Like drinking and gambling?"

"Well sir, drinking hurts the drinker and the people who can't avoid associating with the drunkard. But slavery is the worst. Scripture tells us to free the slave and liberate the captive. It warns against excess in lots of areas, but preventing a person from learning to read scripture, from stay-ing with his own family, wife and children, taking his money, his freedom and abusing him at will. I can't think of a single thing that's worse."

"Stark, don't you think black people are slaves because God wants us to take them out of Godlessness and into civilization. Don't you think they're better off here than in some jungle? Isn't this the best place for them? You've seen how stupid, lazy and impulsive they are. Without some kind of control, they'll just run wild!"

This time, Mathan looked sharply at Logan.

"What? You have a problem with that?"

"May I continue to speak freely, Sir?"

"Well, I told you to, didn't I?"

"Sir, I am certain that any Black people you've met who even come close to the description you just offered are that way because of slavery. A man who is deprived of his own parents, underfed, overworked, kept in ignorance and deprived of all hope for a better future. A man who is beaten, humiliated and insulted can't rise on his own will. He needs an example and he needs a teacher.

"Freedom isn't the end of his needs, it's only the beginning. A man and his family need to be safe from mistreatment. He needs to trust that honest work will allow him to feed them. He needs to learn about the wider world and to have the opportunity to invest in land and business. To be treated fairly."

"I've read all that, Stark. But, why don't we just send them back to recolonize and Christianize Africa? They can have their own country and run it however they want?"

Mathan's enthusiasm for the topic loosened his tongue. "General, *this* is their country. They've spent generations building it. Any profits the slaveholder achieves are rightfully the wealth of his slaves. They're not laborers who can choose where they work and save their money. They're not indentured to pay back some debt. They're not apprentices paying a craftsman for the benefit of a skill. Their labor raised the money to build those plantations and made those families wealthy.

"Black people shouldn't be sent away. They're as essential to our country as other immigrants. The difference is that we're allowing the Irish to flourish, but we take every last cent from enslaved people. They should harvest the fruits of their own labor."

"Damn, Stark," said Logan in a low tone. "You truly believe that, don't you?"

"I do Sir."

"Well, I know the President wants to preserve the Union. I *suspect* he wants to end slavery. For now, we have to stop this insurrection and find a political solution." Logan paused and looked back at Mathan, "Thanks for your honesty, Stark. If a man's advisors all agree with him, there's no reason to have advisors."

They rode on for an hour with little conversation.

A cavalry Sergeant pulled his mount up a few yards in front of Logan's Headquarters Company. "Message for General Logan."

Mathan looked back at Hotaling, Logan's Chief of Staff who'd overheard and waved the messenger toward him. "What is it Sergeant?"

"Sir, Colonel Ingersoll[18] thinks you should see something."

"Something? What does RG want me to see this time?" asked Logan from his mount a few yards behind.

"Slaves sir. He found some slaves just off the road. Asked me to bring you."

"RG has a soft spot for those people." Logan grimaced as he looked around. Stark, Hotaling, come with us. The rest of you, keep moving. We'll catch-up. I want the Brigade secure in Jackson before sunset.

The cavalry Sergeant and about ten of his men led Logan a quarter mile up the road and only steps off to the side. The scent of slaughter hung in the air and flies were everywhere. Colonel Ingersoll was dismounted and watched several of his men digging in the soft earth. He turned to face Logan. "General."

"Good afternoon, RG. What's this?" asked Logan, seeing both shock and rage on Ingersoll's face. Ingersoll realized his mount blocked Logan's view, so he nudged it out of the way and awaited a reaction.

It took a moment for the scene to register. "My God," said Logan looking away from the tortured bodies. Gathering himself, he looked again. Sprawled across the road were the remains of two men and a woman. Both men were bound and hung above pools of blood. Heavily trodden ground indicated that at several men had been present when the two were

---

18 RG Ingersoll was an Illinois attorney whom Logan knew from his prewar legal practice

emasculated and disemboweled. The young woman's fate was similarly obscene. Logan grimaced. "Runaways?" asked Logan.

Ingersoll looked up with a pained expression. "Does it matter? They were brought here as examples to any Black people who think about running."

Logan glanced again but had to turn away. "It matters. Especially if they were under our protection and we failed them."

"Sir, my men have been picking up fugitives all along our route. Probably a hundred in the past two days. We put the men to work on the roads. We give the women rations and whatever spare clothing we have." He paused looking into Logan's eyes. "I know we differed on the matter of emancipation when we were in Illinois, but this is an abomination. This is pure barbarism. Pure evil!"

Logan lowered his head for a moment and let the image settle in his mind. "RG, you're right." He looked at the freshly opened graves. "It's good that you're seeing to their burial." Logan looked at Ingersoll without speaking. He slowly turned his horse back toward the column and rode slowly. Mathan and Hotaling followed silently.

Logan and his men would find Jackson to be a prosperous small town. It looked new because it was nearly three times the size it had been just ten years before. Although his men found the town pleasant enough, the countryside was forbidding.

From June through November, Logan's Brigade struggled to drive off bands of marauding Confederate cavalry. The population was hostile, the terrain was difficult, and Logan was forced to use foot soldiers to contend with cavalry. Their work was endless, thankless, and exhausting.

In the warm summer sunlight, Logan's heard three women talking loudly, outside his office window. He looked outside to see a younger woman walking toward a kitchen in the company of two, older women. He recognized the older women as "contrabands" who had been with the Army for several weeks. Turning to Hotaling, Logan said, "Is that girl a fugitive too?"

"Think so," said Hotaling as he and Logan entered Logan's office. "Been around for a couple of days. Very attractive young woman."

Logan glanced up at Hotaling, questioning his motive. Hotaling caught the look and answered, "Sophia's on my mind. Sick as my Sophia is, I couldn't help contrasting her state with that young woman there."

Next morning, Hotaling visited Logan's office. This time, he needed approval for a couple of young officers to take leave to visit their homes in Illinois.

Logan thought their reasons were sound and signed the papers without comment and without looking up, pushed the papers across the desk.

"Remember that young woman we saw yesterday, the attractive one?" asked Hotaling in a low tone.

The uncomfortable edge of suspicion crept into Logan's mind as he looked up at his old friend. "What about her?"

"She's leaving. Told me her father was near death." Hotaling paused. "Problem is, her father is also her Master."

"I won't ask how come you know so much, but she's gone you say?"

"Leaving soon."

"Get one of the Sergeants to bring her here, right away. Have them bring a couple of the other contraband ladies with her. I need to have a word."

Twenty minutes later, there was a knock on the door, "Sir, the women you asked about are here."

Logan looked up, pointed to some chairs across the room and said, "Thanks Sergeant bring them in. That will be all."

Logan Didn't rise when they entered, but he pointed to the chairs across the room from Logan. The younger woman noticed the lack of courtesy while the other women didn't give it a thought. "Your names ladies?" Logan asked in a more formal tone than he intended.

"I'm Lucy," said the eldest.

"I'm Phyllis," answered the second woman.

"Zola," said the third sullenly.

"Miss Zola, I understand you intend to return to the place from which you recently escaped?"

"Yes sir."

"May I ask why you would want to return there?"

"The Master, sir," she answered with downcast eyes and a softening tone. The women near her stirred in their seats and seemed uncomfortable.

Logan noticed. "Do either of you know anything about this?"

Their reactions told him they were reluctant to share what they knew.

"Ladies, please speak freely. Nothing will happen to you." He tried to hold their eyes as they glanced furtively at each other. Zola twisted her apron with hands Logan noticed were soft.

Lucy took a deep breath and straightened her back but looked away from Logan, choosing the floor as a safer place. "Her Master wrote her a letter that says he's nearly dead and needs to see Zola one more time."

Zola looked up to check Logan's reaction.

"Zola," began Logan, "is this 'Master' the one you're planning to see?"

"Clearly anxious, she held Logan's eye. "Yes, sir. It's where I used to live." Pausing a moment. "Where I used to live before he hired me out to the place I left to come here." Then she added, "My Mamma is still on the Master's place."

"And why did you take the risk of running away to us in the first place?"

Zola turned her face away, but Logan could see her eyes tearing and her cheeks flushing.

Lucy spoke softly and lowered her eyes. "They were using her."

Logan felt Phyllis watching him for his reaction. Logan was genuinely attentive, his face hardening as he realized what had happened to Zola.

Phyllis noticed and added, "General, that Master of hers, he's also her father." Taking a breath she added quickly, "He sent her off so his friends could use her the way he used her and her own Mamma, and like he used me too."

Logan's face naturally dark complexion became even darker with those words. Anger threatened to boil over into rage.

Zola began to weep softly and Lucy put her arm around the young woman's shoulder.

Logan's voice was low, slow and ominous. "You mustn't go anywhere near them, Zola. Not now. Not ever." Then he added more gently, "I'll see you and your friends are moved to one of the contraband camps close to Memphis. You'll be safe there."

Zola's eyes rose quickly, "I have to go back and see him! He won't hurt me, and he won't keep me. He said he loves me, and he'll give me my freedom papers when I come back!"

"I don't trust such promises," pronounced Logan flatly, "and I insist that you remain here until we can get you to Memphis."

Phyllis and Lucy murmured agreement.

"Ladies," began Logan as he rose from behind his desk to indicate the meeting was ending, "you watch over her, won't you? I don't think Zola, here, is making good decisions."

The problem crossed Logan's mind several times in the following days, but he believed the problem was resolved as best it could be under the circumstances.

A few days later, Phyllis and Lucy were waiting outside the Headquarters building when Logan approached. He nodded at them as he passed. His thoughts about Zola kept his eyes on them longer than he would had he not been concerned. Phyllis recognized his feelings and took half a step forward without speaking.

"Yes?" asked Logan. "I'm surprised to see you still here."

"That Zola?" Phyllis asked.

"Yes, of course. Where is she? Weren't you two supposed to watch over her until you got to Memphis?"

"Sir, we're so sorry, we didn't know. She ran off in the middle of the night. Her master wasn't sick, he just tricked her. He gave her right back to that man she ran away from when she first came to this place. And then he made sure she can't run away anymore."

Logan felt a crushing weight deep in his belly. He didn't know exactly what Phyllis meant, but it didn't change anything. Something shifted inside him, like the rumble that precedes an earthquake. A force that brings down structures that stood for ages.

CARBONDALE, ILLINOIS, AUGUST 1862

Barely 24 years-old, Mary Logan was deeply concerned about her husband's ill health. Logan suffered pain from his wounds, pain in his joints and pain in his belly. By August, he was so tired and dispirited, he got permission for three weeks' leave to recuperate at home.

Acclaim for his achievements at Belmont and Fort Donelson had faded into the past. He no longer held a seat in Congress and his present duties were under the command of McClernand, a man he had long detested for his selfishness, vanity, and arrogance. McClernand interpreted all success as the result of his personal genius while he blamed every disappointment on others' incompetence or malignity.

Mary asked, "John, won't you support a candidate in this Fall's elections? The Party[19] could certainly use your help. Abolitionists are drawing some support and you can put that right."

John adjusted his legs on the footstool and looked at his slippers before looking up at his young wife. "Mary, I'm a soldier. I'm a Union man. I'm for winning this war and preserving the Union. I don't…"

---

19 Mary Logan refers to the Democratic Party, of which Logan was still a member. He joined the Republican Party in 1866.

Mary cut him off, "We can't afford to lose the support of the party! This war is going to end, maybe this year. You're going to want to run again and if you disappoint the party, you'll be left out in the cold."

"If I support the Democrats, the Republicans will be upset. If I support the Republicans, well… you know."

"John, you *must* take a side! The Copperheads are gaining support all over the state. They'll end the war the first chance they get and on any terms the South offers."

Logan looked up as irritation turned to anger. "Those bastards. Damn them!"

"The Democrats—"

Logan cut her off, shouting, "Damn the Democrats! Damn the Republicans! Damn the Copperheads to hell! We're in the middle of a war! I've seen what those secessionist bastards really want. They want to become princes and kings. They want their own little fiefdoms and they'll make other men pay any price to achieve it!"

He caught his breath and went on. "Mary, I've told you before, if they succeed, they'll try to take California, they'll make a deal with Mexico and Spain. Or France! Or England! This won't be the last war. It will be the first of many. Another Mexican War. Another war with England over control of our own trade. I see only one way. That's Union. I'll speak for Union and I'll write for Union. I'll fight for Union, but I will not choose a party." He fell back into his chair and looked past his young wife.

He said to Mary what he'd said so many times before the war, "I'm not an abolitionist and I'm not working to emancipate anyone. I'm pro-Union and that's all." But this time, his voice was flat. Doubt had entered his mind.

"You'll lose their support, John. The war will end, people will forget and you'll be riding the circuit again, defending murderers and swindlers.

"Mary, that's enough, I'm tired and I've decided. I will speak for the Union, if those idiots think the party is more important than the Union, I want no part of them anyway," he added bitterly.

Mary began to reply, and Logan said, "I said that's enough! No ..more discussion. I came home to see you and our little girl. To rest. I have to go back next week, and I want these last few days to be free of politics."

Mary sighed and nodded. "You know best, John," she concluded with a hint of sarcasm. "I'll continue to visit with the ladies, all the same."

As Mary left Logan lay his head back and closed his eyes. For a moment, the house was still, and he drifted into a shallow sleep Images of his youth returned. The grieving mother of a family torn apart by slave traders. The abject despair of a father watching his wife driven away. He saw the fugitives' tortured bodies. Images of the murders took him to Donelson and the screaming rush of Rebel soldiers lancing through the trees. Invisible men, bullets whirring past his face. The explosion on his hip. Mrs. Allen's hand on his forehead before Mary appeared on the boat. A man with no face writhing in the mud. Riding after horsemen he could never catch. He snapped awake with a groan and found himself wet with perspiration.

JACKSON, TENNESSEE, SEPTEMBER 1862

Mathan was resting in the lobby of the hotel Logan's Brigade used as headquarters. He'd recently finished reading two letters from Rachel that had reached him earlier that morning. The first, short letter was written a couple of days after their last encounter near Pittsburg Landing, while her hospital was in the midst of relocation. It began with an apology for the "misunderstanding," that led to his abrupt departure. Rachel attributed Irwin's apparent familiarity to their many long days of shared labor and understandable friendship. She went on to say she cared for Mathan deeply, was going to Kentucky as part of General Nelson's medical staff and that she would write again soon, missing him very much.

Mathan didn't reflect on the first letter, choosing to open the second one immediately. He might save himself pain and uncertainty by reading them together. The second letter was written in early September, saying in part,

"My Dearest Mathan,

I'm writing to you again because I don't know whether you've received my earlier letters. I've written every other week since last I saw you. This is my sixth letter and much has happened.

The night I saw you last, we left Corinth. Our hospital was rushed to Louisville, but all was quiet, and I was able to take two weeks to visit my family. I didn't visit the college, so I have no first-hand news of our

friends. My parents are well, and I have to say, it was more difficult to say good-bye after our visit, than I had imagined.

After I returned to Louisville, we followed the Division toward Richmond where there was a terrible battle. You may have heard General Nelson's men were routed and over 4,000 were lost. The General was wounded, and Doctor Irwin was taken prisoner. My hospital was far to the rear where we managed to avoid most of the trouble.

The remainder of the army returned to Louisville, a few days ago and we have been inundated with wounded soldiers, as you might imagine. I don't know what will happen next. I understand the Rebels are coming toward Louisville or Cincinnati and I fear another battle like Pittsburg Landing, any day.

I want you to know that I remain true to our promises and treasure my memories of you just as I dream of our future. You have a special place in my every prayer and I think of you always. Be patient with our separation, we will find our ways to one another. Until that blessed day, remember me, take care, and write often.

With Deepest Affection,

Rachel"

Mathan was both relieved and resentful when he read her letter. She promised herself to him, but she said nothing about the doctor. It was better than he feared and worse than he hoped.

It was southern-summer hot outside and Logan's absence had reduced the workload. It was too early for dinner, and Mathan didn't want to do paperwork, so he just sat in the lobby with his thoughts. Colonel Ingersoll passed through the lobby and saw him. "Major Stark! How are you today?"

Mathan pressed his hands to the arms of his chair, coming to his feet, but Ingersoll's hand was on his shoulder. "Sit, Stark, sit."

Ingersoll had an oval face with a high forehead, further accentuated by a receding hairline. He sported a walrus moustache like Logan's, but Ingersoll balanced his with a triangular goatee. Only a couple of years older than Mathan, he had a reputation as an iconoclast. "You're getting some rest with Logan out of town?"

"The General will be back soon. I expect he'll have some plans for us."

"I'm sure he will. But, I'm glad to talk to you." Ingersoll dropped heavily into a thickly padded leather chair next to Mathan. It creaked as he turned towards the attentive Major. "I knew Logan before the war. Knew his young wife, Mary also."

Mathan said nothing, holding Ingersoll's eyes but revealing as little as possible.

"We shared a friendship with Mrs. Logan's father, John Cunningham. You know about their past?" Ingersoll sensed no recognition on Mathan's face, so he continued. "Cunningham was Logan's commander during the Mexican War. They became friends on their march to Santa Fe and back. Cunningham promised the General, a Second Lieutenant then, he could marry his daughter." He snorted, "She couldn't have been ten years old at the time!"

Mathan's eyebrows rose and the corners of his mouth began to turn down in disapproval.

"Well, the point is, I've known our General for quite some time and I've heard that your background and beliefs are, how shall I say this… somewhat divergent from his on the question of emancipation.

Very soon the Army will send us at least a Regiment of Black troops, maybe more. This is going to be a test for him and I'm hoping you'll keep your eyes and ears open. I hope you might find a way to influence him to embrace the new Regiment. To welcome them. To employ them as fighting soldiers."

Ingersoll looked at Mathan meaningfully. "I know he places great trust in you."

Mathan nodded, unwilling to comment but interested in Ingersoll's thoughts.

"I'm also acquainted with Colonel Ozburn. Ozburn has been a friend of Cunningham and like a brother to the General, together since they were boys. Ozburn married the General's young cousin, his favorite as I recall."

By now, Mathan was more relaxed, realizing his role was to be Ingersoll's audience, not his companion.

"It's no secret to General Logan that I am wholeheartedly in favor of abolition and so are most of my men. At the other extreme is Ozburn. As hard-hearted a man as I know. Professes Christian values on Sunday mornings but ignores every tenet of the faith the moment he exits the church. Logan and he began the war in perfect harmony on the question of abolition." He paused to accept Mathan's nod of agreement.

"Besides sending Black soldiers, it seems there may be action on the issue of emancipation from the President's office. Some official step toward the eventual abolition of all slavery. Certainly, I hope so. Hope so very much." Looking into Mathan's eyes he added, "I know you share my feelings. I saw your reaction to the murders we found on our way here this summer. I've seen you ensure the safe return of fugitives from the contraband camps near Corinth to Grand Junction. It's not lost on me that you arranged for my 11th Cavalry to escort them part of the way and assure their safe passage. I am grateful for your sentiments and your actions."

Mathan managed a "Yes Colonel, I was happy to help them."

"So, here's the reason I'm speaking to you. As I said, it won't be long before our Division receives one or more of those Regiments of Black soldiers. You have influence with him. I know you won't overplay your hand.

You mustn't. But we may have more influence on his decisions if we're in mutual support on the subject." He paused and let the message sink in. "Don't you agree, Stark?"

Mathan had learned enough to wait a moment before he replied. "I didn't know of your previous acquaintance with the General. It sounds like you've known him for a long time." Mathan sensed Ingersoll's impatience with the bland response. Mathan continued, "General Logan is aware of my background and my views on abolition. He knows I share his commitment to the preservation of the Union. I would never think to press my opinions on abolition, much less advocate for them. I'm just one of his assistants."

Ingersoll sat back, his eyes moving from Mathan to an unfocused gaze across the lobby. A smile slowly crossed his face. He concluded, "You understand me, Stark. I trust your beliefs will guide your actions in the future as they have guided you in the past." Then he turned his face to Mathan and leaned in. "If I can ever be of help to you, Stark, say the word." The young Colonel sat back in his chair, allowing the conversation to set in Mathan's mind. He rose heavily and smiled at Mathan. "Have a good day, Stark."

Mathan watched Ingersoll walk slowly to the door of the hotel, where he paused, held the door open and looked back. "Don't underestimate your role," he said. He paused. Mathan looked at Ingersoll but neither moved, nor blinked. They held one another's eyes for more than a moment before the Colonel pulled the door fully open and left.

Mathan felt the weight of Ingersoll's expectation. It might be time to become more than a good soldier. It might be time to say something to Logan. The thought of Logan's anger made Mathan shudder, but it didn't make him forget his beliefs.

CORINTH, MISSISSIPPI, OCTOBER 1862

Mathan walked across the camp. The beauty of scarlet, orange, gold and amber leaves sparkling in the sun around Logan's camp nearly moved him to tears. Major Hotaling assembled Logan's staff while Mathan went to each encampment, collecting the Regimental Commanders. Sergeant Himmelstoss was beside Mathan, casting a broad shadow in the late morning light.

"Nothing much came of our dash down from Jackson, did it?" Asked Sergeant Himmelstoss quietly. "At least, I'm glad Colonel Leggett let you bring me to the staff, Major," said Sergeant Himmelstoss as they returned from Leggett's camp.

"I suppose the medics will learn to do without you, but we need you with the Headquarters Company. I think we're going back to Jackson tomorrow or the next day and I like having you with us." Mathan paused, remembering his first encounter with the wheelwright in the middle of a river. "I'll always be in your debt."

Himmelstoss looked down at his young officer. "I've told you before, that was Pastor Allen and his brother. You should thank them. I just rowed the boat."

"I've thanked Pastor Allen. And I'll thank him every time I see him." They walked a bit further and Mathan added, almost under his breath, "Don't know when that will be."

The big man grunted. "Well, he's a good man and it was good that you got him and his wife back from Doctor Irwin and his lot. They'd be somewhere in Kentucky by now, who knows what could happen to him there." Himmelstoss paused and looked at Mathan with an affirming nod of his head, "Mrs. Bickerdyke will watch over them." After a pause Himmelstoss asked, "They're in Memphis with Mrs. B, now, aren't they?"

"I believe so."

"And young Miss Rodgers?"

Mathan didn't answer quickly. Rachel and he had exchanged letters in recent weeks, the most recent arriving just the day before. She only referred to her relationship with Irwin once, saying he had been released from captivity in an exchange of prisoners and had been in Louisville until Nelson was murdered by one of his subordinate Generals (who bore the unfortunate name of Jefferson Davis). Rachel planned to return to Memphis at her first opportunity and resume work with Mary Ann. There were many more Ohio men in Memphis than in Louisville and Mathan was the first among them in her heart.

"She'll be safe," said Himmelstoss, completely missing Mathan's true concern.

They arrived at the Headquarters area, finding stools, benches and crates arranged in semicircles around Logan's chair. Mathan and Himmelstoss took their places in the third and fourth of the concentric rings. The "inner circle," was reserved for Logan's Adjutant and the Regimental Commanders. The second circle was occupied by Regimental Adjutants and Logan's most senior staff. The third ring was for selected staff officers from the Brigade and Regiments. The gallery, in this case, those standing on the periphery, were administrative assistants, senior noncommissioned officers and men like Himmelstoss, happy to have become a personal assistant to Mathan.

Logan chatted quietly with Leggett who was seated nearest him. Mathan couldn't make out their conversation, but they smiled amiably and chuckled as they surveyed the meeting. Logan raised his voice.

"Gentlemen, I have several important items to review with all of you today. Some big changes for everyone." The murmurs silenced as all eyes turned to their Commander.

"First, we'll be leaving Corinth tomorrow. We got here too late to fight, and it looks like they need us somewhere else. We're not going back to Jackson."

The men murmured and waited. "We're headed to La Grange, near Memphis. For the most part we'll use railroads for the movement." There was a sigh of relief. It was much faster and easier to move men by rail than on foot, particularly as the weather could turn cold any time. Most officers looked at one another quizzically. Mathan noticed Leggett who didn't seem at all surprised. Instead, he calmly kept his eyes on Logan.

Logan began slowly. "Our Colonel Leggett," Logan paused like the politician he had been, surveying the audience to build tension, "will be leaving his Regiment, the 78th Ohio Volunteers." Leggett was as inscrutable as a sphinx. "Mort, would you like to announce your successor?"

"Thank you, sir," said Leggett, rising slowly and finding his Adjutant in the second circle. Greeny, would you please stand?" All heads turned to face the Lieutenant Colonel. "Although I am very sorry to leave the men of the 78th Ohio Volunteer Infantry for other duties, I am delighted to leave you in the exceptionally capable hands of our newest Colonel and your commander, Greenberry Wiles!"

Applause were spontaneous and generous. Wiles smiled, raised one hand in thanks and took his seat more quickly than any politician in history. When the applause subsided and while officers nearby were softly congratulating Wiles, Leggett took his seat and nodded thanks to Logan.

"Many of you have met General James B. McPherson, but for those of you who haven't I'd like to tell you about him. General McPherson began his career at West Point and did very well. He was one of the best and that's why he became an engineer instead of a cavalry, infantry or," he paused for effect. "an artillery officer like some of the West Pointers we know." The officers laughed.

"Major General McPherson has risen from the grade of Captain to Major General in one year. There is no doubt that he has the confidence of our Generals and I've recently spoken to him. This brings me to the next bit of news I have to tell you."

Logan began in a lower voice. "I am very sorry to say that, I … I must leave the Third Brigade." This brought a universal groan of disappointment and more apprehensive murmurs. Then he added brightly, "I will assume command of General McPherson's Third Division from General Ogelsby." His men rose to their feet applauding steadily with calls of "Well-deserved!" and "Congratulations, Sir!"

Mathan took all this in with growing concern. Logan was promoted to Division Command and would leave. Leggett was leaving the 78th for who knew where. Mathan felt adrift.

"There's more, gentlemen. Some of you have met General McClernand. I hope you've enjoyed your acquaintance with him, because it is about to come to an end." This caused a stir among the officers, particularly in the front row.

"There's more, important news. Settle down, if you would, please." The men slowly took their seats and waited for the next announcement. "Three things!" said Logan firmly in the face of their immediate silence.

"First, Colonel Leggett is promoted to Brigadier and will command the Third Brigade in my place!" Cheering was as loud at it had been for the announcement of Logan's new duties. The first circle pressed forward to congratulate Leggett and to shake his hand. Not waiting for the voices to quiet, Logan's voice roared above the ongoing expressions of approval. Logan bellowed, "And the Third Brigade is coming with me!"

Pandemonium reigned. The 78th would be well-led, the other Regiments universally approved of Leggett and most of all, they would remain together under the command of someone they loved and trusted.

Celebration continued until Logan held up both hands in a sign they should reseat themselves. "And the last bit of news." He waited until he had every officer's attention. "General McPherson's Third Division…" Logan paused. "And for you who are slow at math, that would be us," he smiled. "The Third Division of General McPherson's Seventeenth Corps will relocate to Memphis where we'll lead the Army into Mississippi and take Vicksburg!"

The final announcement opened floodgates of emotion and pride. McPherson was Grant's favorite West Pointer and Logan was Grant's favorite "political" General. Celebrations began even before Logan smiled broadly, raising both hands, announcing, "That's all for now!"

Mathan had been near grief before Logan's final announcement. He realized he would probably remain with the Brigade and Leggett, or he might go with Logan. He might even get a command of his own, although he had mixed feelings about that. At least in Memphis, would be free of the constant raids that had occupied nearly every day since they arrived at Jackson in June. And he might see Rachel again.

HOLLY SPRINGS, MISSISSIPPI, DECEMBER 1862

Early on a very chilly morning, outside the small Northwestern village of Holly Springs, the dashing, young General Earl Van Dorn leaned back in his camp chair, grinning at the three Yankee cotton speculators who stood before him in their underwear. "Thank you for your clothing and military passes gentlemen, they'll be very helpful. I hope to return them to you tomorrow sometime. Until then, please stay close to your guards here. You'll have a fine story when all this is over."

Turning to the Sergeant in charge of the guard detail, Van Dorn said under his breath, "Give them a couple of blankets and keep them with the other prisoners. We'll decide what to do with them later."

As the guards pushed the three chilly speculators out the door, Van Dorn turned to three men attired in the prisoners' clothes. "First thing in the morning, use your passes to get by the sentries and have a look-around Holly Springs. Get back to me before supper. I want to know where they've stored the supplies but most of all, who's guarding them, how many are there and where they are. Understand?"

The three spies were welcomed to Holly Springs, where Grants' Army stored equipment and supplies intended for the overland invasion of Mississippi and the capture of Vicksburg. The spies had no trouble scouting the town and its defenders, returning unnoticed to their commander late that night. They gave Van Dorn and his staff a full report.

With exactly the information he needed, at dawn the next day, Van Dorn sent 3,500 of his cavalrymen to attack the town. By noon of the same day, only 130 of the 1,600 Union defenders had escaped. The rest were killed or captured and Van Dorn's men carried away what they could.

Knowing reinforcements would soon arrive, Van Dorn ordered the burning of three fully loaded trains and countless warehouses packed full of supplies. He promptly paroled his prisoners, riding away before dark, having made it impossible for Grant to continue to approach Vicksburg from the North or East.

During the following week, Van Dorn's horsemen ranged across Southwest Tennessee, destroying bridges, tearing up tracks and disrupting communication between Memphis and the rest of Tennessee. Before word could reach the town of Bolivar, four ambulances carrying a dozen sick and wounded Union soldiers left for Memphis.

The ambulances were supposed to cover the 20 miles to La Grange on the first day, then continue to Memphis the next day. An Assistant Surgeon, a nurse, four drivers and three Black assistants were captured by a troop of Confederate cavalry. Rachel was the nurse and she trembled with fear while her captors considered their options.

The question was resolved when a cavalry Captain visited General Van Dorn. As the General smoked his cigar outside his tent, the young officer from Vicksburg approached asking, "General, may I have a moment of your time?" Van Dorn looked up from his conversation with one of his Colonels and said nothing but stared at the unusually tall, slender young man.

The Captain began uncomfortably, "Uh, sir, we've paroled those Yankee wounded and their drivers. They were let go on foot. We'll turn the runaways over for bounty in the morning."

"That's fine Captain. Why are you here?"

"Well sir, I'd like to hang on to that Surgeon and the nurse."

"Captain, I understand the Surgeon is a Yankee officer. We can certainly hold him for an exchange. But isn't that nurse a woman? A civilian? What's she doing by herself out here anyway?" asked General Van Dorn.

"Um, Sir, I, really don't know why she's here. Said something about a 'Sanitary Commission' and a pass, but she must have lost her pass. She didn't have any papers." He paused as Van Dorn stared at him with incredulity.

"Anyway sir, there are six ladies from Vicksburg who've been stuck up in Memphis for months and can't get a pass from the Yankees to go down the river and home again. I figured the Surgeon and the Nurse would give us some leverage for an exchange."

"Captain, she's a civilian and she hasn't done anything wrong," said Van Dorn rolling his eyes and shaking his head. "Unless she's one of the 'public women,' you should have just, let her go with the parolees."

"Sir, couldn't we hold her on suspicion?"

"Suspicion of what, exactly?" asked Van Dorn with exasperation creeping into his voice.

The Captain paused for a long time. "Umm … spying?"

"Spying!" Van Dorn blurted, "Spying by tending to a few ambulance loads of wounded on their side of the lines? First you 'lose' her papers, then you accuse her of spying?"

"Sir, um, I'm thinking, suspicion is enough to keep her in our custody, at least until we can sort it out in Vicksburg."

"Suspicion of spying, huh?" Van Dorn thought it over and looked at his second-in-command, who assented. "Well, I suppose so. We're going back to our bases and you militia boys will go home. You'll have to look after her and that Surgeon. Long way to Vicksburg. Use the railroad, report to the cavalry commander there then rejoin us as soon as you can."

"Thank you sir!' said the Captain, snapping to attention and saluting over the general's head.

Lazily returning the salute, Van Dorn said, "You're dismissed Captain."

The drivers, orderlies and ambulatory patients were "paroled," meaning they could continue on their way, but could be executed if they violated their oath not to fight before being exchanged. The sickest men had been crowded into a single ambulance and put back on the road. The Rebels took all the food, weapons, medical supplies, mules and the other ambulances. The Captain kept Rachel's personal papers.

Rachel and the Surgeon were placed on mules and taken to a temporary camp. The enslaved women were bound and led into the woods. That night, Rachel was horror-stricken by the screams of her coworkers as they were assaulted before being sold for bounty.

Sometime after the women were silenced, a Confederate soldier stopped in front of Rachel and leered at her. He leaned down and whispered, "You would have joined our little party except the Captain said he needs you to tell a good story when he trades you for his sister." He raised up and smiled saying, "It would have been fun. You could have met the whole troop!" After that night and except for the Assistant Surgeon, Rachel saw her former traveling companions only in her nightmares.

Rachel kept a close eye on the Rebel Captain and she noticed that one of the two enlisted men, a Sergeant, was often at the Captain's side. The other enlisted soldier, the one who leered at her the night before, stared at Rachel with an obvious mixture of hostility and prurience. In contrast, neither the Captain nor the Sergeant seemed interested in Rachel in any way beyond her value as a pawn to be exchanged.

Early that, next morning, Rachel and the Assistant Surgeon began their journey in the company of the Captain and the two cavalrymen: first on horseback to the railroad, then in a rickety rail car to Jackson, Mississippi, finally on another train to Vicksburg.

By the time the train groaned to a halt at the Vicksburg station, she was nearly certain the Captain and the Sergeant had more of a relationship than their membership in the same Regiment would indicate.

Stepping from the railroad car onto the platform, the Captain turned to look back at Rachel, standing above him, still in the car, with the Sergeant and the Private just behind her. "Now you get down from the train and stay right here with those gentlemen, while I go into town to make arrangements."

The Captain was well down the platform when the Sergeant draped his coat over her bags and said, "I'll go up to the hospital and see whether they could keep you while we arrange the exchange." Turning to the Private he said, "You watch her and my things while I'm gone."

The Private's eyes didn't move from Rachel's figure as he grunted assent. Fifteen minutes or so, after the Captain and the Sergeant were well away from the station, the Private became bored, then fidgety.

"You stay right where you are and don't you move an inch! Hear me?" The Private shook a finger at Rachel, who looked town for fear of revealing her contempt. The Private walked toward the interior of the station and looked back, admonishing her, "I'll be right back, and you'd better be right where you're standing now." He turned his back and walked away.

Rachel waited. Was he looking for a privy? Tobacco? Food? Beer?

A cloud covered the sun and it quickly became cool. Rachel reached for her cloak but it was beneath the Sergeant's coat. As she moved the Sergeant's coat, she noticed something protruding from a tear in the lining. Curious, Rachel confirmed no one was nearby and no one was watching. She slipped her fingers into the space behind the lining and withdrew two, small, rolled pages.

Her heart raced as she reaffirmed her isolation and unrolled one of the pages with her back to the direction of the Private's departure. With trembling hands, she drew a Bible from her purse and slipped the letters between some of the Gospel pages and began to read. Her heart fairly hammered as she grasped their meaning. The Captain and the Sergeant were lovers. The second letter was even more explicit than the first. Her mind spun from one possibility to the next.

Rachel recognized she was in the possession of an insurance policy but that the letters posed a serious risk to her life if the Sergeant or Captain found them in her possession.

Taking up the Sergeant's coat, she searched out a small gap at the bottom of its lining and quickly enlarged it, creating a hole through which the letters might easily have slipped and discarding any threads that would reveal the recency of the gap. With luck, the Sergeant would say nothing to the Captain and she could produce one of the letters when the time was right. Calming herself, Rachel secreted the letters and replaced the Sergeant's coat just as it had been when he left.

Rachel had a several minutes to restore her composure before the Private returned.

"C'mon!" ordered the Private, "you're going to work now!" Picking up the Sergeant's Coat and his own bag, the Private reached for Rachel's but caught himself. Gesturing to her cloak and bag with his free hand, he growled, "Get your own damned things and let's go." He was careful to walk behind her on the way to the hospital, enjoying the movement of her hips, swaying beneath many layers of fabric.

VICKSBURG, MISSISSIPPI, JANUARY 1863

Rachel was disoriented when she awoke on a narrow cot in the tiny room. Gray light filtered through a small, cracked, unwashed and shabbily curtained window. With confusion came a surge of fear; there had been so many relocations in recent days. Just as her eyes found the room's only furniture, a single chair and a rickety table, it came back to her. She was in Vicksburg. In the military hospital where she was supposed to work as a nurse while she awaited her exchange.

The air was cold and damp. Worry and fear oppressed her. She was alone; the Assistant Surgeon had been taken to a military hospital in another part of the town. She managed to keep a single bag of possessions including one change of clothes, a couple of books and a hairbrush, a Bible with couple of papers hidden inside the back cover.

Rachel had not heard from Mathan since she left Louisville over a month ago and she wondered whether her letters (and Mathan's) had been burned in one of the warehouses during the raid at Holly Springs the Rebel Captain told her about.

Footsteps approached her door. Without a knock or warning, the door flew open and slammed the side of her bed. The hospital's matron scowled, "Still in bed! Get up. Come to breakfast and we'll get you to work. You're not a guest in this hospital! We have patients to care for and you'll help, or you won't eat." She continued to stare at Rachel with contempt.

"Yes, Ma'am." Answered Rachel softly. "Where shall I find … breakfast?" she asked softly.

The matron snorted dismissively and pointed with her chin. "End of the hall on your left. Eat with the servants you like so well. You'll work in the kitchen and laundry for now. They'll show you what to do." She leaned into Rachels' room and looked around, adding "This is where you'll sleep. Leave your things here. They'll probably be safe." The matron pulled the door closed and her footsteps receded down the hall.

There was no water in the pitcher, nor in the basin. There was no pot beneath the bed. Rachel's eyes welled, but she hardened herself quickly and wiped her sleeve across her face. This was lonely, unpleasant and uncomfortable, but she was healthy and they would feed her. She brushed her hair back with her hands, smoothed her dress and followed the direction she'd been given.

At the end of the hall, she found a small room with ten or a dozen black women seated along benches, eating grits and gravy, drinking something dark as they talked softly among themselves. They looked up when Rachel entered.

"Good morning, Miss," said the woman nearest the door through which she'd entered. "Miss Cuthbert said you'd be here today. Said we should make sure you get some food and show you our work." These ladies, called servants, were enslaved. Most worked as cooks and laundresses whose wages were paid to "owners."

"Thank you," said Rachel quietly. "Was Miss Cuthbert the lady in the gray dress with silver hair at her temples?"

"Yes Miss, that sounds like Miss Cuthbert."

"She said I was to work alongside you?"

"Well, Miss," said the oldest lady there. "I'm not sure you'll need to do that."

"Miss Cuthbert said, if I don't work, I won't eat."

"She did? That sounds like Miss Cuthbert alright." She paused and looked Rachel up and down. "You're not a Southern lady, are you?"

Rachel answered and told some of her story, emphasizing the past two weeks and her desire to return to Union lines.

The ladies at the table looked down, not revealing their desire to do the same, and their deep fear that they would be punished if their thoughts were known.

Another woman said, "Miss Rodgers, my name his Estella, and it's time for us to go to work. You come along; we'll look after you."

Rachel threw herself into the care of the Confederate soldiers with the same commitment as she had with her Union patients. Despite their early suspiciousness, Rachel was surprised to become friendly with a few, then several Southern nurses and some of the wounded soldiers' families.

MEMPHIS, TENNESSEE, FEBRUARY 1863

The weather made it difficult to know whether it was dawn or mid-morning. Logan sat in the lobby of the Gayoso House and looked out at the river. There had been a cold rain for most of the night. Lieutenant Colonel John Hotaling walked up behind Logan and passed a steaming cup of coffee over his shoulder. "Have a seat, John," said Logan pointing to the nearest chair with his free hand. Hotaling lowered himself into the seat next to Logan's but said nothing.

Logan began, "Going to be a busy day. Grant's here and McPherson will be too." Hotaling nodded and blew across the surface of his coffee. "How's your assistant working out?"

"Hotaling kept his eyes on his coffee. "Stark's a steady man. Good to have him. Thank you."

"I know you wanted your own command, John," said Logan looking earnestly at his Chief of Staff. "I just can't spare you now, but I'll get an authorization for that promotion as soon as we can. Maybe you can train Stark to replace you?"

Hotaling was disappointed but he understood his role. "Sir, Stark's pretty green still. I'm honored and happy to be here. There will always be other opportunities."

"I like that about you, John!" said Logan smiling and settling back into his old club chair. "You know when the hook is set, and you stop wriggling." He paused and returned his coffee cup to the table between them. "We're going to Vicksburg very soon. Grant isn't a man who takes 'No,' for and answer. Just a matter of bringing them to battle. That's why I need you. With a Division, we have to coordinate three different Brigades and five batteries of artillery with three other Divisions in our Corps and the four other Corps that will be somewhere nearby.

Logan continued, "I think we've settled that business about desertions. That's why I asked Ozburn to come see me. He's had three dozen desertions in the past couple of months. I'll see him in my quarters, but I want you close at hand in case he loses his temper."

"Of course, sir. When is he due here?"

"I told him I'd like to see him at 9:00 AM. That should let us clear up anything that came in last night. We should be ready for our 10:00 AM meeting with the Brigade Commanders after that. Sound alright to you?"

"Yes sir, it does. I'll have the staff ready, should you need anything."

When Logan and Hotaling finished and looked up, they saw Mathan standing at a distance, obviously awaiting their instruction to approach. "Stark!" called Logan. "Come sit down, we were just talking about you!"

Mathan smiled and took a seat across the small circle of chairs arranged in that corner of the lobby. "Good morning, Sirs," began Mathan. "Everything alright this morning?" he looked from Logan to Hotaling.

Logan answered immediately, "Your old friend, Colonel Ozburn will be in today. Nothing to do with you," Logan said smiling warmly at Mathan. "Sometimes, you know a person better by their enemies than by their friends, eh?"

Mathan smiled and looked down at his lap. When he looked up, Hotaling began to speak. "Stark, why don't you go see to our men in the hospitals this morning. I understand the wounded are mostly here at the hotel and the sick are in other buildings. Do you think you could get a report from the surgeons and not return until our staff meeting at 10:00?"

"Thanks Sir. I'm happy to see to it."

"Good. We'll see you at ten, then." Mathan looked from Hotaling to Logan. Both smiled. Mathan rose, nodded in deference and left by the corridor that previously led to one of the wings of the hotel. Those rooms had been converted to a hospital holding up to 1,000 beds, when needed.

Mathan found his way to Mary Ann's office. He'd seen her twice before. The first time to say hello and ask whether she'd heard from Rachel. She said she had, but she knew only that Rachel had gone to Kentucky with Irwin's Division, and from there had visited home. Mathan suspected there were other details, but Mary Ann said there was nothing more to add.

A week later, after visiting troops from his Division, Mathan went again, to Mary Ann's office to say hello. As he neared the door, he heard loud voices.

"Mrs. Bickerdyke! I *am* the Medical Superintendent of *every* hospital in Memphis, I and I *will* take charge! I won't hear another *word*!" said a man's voice, raised to the point window glass might rattle.

The man's voice was familiar and although Mathan could hear clearly from a distance, he stepped up to the door and listened. The man went on, "Mrs. Livermore, couldn't you reason with her? I've insisted these contrabands be dismissed since I arrived here last week. I've told Mrs. Bickerdyke repeatedly! Yesterday, I made it an *order*!" Mathan imagined the look in Mary Ann's eyes, he didn't need see her.

Mrs. Livermore spoke softly saying, "Doctor, I'm sure Mrs. Bickerdyke understands your reluctance to have Black people serve as cooks, laundresses, ward assistants and laborers." She paused, looking from the Doctor to Mary, then back. "I believe she simply disagrees."

"*Disagrees*! I'm the Medical Superintendent of *every* hospital in Memphis! I'm General Grant's *Surgeon*! Who does she think she is!"

Mary Ann spoke for herself, this time in a lower voice. "I am responsible for the care of these men, for their cleanliness, for their sustenance, for their very lives. If I can help them recover, we'll return them to their Regiments. If they can't recover, we send them home to their families or make them as comfortable as we can." She paused then added, "I answer only to God. I have passes from General Grant allowing me to requisition what I need, to go where I choose and to employ those I deem suitable."

"We'll see about *that!*" shouted the doctor as he stormed out of Mary Ann's office. As he strode past, Mathan recognized him. It was the doctor from Shiloh. Irwin, the one who was too familiar with Rachel.

Mathan was trembling when he reached the door to Mary Ann's office. "Mrs. Bickerdyke?" he asked in a soft voice.

"Mathan!" she spoke his name with warmth and welcome. She strode to him and gave him a warm hug. Holding his shoulders, she stood back. I saw you last week, but we didn't have time to talk." She paused and looked around at Mrs. Livermore. "Mathan, this is another Mary, Mary *Livermore*. She represents the Sanitary Commission and is an old friend from Galesburg. She's here to see what we need." She turned back to Mathan asking, "What can I do for you today? Can you stay a bit? I'm busy, but we could talk as I make my rounds."

"Major," said Mrs. Livermore in greeting.

"Mrs. Livermore, a pleasure to meet you," he said as he took her extended hand. "I have about an hour, but I don't want to interfere in your day. I was here to check on some of our men."

Mary Ann turned to Mrs. Livermore and said, "Mathan is my niece's fiancé. He's a fine young man. Educated with her at the Heidelberg College and he's on General Logan's staff, I believe?"

"Yes, Ma'am," replied Mathan softly.

"I'm pleased to meet you Major Stark," said Mrs. Livermore, appraising Mathan from head to toe and back again. "Your niece's fiancé, you say?" And where is she just now?"

Mary Ann looked at Mathan, then at Mary Livermore and said, "Mathan please come in and close the door. We have something to talk to you about."

Mathan said nothing and took a seat across the desk from the two ladies.

"Mary Ann began, "We've heard from Rachel."

Mathan's eyes opened wide and he leaned forward saying, "What…" but Mary Ann held up a hand and told him to sit back and listen to the whole thing.

"She's safe and well as far as we know. She's in Vickburg."

Mathan reacted with alarm but said nothing.

"She was with some ambulances and soldiers coming from Bolivar to us here at Memphis. They left the day of the raid on Holly Springs and the whole group was captured. They took Rachel and the Surgeon as prisoners for exchange." Mary Ann went on, "They paroled the rest but they made up some story about holding her on 'suspicion of spying.' Then they offered to exchange her and the surgeon along with a couple of others for those six women who've been complaining they can't get passage to Vicksburg.

Mathan was now on his feet and near shouting, "That was weeks ago! Why hasn't she been exchanged?"

"I've met those Southern 'ladies,'" said Mary Ann with irritation. "I'd say they're the ones who've been spying, if anyone has. General Grant's man in charge of exchanges said he'd exchange them for Rachel but wanted to keep them here in the hotel for a couple of weeks while their observations go stale. When those ships ran past Vicksburg a couple of days ago, the Rebels just quit talking to us."

Mary Livermore's voice was firm but supportive, "I'm working on lots of things here, but getting your Rachel home is top of the list."

Mathan nodded as he calmed, "Thanks Mrs. Livermore." Then he turned to Mary Ann saying, I'm very worried about her. Can I do anything to hurry this along?"

"No, Mathan," said Mary Ann sadly. "Not just now. We have some ships that ran past the guns at Vicksburg and they're still fighting somewhere down there. That's made it difficult to send a truce boat. We hope to make the exchange before the end of the month."

"Amen, said Mary Livermore, shaking her head solemnly.

Mary Livermore added with a suspicious tone, "By the way Mary Ann, you said Miss Rodgers had gone to Kentucky with a Doctor Irwin? Was that the same Doctor Irwin with whom we were just speaking!?"

"The same. He's the one Rachel helped with his hospital in Kentucky, where our Dr. Irwin got himself captured trying to save his friend, General Nelson," she reflected a moment. "That one's quite the hero. Saves his commander from the Apaches in Arizona last year and tries to repeat the trick in Kentucky. Fortunately, the Rebels treat their prisoners better than the Apaches do. The Rebels exchanged him after only a few days, and he went up to Cincinnati with General Nelson."

"Bull Nelson?" asked Mathan.

"You heard about that too?" Mary Ann asked Mathan, who nodded.

"Heard what, exactly?" asked Mrs. Livermore. I heard he was shot in a duel."

Mary Ann answered. "Nothing of the sort!" General Nelson had a Brigadier working for him, a man with the unfortunate name of Jefferson Davis. Uses the middle initial C. to distinguish himself from our former Secretary of War," added Mary Ann with a sarcastic smile.

"Well," she continued, "it seems General Nelson was unhappy with General Davis' performance of his duties and General Nelson ... You know they called him, 'Bull' for good reason, towered over that tiny little General

Davis. Anyway, Davis went and found himself a pistol and put it to use on General Nelson's heart. Poor man died in a matter of minutes."

Mrs. Livermore clicked her tongue and shook her head.

"Well," concluded Mary Ann, "That's when they reorganized what was left of General Nelson's staff. They liked what Irwin did at Shiloh and they sent him to us here." She looked at Mary Livermore and concluded, "He said he'd last seen Rachel in Cincinnati. Said she planned to visit family, then rejoin us here in Memphis. That was before Christmas. I suppose all the turmoil at Holly Springs the week before Christmas must have gotten her letters lost or burned. At least we know where she is now."

Mathan nodded. He wanted to visit the officer in charge of exchanges. "Mary Ann, Miss Livermore, thank you. I'll be by again tomorrow, if I may?"

When Mathan left, Mary Livermore said, "That boy is heartsick! I want to get those two back together as soon as we can." Then she asked Mary Ann, "Nothing since?"

Mary Ann stepped to the door. "Only this, there was some serious fighting on the Red River below Vicksburg. More prisoners. Maybe an exchange soon." She sighed, "We have things to do. We'll find out as much as we can, as quickly as we can."

Mathan found his way to the Sergeant who guarded the Provost's door. "I'm from General Logan's Office and must speak to the Colonel immediately," said Mathan as he began to circle the Sergeant's desk.

The Sergeant rose saying, "He's not in there!"

Mathan was past him and pushed into the Provost's office only to find the bald, bearded man pouring himself what appeared to be three fingers of whiskey. He looked up angrily, "Who the hell are you and why are you in here?"

Mathan looked at the whiskey, then stared into the Provost's eyes and waited before answering in a low tone. Speaking slowly, Mathan began,

"I'm from General Logan's Division. One of our Surgeons and a civilian are due to be exchanged for some women who want to go to Vicksburg." Mathan saw recognition in the Provost's eyes.

Mathan went on, "The General wants this exchange to take place immediately. I'll accompany the women and ensure the exchange. We want this done immediately, we have a boat and we need the papers." Sensing the Provost's retreat, Mathan leaned forward. "General Logan doesn't want to bother General Grant, but he wants this, now. Today. Understand?"

"Well, I'm, uh … I have to check …" stammered the provost, obviously tipsy. It was clear the fresh glass of whiskey was not his first of the day.

Mathan called his bluff, saying, "Let's go see General Logan, right now. Or I'll interrupt General Grant with you if you want. Let's go talk to the Generals together!"

The provost looked around the room helplessly. "Sergeant, come in here, please."

The Sergeant, who hated the drunk provost had been listening behind the door and appeared with a smile. "Yes Sir!"

"Get the Major the papers for the exchange and tell those six harpies from Vicksburg they're going South on a truce steamer this afternoon not next week. Give the Major all the papers he needs to exchange them. You go too, to make sure the papers are completed correctly." The provost turned to Mathan. Still intimidated, he asked, "Will that do it?"

Mathan smiled and turned to the Sergeant. "Do you have everything we need?"

"Yes Sir. We should get going. We want it to be easy for them to see our truce flag."

"Can I meet you here at 12:30?" asked Mathan.

"I'll be ready. I'll make sure the right people know the Provost approved the plan."

Half an hour later, Ozburn strode past Sergeant Himmelstoss and Major Hotaling without acknowledging either. He continued into Logan's office, tossed his hat onto a chair and dropped himself into the seat nearest Logan without speaking until he was seated.

Logan watched him with a mixture of curiosity and disappointment.

Once seated, Ozburn extended his muddy boots to the side of Logan's desk, rested his folded hands on his belly, put his head back and began, "What's on your mind, old friend?"

Logan looked to Himmelstoss who was standing at the door with Hotaling behind him, on tiptoes to see over the big man's back. Logan nodded, indicating they should close the door, which they did.

"Thanks for coming Doff," began Logan, shifting uncomfortably in his seat while Ozburn looked at him from beneath his brows. "I needed to ask you about some things."

"What sort of things, Jack?" asked Ozburn nonchalantly.

"Well, let's start with the desertions." Ozburn's eyebrows rose, otherwise he remained still. Logan went on. "About 35, I hear. Most in your Regiment. Seems you have as bad a problem as any in the Division, maybe in the whole Army. What's going on?"

"Well, Jack, that last little jaunt into Mississippi was unpleasant enough."

"It was the same for all of us, Doff. I think there's something more. I've heard you've been talking to the other commanders and to your men about the President's emancipation order."

With that, Ozburn straightened himself and looked into Logan's eyes. Anger pulled the corners of his mouth as he answered, "Damned right! I told the men and they told me. We didn't come down here to free n---s! And we don't want any of those damned n---r Regiments!"

Logan locked Ozburn's eyes with his own. Leaning back, Logan said slowly, "That was an order. It took effect the first of the year." He paused and neither man moved or blinked. "It's an *order*! We're going to follow it!" Logan paused, but Ozburn continued to stare. "*You're* going to follow it," added Logan firmly.

"The hell!" exploded Ozburn, drawing his boots beneath him and leaning towards Logan. "I've known you since we were boys. I went to Santa Fe with you and I know what you thought then. I know what you thought and what you said when this whole thing started! You don't believe in emancipation, not one bit!"

Logan sat still, aware of Ozburn's temper. He had already decided to risk it. "Doff, I've... *changed*." Logan's gaze caused Ozburn to break eye contact and throw himself against the back of his chair like an angry teenager.

"God damn it, Jack! The men are here to protect the Union!" Ozburn was shouting now. "That's it. They don't want any n---s carrying rifles or... Damn it! ... Damn it!! They sure as hell don't want to see one of those bastards wearing Sergeant's stripes! They'll *never* follow one! They'll *kill* them first!"

It was Logan's turn to slump in his chair. Then he leaned forward, locking Ozburn's eyes as if he were examining a hostile witness. "Is that what they told you, Doff?" Logan leaned in and growled, "Or is that what *you* told *them*?"

Ozburn's pause confirmed the latter. "It's how we all feel." In a lower but still petulant tone he added, "We won't fight for them. They can all go to hell for all we care." Ozburn glared angrily, but at the floor, not at Logan.

"Doff, that's enough of that kind of talk. There's no choice here. You *must* change your thinking. Times have changed ... *I've* changed! And I'm your commander."

"The hell, Jack," Ozburn spoke plaintively now, leaning across Logan's desk and gesturing with an open hand. "You're damned right about one thing: you're the one who's changed."

With sneering sarcasm, Ozburn added, "You've decided you're a hero now and you want a state-wide office! You want to be a Senator. You want to be the Governor! You're just spewing this abolitionist crap to win voters."

Ozburn pushed himself away from the table and leaned back into his chair. He folded his hands across his belly and added, "Shit, you're probably planning to become a damned *Republican*!"

Logan's face was naturally swarthy, and when his blood rose, his complexion darkened, and it darkened now. Logan half rose from his chair, spread his hands on the desk between them and again, leaned towards Ozburn.

He was close enough to smell the other man's breath. Eyes bulging with anger, Logan searched his old friend's face for any trace of accommodation, but found only Ozburn's cold, almost reptilian eyes.

Logan's voice nearly blew Ozburn out of his chair, thundering, "*Damn you Doff! Damn you*! You don't have the *faintest* idea of '*what I think*!' You haven't seen what I've seen, you haven't felt what I've felt and you sure as *hell*, haven't learned what I've *learned*!"

Logan didn't give Ozburn an inch more space. Logan took a deep breath and continued, "You can't think past what your drinking buddies tell you!" Logan's voice was loud enough to reach every ear in the building. "Slavery is *wrong*! It's *evil* and we're going to put an *end* to it!"

Still holding Ozburn's eyes, Logan stood up straight and asked slowly, "Do-you-understand!?"

Ozburn was silent. He had to look away from his old friend. Recognizing that Logan was immovable, he tried another tack. "Ok, Jack.

I get it. You're in a tough spot. Grant is Lincoln's man and you're Grant's man, so you have to toe the line. You want that promotion. It's OK."

He paused and settled back into his chair more calmly, now looking back at Logan. "But I know what you really believe and I won't disagree with you publicly, if that's what you want."

"You still don't get it do you Doff?" Logan was cold now. "The war has changed things. It's changed politics, yes. But, Doff, now listen to me carefully." Logan enunciated the next words slowly, one at a time, "I ... have ... changed. I've seen things and I've talked to people. And I've *changed*."

Ozburn closed his mouth and with a blank expression, looked at Logan.

Logan collected himself and sat back in his chair, saying, "I need your total cooperation and commitment. Same as every other commander in my Division. Do I have it?"

Ozburn squared his shoulders and leaned his arm on Logan's desk. "I'm as true to my beliefs as you used to be. You can't make me change what I know is true, just because politics has gotten you to change your position. For now."

"For the last time, Doff. What you call 'my *position*,' has changed because my *beliefs* have changed. My commitment includes helping black people. Now, do I have your total cooperation and commitment?"

Ozburn scoffed. "N---rs!" He paused and went on sarcastically, "Sure Jack, of course, whatever you say."

Logan's face darkened again. He placed his forearms on his desk and looked down at the stack of papers that were waiting for him. He raised his head to look at Ozburn with a steady gaze. In low and discouraged tones, he said, "I want your resignation on my desk, before the end of the day. Your health has failed, and I'm allowing you to return to your home and family in anticipation of a full recovery." Logan glared at Ozburn, adding, "Leggett will appoint your replacement."

Ozburn's head snapped up and he glared at Logan. "The hell you say!"

"You can accept my offer, or I'll dismiss you for failure to control your Regiment and send you and all your friends home with papers documenting your inadequacies. Do you understand?"

The consequence of Logan's threat settled into Ozburn's mind. There was a lingering silence. "You wouldn't do that, Jack. We're friends; I'm part of your family!"

"I thought it might come to this," said Logan, pulling two sheets from the bottom of his stack of papers. "Your choice isn't whether you're going home. It's only a matter of how you go, so I have both letters prepared for my signature."

Logan glared at Ozburn. "You're going home. You can go as a Colonel, or you can go home in civilian clothes."

Ozburn looked at the two letters and blanched. He nearly lost his composure and had to swallowed hard to keep from begging. Ozburn looked up at Logan with genuine fear in his eyes. He knew this was no bluff. This time, no words came to Ozburn. With a shallow breath, he slumped back in his chair, chin on his chest, defeated.

Logan resumed in a low voice, "I'm sorry, but this is where we part ways. I won't see you again before you go. Leave your resignation out front with Hotaling or Stark before the end of the day."

Logan didn't stand when Ozburn rose. Instead, he picked up his papers and began to read them. Ozburn resisted the temptation to extend his hand to Logan, knowing he'd be ignored. He picked up his hat and turned towards the door. Placing his hand on the knob, he looked over his shoulder at Logan. "Good-bye, Jack," he said as Logan's eyes rose. The General's cold glare froze Ozburn who dropped his eyes and left without another word. Logan was relieved to see him go.

NORTH OF VICKSBURG, MISSISSIPPI, FEBRUARY 24, 1863

"Sir, we just wait here until the Navy tells us we can go South," said the steamboat Captain to Mathan as they sat still, their steamer tied to the bank.

The Sergeant stepped from the bank onto the stage and made his way carefully aboard the small steamer. "Major Stark, I have a message. There may be a problem."

"What kind of a problem Sergeant?" asked Mathan with impatience returning to his voice.

"We can make the exchange, but we have to leave right now."

"That's fine, but what's the problem then?"

Just then, a Navy Lieutenant appeared behind the Sergeant. "Major Stark?" asked the young officer.

"Yes, what's the problem?"

"Sir, you might recall we sent a ram downriver a while back, the *Queen of the West*?"

"What about it?"

"Well, she was pretty busy, so we sent the *Indianola* past Vicksburg, to help her. Turns out they took the *Queen* and got *Indianola* to run ashore.

They'll exchange the crews today, but Admiral Porter tells us we have to be off the river by an hour after dark or, or else!"

Mathan was on his feet and stepped toward the Lieutenant almost shouting, "What are we waiting for, let's go right now!"

The steamboat Captain looked from the Lieutenant to Mathan and shrugged, "I guess we can get the steam up now." Then he turned back to Mathan and said, Major, have your prisoners ready to exchange and all your papers at hand. We'll need to make this a quick one!"

The prisoners and women had been taken below where they couldn't see the preparations that lined the shores of the river between Memphis and the point of exchange. The six ladies sat, closely packed, below the deck with their bags. Their excited voices carried through the small steamer while twenty prisoners sat passively in the shallow hold with a handful of guards watching them. Mathan stood well back of the Captain, not trusting their huge, white flag to protect them from a partisan with a hunting rifle.

They passed an enormous black barge crawling with men and being loaded with barrels. On one side of the barge were written the words, "Deluded People, Cave In." Mathan's boat was past in a moment and stopped above the range of Vicksburg's guns, where they awaited their escort.

Rachel had been at Vicksburg for over a month when she was called to the Miss Cuthbert's small office. The military hospital was full and three of the wounded Yankee sailors who'd been captured the day before, were now at the civilian hospital. The matron knew of Rachel's pending exchange, so she sent Rachel to the military hospital. The officer coordinating the exchange wanted the Assistant Surgeon, the nurse and the wounded sailors in the same place, so the exchange would be swift.

Rachel stood meekly before the matron's desk. She remembered her time at Heidelberg College and felt a similar combination of resentment and anxiety. The matron began, "As you know, Miss Rodgers, you'll accompany the prisoners who are being exchanged this afternoon. You must have them clean and ready to go to the boat after midday. You will accompany your Assistant Surgeon and you'll join a group of other sailors who will also be exchanged. Do you have any questions?"

"No Ma'am, I don't," said Rachel, fatigue softening her voice. "I'll be ready. I believe it would be best to move the three sailors on stretchers. The long walk in the cold might be dangerous for them."

The matron snorted, "Hmph! It's up to you and your Doctor to sort that out, but you won't have the use of any of our orderlies or servants. You can carry them yourselves or hire some men … if you have the money."

"Ma'am, you must know I have no money. It was taken from me when we were captured and I have no way to earn any here. It's the same for the Doctor and our sailors."

"That's not my concern. You've been fed and sheltered. We've been very generous with you, a woman suspected of spying. We could just as easily sent you to prison."

Rachel shuddered at the thought, but decided to try one, last time. "I imagine that I'll be closely questioned about conditions here in Vicksburg and particularly about the care of our captured soldiers and sailors. I believe if we treat all sick and wounded with similar compassion and generosity, we may eliminate unnecessary suffering for boys on both sides. It would be a tragedy to compound anyone's suffering by punishing them with unnecessary neglect or abuse."

The matron looked up sharply. "Are you threatening to abuse our boys!?"

"Not at all, Miss Cuthbert. I'm saying I think it would be best if exchanges led to the best care for every wounded soldier, no matter who they are or how they were injured."

The older woman grunted. "Alright. Take four servants to carry two of the stretchers. You and your Doctor can carry the third."

"Thank you, Ma'am."

"Get on your way," said Miss Cuthbert coldly. "I will not wish you farewell. Tell your people to end this unholy invasion and go back wherever they came from. Be sure they take you and your young doctor with them!"

Rachel had a couple of hours to pack her few possessions, to prepare the sailors for travel and to say good-bye to the ladies with whom she'd been living and working for the past six weeks.

The sky was gray, the air damp and the ground still showed puddles where a cold rain had fallen the night before. Coal smoke scented the breeze that blew down the river as the three patients and six bearers slowly made their way toward the waiting boat under the eyes of two skinny, smudged teenagers in Rebel uniforms. With only two bearers for each stretcher, and with their few possessions added to the burden, they paused every ten or twenty yards. Their guards had no thought of helping.

It took an hour to cover a distance they comfortably walked in ten. Loading went smoothly. The thought of exchange and a return to their own people seemed unreal. Rachel's mind raced. Before her capture, she heard Irwin had been sent to Memphis. She heard Logan, and so Mathan, were near there as well. She knew Mary Ann was the Matron for the Memphis Hospitals.

They'd been aboard for nearly an hour. Their perspiration dried and it was cold. The navy prisoners said little as they watched preparations to depart. The soldiers, the doctor and Rachel were especially chilled and anxious to go. Around two, the boat's captain was called to the rail. A Confederate officer spoke, too softly for Rachel or the others to hear. Concern grew when the Captain arched his back and looked at the gray sky, shaking his head and sighing. He looked sadly at the cluster of prisoners.

A moment later, the First Mate told the Surgeon the ship's boiler needed repairs and that would take all night. The Surgeon and his nurse were told to collect the wounded and go back to the hospital. They would take them upriver tomorrow.

A few miles upriver, Mathan waited near the landing where the giant black form of a steamship was constructed atop the barge. A huge log was rolled aboard, stripped of bark and painted the same menacing black as the rest of the vessel. The Captain of their boat came to Mathan saying, "We have to go two miles downriver to make the exchange. We can't allow the Rebels to see the *Black Terror* they're building over there."

"*Black Terror*?" questioned Mathan. "Is that what they call that barge?"

"That's no barge, Major. The magic of darkness will transform it into the most dangerous gunboat the Rebs have ever seen." He paused and smiled, "But, if they see it in daylight, the spell will be broken, and it will fail in its special mission."

"It has a special mission?" asked Mathan incredulously.

"Indeed, it does, Major. And we'll know tomorrow whether it succeeded. So, before the sun goes down, we need to complete the exchange and return. Your men are to be silent." The Captain leaned into Mathan with a sly smile and said, "Any who reveals even the hint of *Black Terror*'s secret identity will be shot!"

Mathan smiled and nodded, saying, "Let's go!"

The combination of the river's flow and a breeze hastened the boat's short journey and they were at the exchange point under their large white flag in less than half an hour. There they waited as their large, white truce flag lifted lazily on the cold breeze.

They waited from 3:00 PM until just after 5:00 PM. Although the clouds obscured the sun, it would set around 5:30 and be dark soon after. As they raised steam and were about to cast off, a tiny steam-powered yawl under a white flag appeared in the distance. It quickly came alongside Mathan's ship. The Confederate Lieutenant saluted Mathan and handed him a note. "*Mechanical problems. With your agreement, exchange will take place in 24 hours. All other particulars as previously agreed.*"

Mathan replied in writing, "*Your note of the 25th instant is received. It is agreed to make the exchange tomorrow, February 26th, 1863 at 3:00 PM at the place and in the manner previously agreed.*"

The boats parted and Mathan's party, complete with 50 down-cast Confederate soldiers and six, very angry ladies returned to Lake Providence, where they would await exchange on the following afternoon. As Mathan stood on the deck of his steamer, he saw the enormous *Black Terror* slowly being towed toward him.

When he arrived at Lake Providence, Mathan telegraphed word of the delayed exchange with instructions to please notify Mrs. Bickerdyke. Within minutes, Mathan received a reply. He was ordered to turn responsibility for the exchange over to the local commander and return to Memphis immediately.

Mathan was livid and didn't sleep at all before catching the first boat to Memphis the next morning at 6:00. He arrived in Memphis early the same evening, only to find Sergeant Himmelstoss waiting for him at the landing. Himmelstoss took him directly to Logan's headquarters with the warning that Mathan should be ready to explain his mission to the General. As Mathan entered Logan's outer office, he found an angry Provost glaring at him.

"That's him! That's the Major who tricked me into approving the exchange!"

Logan stepped out of his office and saw Mathan staring open-mouthed at the Provost.

"That's all Colonel." Said Logan calmly. "Thank you for coming up this evening. Please give my regards to your boss and tell him I'll see to the necessary discipline in this matter."

The Provost snorted at Mathan with contempt as he passed on his way out the door.

"Himmelstoss," asked Logan. "Are you part of this?"

Himmelstoss looked at Mathan who answered for him, "No Sir, he's not. This was my doing."

"You're dismissed Sergeant. Stark, come into my office."

When Mathan entered, he saw Lieutenant Colonel Hotaling seated in a chair with his leg across his knee and his fingers tented. An amused smile was on his face as he nodded at Mathan.

"What the hell did you tell the Provost?" Said Logan sharply as he leaned forward, leaving Mathan standing before his desk. "And I want every bit of the truth on the first go, understand?"

"Yes Sir," gulped Mathan. "Sir, I knew my fiancé, Miss Rodgers was being held in Vicksburg for exchange. I knew they wanted six ladies from here to obtain passage to Vicksburg and I knew the Provost was moving very slowly on the arrangements."

Logan nodded and waited for Mathan to go on.

"Well Sir, when I went to speak to the Provost, I noticed he appeared to be, um… The Provost had been drinking enough whiskey to make him unstable on his feet and unable to articulate clearly, Sir. I explained that if I were busy with the exchange, I'd have no time to communicate his state to higher authority."

Logan sat back. "I understand you wanted to get her back here. Isn't she Mrs. Bickerdyke's niece?"

"Yes Sir, she is."

"And hasn't there been a bit of," Logan paused for effect, "tension between our Medical Director and you over Miss Rodger's attention?"

Mathan said nothing.

"When she learned you had taken the exchange into your own hands, Mrs. Bickerdyke asked me to bring you back here. Didn't it occur to you that the exchanged prisoners would come directly to Memphis and that you might be stuck at Lake Providence?"

"Sir, I wanted to see her safely behind our lines. I figured the rest would work itself out in time."

"Well, I have some news for you. Last night, while you were sleeping, Admiral Porter sent a giant barge in the shape of a gunboat past Vicksburg and down the river. The *Indianola*, one of our most important gunboats, was grounded below Vicksburg and the Rebels were going to salvage her and turn her on us. Turns out the *Holy Terror…*"

"*Black Terror*, Sir," said Hotaling softly.

"*Black Terror*, put such a damned scare into the Rebels that they blew up the *Indianola* rather than let us take her back. They blew her up then ran South! They didn't realize until this morning, they'd been spooked by an empty barge with pork-barrels stacked up to look like smore stacks and tree trunks painted to look like cannons!" Logan laughed at the thought.

Mathan smiled weakly but waited to learn how much trouble he'd made for himself.

"For the record, Stark, you've been severely reprimanded, I mean very, *very* severely! And I need you to remember that because I'm probably going to forget it by tomorrow with all the things I have to do. Hotaling over there is so busy, he'll probably forget too, but that damned Provost wanted your hide and I told him I'd take care of you!" Logan smiled at Hotaling conspiratorially. "Do you understand Stark?"

"I think so. Yes Sir. Severely reprimanded. Harshly rebuked. Never forget. Damned thin ice."

"Well said. Well said. Now go get some rest. Seems the ghost ship did its work South of Vicksburg and they wanted to show us everything there is under control and normal. The exchange took place this afternoon

320

as scheduled. The boat with Miss Rodgers and the others should arrive tomorrow some time. Better go get some rest."

Logan added, "You know our Division is about to move South. Your reunion is likely to be very brief."

The next afternoon, Himmelstoss led Mathan to the landing where the exchanged prisoners were to be returned. Mary Ann was already there. She had decided to come early when she overheard Irwin saying he wanted to meet Rachel's boat. Pastor and Mrs. Allen were there as well.

Mathan's heart stuck in his throat when he saw the small steamer come into sight from the South. The decks were crowded with Federal soldiers, and he couldn't make out individual faces at that distance. There was commotion behind him when he turned to see General Logan, Mrs. Logan and General Leggett coming toward them from the direction of the Gayoso Hotel. A Regimental band began to play and a small crowd gathered to watch the prisoners' return.

As soon as the steamer tied up, General and Mrs. Logan shook hands with the Captain. They spoke for a moment before the arriving soldiers pushed to the front and were greeted by the Logans. General Leggett was next to the Logans and looked back at Mathan before he began shaking the returning soldiers' hands.

Mathan, Himmelstoss, the Allens and Mary Ann waited on the other side of the road. It took about ten minutes to unload the soldiers who were followed by several sailors. Irwin greeted the Assistant Surgeon when he came off the boat in the company of the stretcher patients. Irwin spoke to the younger Surgeon and nodded. The two doctors looked at Mathan as they passed but said nothing.

Mathan waited for Rachel to appear. General and Mrs. Logan stepped over to him. Mrs. Logan spoke first. "Major Stark, we're so sorry. Your Miss Rodgers isn't aboard. The Surgeon said he didn't see her again after they returned to the hospital yesterday."

Only later would Mathan learn what happened the night before the Black Terror reached Vicksburg.

Rachel had struggled with the last stretcher to come off the little steamer. It was dark, and she was cold, tired and very disappointed. She returned to her tiny room at the hospital and took one of the Captain's love letters from her Bible and felt for the other, hidden in the collar of her cloak. Her insurance policies.

Turning the tiny letter in her hands, she recalled the Captain's reaction when she told him she wanted her possessions, her money, and the papers he'd taken from her. He sneered at her, "Women like you are lucky to have a room instead of a crib down by the river with your own kind! I hear Miss Amy is always looking for new talent."

Rachel's stomach gripped as she glared at him reciting, "I've never loved a man the way I love you, and I've never felt the soaring passion I've discovered in your arms, my sweet Henry." She paused and a smile began to cross her lips. "Shall I go on, or shall we ask the Sergeant what comes next?"

All color left his face and his limbs froze. No words came as he began to tremble.

"A house near the Soldiers' hospital has decent rooms for nurses. Your letters are safely stored in different places with different people who have instructions to open them should anything unfortunate ever happen to me."

He couldn't afford to call her bluff and he wasn't the sort of man who murdered.

The Captain saw to it that Rachel was moved, had a pleasant room, and wasn't troubled by anyone under his authority.

Friendships with other nurses led to introductions and more conversations. Then still more introductions. As an educated, Northern woman, she was a curiosity. As a nurse, she was accomplished and trusted. It wasn't long before several of the ladies of Vicksburg took her into their confidence. The friendships meant she seldom needed to test the durability of the Captain's fear of exposure.

Moving through the town, chatting with her new friends and working closely with enslaved women, Rachel learned a lot. Like, numbers of soldiers, commanders' names, sorts and amounts of supplies and even the locations of roads, storage facilities and artillery. These details, she committed to memory.

Shortly before the exchange and her opportunity to share all she had learned, the big guns thundered in the dark more loudly and more often than she'd heard before. Slipping out to see what was happening, she encountered several of the Black women who served with her in the hospital. One of the ladies stepped up behind her and Rachel was surprised to see the woman had a shawl covering her face.

"I found this book of poetry and believe you might have lost it. I thought you might want it back," said the woman ominously. "You might want to share it with your friends at General Grant's headquarters. Tell them Miss Jaycee from New Orleans gave it to you."

Rachel accepted the book wordlessly and watched the woman turn quickly and begin to move away.

"Wait!" hissed Rachel. "Are their other books for my friends?"

The woman turned and seemed to be appraising Rachel. "Now, there may be, but what's it to you? You're leaving."

"I'm not the only one who delivers books, am I?"

"Maybe so, maybe no." And the woman walked away quickly. Rachel followed her until the woman reached a very dark alley between two warehouses. "Why are you following me! She demanded."

Rachel whispered. "I have… I have more books and I keep finding them. I think my friends would like to read them. Do you have another way to deliver books to my friends?"

Suspicious but accepting the risk, the woman under the shawl faced Rachel and said, "You can give me books. I might have friends with friends along the river. It's sometimes slow, but they know their way."

The woman looked Rachel up and down before she went on. "Now, I want you to keep that, particular book until you see your friends. You don't think that's the only one of its kind now, do you?"

With that, the woman turned away saying over her shoulder, "Don't you follow me anymore. We'll be in touch with you. Their word will be 'Miss Adele is looking for you.' Your word will be 'Miss Adele is away at Grand Gulf.' They'll show you how to write to your friends and give you some books." With that, she disappeared.

The intense firing from upriver moved closer, then slackened. Rachel was nearly back to her room when she heard a very loud explosion from downriver. After that, things were strangely quiet.

Rachel decided she was more than a nurse. She had been an observer. She would become a reporter. They would call her a spy.

End of Volume 1

APPENDIX I

Organization of the Federal Armies

During the Civil War, armies were organized around Regiments. The 78th Ohio Volunteers and the 31st Illinois Volunteers are two Regiments central to this story. All the military organizations mentioned in this book are as accurately reported as possible.

Regiments were usually commanded by a Colonel and were authorized about 1,000 men, although they may have had several hundred fewer. Civil War Regiments were usually identified by a number and the state from which they originated (like the 31st Illinois and 78th Ohio). Each Regiment included about ten Companies of around 100 men each. Companies were usually commanded by a Captain.

Regiments usually served as part of a larger organization called a Brigade. Brigades had two to as many as five Regiments. The commander of a Brigade was called a Brigadier General (one star).

Two or more Brigades made up a Division. Divisions were usually commanded by a Major General (two stars).

Two or more Divisions could be combined into a Corps. In the Civil War, Corps were also commanded by Major Generals (two stars), and they were senior to Division commanders.

When more than one Corps operated together, they were called an Army, also commanded by a Major General.

Until Ulysses Grant became the commander of all Union Forces in 1864, there were no American Lieutenant Generals (three stars). Later, when Grant was promoted to General of the Armies (four stars), he was only the second person ever assigned that rank, Washington having been the first.

Hierarchy of Civil War Army organization:

Level	Commanded By	Made Up Of
Army	Major General	Two or More Corps
Corps	Major General	Two or More Divisions
Division	Major General	Two or More Brigades
Brigade	Brigadier General	Two or More Regiments
Regiment	Colonel	Ten Companies
Company	Captain	About 100 men

APPENDIX II

Military Ranks of Federal Soldiers

Officers hold "commissions," meaning they are appointed to act on behalf of the government and require Congressional approval of their appointments. This is the source of the term, "commissioned officer."

The most junior officers in the Army are Lieutenants. They are numbered in the order of seniority. First Lieutenants are senior to Second Lieutenants. Above Lieutenants are Captains. Captains commanded Companies but could also perform administrative duties.

Majors rank above Captains. They are senior officers who took care of administrative duties and commanded portions of a Regiment. Ranking above Majors are Lieutenant Colonels.

The origin of the word "Lieutenant" comes from French word "lieu" meaning substitute and "tenant" meaning in place. A Lieutenant can be considered an assistant or a substitute. A "Lieutenant" Colonel is the next rank below Colonel and can take the place of a Colonel. A "Lieutenant" General (three stars) can take the place of a General (four stars).

The seniority of Army Ranks (followed by the spoken title) in the Civil War follows:

Rank	Term of Address
General of the Army	"General"
Lieutenant General	"General"
Major General	"General"
Brigadier General	"General"
Colonel	"Colonel"
Lieutenant Colonel	"Colonel"
Major	"Major"
Captain	"Captain"
First Lieutenant	"Lieutenant"
Second Lieutenant	"Lieutenant"

Non-commissioned officers have official responsibilities although they have not been commissioned by Congress. They are assigned duties by commissioned officers and frequently take great responsibility for training, managing and leading alongside commissioned officers.

During the Civil War, noncommissioned officers bore the following ranks. Each was addressed by their rank.

Sergeant Major

Quartermaster Sergeant

Ordinance Sergeant

First Sergeant

Sergeant

Corporal

Index of Persons

Babcock, John, Was a homeopathic physician in Galesburg, Illinois at the time Mary Ann lived there.

Bickerdyke, Robert, Mary Ann's husband. He died in Galesburg in 1859.

Beecher, Edward, Theologian, and member of the Beecher family of authors and preachers. He was a lifelong advocate of civil rights. He died at the age of 91 in New York in 1895

Bickerdyke, Martha, Mary Ann's youngest child. Died in 1859.

Bickerdyke, Hiram Mary Ann's son. He found it difficult to forgive his mother for choosing to serve in the war.

Bickerdyke, Mary Ann as a girl.

Blanchard, Jonathan, Presbyterian minister, president of Knox and Wheaton College. Noted Abolitionist. He died in 1892.

Bickerdyke, Mary Ann born in Ohio in 1817. She accompanied Sherman and Logan throughout the war, riding next to them at the head of the Grand Review. Afterward, she was a tireless advocate for veterans' benefits while running a hotel in Kansas and working at the San Francisco mint. She died in 1901 at the age of 84 in Kansas and is buried in Galesburg.

Brinton, John M Born in Philadelphia in 1832, a younger cousin of George B. McClellan. Serving as a surgeon on General Grant's staff. First curator of the National Museum of Health and Medicine. He died at age 74 in 1907.

Chandler, Z M, Named as a Company Commander in the History of the 78th Regiment.

Cherry, Anne Irwin and daughter **Mary**. Owner of Cherry Mansion. Courtesy of Hardin County, Kentucky, Historical Society

Cunningham, John M, born in Tennessee, moved to Missouri and Married Elizabeth Fountain. Moved to Illinois and freed his two enslaved people in 1839. Father of Mary Cunningham Logan. In 1866 cholera took his wife and he relocated to Provo Utah with his second wife, Mary. He served as tax collector and died there in 1873.

Davis, Jefferson C. born in Indiana in 1828. At Ft. Sumter when the War began. Promoted to Brigadier General for success at the Battle of Pea Ridge 1862. On a leave for exhaustion when he murdered Major General William "Bull" Nelson in retaliation for a perceived insult. Excused the killing, Davis later commanded the XIV Corps under Sherman and worked closely with Logan. Later he destroyed a pontoon bridge abandoning hundreds of fugitives to drowning or capture. Later, led combat against Native Americans in the Modoc War. He died in Chicago in 1879 at the age of 51.

Dennison, William J, born in Cincinnati, married Anne Neil and was one of the first to leave the Whigs to become a Republican. Governor of Illinois at the outbreak of the War. President Grant appointed him to the Board of Commissioners for the District of Columbia. He died in 1882 at the age of 66.

Dougherty, Henry, severely wounded at Belmont, he was captured and quickly paroled. He commanded at Paducah for several months but left the service on account of wounds. He died in Pennsylvania in 1866 at the age of 40.

Douglas, Stephen A. was born in Vermont in 1813 and moved to Jacksonville, Illinois in 1833 where he met John Logan (John A.'s father). He served in the US Senate for 14 years. He died in June of 1861 at the age of 48.

Douglass, Frederick, born into slavery in 1817, he escaped to freedom in 1838 and married Anna Murray in the same year. His life is legendary. He died in Washington, D.C. in 1895 at the age of 77.

Force, Manning F, born 1824 in Washington, D.C. to the Mayor of that city. He attended Harvard College and practiced law in Cincinnati. Suffering a wound to the face in Atlanta in 1864 he was later awarded the Congressional Medal of Honor. He died in Cincinnati in 1899 at the age of 74.

Fouke, Philip B, born in Illinois in 1818, he practiced law in Belleville and was a member of the US House of representatives from 1859 to 1863. Wounded at the battle of

Belmont he died in Washington D.C. in 1876 at the age of 58.

Gale, George W. born in upstate New York in 1789. Presbyterian minister serving churches in his New York. Founded the Oneida Institute and later Knox College in Galesburg, Illinois. He died in September 1861 at about age 72.

Garrard, Lewis H. born in Cincinnati in 1829. At 17 he traveled the Santa Fe Trail and attended the trials of some participant in the Taos Revolt. He returned home within the year. He died in 1887 at the age of 58.

Grant, **Ulysses S.,** born in Ohio in 1822 his life is legendary. He died in New York in 1885 at the age of 63.

Garrison, William Lloyd, born 1805 in Massachusetts. A publisher and active abolitionist in his teens. Founded "The Liberator," an antislavery weekly. Died of kidney disease in New York in 1879.

Halleck, Henry, born 1815 in Oneida County, New York. He was a prodigal cadet at West Point and distinguished himself as a military theorist and a coauthor of the California State Constitution. He served as General in Chief of the Armies until he was replaced by his former subordinate, Ulysses Grant. He continued to serve in the Army after the war but succumbed to liver disease in Louisville in 1872 at the age of 56.

Hotaling, John R, born in Sharon, New York in 1824 he was trained as a printer. He was wounded in the Mexican War and went to California during the initial Gold Rush. He married Sophia Waterhouse and moved to Illinois. His wife died of tuberculosis in 1863 and he served the remainder of the War on Logan's staff. He remarried Carrie Cass in 1868 and became a postmaster. He died in 1886 at the age of 62.

Hartsock, Jane, was Principal of the Female Department at Heidelberg College from 1859-1860.

Hussey, Zimri, listed in several books about Mary Ann Bickerdyke as a homeopath and professor in Cincinnati.

Ingersoll, Robert G, born 1833 in Yates County, New York. His family moved to Ohio and later to Marion Illinois were he practiced law. He was John Cunningham's law clerk. Captured in Tennessee in December, 1862 and paroled, he was never exchanged and left the Army. After the war he became a famous orator on the subject of humanism and agnosticism. He died of heart failure in 1899 at the age of 65.

Irwin, Bernard J D, born in Ireland in 1830, he immigrated with his parents in the 1840s and graduated from New York Medical College in 1852. His exploits in Arizona in 1861 resulted in the award of the Congressional Medal of Honor in 1894. Irwin was eventually promoted to Brigadier General and remained in the Army until age 64 and died in 1917 at the age of 87.

Jenkins, Alexander, born 1802 and settled in Jackson County Illinois. He served in the Illinois house and as the Lieutenant Governor. His sister was John A. Logan's mother. Jenkins died in 1864 at the age of 62. Photo courtesy of the Logan Museum.

Kieffer, Moses, born 1814, died aged 74 in 1888. President of Heidelberg College from 1855-1863.

Kuykendall, Andrew J, born in 1815. He began practicing law in 1840 and was a member of the Illinois State House of Representatives from 1842-1862 where he was Logan's friend. Elected to the US House of Representatives from 1865-1867 Thereafter he served as a probate judge and State Senator. He died in Vienna, Illinois in 1891 at age 65.

Lauman, Jacob, born in Taneytown, Maryland in 1813, he grew up in York, Pennsylvania before moving to Iowa in 1844. He was promoted to Brigadier General after Fort Donelson. He was promoted again to Division Commander and was relieved of command by General Sherman for poor performance in July of 1863. He remained in Iowa for the rest of the war and struggled unsuccessfully to rehabilitate his reputation. He died of a stroke at the age of 54 in 1867.

Leggett, Mortimer, born in Ithaca, New York in 1821, moving to Ohio with his parents in 1836. He practiced law, published educational journals and was superintendent of public schools in Zanesville, Ohio when the war began. He was the first commander of the 78th Ohio Volunteer Infantry. He was wounded six times. He became a Division commander and fought very successfully under Sherman through the end of the war, attaining the rank of Major General. After the war, Grant appointed him Commissioner of Patents in 1871. In 1873, his son was killed in a fraternity hazing accident, the first such recorded death. Leggett died in Cleveland, Ohio in January 1886 at the age of 74.

Livermore, Mary Ashton Rice,
born in Boston, Massachusetts in
1820. She attended the Female
Seminary in Charleston,
Massachusetts and taught there.
Her work as a tutor in Virginia
before the war made her an ardent
abolitionist. She married the
Universalist Minister, Daniel
Livermore in 1845 and they moved
to Chicago where they published a
Unitarian magazine. After the war,
she wrote, lectured and remained
active in suffrage and temperance
movements. She died in
Massachusetts aged 84, in 1905.

Logan, John A. 1850s Courtesy of
the John A. Logan Museum.

Logan, John A. in later life

John and Elizabeth Logan,
Courtesy of the Logan Museum

Logan, Mary Cunningham, 1858.
Born 1838 in Missouri, daughter of
John Cunningham and Elizabeth
Fontaine. She was educated at the
Convent of St. Vincent's in
Kentucky. Her biography gives a
vivid description of her life and
times as well as insight into her
views on slavery, politics and her
husband's service. She died in
1923. Courtesy of the Logan
Museum

Logan, John A. in about 1862

Logan served with distinction at
Vicksburg, and the Battle of
Atlanta. He eventually
commanded the XV Corps during
the Carolinas Campaign. Logan
was chosen to lead the Western
Army during the Grand Review in
May 1865 with Mary Ann
Bickerdyke at his side. He served in
the US Congress from 1867-1871.
He became a national leader of the
largest veterans' organizations and
was instrumental in establishing
Memorial Day as a Federal
Holiday. He was elected to the US
Senate in 1871 and was the
Republican Party's Vice-
Presidential Candidate in 1884. He
died of "rheumatism" (heart
failure?) the day after Christmas,
1886 at age 62.

Lovejoy, Owen, born in Maine in 1811 and attended Bowdoin College.

He moved to Alton, Illinois in 1837 and was present when his brother was murdered by a pro-slavery mob. After his brother's murder, he organized over one hundred anti-slavery Congregational Churches in Illinois and worked with Lincoln to form the Republican Party. He served in the State Legislature with Logan and in the US House of Representatives (also with Logan) from 1857-1863. He died in New York in 1864 at the age of 53.

McArthur, John, born 1826 in Scotland and came to the United States in 1846. He married Christina Cuthberson in 1849. After Fort Donelson he was promoted to Brigadier General and eventually to the command of a Division and the rank of Major General. After the war he served as Chicago's Commissioner of Public Works and Postmaster General. He died in Chicago in 1906 at the age of 79.

McClellan, George B, born 1826 in Philadelphia, son of a prominent surgeon and cousin to Dr. John Brinton. A graduate of West Point, he did well enough to be selected as an engineer and served in the Mexican War. A strong supporter of Stephen A. Douglas, McClellan won Lincoln's support through very early successes in Virginia. Lincoln eventually grew frustrated with McClellan's ego, political aspirations and most of all, his lack of aggression on the field. Lincoln replaced him in November 1862. He ran for President against Lincoln in 1864. After the war he spent three years in Europe and served one term as governor of New Jersey. He died of a heart attack in New Jersey in 1885 at the age of 58.

McIlrath, James & Robert J., James brought Robert and their family to Illinois from Belfast in 1850, when Robert was six years old. Father and son joined the 31st Ohio Volunteers together and the elder McIlrath was killed at Fort Donelson. Robert was discharged from service in April of 1863. He married India Gloss and farmed, raised cattle and ran a bank. He died sometime after 1905.

John McClernand, born 1812 in Kentucky, his family moved to Illinois when he was very young. Acquainted with Logan's family, he married Sarah Dunlap from Jackson, Illinois. McClernand served in the US House of Representatives from 1843-1851 and again from 1859-1861. He was relieved from duty by Grant for insubordination in 1863. After the war, he served as a District Judge and presided over the 1876 Democratic National Convention. He died in Springfield, Illinois at the age of 88.

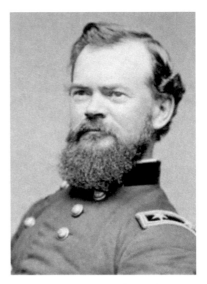

McPherson, James B, born 1828 in Clyde, Ohio. Graduated first in his class from West Point and instructed engineering at the Academy. In California when the war began, he was reassigned as Grant's chief engineer. He was quickly promoted to Major General and led the XVIIth Corps. He commanded the Army of the Tennessee after Sherman was promoted. Outside Atlanta, on July 22, 1864, while attempting to flee capture, he was shot and killed. He was 35 years old.

Murray, Robert, born in Maryland in 1822, he graduated from the University of Pennsylvania Medical School in 1843. He served with the Army in California and New York. When the war began, two of his brothers fought for the Confederacy. After serving as the Medical Director of the Army of the Cumberland, he served as the "Chief Medical Purveyor" (director of medical acquisition) until the end of the war. He became the Surgeon General of the Army and retired as a Brigadier General. He was essential to the formation of the Association of Military Surgeons of the United States in 1891 and died in Baltimore on New Years Day, 1913 at the age of 90, the fourth-to-last surviving veteran of the Mexican War before he died.

Narbona, born about 1766. He became a wealthy and influential member of the Navajo Nation. He led his tribe to a decisive victory against the Mexican government in 1835. Narbona was killed in a melee in New Mexico in 1849, age about 83. Photo, courtesy University of New Mexico Archives.

Mexico in 1862. Retired from the Army in September 1863 and died in Illinois at the age of 66 in 1870.

Nelson, William "Bull", born in Kentucky in 1824, attended seminary for two years before appointment to the US Naval Academy. After serving in the Mexican War, he collaborated with Lincoln to keep Kentucky in the Union. Made a Brigadier General in September 1861, he was good friends with Dr. Bernard John Irwin. Suffered a serious defeat at the Battle of Richmond, Kentucky. Murdered by General Jefferson C. Davis over a perceived insult in September 1862 at the age of 38.

Newby, Edward, born 1804 in Virginia. Elected as a Captain of Illinois Volunteers for the Mexican War, he was appointed Colonel of the Regiment. After the Mexican War he served on active duty in Kansas and New Mexico. When the Civil War began, he served as a Major in the 3rd Cavalry Regiment, helping defeat the invasion of New

Ogelsby, Richard J, born in 1824 in Kentucky. Orphaned, he was sent to Illinois when he was eight and enlisted to fight in the Mexican War. He studied law at Louisville at the same time Logan did and joined the Republican party with Lincoln. He married Anna White in 1859. He was seriously wounded at Corinth in 1862 and resigned from the Army in May 1864. He was elected Governor of Illinois and served from 1865-1869. He was reelected Governor in 1872 but relinquished the seat to serve as a US Senator (with Logan) from 1873-1879. In 1884 he was elected to his third term as Governor. He died in Illinois at the age of 74 in 1899.

Lindorf "Doff" Ozburn, born 1823 in Jackson County, Illinois. He married John Logan's fifteen- year- old cousin "Diza" in 1845. Ozburn resigned from service under pressure from Logan on 24 February 1863 citing "an oblique inguinal hernia" that rendered him unfit for service. He returned to Jackson County Illinois where a vengeful recruit to the 31st Illinois smashed his skull with a four- pound weight. He died in April 1864 at the age of 40.

Patterson, William, listed as a Second Lieutenant in the History of the 31st Regiment of Illinois Volunteers.

Polk, Leonidas, born 1806 in North Carolina, the son of a wealthy planter. He graduated from West Point in 1827 and promptly resigned his commission to enter the clergy. He married Frances Ann Devereux in 1830. In the 1850s he owned a plantation with several hundred people enslaved there. When the war began, his West Point classmate, Jefferson Davis appointed him a Major General, though Polk hadn't served but a few months as a Second Lieutenant over thirty years before. He feuded with General Braxton Bragg throughout the war and neither was particularly successful. He was killed during the Atlanta campaign when an artillery shell went through his chest. He died in 1864 at the age of 58.

Ransom, Thomas E G, born 1834 in Vermont. His father was killed in the Mexican War and Ransom became a civil engineer. He raised the 11th Illinois Volunteer Infantry and quickly became its commander. He was promoted to Brigadier General in November 1862 and commanded under General John McArthur. He was not only wounded at Fort Donelson, but previously in Missouri and subsequently severely wounded at Shiloh and again in 1864 in Louisiana. He was a favorite of Grant and Sherman. Ransom died of dysentery in Georgia in October 1864 at the age of 29, shortly after being promoted to Major General.

Scott, Winfield, born in Virginia in 1786, his father was a veteran of the Revolutionary War and died when Scott was eight. Scott attended William and Mary College and practiced law in Virginia. He was a militiaman in 1807 and an artillery officer in the US Army in 1808. He was a successful combat leader during the War of 1812, wars against Native Americans and Mexico. He was the Army's Commanding General from 1841 to 1861. He died at West Point in 1866 at the age of 79.

Woodcock, Elizabet Ball, was Mary Ann's older sister. The two corresponded throughout their lives.

Smith, Charles F, born in Philadelphia in 1807, the son of an Army surgeon, he graduated from West Point in 1825 and returned as Commandant of Cadets in 1838 when Grant was there. He served with distinction in the Mexican War. Promoted to Brigadier, he led successful attacks at Fort Donelson. Smith died of injuries suffered when boarding a boat at Pittsburg Landing in 1862. He turned 52 the day before he died.

Stembel, Roger N., born 1810 in Maryland, raised in Ohio. He was the son of a distinguished veteran of the War of 1812 and commissioned in the Navy in 1832. He married Laura McBride in 1836. He was seriously wounded near Vicksburg in 1862. He returned to service in 1865. He served the Navy throughout the world and was eventually promoted to Admiral, retiring in 1872. He died in New York in 1900 at the age of 89.

Somerville, Alexander S. Was from Centralia Illinois. He is listed as having been dismissed from the Army in May of 1862.

Stowe, Harriet B, born in Connecticut in 1811, she was the sixth of eleven children born to Lyman Beecher, a prominent theologian and preacher. Her siblings also preached and wrote. A committed abolitionist, she published the first portion of Uncle Tom's Cabin in 1851 and it became the best selling work of fiction in the country. In later life she advocated rights for married women and was involved in several controversies. Her cognitive decline was very public and she died in Connecticut at the age of 85.

Thayer, John M, born in Massachusetts in 1820, he married Mary Tory Allen in 1842, worked as a publisher and moved to Nebraska in 1854. He served as a Brigade commander under Lew Wallace, eventually promoted to Major General. After the war, he was elected as one of Nebraska's first two US Senators. He then served as Governor of the Wyoming Territory, final, elected Governor of Nebraska for three terms. He died in 1906 at the age of 86.

Thurber, Charles H, listed as commander of the 2nd Missouri Artillery.

Valandingham, Clement, born in Ohio in 1820 to a Presbyterian minister. He had a conflict with his college president and was dismissed. He practiced law in Dayton and opposed Logan in the question of "Black Laws." He served in the US Congress at the same time Logan was there. He was convicted of crimes associated with his view on the war and banished to the Confederacy. After the war he returned to Ohio, ran unsuccessfully for public office and shot himself in the stomach when demonstrating how a victim may have accidentally shot himself in the stomach. Valandingham died in Ohio in 1870 at the age of 50 (but his client was acquitted).

Van Dorn, Earl, born in Mississippi in 1820 to Andrew Jackson's niece. He graduated from West Point in 1842 with an unremarkable record. He fought with distinction in the Mexican War and subsequently in combat with Native Americans. He was appointed a Colonel then a General in the Confederacy. He lost at the Battle of Pea Ridge, Missouri in 1862 and again at Second Corinth that Fall. Returning to the cavalry and taking Holly Springs in December 1862. In May of 1863, Van Dorn was shot in the head by a husband, jealous of Van Dorn's relationship with his much-younger wife. Van Dorn died in Spring Hill, Tennessee at age 42. His assailant was never charged.

Walke, Henry A, born in Virginia
in 1809, serving in the US Navy
beginning in 1827. He fought
pirates and participated in the
Mexican War. He commanded a
ship as part of Perry Expedition to
Japan. He participated in the battle
for Vicksburg and ended the war
on the East Coast as a Captain. He
retired in 1870 as a Rear Admiral.
He died in New York in 1896 at the
age of 86.

Wallace, Lewis, born in Indiana in
1827, the son of a West Point
graduate and Indiana politician.
His' mother died when he was
seven and his stepmother was an
advocate of women's rights and
temperance. Volunteered for
service in the Mexican War, but
saw no combat. Married Susan
Arnold Elston, the daughter of his
Mexican War commander in 1852.
After Shiloh, he was sent East
where he led Union troops at the
Battle of Monocacy, earning
Grant's praise and gratitude.
Subsequently served as Governor
of the New Mexico Territory and
Ambassador to Turkey. His novel,
Ben Hur was the best-selling novel
in the United States before 1900. He
died in Indiana in 1905 at the age of
77.

Wallace, WHL, born in Ohio in 1821, he grew up in Illinois, studied law and was friends with Lincoln. Wallace served in the Mexican War. 1851, he married Martha Ann Dickey, the daughter of his law partner. He joined the 11th Illinois Volunteer Infantry as a private but was elected Colonel. He served as a Brigade commander at Fort Donelson and as a Division commander at Shiloh, replacing CF Smith who had injured his leg. At Shiloh, Wallace led desperate fighting that gave the Union time to reorganize and hold on until reinforcements arrived the following day. Wallace was severely wounded and died on April 10th, 1862 in the Cherry Mansion. He was 40 years old.

Webster, Joseph D, born in New Hampshire in 1811. He graduated from Dartmouth College and worked as a civil engineer. He joined the Army in 1838 and served in the Mexican War, resigning in 1854. He returned to service in 1861, joining Grant's staff and becoming its Chief just before Belmont. He was instrumental in organizing the artillery that protected Pittsburg Landing at the end of the first day of fighting at Shiloh. He was promoted to General and served as Sherman's Chief of Staff to the end of the war. He was promoted to Major General and left the Army after the war. He later served as a revenue collector. He died in Chicago in 1876 at the age of 64.

West, Mary Allen, the first child born in Galesburg, Illinois in 1837 to founders of Knox College. She was a prodigy who qualified for entry to college at 13, taught there until 15 and graduated at 17. A vigorous supporter of the US Sanitary Commission and later head of the Illinois Chapter of the Women's Christian Temperance Union. In 1863, she established a school for Black children at a time they were excluded from public education. She became superintendent of Galesburg schools. After the war, she published widely, spoke extensively and advocated effectively for women's rights, temperance and effective child-rearing. Late in her life, she visited California, Hawaii and Japan to promote temperance and died in Japan in 1892 at the age of 57.

White, John H., born 1821 in Connecticut, he moved to Ohio in 1840 and was trained as a cabinet maker. He married Emily A. McCoy in 1845. He Volunteered for the Mexican War holding the rank of Sergeant Major when he accompanied Newby, Cunningham and Logan to Santa Fe. Later, he farmed in Marion Illinois and served as a County Clerk. When Logan formed the 31st Illinois Volunteers, White quickly joined and served as the Lieutenant Colonel of the Regiment. He died on the field at Fort Donelson in 1862 at the age of 40.

Whittelsey, Charles, born in Connecticut in 1808 he attended West Point, graduating in 1831. He resigned from the Army to study law. A successful geologist in the 1840s and 50s. He married Mary Lyon Morgan in 1858. He was with Leggett and McClellan in the Western Virginia campaign of 1861. Commander of the 20th Ohio Infantry and later of a Brigade under Lew Wallace at Shiloh. Following the battle, he was discharged for ill health. After the war, he earned fame as an anthropologist. He died in Cleveland in 1886 at the age of 78.

Wiles, Greenbury F., born 1826 in Maryland and raised in Ohio. He married J. H. Chapman of Zanesville. Helping organize several Companies of the 78th Ohio, he rose through the ranks to Brigadier General. When Leggett was promoted, Wiles commanded the 78th Ohio, eventually becoming a Brigade commander himself. He was in business after the war in Zanesville, relocating to Kansas in 1880. He died in 1899 at the age of 73.